Praise for The Shadow...

P9-CKV-401

"Hunter sucks you in . . . an amazing roller-coaster ride."

—*RT Book Reviews*

"The Shadow Falls series belongs to my favorite YA series. It has everything I wish for in a YA paranormal series. A thrilling tale that moves with a great pace, where layers of secrets are revealed in a way that we are never bored. It continues a gripping story about self-discoveries, finding a place in the world, friendship, and love. So if you didn't start this series yet, I can only encourage you to do so." —*Bewitched Bookworms*

"Ms. Hunter handles this series with such deftness, crafting a wonderful tale that speaks to the adolescent in me. I highly recommend this series filled with darkness and light, hope and danger, friendship and romance."

—*Night Owl Reviews* (Top Pick)

"Jam-packed with action and romance from the very beginning, Hunter's lifelike characters and paranormal creatures populate a plot that will keep you guessing till the very end. A perfect mesh of mystery, thriller, and romance. Vampires, weres, and fae, oh my!" —*RT Book Reviews* on *Taken at Dusk*

"An emotional thrill ride full of suspense, action, laughter, multiple love stories, and an intriguing variety of paranormal species. I could not put this book down and can't wait to start the next book as soon as I finish this review." —*Guilty Pleasures Book Reviews* on *Awake at Dawn*

"There are so many books in the young adult paranormal genre these days that it's hard to choose a good one. I was so very glad to discover *Born at Midnight*. If you like P. C. and Kristin Cast or Alyson Nöel, I am sure you will enjoy *Born at Midnight*!" —*Night Owl Reviews*

"The evolving, not-always-easy relationships among Kylie and her cabin mates Della and Miranda are rendered as engagingly as Kylie's angst over dangerous Lucas and appealing Derek. Just enough plot threads are tied up to make a satisfying stand-alone tale while whetting appetites for sequels to come." —*Publishers Weekly*

"With intricate plotting and characters so vivid you'd swear they are real, *Born at Midnight* is an addictive treat. Funny, poignant, romantic, and downright scary in places, it hits all the right notes. Highly recommended."

—*Houston Lifestyles and Homes Magazine*

── SHADOW FALLS ✦ AFTER DARK ──

Unspoken

C. C. HUNTER

ST. MARTIN'S GRIFFIN ⚑ NEW YORK

UNSPOKEN. Copyright © 2015 by Christie Craig. All rights reserved. Printed in the United States of America. For information, address St. Martin's Press, 175 Fifth Avenue, New York, N.Y. 10010.

www.stmartins.com

The Library of Congress Cataloging-in-Publication Data is available upon request.

ISBN 978-1-250-06709-8 (trade paperback)
ISBN 978-1-250-07211-5 (hardcover)
ISBN 978-1-4668-7503-6 (e-book)

Our books may be purchased in bulk for promotional, educational, or business use. Please contact your local bookseller or the Macmillan Corporate and Premium Sales Department at (800) 221-7945, extension 5442, or by e-mail at MacmillanSpecial Markets@macmillan.com.

First Edition: October 2015

10 9 8 7 6 5 4 3 2 1

To my father, Pete Hunt, I'll always be your little girl. To Cara Bates, my niece, for always being there when she's needed. To my mom, Ginger Curtis, who never fails to tell me how proud she is of me. And to Bob Curtis, my stepdad, thank you for your love and all you do.

Acknowledgments

I could not do this alone. Thank you to my husband, Steve, for being my rock, for doing the dishes, making coffee, and proofreading all my books. Thank you to all my friends who walk with me, whine with me, and share wine with me. Thank you to my assistant, Kathleen Adey, who keeps me on my toes and organized. To my editor, Rose Hilliard, and my agent, Kim Lionetti, who have to put up with this crazy writer.

Unspoken

Chapter One

The sound of the door swishing open filled the small space. Before Della Tsang heard the footsteps, the scent filled her nose. Another vampire. But not just any vampire . . .

Him.

Chase Tallman. The guy she was regrettably bonded with. The guy who'd given her his blood to ensure she'd survive a rare second turn into vampirism that had made her a Reborn—a stronger kick-ass vampire who attracted ghosts. Not that she'd asked for it, or would have wanted it—especially the ghost part.

His footsteps brought him into the closet-sized room. The door whooshed closed. Her heart thumped against her breastbone.

She'd been to hell and back looking for him. Had even gone to France to find him, with no luck.

And now he just shows up.

Here.

In the ladies' bathroom at Whataburger.

The door in the stall next to hers opened and shut. Surely he wasn't . . . He didn't intend to . . . The sound of someone stepping on the toilet lid echoed.

He did.

She glared up. He peered down at her over the stall wall. His dark brown hair looked a little longer. His bright green eyes were glowing with humor.

"Fancy meeting you here." He smiled, no doubt at her position—knees bent, locked, her tush hanging two inches above the pot, her jeans down to mid-thigh. Thank goodness her light blue top was long and flared and covered her lady business.

She jerked up and zipped. Never taking her eyes off him, but wishing she had her hands on him. Like her fingers around his throat. He wouldn't be smiling then.

"No paperwork?" he teased.

He thought this was funny? Seriously? Did the guy want to die? Did he not have a clue how much his deceit had hurt her?

If she didn't need information, she'd kill him. And she'd make it slow and painful.

But she needed information, needed to find her uncle, the man who'd killed her aunt and was letting her father go down for the murder. And Chase had that info. Had it from the start, and had lied about it.

She'd recently learned the truth. The man Chase referred to as Eddie, the man who had taken him in when he was fourteen and helped him through his first turn, and bonded with him on the second turn, was Della's uncle.

Who sent you? She'd asked Chase that a thousand times. And a thousand times he'd lied.

As much as she hated admitting it, she understood Chase's loyalty to the man. Not only was Eddie his father figure, but she knew better than anybody how a vampire blood bond could mess with your head and your emotions. But Chase's loyalty to her uncle meant he'd been disloyal to her. He'd made that choice. And she'd be damned if she'd let her own father go to prison for her uncle's sin.

Bolting out of the stall at the same time he did, she cornered all six feet of him. Her pulse raced with fury.

He held his palms up, shoulders tight, but his eyes exhibited no fear. Instead his pools of green still held a touch of tease. Oh, how she wanted to teach him a lesson. She leaned in, putting her face in his, letting him know she wasn't intimidated by him.

A move she instantly regretted. This close, his masculine scent all around her, the lure, the attraction, all of which she blamed on the bond, chipped away at her sanity. She fought it. Didn't want it.

"What are you so happy about?" she growled.

"You," he said. "Being around you makes me happy."

She flattened her palm on his chest, ready to give him a good thump into the wall.

"Wait," he said.

"For what?" she seethed.

His lips twitched into a bigger smile. He pointed to the wall behind his shoulder. "The sign says you need to wash your hands."

That did it. Her canines came out to play. Her eyes stung, a telltale sign that her dark brown irises, inherited from her Asian father, were growing brighter.

"I'm not an employee." She stared him dead in the eyes. His disloyalty stung. "How's Feng, my uncle?"

The playfulness vanished and damned if guilt didn't fill those pools of green. "I was going to tell you."

"Sure you were."

"I wouldn't . . ." He stopped talking as if the words didn't sound right. It took her about two seconds to realize what he'd been about to say.

"Wouldn't what? Lie to me? All you've ever done is lie."

"Della?" Her name being called from the other side of the door barely registered. The fact that she was in vamp mode hardly concerned her. Or rather, when it did bring on a distress signal, it was too late. The bathroom door swung open.

Chase, in a quick swoop, swapped places with her and used his arm to hide her face from Lilly's view. However, the way he leaned in, his hand on the wall, his lips inches from hers, gave the impression they were making out—swapping spit—in a bathroom. Oh, yeah, like that was something she'd actually do. Everyone knew what kinds of germs hung out in public restrooms.

"What . . . ? Della?" Lilly, her human former friend, blurted out as if shocked. The girl rose on her tiptoes to see over Chase's shoulder. "Is that . . . you?"

Della glanced to the side to hide her eyes and canines. "Yeah."

"Oh, my," Lilly said. "And who are . . . you?"

No doubt the question was meant for Chase. Della didn't glance up at his expression, but she knew he'd put on his charm: all smiles and good ol' boy innocent eyes. "I'm a friend." His voice still held on to the tease.

"Looks like you're a good friend," Lilly said in a playful tone. "Are you the notorious Steve?"

Chase's shoulders tightened. His gaze shot to Della, the humor in his eyes fading to hurt, maybe even jealousy.

Not that he had any right to feel it.

Della forced her fangs in, and attempted to calm her inner vamp. "No, he's just someone I know from Shadow Falls."

Feeling under control, she nudged Chase back, giving herself a couple of inches, but no more. Not enough room for him to slide out. She focused on Lilly and motioned to Chase. "We need to talk. Can you give us—"

"No," Chase said. "I just wanted to say hi. I'll swing by your place later."

"No." She cut him a cold glare. He was not getting away. Della grabbed his arm, her grip locked around his bicep. "I'd prefer to chat now." She slapped a smile on her face for Lilly's sake.

"Don't be silly. It's a girls' night out." He gently pried her fingers free with ease.

Then before she knew his intent, he'd planted a quick kiss on her lips. His tongue swiped across her bottom lip, making her knees weak. That taste . . . That quick taste of him had her breath hitching. Her body humming. Her heart wanting. And she hated her own weakness.

She inhaled, fighting the bond while at the same time resisting the urge to go full vamp on his ass again. But before she could figure out her next move, he'd moved out the door. Gone.

Lilly, whom Della hadn't even thought about in a year, leaned against the wall. She stared in shock at his quick exit. "Wow, he's fast." Then she giggled and shook her finger at Della. "Now, now, Miss Tsang. I think you're keeping secrets."

Ya think? Della wanted to scream. The first secret was a real doozy. Della was no longer human. Hence the reason she lived at Shadow Falls, a boarding school for supernaturals. If not for the trouble at home, she'd still be at school—with friends who understood and didn't judge her for downing a glass of blood every now and then.

She didn't even understand why Lilly had just shown up tonight. If her mom hadn't overheard Lilly's invite, and insisted Della go, she wouldn't be in this jam. But since her family didn't know her secrets, it was kind of hard to explain why she couldn't maintain old friendships.

"No, no secrets," Della lied. "That wasn't at all what it looked like. He's just . . . a guy."

"He didn't look like just a guy."

"Looks can be deceiving." Della walked out. She moved down the hall and inhaled to see if she could still lock on to Chase's scent. She let go of a deep gasp of air. Only the smell of hamburgers and fries scented the air. Still, her gaze shifted left then right, hoping for the off chance he was still around. Nope.

Chase was gone. Why the hell had she let him get away? The answer bumped into her back. Literally. Lilly. If Della had used force to detain him, her old friend would have freaked. Then she might have mentioned it to Della's parents. And with all the crap going on with her dad's murder charge, the last thing she wanted to do was give her parents something else to toss and turn about at night.

She faced Lilly, but someone called her name.

"Della Tsang?"

Della turned and saw Mrs. Chi inching closer. She was an older neighbor who co-owned a small jewelry store with her husband, just a couple of blocks away from Della's house. "I have not seen you in forever, young lady."

"Hi," Della said and noticed her neighbor glance at Lilly. "This is my friend Lilly Shay."

"Hello," Mrs. Chi said. Lilly barely nodded. She hadn't even met the woman's eyes and was already pulling her phone up. Had her mother never taught her manners?

"How is Chester?" Della asked. Before she'd left for Shadow Falls, she'd cared for the Chis' cat when they'd gone on vacations.

"The same. He brought me dead rat yesterday. I call exterminator out and they say I have no rats in my home or the store. Where does that cat go to find them?"

"He gets around," Della said, remembering she'd seen the cat snooping around her dad's shed three nights ago when she'd gone out late to the supernatural blood bar.

Mrs. Chi patted Della's arm. "I will go and grab dinner for Bojing. He is at store . . . closing." She glanced at Lilly. "Have good night. Be careful. It is dangerous for two girls to be alone. The neighborhood is not safe as it used to be."

"We will." Della watched the elderly woman move to the counter. Then plastering on what she hoped was a friendly expression— but still irritated by Lilly's rudeness—she faced the blonde. "Did you finish your hamburger?"

"Yeah."

"Then maybe you can drop me back home." She didn't know if Chase had been serious about coming by or if she could add that to his list of lies. Probably a lie, but she should be there, just in case. She wouldn't let him get away this time.

"But we're going over to Susie's to watch a movie."

"Yeah. Sorry, I'm just not up to hanging out. It's that time of the month." She pressed a hand low on her abdomen. It was of course another lie—Aunt Flow had already come and gone. But Mother Nature had plagued women with the monthly curse, and Della figured that meant women had the right to use it as an excuse whenever needed.

Lilly frowned. "But your mom already . . ." She shut her mouth and even curled her lips as if wanting to pull the words back in.

"My mom already . . . what?" Della asked, sensing Lilly had her own secrets.

The girl rolled her green eyes, and Della remembered she'd never really cared too much for Lilly. Even before she'd gone off to Shadow Falls, she and Lilly had drifted apart. "Spill it," Della snapped.

"Your mom paid me to get you out of the house."

Della stood there, mortified and furious that her mom had paid someone to be her friend. Della had friends. She had the two best friends in the world back at Shadow Falls.

Right then she wanted nothing more than to go home, grab her bags, and get back to where she belonged. Where she didn't feel like a monster.

"It's not like I didn't want to see you or anything. But I wasn't going to turn down twenty bucks."

"Take me home." Leaving the stench of grease and beef behind, Della hurried out of the restaurant, fighting the temptation to fly home herself. When the cold Texas air hit her face, she inhaled and swallowed the tears down her throat. She might be hurting on the inside, but she'd be damned if she'd let Lilly know it.

Della didn't say another word. When the car stopped in front of her house, Lilly looked at her. To the girl's credit, she looked sorry. "Should I return your mom's money?"

"No. Keep it." Della jumped out and stopped outside her front door to listen. Her sister was staying over at a friend's house. With any luck, Della could sneak upstairs without a confrontation. She didn't hear the television on. Slowly she turned the knob and made a mad dash inside.

The living room was empty—thank God. She got to the bottom of the staircase and had her foot on the first step when she heard a whisper of music from her dad's study. Della recalled when she would have been in that study with him, playing chess, laughing, and solving the world's problems. Or at least solving Della's problems. Whatever was going on in her life, her father had advice.

Now, there was no advice. He barely acknowledged her presence. As he had done every night in the three weeks that she'd been home, he'd already barricaded himself in his room. She wondered if he hid in there to avoid her. Then again, with a murder conviction hanging over his head, he was probably hiding from life. Earlier today she'd heard him tell her mom that he didn't know how long he could continue to work. People were whispering behind his back.

I'm so sorry, Dad. The knot in Della's throat doubled. It was her fault. Her fault that the cold-case file of her aunt, Bao Yu's, murder had been pulled and reopened. Her fault that her father was being falsely accused of murder.

Yes, the blood on the knife used to kill her aunt had been a perfect match to her father's. Only an identical twin could carry the same blood. Too bad Uncle Eddie, her father's identical twin, had already faked his death. Something most teens did when they were turned vampire. Living with a human family and trying to hide your new nature was near impossible. Della knew that all too well.

Right then it hit her. If she'd done it, if she'd faked her own death, walked away, none of this would have happened. Her family wouldn't be suffering now.

She had her foot on the second stair when her mom stuck her head out from the kitchen. "Why are you back so early?"

Don't do it. Don't do it. Make up some shit. She opened her mouth, waiting for some lie to form, to slip out, but damned if the humiliation she'd felt earlier didn't peak again and her temper got the best of her.

"Guess you didn't pay Lilly enough." Della tore off up the stairs. This time she couldn't swallow the tears.

Chapter Two

Della got to her room and dropped face first on her bed, her chest a big ball of pain. She heard her mom's footsteps and wanted to kick herself, really hard, for not keeping her mouth shut. Her mom already had too much on her plate. But damn, didn't she know how much she'd embarrassed her?

"Della?" Her mom opened the door.

"I'm tired, Mom. I want to sleep," she said into her pillow, praying her voice didn't shake.

The mattress shifted with her mom's weight. "She . . . told you?"

Della nodded.

"I . . . was trying to help."

She felt her mom's hand on her back. She rolled over and popped up, not wanting her mother to notice her cool body temperature. Every time her mom touched her, Della saw the concern in her eyes.

"I don't need help." Della pulled her knees to her chest and hugged them. "I certainly don't need you paying people to be my friends. I have friends, lots of them, at school."

"But you're not at that school now. It's not like . . . I didn't . . . She was helping me out with my groceries and I mentioned she should come over and see you. Then I didn't have any change to give her, so I just dropped a twenty in her hands and said she could come by."

"Just forget it, okay?" Della asked.

"Maybe if you enrolled back in your old school you'd get reacquainted with your old friends and you'd be . . . happier."

"No. I'm happy. As soon as things . . . calm down here, I'll go back to Shadow Falls Academy."

Tears filled her mom's eyes. "Honey, it could be a long time before things . . . calm down. The trial could be months away."

"It's not going to trial. They're going to realize it's a mistake and dismiss the charges." At least according to Burnett, one of Shadow Falls's owners and a member of the Fallen Research Unit (FRU), the supernatural equivalent of the FBI, and the half-warlock lawyer he'd sent to assist in her father's defense.

Tears filled her mom's eyes. "I want to believe that, Della, but we have to be realistic."

Realistic? Della stared at the pain in her mom's eyes. The realization kicked Della in the stomach. No, right in the heart. "Oh, God, you think . . ." Emotion filled her throat. "You think he did it. You think Daddy killed his sister? How could you believe that? You know him better than that."

"I don't think . . ." Her mom swallowed hard. "It's just the evidence—"

"I don't give a shit about the evidence. Dad didn't do this."

"I believe that." Her mom wiped a few tears from her lashes. "But honey, he doesn't remember what happened. He was knocked unconscious. He can't even testify to his innocence."

The room's temperature instantly started falling. Falling fast. Only one thing could make a room go that cold, that quick. They had company. The dead kind.

He was not unconscious!

The words rang in Della's head—for her ears only. She let her gaze shift up. There, in front of the window, midair, hung the ghost of her aunt. She wore the bloody gown again. It flowed back and forth as if some unfelt breeze stirred it. Tears ran down her cheeks, but she looked angrier than she was sad. She hadn't shown herself since Della left Shadow Falls.

Let my mother talk, Della said in her head.

It was the first time her mom had said anything about her dad's account. Her dad would never talk to Della about it, so this was as close as she could get to hearing it from him.

"Tell me what happened, Mom." The more Della knew, the better her chances of helping, but would her mother tell her?

Her mom rubbed her hands up her arms, fighting the cold. "I shouldn't have said anything."

"No," Della said. "I deserve to know."

"Honey, your father—"

"I'm part of this family. It's hurting all of us. We can't keep secrets."

A tear slipped from her mom's lashes. "That's just it, I don't know anything." The cold caused steam to rise from her lips. Della hoped her mother couldn't see it. "The only thing he's told me is that he woke up when the paramedics were there. His sister was . . . dead. He said there was blood everywhere. To this day he has nightmares about it. He got so upset that his parents sent him to a psychologist and they committed him for a while at St. Mary's."

"The mental institution?" Della asked.

Her mom nodded.

"Sharron," her dad called out her mom's name.

Her mom's gaze filled with guilt. She wiped her tears away. "Yes, hon. I'm in here."

Footsteps sounded on the stairs. He stopped in the doorway. His gaze went to Della and—as he always did when he saw her— he flinched. Maybe not physically, but mentally. He'd blink and his pupils would change sizes. What was it about her that caused him so much pain?

"You're home." Disappointment echoed in his tone. His eyes shifted to her mom. "I thought she went out." He tucked his hands into his pockets.

"I came back. You were in the study so I didn't bother you." Della hoped she sounded normal, but it was hard when the ghost stood there, blood dripping from her white gown, staring at Della's dad with murder in her eyes.

"Why is it so cold up here?" he asked. "Have you been playing with the thermostat?"

"No, sir," Della said.

He walked out. Della sat there, holding the hurt inside while freezing on the outside. Glancing back at the ghost, Della prayed that it didn't start snowing. The ghost had done that once before.

Her mom watched her dad leave. She stared at the empty doorway for a second before she turned back to Della. Relief and more guilt filled her mom's eyes. She squeezed Della's hand, as if in some kind of unspoken apology. Thankfully, it was so cold that the chill in her mom's hands matched Della's body temperature.

Then her mom dropped Della's hand and stood up. She was almost out the door when she looked back. "I just want you to be happy, baby."

With the sound of her mom's footsteps treading down the stairs, Della glanced back at the angry ghost, who stood shaking her head.

Lies. It's all lies. He remembers. He remembers everything!

"Do *you* remember?" Della asked, knowing how unreliable ghosts were. Apparently, death, especially a violent death, did a number on your psyche, making memory recall and communicating difficult.

Enough to know he's lying, she said.

"You think he killed you?" Della asked.

The spirit stood there, pain and regret so clear on her face.

"What if it wasn't my father, but your brother, Feng?"

She tilted her head to the side as if remembering. *No, Feng was already . . . He died. There was a car accident.*

Maybe it was time to tell her aunt the truth. "No, he's vampire like me and your daughter, Natasha. Remember, you had me find Natasha? And there was Chan, too. Chan faked his own death to protect his parents from finding out that he was vampire. Just like Feng did."

Bao Yu's eyes glazed over. A dead glaze. Did she not understand?

"Tell me. Tell me exactly what happened." Della braced herself to hear details. When her aunt still didn't speak, Della added, "Or show me." Her chest tightened at the suggestion. Ghosts could pull you into their thoughts, where you basically lived through their experiences. A month ago the ghost had given her a quick glimpse of that night. The vision of someone standing over her dead aunt with a knife. Someone who looked just like her father.

If she could find her uncle, Burnett would attempt to get a supernatural judge on her father's case. Maybe even get it dismissed. But they needed proof. They needed her uncle.

"I'm serious," Della said. "Show me."

It's too ugly.

Della clenched her fist. "In the vision you did show me, Feng was standing over you with a knife. Did he kill you? Think, Bao Yu. Think."

No. Feng, he . . . he didn't have the . . . Chao, he . . . The spirit closed her eyes, as if reliving the vision. *It wasn't Feng. It was Chao.*

The apparition faded.

Gone.

Della muttered words her mom would ground her for saying.

Then with her vampire hearing, she listened to her parents talking, whispering below. While it was rude, she popped out of bed and went to stand in the hall to listen. Her three weeks here had gained her nothing, no new information. How was she going to help figure things out if her parents wouldn't confide in her?

"Why?" her mom asked, speaking to her father. Her voice was a mere whisper, but her tone was tight, filled with angst. "Why do you treat her like that?"

Della's breath caught.

"Like how?" Her father's words bit back. "All I did was ask her if she'd messed with the thermostat."

"It's not what you asked, it's how. Didn't you hear her answer, 'No, sir'? Like you're a drill sergeant. It's as if everything you say to her is an accusation. She's our daughter! Don't you love her?"

Della swallowed the painful lump.

She waited for her father's answer, afraid of his answer.

"She's just . . ."

"Just what?" her mom asked.

"She's changed. She's not the same."

Changed? Della leaned against the wall. Hell, yeah, she'd changed. She'd become a vampire, but he didn't know that. And no way in hell could she tell them.

"Of course she's changed. She's growing up."

"No, it's more than that. And I did nothing wrong," her father snapped. "I've got too much going on to worry about . . . this. I don't understand why she's here. It makes things harder. Send her back."

Della put her palm over her mouth. Tears, tears hotter than her skin, rolled over the back of her hand.

"She's here because she loves you!" her mother said. "Can't you see that?"

Footsteps sounded and the study door slammed in his wake.

Della slid down the hall wall, hugged her knees, and sat there, letting herself cry. She'd come home because Marla, her sister, had begged her to. Now Della had to wonder. Would it be in the best interest of everyone if she went back to Shadow Falls?

How many times would she have to be reminded? She didn't belong here anymore.

She stood up, walked back into her bedroom, and found her phone. She hit the name of someone she knew she could count on—someone who was becoming more of a father to her than the man downstairs.

She called Burnett.

Chapter Three

Chase Tallman stood outside the entrance to Della's house, his hands tightened in fists. Anger burned his eyes. Someone needed to teach that man a lesson, and damned if Chase wouldn't like to volunteer for the job. Could he not see how much he was hurting his own daughter? The fact that he didn't know his daughter was listening didn't excuse shit.

He could feel Della's pain. Feel the knot curling up inside his chest.

Parents were supposed to love you unconditionally. His had. He had never doubted it. Della deserved that too, damn it!

Chase had landed on the house's eaves, beside Della's window. She hadn't been in her room, but then he saw her outside her bedroom door, her shoulders dropped in defeat. Della Tsang didn't do defeat. Behind that tough exterior, there was a vulnerability to her, but she seldom caved in. What was wrong?

He jumped down beside the door, and overheard Chao Tsang's hurtful words. Every single one of them.

Maybe Feng Tsang, or Eddie Falkner as Chase had known the man who took him in after his parents' death, was wrong. Maybe Chao *had* killed his sister. For Della's sake he hoped not, but right now Chase didn't have a high opinion of her father.

He flew back up to the roof, wanting to comfort Della. Her taste, that quick kiss he'd stolen, still lingered on his tongue and he craved more. But all he wanted to do now was hold her. Console her.

She had her back to the window, her phone to her ear, and obviously her guard down or she'd have sensed him.

He tilted his head to see who she was talking to. With about ten feet and a glass pane separating them, all he could make out was that the voice was male.

His memory shot back to Lilly mistaking him for Steve. That had stung. Had Della called Steve for comfort?

"I need to come back to Shadow Falls. Can you call my father and tell him I'm falling behind on my grades?"

So it was Burnett on the phone.

She paused, then spoke again. "I don't care. Make something up. He'll agree to it." Her shoulders tightened. "Yes, he will. He doesn't want me here." She held her breath. The pain sounded in her voice. "Tomorrow's fine."

Chase exhaled a pound of frustration and fury. Fury aimed at her father for being such a bastard, and frustration because . . . Chase didn't want her back at Shadow Falls.

Considering Burnett's distrust of Chase, if Della went back, it would be almost impossible for him to see her. These last three weeks away from her had been hell. Right then his need to be close to her pushed him to accept what he had to do.

It would change everything, but it was the right thing. He'd have already done it, if Burnett hadn't screwed things up.

Chase considered opening her window and telling her his plans, but he recalled her anger at him. She'd try to stop him. He couldn't let that happen.

Knowing that Della would either hear him or catch his scent any second, he drew a heart in the condensation on the window and left.

He'd gotten less than a mile when he picked up the scent of some weres . . . and blood. Diving low, the smell got stronger. Thankfully, it was animal blood. He pulled up higher and went to take care of business.

"What happened?" Burnett asked.

Della gripped her phone tighter. "Nothing."

"Della?"

Fine, it had been a lie. But not really. Sometimes "nothing" just meant it hurt too much to say it aloud. A creak sounded outside and she swung around. "Hold on a minute!" She shot to the window, lifted her nose. His scent held there. Then she saw the heart.

"Damn," she muttered.

"What?" Burnett asked.

She didn't know why, but she wasn't ready to tell Burnett about Chase. Embarrassment, probably, that she'd let him get away. Not because she wanted to protect Chase.

She owed him nothing.

Later, she'd tell Burnett. Hopefully after she'd gotten the information from Chase and knew her uncle's whereabouts.

"I thought I heard someone." She leaned into the window and searched the sky.

"And?" Burnett asked.

"No one is here."

"When is the last time you fed?" he asked, probably thinking she wasn't on top of her game. And he might even be right. She'd let Chase get away. Not once, but twice.

"When?" he repeated.

She knew he wouldn't count the two bites of hamburger and three fries she'd had at the restaurant. No, he meant blood.

"Tuesday." She'd gone to the blood bar.

"Can you get out of the house tonight? I'll meet you with some blood at the park beside your house."

She hated that he felt as if he had to take care of her. "I can wait until I get back."

"No, it's not healthy!"

"Maybe I'll go to the bar." She wouldn't, but he didn't need to know that.

"No, don't go to the bar tonight. It's almost a full moon. Weres will be out and the supernatural bar is the first place they'll go. I'll meet you at the park beside your house."

Her stomach grumbled at the thought of blood, proving Burnett right. She needed to feed. But something about living back at home had her ignoring that hunger—as if doing without blood would somehow help her fit in with her family. Make her more human. Damn, she was pathetic.

Her gaze fell on the fading heart, and she recalled another reason she couldn't leave. What if Chase showed up again? "Really, I think I can wait. Why don't—"

"Della." His tone was dead serious. One that said any argument would be futile.

"Fine. But it will have to be later, when my parents go to bed." Maybe by then Chase would have come back, or she would have found him.

"I'll text you with the details around midnight." He hung up.

Della slipped her phone into her back pocket and stared out at the night—feeling alone.

The moon, almost full, hung in the dark sky. Her instinct nudged her a warning—giving more credence to Burnett's caution. Weres were gathering strength from the lunar glow right now.

While she no longer hated the species as a whole, her vampire predisposition would never let her trust a stray she might stumble upon. They could be rogue.

But it wasn't a were that worried her now, or what caused the

empty spot in her chest. Nope, that would be her father and a con-
niving, lying vamp.

*Where are you, Chase? What kind of game are you playing this
time?*

Why had he come and then disappeared? Why had he seemed
so dad-blasted elated to see her? Did he know her uncle had killed
her aunt? Did he know that she, Burnett, and the FRU were searching for the man? The same man who'd helped Chase survive being
Reborn. Was Chase protecting him?

He had to be, didn't he? Why else would he have disappeared
out of the blue after she texted him the photo of him and her uncle?

She pressed her forehead to the cold glass pane, remembering
their brief kiss, and fought the yin and yang emotions that came
whenever she allowed herself to really think about Chase. Senti-
ments she spent a lot of energy denying, but that in brief moments,
like right now, she couldn't refute.

That damn bond had emotionally tied her to him. Not that it
changed anything.

Was Chase smart enough to know that no matter what feelings
she might harbor for him, given the choice between him and her
father, her father would win? It would probably be like ripping her
heart out. But who needed a heart? The dang organ just caused
problems.

Chase walked into a house in one of Houston's middle-class sub-
urban neighborhoods. Eddie had recently rented it under the name
Jacob Mackey. He'd taken a month off from his position as a research scientist—a job the Vampire Council provided him. The position had saved not only his own life, but Chase's, and Della's,
and those of about twenty other vampires who had gone through
the rebirth stage in the last five years. Eddie was the doctor and
scientist who had discovered the transfusion treatment, along with

numerous lifesaving procedures that had helped their kind and others.

Not only was Eddie dedicated to providing better health care for the vampire species, but he'd been Chase's surrogate father since the plane crash. Then when Chase went through the rebirth, he'd willingly bonded with him. Chase owed him. And more importantly he loved him. Not that they expressed endearments, but actions spoke louder than words.

Which was why this was all going to be so difficult.

Chase moved into the living room, where Eddie sat in his old brown recliner—the only piece of furniture that he moved with him whenever he relocated. On the end table was the framed photo that also went with him. Kirsha. Eddie's bond mate that had died only a year after they'd been together.

Baxter came running and nudged Chase's leg with his nose.

Eddie held a newspaper in his hands, and only when Chase dropped down on the sofa did Eddie look up.

He studied Chase. Eddie could read him so well, it was pointless to try and hide anything. Not that Eddie hadn't ever had secrets from him. Until Della had told him about Bao Yu, he hadn't known about the murder.

"What's got your eyes so bright, son?"

"Chao Tsang, your twin. Perhaps you have it wrong. Maybe he did kill your sister."

Eddie sat up, lowering the recliner with a firm thump. His expression was serious. "That's ridiculous. I told you what happened. We find Douglas Stone and we'll have our proof."

"You said you didn't see the murder. And the more I get to know your twin, the more—"

"Stop," Eddie said. "Why would my brother do this?"

"Why would he treat his daughter with such disrespect? Do you have any idea how much he's hurting her?"

Eddie took a deep breath, and emotion filled his eyes. "You feel for her. She's your bond mate, so that's understandable, but don't toss out harmful statements. Chao is already facing charges."

"As are you," Chase countered. "The FRU are looking at you for this! This whole thing is a mess. Leave. Don't tell me where you're going, don't call. Let me do what I have to do. When Douglas Stone is found, and the FRU is no longer hunting you, I'll let the Vampire Council know and they can contact you."

He shook his head slowly. "No. You do what you have to do. Don't worry about me."

Chase ran a hand over his face. Damn, this was hard. "We need the FRU's help."

"The council is on this," Eddie insisted.

"You, yourself, told me that you've had the council looking for Douglas Stone for over sixteen years. They haven't found him. What makes you think they'll find him now?"

"They realize the urgency now that this has escalated."

Chase stared up at the ceiling trying to find an easy way to say this, but there wasn't one. He looked at Eddie. "I'm resigning my position with the council."

To his credit, Eddie didn't look surprised. "To work for them? The FRU?"

Chase nodded.

"The bond you have for her is that strong?" Eddie asked, only the tiniest amount of hurt in his voice. What Eddie was really asking was if the bond he shared with Della was stronger than theirs. It wasn't any stronger. He was indebted to Eddie, in so many ways, but what he felt for Della was different.

"Does she not feel it?" Eddie continued. "Why does she not join you at the council?"

"She's stubborn. Like you." Eddie looked at the picture of Kirsha. Chase knew Eddie couldn't, wouldn't argue. He knew how special a bond mate was. Hell, the man had never married again, and it had been over ten years. He might have entertained a few women, but

Chase remembered him telling him that his heart would always belong to just one.

"Have you tried to convince her?" Eddie asked.

Chase realized he needed to be completely honest. "It's not just the bond." He swallowed. "I see the good the FRU is doing."

"And you don't see what good the council has done?"

"Of course I do, but the council has always run with the us-against-them policy. All supernaturals need to come together. The FRU is working toward that. It's a good goal."

"Because we think taking care of our own comes first, we are the enemy?"

"No. Not the enemy. The council needs to exist. But to govern, we need to unite—not only with the other supernaturals, but with the federal government and the human police."

"If the FRU has their way, the council won't exist."

Chase got the feeling that Eddie's complete distrust of the FRU was more than just a political stance. But it was something Eddie never spoke of.

"Then someone needs to show the FRU that's wrong. I could be that someone." He tightened his hands. "Look, I'm not saying their procedures are perfect, but I agree with a lot of their policies. United we can accomplish more. Have more resources. Sources that could help us find Stone."

Eddie went back to the window, staring out into the night. Guilt washed over Chase. With Chase being raised like his son these past years, Eddie expected him to follow his advice.

"I know you don't respect my decision," Chase said.

"Do I agree with it? No." Eddie turned around. "But I respect you enough that I will not try to stop you. You are your own person, Chase Tallman." A sad smile appeared in his eyes. "You are so much like your father. He and I never agreed on politics either."

"Then respect me enough to do one more thing for me," Chase said. "Go somewhere else. Somewhere the FRU can't find you. Somewhere I don't know, so when they ask me where you are, I won't have to lie. Because if they can't find Stone, they'll want you for this."

"Or they'll convict my brother." Eddie exhaled. He looked back outside at the darkness. Several slow seconds ticked by before he turned back. "If they can't find Stone, I'll turn myself in."

Chase shot off the sofa. "What?" He shook his head. "No! They'll imprison you."

"Or they'll imprison my brother. He holds no fault here. I can't say the same."

Chapter Four

"You didn't do this." Chase's eyes burned with frustration.

"No, I didn't kill Bao Yu. I would have taken her place a thousand times. But I joined the Vultures gang, Chase."

When Chase learned Della's aunt had been killed, Eddie had told Chase the story. "You were young and scared."

"But it was my mistake. I own it. It was because of me that they killed her."

"That doesn't make you guilty," Chase insisted.

Eddie frowned. "In a way, it does, son."

Eddie's calm attitude had Chase clenching his jaw. "How? You chose not to kill someone, now you are going to pay the price for them killing someone you loved." He paced the path between the sofa and coffee table once. Then twice. There had been times when Chase had wished he too had died with his family, but Eddie made him see that life was worth living.

"I made a mistake," Eddie said. "I'm more responsible than Chao. And before I'll let him pay for this, I will pay." Eddie's dark eyes met Chase's in a firm look. "Now respect me and my wishes like I respect yours."

Eddie was dead serious. Emotion tightened Chase's chest. "I'll find Douglas Stone. I'm not going to let you go to prison." And he meant it.

Eddie put a hand on his shoulder. "I have no doubt you'll do everything you can." He gave Chase's shoulder a heartfelt squeeze. "Meanwhile take care of my niece. You call her stubborn, and you are right: The Tsangs are headstrong. But son, you have your own obstinate side." His smile widened. "The two of you are going to make quite a pair."

The advice came from the heart. Chase owed this man so much, and right or wrong, he felt as if he were turning his back on him.

Then it occurred to him that what he felt for Eddie, Della felt for her father. Whether Chase liked the man or not, even if he wasn't deserving of his daughter's affection, Della was emotionally connected to him.

"You need to get to know her," Chase said. "You would be proud of her."

"I have no doubt. I can see you care for her. Does she feel the same for you?"

"Like I said, she's stubborn."

Eddie smiled. "But you will win her over."

Chase put his hand on Eddie's. Why did this good-bye seem harder? Part of him longed to be exactly who Eddie wanted him to be, but Chase wasn't blind to the rights and wrongs of the council's ways.

Chase moved over to Baxter and gave him a good ear rub. "Take him to Kirk's. I'll get him from there." Not that Chase was looking forward to facing Kirk, either. Kirk Curtis was Eddie's best friend and a member of the council. Kirk had even been with Chase when they found the crashed plane.

Eddie nodded. "Are you sure this Burnett James is going to accept you after what happened? You've said he's a hardass."

The same question had been bubbling in Chase's subconscious. "A letter releasing me from the council would help."

"Kirk can provide that. He's at his office right now." Eddie paused. "And if that doesn't work, come back, where you belong."

"It'll work." Chase refused to believe otherwise. "It has to." His gut knotted, thinking about the possibility that his request would be denied. But even the best-case scenario of Burnett agreeing was going to be hard. For there was no way Burnett was going to let him back in without giving him some comeuppance.

If Burnett excelled at anything, it was dishing it out. And if there was one thing Chase sucked at, it was taking it. He'd never liked eating crow.

But he'd better work up an appetite. For Della, he'd do it.

Nodding goodbye, he walked out of the living room. Baxter followed him, gazing up at him, his tail thumping. Chase knelt down. "I'll be back soon to take you with me. Promise."

Chase's phone, tucked in his back pocket, dinged with an incoming text. He stood up and pulled it out.

His heart jolted when Della's name appeared. When he'd first left on a mission, trying to find the lowlife rogue who'd killed Eddie's sister, she'd tried to contact him. It had hurt not to be able to answer her. It had hurt more when she stopped trying to contact him. He read her text.

What game are you playing now?

"Just the one to win you back," he said to himself as he walked out.

Della had cratered and texted Chase again. Now she stared holes into her phone waiting to see if he would answer.

When no ding came, she paced her room for another ten minutes.

Back.

Forth.

Back.

Forth.

Feeling caged in, she noted the clock on her bedside table. It wasn't eight o'clock. Her parents were still moving about downstairs and normally didn't even go to the bedroom until after eleven.

She went to the window, slid it open halfway, and took a big breath of cold November air.

Was Chase still close by?

The slightest hint of his scent lingered outside her window, but it wasn't fresh. Glancing over her shoulder at the clock again, her stomach quivered with the need to hit the dark sky and search for the lying bloodsucker.

Maybe just a few laps around the block? Perhaps he lingered close by? Moving over to her closet, she yanked off her pastel-colored top and donned a black fitted tee. Then out of her suitcase, she pulled the black wig and the extra-large shapeable pillow she'd brought with her from camp. She stuffed the pillows under the blanket to make it look like a body, then slipped the wig under the top of the cover, leaving just enough of the straight dark hair hanging out to make it look convincing.

Stepping back, she looked at the imitation of her. It looked as if she were the hunchback of Notre Dame. She went back to rearrange the pillows. With just a little fluff, she stepped back again to check her handiwork.

Friggin' great, now she looked like a Hooters waitress with size Ds. She yanked back the covers and gave her pillowed self a breast reduction.

She moved toward the door to make sure it looked convincing for when her mom did her normal peek-in to confirm Della was sleeping. Right then she imagined her mom discovering the faux Della and how upset it would make her.

Blinking, she glanced away, but her gaze stopped on the framed picture on her dresser. The one taken before a father-daughter dance. She'd been eight. Her father had knelt down and put his arm around her. She could still recall how special he'd made her feel that night.

Then she remembered her mom's words from earlier. *She's our daughter! Don't you love her anymore?*

A knot tightened her throat. She looked back at the window; she had to find Chase, find him and get him to hand over her uncle. Standing up, she grabbed her phone and fit it in her back pocket, then went to the window and eased it open. Slowly, so it couldn't be heard below, she climbed out on the roof, turned, closed her window, and took a flying leap into the dark sky.

Twice she flew around the neighborhood, hoping to get a fix on Chase's scent. She got nothing. Well, not nothing. She got a hint of a few weres. And from about a hundred feet up, she spotted three young guys. Were they the weres? And if so, were they just cruising the neighborhood, or were they looking for trouble?

Flying lower, the scent got stronger and she got a good glimpse of them. They weren't dressed in gang attire, so chances were they weren't rogues, just some young guys, who happened to be weres, out on a Saturday night. She couldn't condemn them for that.

Right before she moved higher, one of the weres must have gotten her trace. One and then all three looked up. She saw their three faces, all scowling in dislike. Not wanting any trouble, she hurried back home.

Della had just shut her window when her phone rang.

Chase?

She hurried to get the cell out of her jeans.

"Hello?" she answered before looking at the number.

"Della?"

It took a second to recognize Natasha's voice and another for Della to feel guilty for not contacting her since she'd left Shadow Falls. For a good reason, of course, Della didn't want to have to explain to her cousin that her own father was accused of killing her mother. She and Natasha had grown so close since she and Chase had rescued her and her boyfriend, Liam.

"Hi, Natasha."

"Guess who Liam saw earlier today when he was visiting his mother?"

"I have no idea," Della said.

"Chase. And he asked Liam if we would house sit for him. Of course, we know he's just being nice and giving us a place to stay. Have you seen his cabin? He could rent it out in a snap."

"Yeah." Della remembered the warm interior of leather and wood. The cabin, secluded in the woods, spoke of relaxation. And her cousin was right. Chase could have easily rented it.

She recalled how happy Chase had been when they'd found Natasha and Liam.

It had been less than a month ago, but it felt like forever. She'd been about to give herself to Chase. Damn, she'd been a whisper away from sleeping with the lying vamp.

She moved to the window, where his scent was still lingering.

Liam and Chase talked forever," Natasha said.

Had Chase had told Liam about the murder case?

"Are you still staying at your parents'?" Natasha asked.

"Yeah."

"I've been worried. Look, I know about your father being charged with my mother's murder."

"Chase told Liam?" Della asked.

"No, Burnett explained it when I asked about you. I can't imagine how hard that must be."

Della took a deep breath. "He didn't kill her."

"I know. Burnett told us about our other uncle and how you two think he did this. But then Chase told Liam—"

"I don't care what he said. My dad didn't kill—"

"Chase doesn't think your dad did it."

Della heard the words but couldn't digest them. "Then why is he protecting a murderer? Why hasn't he turned in Feng?"

"He said Feng, or Eddie as he calls him, didn't do it either. But they know who did kill her. And they're looking for the guy and trying to get your dad off, too."

Della stood there, trying to wrap her brain around this. "But he lied to me the whole time. And then he took off when I found out he knew our uncle."

"I can't defend his actions," Natasha said. "But I know he cares a lot about you. And Liam said he was trying to make it right."

"The only way to make it right is to turn Feng over to the FRU. Let them decide if he's telling the truth." Della took in a deep breath. "Where is Chase?" She held her breath, waiting. Hoping.

"No one knows." Then after a second, she said, "Oh, Burnett is trying to find a way for me to still be alive. To say I was kidnapped and they just misidentified the body."

Della became lost in the absurdity of it. She'd been thinking everyone would have been better off if she'd faked her death, and here her cousin was trying to undo hers. Which one was right?

"If anyone can do it, Burnett can," Della said

The line got quiet. Then Natasha spoke up. "I know you still have your family, and maybe I'll get mine back, but . . . right now, you are the only family I have. I would really like to see you and just talk. Please."

"I promise, I'll stop by soon."

Chase parked in front of the Shadow Falls entrance. Burnett had probably already heard his car and picked up on his scent. Was he gearing up to give Chase shit, right this moment?

Running a hand over his face, he reminded himself not to give the man any lip. If Burnett was going to allow Chase back at Shadow Falls, Burnett would demand respect.

Chase didn't have a problem with respect. He had a problem with Burnett. Not that Burnett didn't deserve respect. Chase wouldn't be here if he didn't. But Burnett didn't respect Chase. And while Chase didn't like admitting it, the agent's lack of regard was probably for good reasons. More than once Chase had lied to the man.

Are you sure this Burnett James is going to accept you after what happened? Eddie's question had brought Chase's fears to the surface.

Because Chase wasn't a hundred percent sure Burnett would take him back, he decided to cover his bets.

Before coming here, he'd stopped off at the FRU office and slipped in his application to work for the bureau through the mail slot. In the same envelope he'd included a copy of his letter of resignation from the council and his own personal requirements: He would live at Shadow Falls and work under Burnett.

His goal was that the FRU would put pressure on Burnett to say yes to Chase's offer. They were, after all, Burnett's boss.

Hell, for all Chase knew, Burnett had already received a call from the FRU office. A flicker of light in the school's main office came on.

So Burnett was waiting for him. Taking a deep breath, Chase went to face the music.

How hard could it be? He'd already faced Eddie and Kirk. And while telling Eddie had been emotionally harder, Kirk, like an uncle to Chase, had been less understanding. Not that it had surprised Chase; Kirk, as part of the vampire council, saw Chase's actions as disloyal. *I personally trained you.* Kirk's words still echoed inside Chase's head and heart.

Chase was almost to the Shadow Falls gate when he heard Burnett's voice. "I'll text her in a few minutes and let her know you will be showing up instead of me. Don't forget the blood. And don't mention this."

For some reason Chase knew Burnett was talking about Della. And the "this" had to be about him.

Through the darkness Chase spotted Lucas Parker stepping out onto the office porch. Lucas was taking Della blood. If Chase had known she needed blood he could have supplied it.

He felt like an idiot. Of course she would need blood. She'd been living with her parents, pretending to be human. Since he'd been turned he'd never had to live with humans, and therefore hadn't considered this. He felt a ding to his ego knowing he'd let Della down.

Again.

Just one more thing he had to make up to her.

Lucas's footsteps came closer and Chase looked up. The dark-haired, blue-eyed were approached with a smile. While Lucas was a were, Chase didn't have a problem with the guy. Chase could even relate to Lucas. The were had gone against his own family and joined the Were Council while fully intending to work with the FRU.

Lucas stopped. "Good luck." It was as if he knew exactly what Chase was up against. "Say 'yes, sir' a lot and don't mouth off."

Shoulders tight, Chase made his way into the office.

He stepped through the front door. The only light on was in the back office. Burnett's office.

Trying to hide his unease, he walked in. Burnett sat behind his desk. His eyes were a light yellow, telling Chase the man was already angry.

The older vampire had a few inches and about twenty pounds on Chase. Not that Chase was afraid—at least not of physical harm. The man had other means to hurt him.

Della respected Burnett. In a way, Burnett was more of a father figure than her own dad. If Burnett was dead set on keeping him and Della apart, it would make this harder.

Not impossible, because Chase wouldn't allow that, but harder.

Burnett looked at the chair across from him in an invitation, though not an overwhelmingly friendly one. Chase pulled the folded envelope from his pocket containing another copy of his resignation and his requirements and placed it on the desk.

They sat there. In silence. Time ticked by slowly. Was this some kind of a test? Deciding to take a chance, Chase cleared his throat. "I realize—"

"Back again, are you?" Burnett interrupted.

Chase nodded. When the man didn't reach for the envelope he

figured he'd spoken to someone from the office and knew what was inside. And if his expression was any indication, he didn't like it.

But was he angry because of Chase's demands that he work under Burnett and stay at the camp, or was he just angry at Chase?

"This time is different," Chase offered.

"You expect me to believe that?"

"I brought—"

"I know," he seethed.

Chase again tried to decide how to play this. "I would be an asset to the FRU."

Burnett's eyes glowed brighter. "To the FRU, yes. To Shadow Falls, to Della . . . no!"

Chase stiffened. "We are bon—"

"I don't give a rat's ass what you are. You hurt her!" He slammed his fist down on his desk. The heavy piece of oak furniture bounced off the floor. "She has enough pain from her father. She doesn't need the likes of you messing with her."

Chapter Five

"I never intended to hurt her." Chase felt his own eyes grow bright.

"Your intent doesn't mean shit!" Burnett said. "You saved her life and then you left her. Not once, but twice!" His fist hit the desk again.

Chase wondered how many blows the desk would take before collapsing. Better the desk than him.

"Don't you think that hurt her?" His bright eyes dared Chase to deny it.

"I suppose it did," Chase admitted. "The first time, I left because I knew once you figured out I was working with the council you wouldn't allow me to stay. The second . . . I left to fix a problem, not to create one."

"You left to protect Feng Tsang and let Della's father take the fall."

Chase lifted his gaze. "I left to find the person responsible for committing the murder."

"That would be Feng Tsang," Burnett said. "Della saw in a vision—"

"I don't know what Della saw, but Feng did not kill his sister. But he knows who did."

Burnett did not look convinced. "Do you know where Feng is?"

Chase met his gaze sincerely. "No."

"If you did know, would you tell me?"

He could lie and control his heartbeat, but he suspected Burnett would guess. "No."

"So you're still protecting him?"

"I'm trying to protect the innocent. That includes Della's father."

Burnett leaned in again. "Funny, that's what I'm trying to do. And you know who's more innocent than Chao Tsang?" He paused. "Della."

He got Burnett's meaning. "You don't need to protect Della from me."

"The hell I don't!" His palms flatted on his desk. His canines extended as a not so subtle reminder of how dangerous he could be.

Chase had to grit his teeth not to tell Burnett to go to hell. Instead he sat in silence. Total silence. Somewhere in the office was a clock, and it marked the seconds as they passed. Chase stopped counting at sixty.

Burnett finally leaned back, not in a relaxed pose, but he no longer looked poised to pounce. "If you know who killed Della's aunt, why don't you just bring their ass in to the FRU?"

"I need some help," Chase admitted.

"And the council won't help you?"

He pulled his shoulders up, not in defense, but in honesty. "They have tried. His name is Douglas Stone."

Burnett sat still. "Who is he?"

Before Chase could answer, Burnett's phone dinged with a text. He read it and instantly his eyes glistened with anger. When he looked up all that fury was aimed as Chase.

Was it at him, or at whoever left the text? Didn't matter, Chase surmised, because right now he was the only target.

"And now you come begging for our help," Burnett seethed.

It was the word *begging* that did it—pushed Chase over the edge.

"I am *not* begging." He inhaled to calm his fury, especially in the face of Burnett's rage. "I'm offering my services to the FRU."

Burnett leaned in again. Chase had seen the man angry, but never like this.

"Then offer it to them, Mr. Tallman. Don't involve me or Shadow Falls in your deal."

Chase squared off. Was that what the text had been about? "Surely the FRU knows the value of having another Reborn in their employment. My conditions . . ."

The man's canines came all the way out and his eyes glowed.

Just like that, Chase realized his mistake. He should never have tried to use leverage against Burnett.

"My intent was—"

"Take your intentions," he shoved the envelope across the desk, "and get the hell off my property. No one—not you, not the FRU— tells me what I must do! Don't you think for a minute I wouldn't walk away from my position with the agency to protect those that I love? And no one—*no one*—forces my hand!"

Right then Chase realized that was exactly what he'd done wrong. Tried to force Burnett to accept him back.

The desk between them was suddenly slung against the wall. Burnett James stood up in full vamp mode.

Yup, it had been a big mistake.

"Go!" Burnett seethed. "While you still can!"

Chase stood up. "Look, I realize—"

"Go!" he ordered.

Chase heard the warning in the vampire's voice and saw it in his eyes. Desperate, but not stupid, he turned and walked out.

Damn it to hell and back! Chase seethed as he hurried off the porch. He'd screwed up. At this rate, he was never going to win Della back.

At this rate, maybe he didn't deserve to. He should have known this would backfire.

. . .

Della landed in the park in the mix of the trees and rubbed her arms to fight off the cold, again wishing she'd worn a jacket. The moon gleamed on the metal playground equipment in the clearing about a hundred feet away. Another chill tiptoed down her back. There was something eerie and almost ominous about an empty playground—as if it had been robbed of its innocence.

A swing squeaked as a cold breeze stirred it. The noise seemed loud, as if it were a call for help in the night's silence.

She looked around at the dark shadows and lifted her nose to make sure no one lurked nearby.

Her phone beeped. Probably Burnett.

As she pulled her cell from her pocket, she heard a car pull up and cut off its engine. Someone opened a car door and then she caught the scent of a were. She shifted deeper into the trees, glancing up to plan her exit if the were came at her. Right as she clicked on Burnett's number the scent became familiar. She knew before she read the text what it would say.

Burnett hadn't come. Had Lucas brought Kylie? She inhaled again.

No Kylie. Disappointment stirred. She could have used some girlfriend time.

Turning, she watched as the good-looking were crossed the parking lot. The dark-haired, six-foot-plus eighteen-year-old held a Thermos. Her stomach grumbled.

"Hey . . . ," Della said and then, "thanks." She took the Thermos.

"No problem," he said.

"Why didn't Burnett show?"

"Something came up," the were said.

"A new case?"

"I don't think so," Lucas said.

Della wasn't sure if he was hiding something or just being vague.

Lucas wasn't exactly the talkative sort. Most weres weren't. Not that Della disliked him. He loved Kylie, one of Della's best friends, and he was good to her.

"Do you mind?" She held up the Thermos.

"No. My job's not complete until you do."

They moved over to the playground.

She glanced back just then, realizing what he'd said. "Did Burnett instruct you to watch me drink?"

When he didn't answer, she knew he had. "That's ridiculous."

"He just knows how hard it is to be vampire while trying to coexist with humans."

She found just a little comfort in knowing it wasn't just her.

"I hear you're coming back to Shadow Falls." Lucas stood beside a swing set.

A new wave of hurt filled her chest. "Yeah." She offered one quick word, then lifted the nozzle and drank. The sweet berry fluid of O negative spilled on her tongue and she had to remind herself to slow down and savor it. Burnett had sent his good stuff.

"I saw Kylie and Miranda before I left. I told them," he said. "They're thrilled. Miranda hasn't had anyone to fight with since you left."

"We don't fight that much." She dropped into a swing and kicked the ground with the heels of her boots.

"Right." Lucas chuckled. "They miss you."

Della latched her hand around the chain. She just sat there, the round plastic rubber of the swing's bottom hugging her butt, and drank her blood and thought about her two friends.

"Me, too," Della finally said. Not that she didn't talk to them—she did, about twice a day. But she still missed them. Missed everything and everyone at Shadow Falls. It was home. So why did the thought of going back hurt so much? The answer bubbled up from the ache in her chest. Because her dad didn't want his own daughter around.

After taking several more sips, she saw Lucas tilt his head to the side as if listening. Normally, a vampire's hearing, sight, and strength were stronger than a were's, except around the time of a full moon. That's why vampires had to be on higher alert during this time. Still, she angled her own head and listened to see if she picked up on anything.

Sirens. Several of them. She stood up and gulped down the last of her dinner. "Let's go check it out." She wasn't ready to go back to her room and get caught up in the hurt again.

They tossed the Thermos in Lucas's car. By the time they'd exited the woods, three cop cars, with sirens and lights flashing, were in the parking lot of a strip mall about a block from the entrance to Della's subdivision. In it were the Chis' small jewelry store, an all-night convenience store, and a pizza joint. Had someone tried to walk out without paying for a six-pack?

Lucas stopped before moving closer to the crowd and his expression tightened. Della, still fighting the cold, lifted her face and caught the scent of what had brought on his frown. Blood. Lots of blood as well as traces of . . . "Weres," Della said aloud. Though the scent was weak.

She recalled seeing the three weres walking down the street earlier. In her mind's eye, she could picture all three of their faces, too.

"We should call Burnett." Della shivered again from the cold.

"We don't know if the weres were involved," Lucas said, in defense of his whole species.

She couldn't blame him. He was right. Of all the species inhabiting the earth, humans did more than their share of causing trouble. And shedding blood.

"It was a robbery," someone said into a phone. An ambulance pulled up and two uniformed guys jumped out of the vehicle.

Looking between a couple standing in front of her, Della expected to see the paramedics running inside the only opened business, a convenience store.

But they passed that door and . . . "Not the Chis' store," Della muttered and slipped her way up closer to the front of the crowd.

Crap! It was the jewelry store. Had someone broken in? But whose blood was it? The Chis closed the shop at seven. By now they were home in bed.

Another cold blast of November air sent goose bumps climbing up Della's bare arms. She slipped her hand into her jeans pockets to warm her fingers.

All of a sudden Della heard a meow. She looked to her right and much to her relief, Mrs. Chi stood there with Chester, the big orange tabby, in her arms.

"Oh, thank God," Della said. "What happened, Mrs. Chi? Is Mr. Chi okay?"

"I don't know," Mrs. Chi said. "I . . . I . . ."

The cat vanished. Poof, her arms were empty. Mrs. Chi gasped right along with Della, and then the woman looked around on the ground. "Chester? Chester?"

From inside the store, Della heard one of the cops say, "The cat's still alive. Someone get this cat to a vet." Della suddenly recognized the cold. The kind of cold that came with death—that came with the dead.

Chapter Six

Her chest gripped, and she felt pain behind her rib cage. Goose bumps tripled and chased each other on Della's skin. She looked at her elderly neighbor, remembering that when she'd been turned and Mrs. Chi had heard she'd been sick, she'd brought Della egg drop soup. Was the woman . . . ?

Mrs. Chi glanced up at Della. "Have you seen my cat?" Then panic entered her dark Asian eyes. "What happened? I brought hamburgers and then . . ." She faded, turning into nothing more than a smear of wispy fog in the night. Or was that smear the mist in Della's own eyes?

"No," Della said. "Talk to me. Who did this to you?"

"Who did what?" Lucas asked, now standing next to her.

Della ignored him and pushed her way through the crowd, wanting nothing more than to prove herself wrong. Right before she went to jump over the yellow tape that an officer had just rolled out, Lucas caught her.

"You can't go in there." He leaned in. "Della? What's going on? You're acting freaky. Kylie freaky. Ghost freaky."

Della ignored Lucas and listened to the cops' dialogue. "How many?" asked one of the paramedics.

"Two," someone answered. "I'm told it was their store. Someone pumping gas saw the old man on the floor through the window."

Chase had taken his car down some back roads where he could drive fast. He'd even taken the top down, hoping the frigid air would help him think of how to get his ass out of the sling he'd gotten himself into.

As his motor roared he recalled something his dad had told him years ago. Chase had thrown a ball and accidentally broken his next door neighbor's window. The old man who lived there had been a grumpy ol' ass. Chase hadn't wanted to face him. His mom had agreed to do it, but when his dad found out their plan, he hit the roof.

When you make a mistake, son, you face it.

He's gonna yell at me, Dad.

Well, yeah. You broke his window. He has the right to yell.

Chase turned his car around and headed back to Shadow Falls.

He parked his car. The lights were off in the office. Burnett was probably at the cabin he and Holiday shared. He walked through the gate, knowing the alarm rang.

When he stepped up on their porch he heard Holiday talking, no doubt trying to calm her husband down. It seemed that was the woman's mission in life.

He knocked.

"Be smart and leave!" Burnett's words and anger carried through the door.

"I'm not leaving," Chase said.

The door swung open. A bright-eyed Burnett stood there.

"Can I come in?" Chase asked.

"I'd prefer you didn't," he said, but shifted back.

Chase stepped inside. Holiday rushed in from the hall with Hannah, her dark-haired little girl, in her arms and placed the baby in Burnett's arms.

"What are you doing?" Burnett asked.

"You asked me to not let you kill him. I figure you won't kill him if you're holding Hannah." The woman's green eyes looked determined. "Plus, she needs changing and it's your turn."

Burnett cradled the small sleepy body against him. "I still have one free hand." He looked at Chase. "Why are you back?"

Chase swallowed the lump in his throat. It wasn't fear, it was pride. "Because I remembered something my dad told me. *When you make a mistake, you face it.* I made a mistake, sir."

"If you mean coming back here, I agree."

"No. I made a mistake trying to force your hand. You demand respect, and believe it or not, I do respect you. What I did was probably the most disrespectful thing I could have done. I'm asking you to overlook my stupidity. Let me stay here."

"Because of Della?"

"Yes. But not just that. I want to work for—"

"They can train you." Burnett's tone was colored with anger.

"I don't just want to be an FRU agent." He met the man's stern gaze. "I want to be a damn good FRU agent. I want to learn from the best. And you are the best I've seen. Della has told me that you take risks and will break rules to do what is right. That's the kind of agent I want to be. I'm asking you to take me under your wing. Teach me how to do this. To work within a set of guidelines and still be true to yourself."

Burnett stood there, his eyes still hot. His daughter looked at Chase with a toothless grin. The contrast between the two looks alone made the moment feel awkward.

"I'm asking for one more chance," Chase said. "Let me earn your respect. I'll do whatever it takes."

Burnett's expression lost some heat. He looked at his wife. She nodded. Her husband exhaled, looked back at his daughter and frowned, then glanced back at Chase. "Anything?"

"Anything," Chase said.

"Do you know how to change a poopy diaper?"

The smell hit Chase's nose and his Adam's apple trembled. He took a step forward to do his duty. "I can learn."

"Not on my baby," Holiday said. "It's your turn, Daddy." She pointed down the hall.

Burnett glanced back at Chase. "But I need—"

"To change a diaper. It's my turn to talk." Holiday motioned for her husband to leave.

Burnett walked away with his smiling daughter in his arms. As he left, Chase heard him say, "Hannah, how can you be so sweet and smell so bad?"

"Thank you," Chase said, sensing Holiday's nod earlier meant more than he could guess.

"Don't thank me." Holiday moved closer. "What you said was powerful."

"I meant it."

"I believe you." She looked down the hall to where Burnett and Hannah had disappeared. "You know my husband might be hard as nails on the outside, but on the inside he's the most decent man I know. He's taken an oath to never cause unnecessary harm. He follows that. Although a few times I've had to remind him of it."

Chase nodded. "He's very lucky to have you."

"Me, on the other hand," she continued. "I never took any oaths. And Chase Tallman, if you hurt Della one more time, I'm going to remove your boy parts, grind them up, and feed them to the hungry rats and scorpions. Is that clear?"

Chase nodded. He would have said, *yes, madam,* but he'd about swallowed his tongue. It wasn't just the removal aspect of what she'd said, but the hungry rats and scorpions. Those two words should never be used in the same sentence with boy parts.

"Now, go. If you need a place to sleep tonight, cabin fourteen is empty."

. . .

"We should probably leave," Lucas said for the eighth time.

What if Mrs. Chi came back and could tell Della who'd done this? She needed to know. Needed to find the idiots and make them pay.

"I saw them," she muttered, her gaze on the front of the jewelry store as they wheeled a body out on a stretcher. Her chest filled with a knot of hurt.

"Saw who?" Lucas asked.

"The weres. There were three of them."

Lucas spoke in a whisper. "We don't know if weres did this."

"Their scent is here," Della said. "I'm sorry if this insults you, but we are both pretty sure what happened."

"Just because they were here doesn't mean they killed anyone," he said in a low voice.

"We won't know that until someone looks at the evidence. And if someone doesn't inform the FRU, this evidence might not be available to them."

Lucas closed his eyes as if trying to digest her words.

"Let's contact Burnett." Della pulled her phone out of her pocket and typed a text.

Chase dropped a hand over his eyes and sighed. The stench of fresh paint filled the space and was giving him a headache.

A knock at the cabin door echoed through the thick wooden walls. He didn't have to guess who it was. He'd heard and sensed Burnett land outside the second his head hit the pillow. And he'd been counting his lucky stars that Burnett hadn't planned on interrogating him tonight. He'd eaten just about all the crow he could stand.

"Come in," he said, getting up, knowing Burnett could hear him.

By the time he got dressed and entered the living room, Burnett was sitting on the sofa—in the dark. His eyes weren't bright, a good sign. The man nodded to the chair across from him. Chase followed orders and sat.

"Douglas Stone." Burnett said the name—nothing else. He didn't actually say he wanted information, but it was implied. And since Chase had already pissed the man off, he decided not to push it.

He stood and walked to the table in the adjoining kitchen and pulled out the file from his backpack. Walking over, he handed it to Burnett.

"It's everything we have on him."

Burnett opened the file and thumbed through it. The only sound in the dark air was of the papers rustling. He finally looked up.

"Most of this information is fifteen years old."

Chase nodded. "I know."

Frustration tightened the older vampire's expression. "Do you know how hard it is to find someone with this outdated information?"

"Difficult. I know. Not impossible."

"But improbable," Burnett hissed.

"There is one new report from a council affiliate at the end of the file. A Douglas Stone was questioned in a different murder."

Burnett turned a few more pages, read, then looked up. "In France?" He inhaled again. "That's what you were doing there?"

Chase nodded, hoping the fact that he'd actually saved Miranda Kane would make Burnett less inclined to be an asshole.

"Was Della's uncle with you?"

"Yes."

Burnett continued to stare. "But you don't know where he is now?"

"No."

"Because you told him not to tell you?" he accused.

Again, Chase decided to tell the truth. "Right."

Burnett looked down at the file. "In France, you came up empty again and couldn't find him?"

"We have proof that someone fitting his description, using the name Don Williams, flew back to the U.S. All of our attempts to locate a Don Williams in France and neighboring countries have come up empty. It must have been an alias. Right now they're searching here in the U.S."

"And?" Burnett asked.

Chase paused. "Nothing has come up. I've searched for weeks. But the FRU has tons more resources to find people."

Burnett arched an eyebrow. "We do. Unfortunately, when looking for the real scum of the earth, it's not those resources that usually turn something up. It's who you know, other scumbags, who are willing to talk."

"So I should go through my scumbag list?" Chase asked with a touch of sarcasm, but then he had an idea and immediately adjusted his attitude. "I see your point."

Burnett nodded. "Oh, I heard from the FRU again. They are expecting you to work full-time. Have you actually finished your primary education?"

"A year ago," Chase said.

"And college?" Burnett asked.

"I took one semester and I might go back on my own later, but I'm eager to start my career with the FRU."

Burnett closed the file. "Working under me and living here, there will be rules."

Chase didn't care much for rules. "I'm sure we can compromise."

Burnett's eyes grew just a bit brighter. "I don't compromise. You'll either follow them, or you'll find yourself living somewhere else."

Chase's gut tightened. "What are the rules?" If Burnett said he couldn't be near Della, all bets were off.

Burnett's phone dinged with an incoming text. He pulled his cell out, read the message, and frowned.

Not that Chase expected it to be good news at this hour.

Burnett stood and tucked the file under his arm. Then he pointed to the envelope on the sofa.

"That's your contract, and it covers their rules. We'll go over mine later. I have to go." He tapped the file he held. "I'll keep this."

"What's wrong?" Chase asked. "Can I help you with something?"

"No." The adamant way the man gave that one-word response worked its way into Chase's suspicions.

"Is it about Della?" Chase stood up.

"I said I didn't need help." He started out.

"Wait, you can't—"

Burnett swung around. "Yes, I can! You said you wanted to earn my respect. So start earning it by listening. I'm taking care of this."

Chase met Burnett's stern glare. "Is Della in danger? Tell me she's not in any danger and I'll do as you ask."

"She's not in danger." He left.

Chase dropped in the chair and ran his hands through his hair. Then he grabbed his phone and sent Della a text.

Are you okay? What's up?

No answer dinged back. Was she still pissed?

Everything inside him screamed for him to find Della, but damn it, he sensed this was his first test from Burnett. Inhaling, he recalled the honesty in the camp leader's voice when he assured him she wasn't in any danger.

Could he trust him?

What if he was wrong?

Chapter Seven

Coffee. Della didn't drink the dark bitter brew, but the waitress hadn't asked. She just dropped two cups on the table as if it were a requirement.

So Della now held the lukewarm cup and turned it. Lucas sat across from her. He hadn't touched his coffee, but he'd wolfed down a burger.

Over the phone, Burnett had insisted that Della and Lucas leave before the media showed up and plastered their faces on the news.

"What if Mrs. Chi comes back?" Della had insisted.

"If there's one thing I've learned about ghosts since I married my wife is that if they want you, they'll find you. There's an all-night diner right around the corner. Go there. I'll see what I can find out and meet you."

Della picked up her phone and saw that it was almost two. What was taking Burnett so long? She stared out the window into the dark cold night. Her mind slipped away from the Chis to Chase. Had he come back to her house looking for her? Was she going to tell Burnett about his little bathroom visit?

Determined footsteps moved down the sidewalk. Della looked to the diner door, waiting for Burnett to appear. Dressed in faded jeans, a black shirt, and black leather jacket, he looked like a force to be reckoned with.

She worried he'd consider the Chis' murder more of an inconvenience than an important case. But the moment she saw his gaze on her, she knew differently. For all his gruffness and even his appearance, there was innate goodness in him.

He dropped into a chair beside her, giving both her and Lucas a nod. The waitress, a thirty-year-old bleached blonde, came swaying over, seductively, with a cup and pot of coffee dangling from one hand.

"Hey there, sweetie." She slid the cup to him, leaning over as she filled the cup, as if to make sure he got a good peek at her cleavage.

Burnett nodded, and much to the woman's dismay, he didn't even offer her boobs a glance.

"You need anything?" she asked. "Anything at all?"

"No, thank you. That will be it," Burnett's tone pretty much dismissed her. He wasn't so much rude as matter-of-fact.

The waitress walked off, a lot less seductively. Burnett's gaze shifted to Della. "Sorry for your loss."

Della swallowed a lump in her throat. "She was just a neighbor, but she was . . . nice. I saw her tonight at Whataburger. She was getting her husband dinner. She told me to be careful."

"What time did you see her?" Burnett asked.

"A few minutes after seven."

He picked up his cup. "The food was still in the bags." He sipped from the rim of coffee where steam swirled up. He made a face and set the coffee down. "Someone could have followed her, pushed their way inside, or they were already in."

"So no forced entry?" Lucas asked.

"No."

Della gave her own cup another twist. "If someone knocked, they would have opened the door."

"Even to strangers and after hours?" Burnett asked.

"Yeah." Della stared into the cold dark brew in her cup for several seconds. "For that matter if someone asked for the money, they'd probably have given it to them too." She looked up. "Was it weres?"

"There are mixed signals. It was a bloody crime scene, and I picked up traces of weres, but usually weres like to throw some muscle around this time of the month. Nothing looked overly ransacked."

"Maybe they were easy marks and didn't require any muscle." Della's stomach clenched.

"Could be. I've secured the paranormal mortician for the autopsy. We'll know more when she's finished. It probably won't happen for a few days." His gaze slipped to Lucas. "What do you think?"

"He's going to defend his own kind," Della snapped.

Burnett frowned. "Let him answer."

"But he's already told me. He doesn't think they—"

Burnett cleared his throat. Della realized he was right. It wasn't Lucas she needed to aim her fury at.

"Sorry," she said to the were. "I just . . ." That damn knot appeared again.

"It's okay." Lucas leaned in. "It hurts . . . to lose people we care about."

Della recalled that Lucas had lost his grandmother not too long ago.

Burnett settled back in his chair. "So what did you get?" he asked Lucas again.

"I picked up six different traces. Three were weak, like halfbreeds."

"Six?" Della asked. She realized what she'd missed. Something important. "The traces I got at the jewelry store, they didn't . . . ring familiar. I don't know if they belonged to the same guys I saw earlier."

"You saw them?" Burnett asked.

"It was around seven-thirty. I went out . . . for a bit. I picked up their scent and dropped down. They were walking about half a block from the store."

"When you got their trace, did it include blood?"

"No," Della said. Had she even seen the killers? She needed to quit making assumptions.

"How good of a look did you get?" Burnett asked.

"Pretty good. They were around my age, maybe a little older."

"Were they in gang attire?"

"No," Della said. "They looked like some young weres out on a Saturday night."

"That may have been exactly what they were," Burnett said. "But even if they are innocent, they might have seen something. Do you think you could describe them?"

"Yeah," Della said.

He had her describe their facial features and typed her answers into his phone.

Pocketing his phone, he turned the cup in his hands as if hesitating to broach another subject. "Did the spirit give you anything?"

"No. She was confused." Then Della remembered her cat. "Her cat was with her and then wasn't. I heard someone say the cat was still alive and for someone to get it to a vet." Della swallowed another lump. "We know weres and felines don't mix."

"And the fact that it had any life in it at all could mean it wasn't weres," Lucas added.

Della couldn't argue.

Burnett sighed. "We'll know more when the autopsies are in."

"Has the family been notified?" Della remembered that their daughter lived in California.

Burnett looked down at his cup. "The police are taking care of it."

Della got a vision of Mrs. Chi holding her red tabby. She'd loved Chester. "Can you find out where they took the cat?"

Burnett nodded.

Silence filled the diner. Only a few forks clicked against plates. "I want to work the case," Della said.

Burnett raised one eyebrow. "You're already working one."

"You work two or three cases at a time," Della countered.

"I'm not seventeen." He frowned.

"I'll be eighteen next month!"

Burnett glanced at Lucas. "Why don't you head back? I'll see Della home."

Della rolled her eyes. She didn't need to be seen home!

Lucas reached for the bill. "I got it," Burnett said and moved into Lucas's chair.

Della watched Lucas leave, then faced Burnett. "Your male chauvinist pig is showing again. You might want to suck it in a little bit."

Burnett's brows pinched. "What?"

She shook her head. "Lucas has a longer walk to get back to his car than I do to get back to my house. Why didn't you see him to his car?"

Burnett blinked. "I wanted to talk to you . . . alone."

"So that comment about seeing me home was just a ruse? Is that what you're saying?"

He opened his mouth to answer, then shut it. And she knew why. She heard his accelerated heart rate.

"I thought so."

"Friggin' hell. Fine! Kick my ass for wanting to make sure you're safe."

"No, kick your ass for thinking I can't take care of myself. And don't say it's because you care. Because you care about him, too. It's because I'm a girl."

He raked a palm over his face. "Okay, I'll admit it. I might be a little more protective of the girls in my life than the guys. Does that make me a male chauvinist pig? I don't think so. But I can hear Holiday in my head saying it does."

She smiled in victory. "You should listen to your wife more often."

His eyes brightened a hue. "I give you permission to call me on it each and every time, but you might as well get used to it. I'm not going to be able to change because I'm not going to stop caring. No more than you or Chase will stop being pains in my ass."

Della leaned back, respecting his acceptance that she wouldn't give in. Because hell, yeah, she'd keep . . . "You've seen Chase?" she asked.

Burnett didn't say a word. He didn't have to.

"Did he hand over Feng?" she asked, hoping even when her heart knew that Chase would protect Feng, just as she would her father.

"No. He's saying a man named Douglas Stone killed your aunt."

"And?"

"And I only got my hands on the file about the guy two minutes before I got your text."

"A file?"

"The Vampire Council has been looking for him. But they haven't been able to find him."

She slumped back in her chair. "Do you believe any of this? It's kind of convenient, isn't it? My uncle is accused of murder and suddenly he knows who killed his sister."

"You're right. It could be a lie. But he didn't *just* remember who did it. The file shows that the council's been looking for this guy for over fifteen years."

"Then why, if Feng's innocent, hasn't he come out of hiding? Why hasn't he stepped forward and told the FRU this?"

Burnett rested his hand on the table. "Maybe because he knows if we don't find this guy, he'll be accused. Or maybe . . . he's hiding something else."

"What more could he be hiding?" Della asked.

"I don't know."

"But you believe Chase?"

"I believe Chase believes it. I'm just not sure if he's right."

"So Chase just shows up right before you come here and hands you a file of who he thinks killed my aunt?"

Burnett pulled his cup closer. "There's a little more to it than that."

Something in the way Burnett didn't meet her eyes when he answered told her there was a lot more to it than that.

"Oh, hell. What is it you're not telling me?"

Burnett looked up. "Chase resigned from the council."

"He . . . did? He was so loyal to them."

Burnett gave his cup a turn. "And . . . he put in his resume to the FRU."

She shook her head. Less than a month ago, when Della thought their relationship was actually going somewhere, she had suggested that Chase do this very thing. He'd countered that she should come to work for the council. They'd butted heads.

Then instead of either of those things happening, she'd discovered all his lies, his deceit, and he ran off.

So why was he doing this now? Did he have ulterior motives?

"Are you hiring him?"

"I don't hire agents." He paused. "But yes, the FRU is hiring him."

"But he came to you about it?" she accused. "So you helped—"

"Actually, he went to them first."

Burnett picked his cup up. "There's one other thing. Two, actually."

"Why do I have a feeling I'm not going to like this?"

When he didn't answer right away, she exhaled. "Just tell me."

"Chase will be working under me. And living at Shadow Falls." He set his cup back down. The clank of the white ceramic cup on the table seemed to punctuate his words.

"Well, isn't that just jim-dandy. Why?" she asked.

"Several reasons." His eyes tightened. "While I believe Chase when he says he doesn't know where your uncle is, it certainly couldn't hurt to keep a close eye on him in case Feng decides to contact him. You have to agree with that."

Agree with it, yes, but she liked it about as much as she would a punch to the gut. She pulled her cup close, then, almost as if to punish herself, she took a sip.

Damn, it was nasty. She had to work hard not to gag. "What's the other reason?"

He leaned forward a bit. "Chase infuriates me. He's arrogant and hardheaded."

Does he remind you of anyone? Della almost spouted off, but bit it back.

"In spite of being misguided at times, his intentions are good. With some training, he would be a big asset to both the FRU and Shadow Falls."

Hearing positive things about someone who'd hurt you was like touching a lemon after getting a paper cut. It stung. All the way to the bone.

Burnett cut her a hard stare. "You and Chase, you'll get along."

"Oh, sure we will. Like cake and ice cream." Or fire and gasoline. "Do you know where he is right now?"

Burnett gave her a hard stare. "Don't think for one minute I'm saying you have to make amends with him. That decision is yours and yours alone. And if he tries to put any pressure on you—in any way—I'll kick his ass so hard he'll find himself in France again before he catches his breath."

"Don't worry," Della said. "If he puts any pressure on me, he won't be breathing." She stood up. "Is he at Shadow Falls now?"

Burnett frowned. "It's almost two in the morning. You're going back to your house. I'll call tomorrow and speak to your father about you coming back to Shadow Falls. You can interrogate Chase then."

Chapter Eight

Worry had been eating away at the lining of Chase's stomach for an hour. He finally dressed and went out for a few laps around the camp. He flew low, ducking in and out of the trees, just trying to spend some of the negative energy flowing through his veins. He wanted to see Burnett return, and make sure Della was okay, before he ran off to interrogate a few scumbags. Yup, Burnett's little speech had given Chase a few ideas.

Della still hadn't responded to his text. Not that he was all that sure she would. Something he intended to fix very soon. He wanted to get back to where they were before. When she was happy to see him. When leaning in and stealing a kiss wouldn't actually put him at risk of losing an eye.

Recalling that kiss, he realized he wanted more. He wanted all of her. He wanted to protect her, to touch her. To have her at his side day and night.

Would it be enough that he'd quit the council and come to work for the FRU? Or would she still be inclined to make him pay for his past mistakes? He hoped like hell she wouldn't. But knowing Della, forgiveness wouldn't be handed over too easily.

As he followed the property line, he spotted headlights pulling into the school's parking lot.

As Lucas stepped out of the car, Chase approached. "Hey."

"You're out and about late," Lucas said.

Chase debated how to play to this, then decided not to play.

"Is Della okay?"

"Yeah, she's fine."

"What happened?" Chase asked.

"An elderly couple, neighbors of Della and her parents, were murdered. Della seemed to know and care about them quite a bit."

"Damn," Chase said, remembering Della hearing her father's rude conversation last night and knowing she didn't need any other crap right now. "Have they caught who did it?"

"Not yet. Burnett's looking into the autopsy."

"So it's an FRU case? The killers were supernatural?"

"Possibly." Lucas started walking to the gate.

"Vampires?" Chase asked, knowing that would make it harder on Della.

"Weres," Lucas said. "But it's not for sure."

"Where were they killed?" Chase remembered the were scents he'd gotten when leaving Della's house.

"A strip center in front of her subdivision."

"Damn. I got a scent of a couple of weres, and blood, hanging right outside her neighborhood earlier tonight."

"Blood? And you didn't check it out?"

"No. I mean, I dropped down, but the blood was animal."

Lucas's frown held. "Was it feline?"

"I . . . I'm not sure." Weres, being hunters by nature, were better at distinguishing different types of animal blood. "Why?"

"A cat was injured, too."

"Shit," Chase said. "It could have been them."

"You might want to let Burnett know."

"I will." But he'd do it after his appointment, an appointment Chase had strong suspicions Burnett would object to. Face it: Burnett was about to set down the rules, so Chase had better do all he could before he swore himself to them.

They walked past the office, heading back to the cabins. Chase tried to think of a way to ask more about Della.

"So Burnett wouldn't let you come tonight?" Lucas asked.

"No," Chase said, another straight-up answer. It felt good not trying to hide things anymore. He could get used to this.

The were shrugged. "Probably just as well. Della's pretty pissed at you."

"She told you that?" What else had she mentioned?

"No. She told Kylie." He frowned. "And Kylie made me promise not to say anything. Which means I need to learn to keep my mouth shut."

"Don't worry," Chase said. "I don't think Della's dislike toward me is a big secret right now."

Della headed back to her house. Thankfully, Burnett hadn't insisted on escorting her. But he hadn't been able to send her off without a warning. "Be careful."

Like she would be anything but careful.

"Text me when you get there."

She rolled her eyes, but didn't waste her time giving him more hell.

As tempting as it was to defy Burnett and go find Chase, she knew Burnett would come unglued. And an unglued Burnett would not be easy to handle. Yet, still buzzing with unwanted emotions, she took the long route just to blow off some steam. And to check the area for any stray weres. Even with her heart overloaded with Chase, her uncle, and her dad's murder case, she intended to find whoever had killed her neighbors. Find them and make them pay.

Following the line of trees, she dropped down low near the strip center, close enough to pick up any scents. Nothing. Even the earlier traces had faded. Dodging treetops, she headed back to her place, then spotted the thicket of trees at the park. Deciding to just give it a quick pass, she changed course.

The moon, almost full, cast sprays of light into the trees, causing shadows. At first she got nothing, then it hit. The musky scent of were, more than one. Knowing the dangers of confronting a were this close to a full moon, she decided to just fly by. If they looked suspicious she'd give Burnett a ring.

See, Burnett? I am careful!

Darting a little lower, the scents grew stronger, and familiar. But because she hadn't fully paid attention to the scents at the jewelry store, she wasn't sure if the trace came from the guys she'd seen earlier. She needed to see the guys to confirm.

Before she spotted the weres, she spotted someone else. A girl. A human girl, if Della's nose was right. She was running, sweating, fear seeping out of her pores. Della lost the visual as another thick clump of pine trees rose from the ground. But what she didn't lose was the sound of the girl's scream. It rose up and the sheer terror in it sent a shiver down Della's spine.

Well, crap. Careful had just gone out the window.

She started down.

When she got past one cluster of trees, she saw the blond girl, probably no more than fifteen, surrounded by weres. Oddly, their scents weren't very strong, so maybe not full weres. Which would mean they may not have full strength, either.

"I called the cops, you idiots, and they're coming," the girl screamed, sounding brave, but the shakiness in her voice gave her away.

Della counted four of them. Confident, or almost confident, she could handle all four—depending on just how much lunar strength they had—she headed down. Feeling her eyes grow hot, and her front teeth lengthen, she landed to the right of their little circle.

They knew when she'd landed, or probably a second before, because they turned away from the girl to face her. No doubt their dislike of vampires made her the more attractive victim. These were not the boys she'd seen earlier. She couldn't be positive if they were the ones she'd halfway smelled at the jewelry store. But they were still being bad boys.

In the corner of her eye, Della saw the girl running away and felt some relief that she wouldn't have to worry about her.

"Sorry to intrude," she smarted off while assessing her situation. She knew she'd be fine if she could just keep her distance, and their attention, without them getting their dirty paws on her. She tuned her ears to listen to the girl, judging her distance. When the girl got to freedom, or arrived in a public place where the weres wouldn't attack, she could simply fly out of there and leave these rogue dogs grounded without even breaking a nail. Then she'd call Burnett.

Such a good plan. And one that would have worked if her ears hadn't been so tuned in to the girl that she missed the two weres who'd come up behind her. Each grabbed an arm.

Definitely half weres, because their scents weren't that strong either.

Oh, shit. She felt a fist slam into her ribs and she gasped for air. She had one moment of concern that it might not just be a nail that she broke. Not that she was going to make it easy on them . . . or let them win.

She was just going to have to open up another can of whoop ass.

"Oh, so ya'll wanna fight, do ya? Why didn't you tell me that?"

Yanking out of one of the dog's clutches, she coldcocked the other who came up to confront her. He dropped to the ground.

Another rushed in front of her, his fist drawn. She kicked that bastard right in the gonads. He yelped like a young pup.

Then she used the creep still holding on to her as a bowling pin to down the two others coming at her.

She was preparing to fly when two others jumped her from behind.

Damn. She swung a fist.

Damn. She started kicking.

Damn. She took a hard punch to her stomach.

Chase landed to the side of the strip center, still decorated with yellow crime scene tape. He drew in a deep breath. The tiniest bit of were scent lingered but not nearly enough to be able to identify it as one he'd gotten earlier. Looking north toward Della's house, the temptation bit. Bit hard.

Had Burnett told Della about him?

Was she thrilled, nonchalant, pissed?

Damn, he wanted to see her.

He almost took off toward her house, but heard Burnett's warning. *You said you wanted to earn my respect. So start earning it by listening.*

Pushing his desire aside, he took off, but once airborne he saw two police cars, lights flashing, driving down a street—a street that led to the park.

Thinking it might have something to do with the weres, and feeling a bit bad he hadn't checked things out earlier that night, Chase shot forward, hoping to get a peek of what trouble transpired before the cops arrived.

From his not-so-good vantage point, he spotted and smelled the trouble. Weres. Definitely weres, or at least part weres. A group of them. He thought he counted six—no, eight—all going against one. He inhaled and instantly knew a couple of those guys were the same ones he'd come across earlier. Another deep breath and his nose picked up the scent of a vampire. The victim, maybe? Then the scent exploded in his brain, and went right to his heart. The air in his chest froze.

"Friggin' hell!" he seethed, and prayed he wasn't too late.

Chapter Nine

A few feet from the struggle, Chase saw Della was still standing. Bleeding, but standing. And the smell of his bondmate's blood made him thirsty for more blood. With a growl that came from his soul, he tossed them away from Della two at a time. Their bodies landed among the trees, one even getting caught on the limbs of a pine.

Still caught up in the chaos of the fight, Della clipped him in the jaw. It hurt like hell, but he didn't budge. "It's me." Chase tried to reach for her but she backed away, fist still swinging.

All of a sudden, recognition hit her expression. "I thought—" Her breath caught and she wiped a hand over her lip and smeared blood across her cheeks.

"Are you okay?" he asked, air still trapped in his chest, fury still making his blood burn and his eyes bright.

"I could have taken care of it myself," she snapped.

The fact that she still had her pride intact told him she was okay. "Yeah, but I didn't want you to have all the fun." Sirens filled the night and blue lights flashed through the trees. The sounds of cars screeching to a halt at the park's edge echoed.

"We gotta go!" he said and smiled. She didn't take flight. He heard the footsteps fast approaching and rushed forward, caught her by the waist, pulled her against him—where she felt so damn right—and took off into the dark sky. They were barely above the trees when he heard cops yelling at the weres.

She fought him for a fraction of a second.

Looking down, she must have spotted the police. She remained silent, her body so close to his, and his heart thumping at the closeness as he flew them farther away. God help him, but he could swear her heart was racing faster than his.

Was it because of him, or was she still reacting to the threat of the fight?

"Land," she finally seethed.

"Just a little farther." He savored the closeness and he pressed his face into the curve of her neck. The sweet scent of her skin and her shampoo filled his nose.

Knowing she wouldn't tolerate it much longer, he landed in an alley, a block from her house.

She ran from his arms as soon as their feet hit the ground. Swinging around, she stared at him with bright eyes. "Where's Feng?"

He inhaled and tried to convince himself that some of her anger was residual, left over from the fight. "I don't know."

"Because you told him not to tell you?"

He almost denied it, but he was tired of lying to her. "Yes. Feng didn't kill her, Della. I'm going to find the person who did. And I'm going to get your dad off."

Della just stared, hurt reflecting in her eyes. "Why doesn't my uncle come in and talk if he's innocent?" Unable to stop himself, he reached up to push back a strand of her dark hair. She stopped him with a raised hand, but he noticed the bruises on both her knuckles and her face.

"Are you sure you're okay?" The desire to race back and hurt the bastards who'd hurt her burned in his gut.

"I asked you a question!" She inched closer, her eyes a bright green.

He had to think a second to remember what she'd asked. "If Eddie came in, the FRU would just pin the murder on him. They wouldn't even look for this other guy."

"You don't know that," she accused. "And his name isn't Eddie!"

"Yes, I do know that, and so do you. And since he pulled me out of that plane crash and saved my life I've known him as Eddie." Right then, he felt it, that odd kind of cold he got when Della's dead aunt had been hanging around. He tucked his fists into his jean pockets.

Della stared down the dark alley, her fist clutching and then releasing. Was that still the panic, or was her aunt back to cause trouble? Then she swung around to face him. "We need to go back."

"Back . . . ?" It was almost too cold to think.

"To the park. One or more of those weres might be a murderer."

"Yeah, but the cops are there."

"Doesn't matter." She started forward as if to take off in flight.

He caught her. "It matters. If we just show up they'll suspect that we were part of it. I don't think Burnett would appreciate having to bail us out of jail."

"They could be the ones who killed some people I cared about." Her voice shook and her breath caused a puff of steam to lift from her lips. She looked again down the alley.

"Is that who's here?" he asked.

Della's head snapped back. "Can you see her?"

"No." At least he hoped not. He wasn't going to chance it and look down that alley. "I feel the cold."

"She was my neighbor." Her voice was edged with pain and grief.

He realized Della hadn't pulled away. He'd give his right arm if she would just lean on him a little. Della wasn't the type to lean on people very often, but when she did need it, he wanted to be the person she'd turn to.

"I'm sorry," he said.

"You're not the only one who's sorry. Which is why I have to go back."

He tightened his hold. "Going back there is a bad idea." But she had a point. The FRU needed to interrogate the weres before the regular cops released them.

"I'll call Burnett." No doubt Burnett would be furious that Chase was with Della. Probably earn Chase a good chewing out, but it didn't even matter.

Della's phone dinged with a text. As if she suddenly realized he was touching her, she glared at his hand on her arm and pulled away, then snatched her phone from her pocket. After reading the message, she looked up, puzzled.

"What?" he asked.

"It's Burnett. He wants to know if we're okay."

Chase frowned. "He knows?"

"It seems that way." She started texting back.

Before she finished, Chase got the vamp's scent. So did Della, because her fingers stopped moving. Chase's gut knotted, preparing to get hell.

Burnett hadn't gotten secure on his feet when Della said, "Don't start giving me crap. All I did was take the long way home. And if I hadn't, some poor girl would—"

"I'm not giving you crap," Burnett said.

Is that because he's saving it all to give to me? Chase stood quiet, dreading what might be forthcoming.

"You okay?" Burnett asked Della.

"Fine." She sounded offended by the inquiry.

"Did you get any traces off them?" Burnett asked. "Are they the same ones from earlier?"

"They aren't the boys I saw walking. I didn't get a good enough trace to know if they were the same scents from the jewelry store. I think they're only half were."

"But they are the ones I smelled earlier with animal blood on them," Chase said.

Both Della and Burnett looked at him.

"You were here earlier?" Burnett asked.

Della didn't appear surprised; she knew he'd been in the area. But she hadn't told Burnett. Was she trying to protect him from the big bad Burnett? Chase liked that thought.

"Yes, before I came to Shadow Falls. Around seven."

"So about the time of the murder," Burnett said. "Did you get a visual?"

"No, just a trace."

Burnett stood there as if trying to grasp it all. "The blood, was it—"

"I didn't hang around to identify it as feline." When Burnett looked surprised, Chase added, "I saw Lucas when he came back. He told me about the cat. That's why I came here, to the murder scene . . . to see if I could still pick up the were scents." *And to go check out some scumbags.* But he didn't say that.

Burnett didn't appear pissed. Was he just holding back until he had Chase alone? Burnett stared at the sky as if trying to come up with a plan. "Della," he said. "Head back home. Straight home."

Della frowned. "But—"

"Don't argue. If your parents find you're gone, it would just cause more trouble."

Chase saw the spark of anger in her eyes, but she nodded. She respected Burnett that much. That was part of the reason Chase respected him too.

"Will you text and let me know if you get a confession?"

"Yes."

She took off without offering Chase a goodbye or even a go-to-hell glare. He'd have preferred the glare to nothing. Nothing stung a little.

Burnett turned his dark, accusing gaze on Chase.

"I wasn't planning to see Della," he said.

"I know." He started walking back toward the park.

Chase caught up with him. "How do you know?"

"I had you followed."

The words raked across Chase's nerves. "That's underhanded, isn't it?"

"No," Burnett said, unconcerned if Chase was pissed.

"So you have the right to have me tailed?"

"Until I trust you, I do."

And how the hell long would that be? Then logic hit. "You didn't have me followed. I'd have picked up their scent."

"Not if it was Perry," Burnett clipped out.

Perry was one of the best shape-shifters out there. And the really good shifters could shift their scents so they weren't distinguishable. But Perry was supposed to be in France . . . with Steve.

"Are Perry and . . . Steve back?"

"Got back yesterday." Burnett cut Chase a quick glance. "And there will be no trouble, got that?"

As long as Steve stayed away from Della, Chase had no problem. "I hear you."

"You had best do more than hear," Burnett warned. "At the first hint of trouble you'll be house hunting. Steve is my student. You are an unwanted boarder."

Chase gripped his jaw to keep from smarting off.

After a few more steps, Burnett added, "And since you don't seem interested in sleeping tonight, why don't you go with me to interview the weres?"

Chase recalled his other appointment. He figured he'd missed that window of opportunity. Tomorrow.

"Sure."

"No!" The scream, her mom's scream, had Della jackknifing out of bed at seven that morning. Had she dreamed it? Must have, right? She fell back on her bed.

It had been three in the morning when she'd gotten a text from Burnett saying they were still waiting for permission to move the weres to the FRU offices. It had been four when Della let go of her anger and the memory of being so close to Chase and let slumber pull her in. The scream echoed again. She popped back up and yanked open her bedroom door, flying down the stairs in two seconds flat.

It *was* her mom.

"What's wrong?" Della yelled, flashing into the kitchen and into the room's icy temperature. The distinct cold was a dead ringer for the . . . dead.

Her mom stood in front of the table, her hands knuckled around the back of a wooden chair. Her gaze locked on . . . Della's heart stopped. There sitting at the table was Mrs. Chi, her throat gaping open, exposing an Adam's apple and veins and some other nasty stuff.

Was that how she'd died? Someone had sliced her throat? Della's own throat hurt.

She swallowed back her gag reflex and looked at her mom. Something was terribly wrong. And it wasn't just Mrs. Chi's throat. It was . . . it was . . . How the hell could her mom see Mrs. Chi?

"What . . . is it?" Della pushed out the three-word sentence, telling herself she'd simply misunderstood. Her mom wasn't seeing the ghost. Could she?

"Mrs. Chi," her mom muttered, terror and tears in her eyes.

Holy shit! Her mom *could* see Mrs. Chi. How was that even possible? Maybe this was a dream. She pinched her leg. It hurt. This wasn't a nightmare.

"Don't look at her." Della pulled her mom's shoulders around so she'd face Della and not the dead woman.

Her mom blinked at Della as if confused. "They didn't show her. They just said . . ."

That's when Della realized that behind the table and behind Mrs. Chi's bloody body, was a television. On the screen, a news reporter stood in front of the Chis' store, recounting the horror that had taken place last night. Della's chest burned again at the injustice of it.

She cut her eyes toward Mrs. Chi. *So sorry.*

Taking a deep breath, so cold her lungs were in danger of getting frost bitten, she tried to stop the panic from building. Stopping it wasn't easy, not when Mrs. Chi looked down at her blood-stained blouse in puzzlement. She lifted her head, exposing her sliced throat again, and her eyes met Della's. *What happened?*

Footsteps sounded behind her. "What's wrong?" came her father's panicked voice.

"The news." Her mom, tears making her eyes shine, motioned to the television. "Mr. and Mrs. Chi were found murdered in their shop last night. That poor, poor couple. Who could do something like that?"

Murdered? The elderly woman shot up from the chair, and a . . . a bloody basketball rolled across the kitchen's white tile floor, leaving a bloody streak until it bounced against her father's bare feet.

Of course he didn't feel it. Didn't see it. This was for Della's eyes only. Lucky her! Not. What the hell was Mrs. Chi doing with a basketball?

Mrs. Chi walked in front of Della. Her slanted eyes filled with puzzlement. *Where's my husband? Where did he go?*

Chills ran down Della's arms.

"How . . . how could that have happened?" her dad muttered, his gaze on the television, where the reporter continued talking. Then he swung around and stared right at her.

Did she still have bruises? She ran her tongue over her lip, it was all healed. Her face should be, too. So why was he . . .

"How could it happen?" he asked again, as if . . . as if she herself had the answer.

"I . . . don't know." Della answered, trying to read the emotion in his dark eyes. Emotion that looked a lot like . . .

He blinked. "That's awful." He stormed out of the kitchen almost as quickly as he'd come in.

Della rubbed a hand up her arm to fight off the cold, both from Mrs. Chi's presence and from her father's expression. Then she glanced at her mom. "What was that about?"

"What?" her mom asked, dropping down in a chair.

"Daddy . . . he acted as if . . ."

"As if what?"

"Nothing," Della said and stared after her dad. Suddenly an answer started to come together—bits and pieces connecting, and with it came a lot of pain. Was that why . . . ? Oh, God, she thought she finally understood what was really going on—what had been going on for months. With the understanding she felt the foundation of her life crumbling right under her feet. And there wasn't a damn thing she could do about it.

Except go down with it.

Chapter Ten

Chase sat in Burnett's office at the FRU headquarters. He knew it was Burnett's because the walls were decorated with images of Holiday and Hannah. For one second, his tired mind wondered what it was like. To have a kid. With Della. Not that he was ready for that. Heck, he had to steal kisses. He couldn't hold her when he wanted to. Or sleep with her when he wanted to. And he really wanted to.

His body recalled how it had felt to have her so close to him when he'd flown away from the weres. He let out a deep gulp of frustration, wishing that the remedy would come sooner rather than later.

The computer hummed, still thinking about Chase's request. He had asked Burnett's permission to use the computer, which had a few FRU programs on it, to do a search for anyone named Douglas Stone or Don Williams. It had found six people in the Houston area with the name Stone and ten with the name Don Williams.

Now Chase waited for it to spew out the addresses and information on them. Better to stay busy than just sit and twiddle his thumbs. But watching a computer screen wasn't exactly busy. He stretched his neck to one side then the other. The chair squeaked and his neck popped, relieving very little of his tension.

The computer kept churning and so did Chase's patience—from lack of sleep, no doubt. He really only needed three or four hours, but he'd been running on two a night for the last week and none at all tonight, so that didn't help. Neither did thinking about Steve being back at Shadow Falls. Not that he was . . .

Chase Tallman wasn't jealous. Nope. But damned if he didn't feel something. Something that felt wrong, like too-tight underwear. And why the hell had he spent so much time wondering exactly what Della had told her girlfriend about the shape-shifter?

Leaning back in the chair, a frown pulled his lips downward and he raised his arms over his head, glancing from the computer screen to the blinds. The first rays of sun spilled through the slits and he groaned. The weres still hadn't arrived from the local jail. They had only arrested four, three had gotten away, but one, the one they'd pulled from a tree, was hospitalized. Perhaps Chase should have felt a little bad, but he didn't.

No telling what they'd have done to Della if he hadn't gotten there. Sure, he knew Della could handle herself pretty damn well, but not with that many weres this close to a full moon—even half weres. So yeah, he kind of wished they'd all sustained injuries.

What he did feel bad about was not being able to give any physical descriptions of any of the weres that got away. He'd been so intent on protecting Della, he'd never looked at a face. And according to Burnett, who'd texted Della the same question, she hadn't been able to offer much either.

The computer finally changed screens and gave him the information on the Douglas Stones and Don Williamses. Chase sat up so fast, the chair cried out as if complaining the wrong person was sitting in it—as if it knew he wasn't Burnett.

He hit print. Folding it up, he tucked it in his pocket.

The door to the office swung open. Burnett stuck his head in, looking way too rested, considering he hadn't slept either. "The weres are here. You ready?"

"More than." He popped up and met the man at the door.

"What did you find?" Burnett asked.

"Lots of names," Chase said and pulled out the list and handed it to him.

"It's a long shot," Burnett said, as if considering it. "But I've seen them pay off."

"I sure as hell hope so." His gut said his relationship with Della depended on solving this case. And solving it fast.

"You want to do the interrogating?" Burnett asked. "Show me what you got."

"First, let's see if you recognize any of these guys' scent as the one with the animal blood," Burnett told Chase. One by one Burnett led him into three small rooms with a two-way mirror and shared air ducts.

Their scents were familiar, but from the scuffle at the park, not the ones he'd traced earlier.

"Maybe it was the ones who got away," Chase said.

"Go find out." Burnett motioned to the mirror. "All of their legs are chained, but we didn't cuff them, so don't get too close. I'll be watching if you get into any trouble."

"I got this." Chase swung the door open to the first room, then slammed it shut.

The were, no older than eighteen, had his head down. He jerked upright, his eyes glowing golden yellow. The sound of heavy iron shackles wrapped around his ankles clinked on the concrete floor.

Chase let his own eyes grow bright just to show the half were he meant business.

He moved to the opposite side of the metal table, where a pen and a piece of paper rested. He placed his palms on the tabletop. Leaning in, he took a deep gulp of air. As he did, he spotted a smear of blood on the guy's knuckles, Della's blood. He felt his eyes grow hotter and he forced himself to hold his emotions in check. But damned if he didn't want to grab the twerp by the neck and give him a few swings around the room.

"You're the same guy who . . ." The were smirked. "A little young to be an agent, aren't you?"

"My age doesn't concern you. What matters is that I've got what it takes."

He laughed. "Oh, you act so tough walking in here, but how many of your friends do you have watching out there?" He motioned to the mirror he obviously knew was a window.

"Not nearly enough to stop me from kicking your ass if I want to," Chase tossed out.

The were bolted out of his seat, nearly overturning the table. Chase, ready to act, caught him by the throat, and squeezed just tight enough that the ass-wipe knew he was serious. Then he pushed him back into his chair.

The were gasped for air.

"Now, stay down and listen. You might be able to get yourself out of this mess with a lighter sentence."

"For what?" the rogue spit out.

Chase stared the were right in his orange eyes. "The girl you and your friends ganged up on is a friend of mine."

"We didn't go looking for that bitch, she came to us."

Chase leaned down, his nose almost touching the rogue's, almost daring the were to try something again. "If you hadn't been after that young girl, she'd have never joined you!"

"We weren't gonna do anything bad to that chick. Just scare some sense into her. She should have known better than to be out in the park at that time of night."

"You've got an excuse for everything, don't you? What excuse are you going to give me for not writing down the names of everyone who was with you?"

His eyes brightened and a low growl left his lips. "Because I'm not a snitch."

. . .

Della's mom pulled up and parked in front of the Shadow Falls Academy sign. Something about this trip back to school felt different to Della. More permanent.

More painful.

It was the right thing, even what she wanted, but it stung knowing she wasn't wanted at home, knowing those trips home might very well be coming to an end.

She had known her dad would jump at the chance to send her back, but for God's sake, three minutes after he'd hung up with Burnett he'd told her mom to inform Della to pack her bags.

Her dad's insistence had sparked an argument between her parents. And given credence to what Della was beginning to suspect.

In the end, her mom relented to her dad's demands. Della didn't blame her. Not really.

No doubt her mom was upset about Mr. and Mrs. Chi in addition to being devastated over the fact that her husband was accused of murder. She simply didn't have much fight left in her.

But it would have been nice if she'd had just a little. A little for her daughter.

Marla, on the other hand, had fought. Not with their parents, but with Della. *"Just go. Just go and leave me here to deal with all of this!"*

Della had wanted to scream at her sister that she was doing everything she could to help. And that going back wasn't her idea, but her father's. He didn't want her there. She'd longed to say it wasn't her fault. But it was her fault and she knew that. The reason her father was awaiting trial was because Della had inadvertently gotten the file pulled and the cold case reopened.

But guilt or fault didn't matter. So she just let Marla think that leaving was Della's idea.

"Should I come in?" her mom asked, bringing Della back to the present—sitting in the car.

"No." Della looked up at the iron gate, swallowed the lump that kept appearing in her throat, and reached for the door handle. "I'll see you in a few weeks." Or she prayed she would. Prayed her father wouldn't take away those short visits from her too.

Her mom caught Della by her forearm. "If you would agree to return to your old school, you could stay at home."

No, I can't. Della swallowed. She'd spent all morning thinking about her father. Trying to figure out how it could be. How could he know?

"I love it here, Mom," Della said, hoping the truth sounded in her voice and not the pain. Her mom was hurting enough. She didn't need to borrow Della's pain.

"And I love you," her mom said, tears filling her eyes.

"I love you, too," Della answered and it came from the bottom of her heart, where it hurt the worst.

"I don't understand," her mom's voice shook. "A year ago, our life was so normal. Now my husband's being accused of murder, my oldest daughter lives at a school for troubled kids, and my neighbors are being slaughtered. How did life get this way?"

Della reached for her mom's hand, forgetting about her temperature. Thankfully, her mom didn't seem to notice, but she pulled it back quickly. "It's gonna be okay. Dad's not going to get convicted. I'm almost eighteen, so I would have been leaving the nest soon anyway. Right now this is the best place for me, and . . . the people who killed Mr. and Mrs. Chi are going to pay. I'll make sure of that."

"You?" She blinked and a few tears escaped. "How are you—"

"I mean the police," she answered in a rush.

Her mom got a sad smile on her lips and wiped her tears from her face. Then she reached out and touched Della's cheek. "Sometimes you look so different, and other times . . . I still see the same ol' Della in there."

"I'm still here," Della said, fighting to hold it together while she wondered what her father saw when he looked at her. Did he ever see the old Della? Or did he see the monster in her?

Her mom shook her head. "You'd better go. And study. Your dad said that Mr. James said you were falling behind."

"I will." Della grabbed her suitcase from the back and stood by the gate, the cool wind blowing her hair, as she watched her mom drive away—watched until her mom's gold Malibu was only a speck in the distance.

"You back?" a voice asked, and Della turned to see John, a shape-shifter, walk up.

"Yeah." She bit her tongue to keep from smarting off that it was none of his business, because that would have just been rude. It wasn't his fault she was in a piss-poor mood.

She shot through the entrance. She had a certain vampire to interrogate. If Chase thought last night's questions were the end of it, he had another think coming. But first things first.

She walked into the school's office, having gotten their scent a few steps inside the gate. Dropping her suitcase and stuff on the floor, she walked into Holiday's office. The red-haired fae sat at her desk, her thick rope of hair pulled over one shoulder, a crossword puzzle open on her desk.

Burnett stretched out on the sofa, with adorable Hannah, wearing only a Pampers, sitting on his stomach. The tough-as-nails vampire looked to be in a Sunday-morning carefree mood. His feet crossed at the ankles, his shoulders loose, his hair even a little mussed. Or perhaps it was an exhausted Sunday morning; she knew he'd worked all night.

He'd texted her at five this morning telling her the weres weren't talking. "What's wrong?" Holiday asked, her fae gifts picking up on Della's bottomed-out emotions.

Della took in a deep breath and it shuddered deep in her chest. "My dad knows."

"Knows what?" Burnett asked, sitting up, pulling his daughter to his chest.

"He knows I'm vampire."

Chapter Eleven

"What?" Burnett sprang to his feet, placing Hannah in his wife's arms. "How? You told him?" Burnett asked.

"No." Why in the hell would she have done that?

"Wait. Did he confront you?" Holiday asked.

"No, but it finally makes sense. All this time, I didn't understand. I knew he was disappointed in me, but he looked at me . . . differently. I didn't know what it was and I couldn't put my finger on it. But this morning when they found out about Mr. and Mrs. Chi being murdered, my dad . . . he looked at me like . . . like I'd done it." She swallowed. "He's afraid of me. He knows . . ."

Her voice shook. "He knows I'm a monster."

The second the words were out, Della would give anything to pull them back in. To wad them up in her fist and hide them deep in her pocket—so deep she might be able to forget. Because damn it, in those few words she'd voiced the pain and shame that she'd felt since she'd discovered she'd been turned—since she'd learned that to sustain life, she needed blood.

"You are not a monster." Holiday moved around the desk toward Della. Probably to touch her, to try to take away the pain she felt. It wouldn't work. Not this time.

"Della?" Holiday touched her arm. "Hannah's vampire. Look at her. Do you think—"

"It's not what I think that matters," she lied. "It's what my dad thinks . . . and what my mom and sister will think." *It's what the whole damn world would think if they knew vampires existed.*

"I think you're reading more into this than there is," Burnett said. "How could he know?"

"Because he saw his twin brother in vamp mode kill his sister."

Burnett looked confused. "But I thought . . . He saw his brother? He witnessed the murder?"

"He had to. My mom told me that Dad said he couldn't remember anything that happened that night. That he was unconscious. But my aunt's ghost says he wasn't unconscious after all."

"But your aunt could be wrong," Holiday spoke up. "We've talked about this. When someone is dying they . . ."

"But it makes sense," Della insisted. "Don't you see? Mom said he still has nightmares about it. How can you have nightmares about something you can't remember? She said that he was hospitalized after the murder, not because he was hurt, but because he was so distraught. He knows. And now he's afraid I'm going to do to them what Feng did to Bao Yu."

"I think you might be jumping to conclusions here." Holiday gave Della's shoulder another soft squeeze. She felt the calm sink into her skin, but it never got to her heart.

"Jumping? No, I'm embarrassed I didn't figure it out earlier."

"Look, I think . . ." Burnett stopped. He tilted his head to the side ever so slightly, telling Della he'd heard something.

She did the same and heard the footsteps in the front of the cabin. She raised her nose and got two scents. One was canine. The second . . . Chase. A jolt of unwanted anticipation swept through her. She pushed it back.

Back.

Back.

Back.

She turned and faced the front of the office. "Get ready, I'm coming," she said, just loud enough for him to hear, and took a step toward the door.

Chase prepared himself to see her, but distracting him from getting too excited was the echo of her words. Not her warning—that, he expected—but the earlier confession: *He knows I'm a monster.* His chest tightened, and a deep somber feeling hit him right in his solar plexus. Then the emotion turned to anger. Anger at her father again.

"Don't do it, Della!" Burnett's voice came next.

Chase didn't move, fighting his growing dislike for Della's father, and the disappointment that she wasn't this second standing in front of him. Only when he was convinced Della wasn't coming, did he continue. He got only a few steps when he realized Baxter wasn't following.

"Come here, boy," he called to Baxter, who must have gotten Della's scent because he was trotting toward the office. "No, Baxter."

The dog stopped and glanced back as if to say, "But Della's in there."

"You'll see her later," Chase promised when the dog begrudgingly came. "Believe me, I'm as eager to see her as you are." Anticipation tightened his shoulders, but his mind ricocheted back to another emotion.

Did Della really believe she was a monster?

Of course she did. He recalled with clarity feeling almost the same thing when he'd first been turned. But he'd had Eddie to counter all of the emotional crap. She'd had no one. Well, she'd had Chan, but considering she'd still been living with her nonvampire parents, she hadn't gotten the same amount of guidance. And if he figured it right, it had been months before she'd gotten to Shadow Falls.

Did she know how rare it was for a fresh turn to survive those first few months without a vampire mentor? Or at least to survive with any morality. Most of them went rogue, or killed themselves. He made a mental note to make sure she understood how special she was to have survived all she had.

He made it around the first bend when the hairs on the back of his neck rose. Feeling as if he were being watched, he stopped and looked around. He saw and sensed nothing but nature.

Neither did Baxter, who looked up at him confused.

That didn't mean they were alone. A shape-shifter could still be lurking. And one in particular came to Chase's mind. "I don't want any trouble," he said. "But Della and I belong together. You need to respect that."

Right then he felt something land on the back of his neck. He saw the bird flying away and he didn't have to reach back to know it was bird crap.

Every instinct in his body said to take flight to teach the twerp a lesson, but he heard Burnett's warning: *First hint of trouble and you'll be house hunting.*

Swearing under his breath, his gaze still on the bird in the sky, he caught another sound and scent coming from behind him. So did Baxter. His growl echoed in silence, and they both swung around.

Della stared at the office door.

Had Chase been eavesdropping? Probably. The lowlife vamp had no shame. But she'd bet getting his ass kicked by a girl would offer him a little much-needed dose of humility.

"You two have to get along, or avoid each other," Burnett spouted out, as if fully aware of what had turned her eyes a light yellow. "No bloodshed."

Della frowned. "You always take the joy out of things."

Burnett shook his head as if her smartass remarks didn't suit him. "Sit down." He waved at the chair in front of Holiday's desk.

"Aren't we done?" she asked, so damn ready to face Chase on the off chance he would offer her something he hadn't offered Burnett. An ass-whooping didn't always have to draw blood.

"No. I've got some more news on your father's case and on the murders last night. So drop your butt in the chair and get kicking *his* butt off your mind."

News of her father's case? Chase instantly became second priority. She pulled the chair out and sat down. "What have you got?"

Holiday went back to her chair. Burnett leaned his backside on the edge of Holiday's desk. Hannah let out a sweet coo, but the tension in the room seemed to pull the innocence out of it.

"We've gotten a new DA assistant assigned to your dad's case. Jerod Mason, he's fae, but works a lot of supernatural cases that fall into the regular courts."

"DA? You've got one of our own helping to put my dad away?"

Burnett frowned. "Sometimes the best defense is having an ally in the offense. Jerod is going to pass info to your dad's lawyer."

"What about the judge? You said you were trying to get a supernatural judge who could look for a reason to toss the charges out." Her stomach ached thinking how things could go so badly.

"That hasn't come through yet." He spotted Della's frown and held up his hand. "It still might happen. These kinds of things can take a while. Meanwhile, I spoke with Jerod this morning. He plans on picking up all of the files tomorrow and when he does he's going to get us copies, as well as your dad's lawyer, so we'll know what your father is up against."

Who was Burnett kidding? She already knew what her dad was up against. A murder charge. One that could put him away for life, or worse. Texas was big on the death penalty. Della's heart thumped in fear just thinking about it.

"Do we have a date yet? For the trial?"

"No, but Jerod said that the word is that the DA's office is pushing for it to be soon. We've got a few people working in the courts and we're trying to make that happen."

"Why soon?" Della asked, dreading seeing her dad go through this.

Burnett's expression softened, as if what he had to say wouldn't be so easy to take. "The less time they have to dig things up the better off we'll be."

"This can't be easy for your dad," Holiday added. Hannah let out a sweet coo, so sweet it felt as if it didn't belong anywhere near this conversation.

Della's chest tightened with the guilt for causing this. "You're right." She swallowed. "I heard him tell my mom he didn't know how long he was going to be able to keep his job."

"We're going to do everything we can," Holiday said. "You know that."

Della nodded, but the thought clawing at her sanity was . . . . what if "everything" wasn't enough?

The instant Chase and Baxter swung around, Steve came walking from the woods.

Confused, Chase cut his gaze up to the sky where the bird was still visible, then he looked back at the shape-shifter.

Steve wasn't grinning, but his brown eyes held a hint of humor that royally chapped Chase's ass.

"You thought that was me." Now the shape-shifter smiled.

"Yeah, I did," Chase said, certain his own expression didn't come off so upbeat. "So it was a friend, huh?"

Their gazes met. Tension filled the early Sunday air. Chase inhaled and the guy's scent filled his nose. The scent reminded him of Della because Chase had always smelt it on her when he first met her. Something he really preferred not to think about.

Steve looked skyward where the bird flew in circles. "Nope. Not as far as I know." The guy's heart rate didn't indicate he was lying. "But he is now." Steve smiled, showing no fear. Something Chase admired even when it stung.

Since he'd learned of this guy's feelings for Della, he'd wanted to find things about Steve to dislike—things to discredit him in Della's eyes.

But other than his flirtation with the daughter of the vet Steve worked for, Chase hadn't been able to find any dirt on the guy. That made things harder, but it also spoke of Della's choice in who she let into her life.

Chase swallowed his pride and decided to take the high road. "I guess I was wrong. Sorry."

Steve glanced away for a second as if debating something. When he looked back he had determination written all over his expression. "That's not the only thing you're wrong about."

Chapter Twelve

Afraid he knew where this was leading, Chase clenched his jaw so hard he was amazed his teeth didn't crack. *Don't lose it. Don't lose it.*

"What else am I wrong about?" He breathed in through his nose, hoping the oxygen would help calm him.

"About me respecting that you and Della belong together."

His eyes grew warm as they did when he started to change into vamp mode. "Careful," he cautioned and gave himself the same warning. His gut said Burnett wasn't making idle threats about kicking his butt out of Shadow Falls.

Steve shook his head, ignoring the warning, and that pissed Chase off more.

"You see, the only thing I have to respect is Della. Not you. And not what you think you two have. And personally, I think she's capable and adamant enough to make her own decisions. And you, Mr. Tallman, need to wrap your head around that."

Steve turned and walked away.

Chase gripped his fist so tight his hand ached. It wasn't his head having a hard time accepting the guy's words. It was his heart. But if Steve thought Chase was just going to roll over and give up, the shape-shifter had better think again.

. . .

Della remained in the chair across from Holiday's desk. She wouldn't—couldn't—allow her father to go to jail. But how she was going to stop it was still a mystery.

Burnett spoke up again. "For the Chi case, we got prints. Unfortunately, there were a lot of prints in their shop. So far, there's no match to anyone in the FRU fingerprint database. And we got a shoe print. They're trying to identify it."

"The autopsies haven't been done yet?" Della asked.

"No. But I'm hoping we'll have results tomorrow."

"What about the weres that were arrested?"

"None of their prints matched either. Chase says they aren't the ones he'd traced earlier with the animal blood. It could still be the same group, and the ones guilty of murder got away."

"So make them tell us who they were with!" Della snapped.

Burnett sighed. "We tried. None of them would give us anything."

"Let me talk to them," Della insisted.

Burnett laced his fingers. "Chase interviewed them. Did a great job, I might add. They're either that loyal or that scared. And I would bet they're scared."

Della shook her head. "So we don't have anything?"

"Yet," Burnett said. "It's early."

Holiday readjusted Hannah on her hip. "Burnett said you saw Mrs. Chi's spirit? Did she give you any clues?"

A bloody image of the woman sitting at her mom's kitchen table flashed in Della's mind. "No, she doesn't even know what happened to her. But . . ." Della reached up and touched her neck. "I think her neck was cut."

"That would be right," Burnett said. "It was stated in the report."

Della inhaled, trying to deal with the ugly truth.

"I know this is hard to talk about," Holiday said. "But sometimes they try to tell us something in odd ways. They say something strange, or might be wearing something that doesn't fit their character. Can you remember anything odd about her visit?"

"No," Della said, wanting the image of her out of her head. Then she remembered. "Wait. That's not true. She had a basketball. It was bloody."

"A basketball?" Burnett asked.

"Yeah," Della said.

Holiday shifted Hannah to the other side of her lap. "And I'm assuming Mrs. Chi didn't play ball."

"No."

Holiday raised a brow. "Then this is a sign. Either the killer had a ball with him, or she's seen the killer play ball. Or maybe both."

"Is there a park with a basketball court near your house?" Burnett asked.

"Yeah," Della grasped on her first ray of hope at finding the killers. "At the front of the park where we caught the other weres." She stood up. "Should we go there now?"

"No, I'll send Lucas." Burnett pulled out his phone. "If he runs into any weres they might be more forthcoming with him."

"But—"

"Don't even start." Burnett looked up from his cell. "First, I already told you that you weren't working this case. And second, if you go there, they'll recognize you or your scent from last night."

"And I'll recognize them," she said. Right then the lights in the room flickered and went off. The dead silence of a power outage filled the room.

Burnett moved to the wall where the controls were for the alarm system. While he hit a few buttons, he continued speaking. "Being this close to a full moon, it's best to let another were handle this." A light beep came from the controls.

"Problems?" Holiday asked, looking at the alarm.

"Probably not."

The lights flickered on again. He looked back at Della. "Now go catch up on some rest. You look like shit."

Holiday pulled her daughter closer, pressed a hand over her ear, and shot her husband a frown.

Burnett made an apologetic shrug. "Sorry. I mean, you look . . . awful."

Della glanced at Holiday. "He's such a sweet talker. How did you get so lucky?"

Holiday chuckled, then stood and touched Della's shoulder. A warmth traveled into Della's chest and for one second Della wished she could just give in to it and forget about all her other problems.

"He occasionally says the right thing. And as poorly as my husband put it, you do look tired. Go get some rest. Miranda and Kylie should be here in a couple of hours. And I know they are going to be over the moon that you're back. And there'll be no resting then."

Della heard Burnett telling Lucas about the basketball court. She looked back at the stubborn vamp, then frowned again at Holiday. "It's not fair. I need to work this case. I knew them. I care, damn it!" Her voice shook, escaping around the knot forming in her throat. "Why can't he see that?"

Holiday sighed. "You are working this case. Mrs. Chi is coming to you with clues. And when you're exhausted your chances of channeling a ghost are less likely. Plus, I'm sure Burnett will fill you in as soon as he hears from Lucas."

Della, certain she couldn't change Burnett's mind, and doubtful Holiday was going to help her out this time, shot out of the office.

She exited the cabin door, and had one foot on the porch when Holiday called out from the doorway.

"Yeah?" Della asked. Her gaze fell on Hannah as the baby gave her a big smile. Della felt almost guilty being in such a bad mood.

"If Chase gives you any problems, I want you to come to me. You got that?"

"I think I can take care of him." Della frowned, not liking the fact that everyone seemed to think that she couldn't handle Chase.

"Yeah, but why should you have all the fun?" Holiday smiled with empathy.

Della recalled Chase saying almost the same thing. "What cabin is he staying in?"

The camp leader hesitated.

"I need to talk to him. I'll find him either way," Della said. "It'll just take me a little longer and I won't have as much time to rest."

Holiday frowned. "Fourteen. But remember . . . no bloodshed. Only I get to do that!"

"Fourteen," Della repeated and watched Holiday close the door. Turning to leave, she noticed the bird that stood perched on the porch rail. But with only one thing on her mind, she kept going. She'd gotten down the first step when she felt that odd kind of tingle down her spine. The someone's-staring-at-you kind of tingle.

She looked left. No one.

She glanced right. Nothing.

Then she remembered the damn bird. She swung around.

The black grackle—so black that it looked almost blue—cocked its head and stared right at her. She recalled crossing paths with the shape-shifter, John, when she'd first arrived.

"John?" she asked, waiting for the bird to speak. The feathered creature just stared. "What?" she asked. "What do you want?" It remained silent.

She waved her hand out to see if it would fly away.

It didn't.

A normal bird would have scurried away.

Convinced it was John, she took a step closer. "Fly away or I'll pluck a feather," she warned.

The bird flapped its wings, but didn't leave its perch. Not very John-like. The teen, only half shape-shifter with limited shifting abilities, was as skittish as a mouse with an inferiority complex. Nor could the teen completely disguise his scent. She took a deep breath. Nothing. Nothing but bird.

"Okay, if you're not John, who are you?" Then just like that, the possibility of the bird being a different shape-shifter, one with disguising abilities, filled her mind. But Steve wasn't due back here for another week.

"Steve?" she whispered his name, even though this bird was a common grackle and Steve had a fascination with falcons.

Footsteps suddenly echoed from the path that led to and from the cabins. Thinking it might be Chase, Della pulled in a noseful of air and turned to see who it was. Her breath caught when the figure, walking slow and easy, made the corner.

Her mind started noting details.

Tall.

Wide shoulders.

Dark hair, slightly curly.

Eyes brown.

A soulful gaze. A soulful gaze focused on her. Directly on her.

Steve.

Her heart did a leap. And so did the bird behind her. She heard its wings pushing against the wind to flee. Part of her wanted to join the creature in flight. Seeing Steve made her feel emotions that she wanted to run from. Emotions that weren't even clearly defined.

Ahh, but Steve's scent stirred up memories. Memories of them together. Laughing.

Kissing.

Sharing.

Then came the memory of him saying goodbye.

As he continued walking forward, she realized that if they spoke here, their conversation would be privy to any vampire ears nearby.

And since one particular pair of male ears was in Holiday's office, she leapt off the porch and met the shape-shifter at the exit of the trail.

He stopped and smiled.

He made her world feel a little crazy.

"Hey," he said.

"Hi." She fought the awkwardness stirring in her chest. She'd seen him briefly in Paris when she'd gone with Miranda and tried to find her uncle. It had felt just as awkward then. When she left he hugged her and said they'd talk when he got back. It was talking time, but for the life of her she didn't know what to say. They stood there. The silence, louder than nature, echoed around them.

Finally a subject landed on her tongue. "I thought you weren't supposed to be here until next week."

"Yeah, they let us go early." He slipped a hand into his jeans pocket.

"So Perry is here, too?" Della's mind went to Miranda.

"Yeah."

For one second, she wondered if the bird had been Perry. If so, why hadn't he said anything?

She felt Steve's gaze shift over her and recalled Burnett telling her she looked like shit. Just how a girl wanted to look when she ran into an ex—or almost ex. Not.

"You're back here early too," he said. "Everything okay . . . at home?"

The awkwardness level increased tenfold with his question. The old Della would have told him. Opened her heart and let all the pain and anguish pour out. He would have wrapped his arms around her—brought her head to that soft spot between his shoulder and chest. His caring embrace would have felt good. It would have eased some of her pain.

But that was the old Della.

The new Della didn't know what to do. The realization scared her. She liked feeling in control, a step ahead. She could never be on top of her game if she didn't have a game plan. Or at least know the rules.

And where Steve was concerned she hadn't considered a strategy and didn't own that rule book. If she did, she sure as hell hadn't cracked the spine. Hell, she was outright clueless.

"Yeah, it's fine," she lied. The words had no sooner tripped off her lips than she regretted them, because she saw in his eyes that he knew she lied.

"I'm sorry." The apology slipped out before she could even consider the wisdom of offering it.

"It's okay," he said. "Really."

She wasn't altogether sure what the "really" meant, but the okay part was just Steve being nice and considerate. Steve being . . . Steve.

Suddenly, she remembered where she'd been going.

She remembered Chase.

A big lump of emotion formed in her gut. "I need to go. I have to . . . see someone."

"We'll talk later?" he asked.

"Yeah. Of course." Maybe by then, she'd have her shit together and not be stuck in this awkwardness. Maybe she'd have a damn plan.

Nodding, she took her first step down the path.

"Della?" he called out.

She stopped moving, but didn't look back. She needed a second to prepare herself, almost afraid of what he was going to say.

Chapter Thirteen

Chase walked into the cabin, got Baxter some food and water, and pointed the dog to his new bed. The dog was too busy sniffing around to care. Finally, after checking out all of the rooms and all of the corners, the dog started following him around.

Opening one of the boxes he'd brought over from his cabin, Chase set the picture of his family on an end table.

Running his finger over their faces, he stared at them for a few minutes, letting himself miss them. It didn't hurt like it used to, but he'd bet there wasn't a day that went by that he didn't think about them.

Baxter moved in and poked his leg with his snout. "It's not the Hilton, but we've stayed in a lot worse," he told the dog.

Baxter looked up with all-knowing eyes. He could almost read the animal's thoughts.

"Yeah," he said. "She's the reason we're here."

Still amped up after his conversation with Steve, he moved to the kitchen table and pulled his laptop out of his backpack to plug it in. He found the list of Stones and Williamses he'd gotten from Burnett's FRU computer in his pocket. He started pulling up maps, planning to visit each and every one.

Some of them for the second time. Because after a closer look, he'd noted that a couple of them were ones the Vampire Council database had spit out as well. He'd tracked down several of them.

Feeling his mood and his lack of sleep pull at his shoulders, he rubbed his neck. Looking back toward the bedroom door, he considered trying to rest, but he'd hoped Della would come looking for him.

Refocusing on the screen, he almost jumped when Baxter let go of a deep bark. The dog stared at a window.

Chase listened, and all he heard was a bird fluttering from tree to tree.

"Just a bird," he told Baxter, then inhaled to make sure he was right. The air gave him nothing, but he instantly became aware of a fresh paint smell. And from the looks of the smallest bedroom, they hadn't finished painting.

Pushing away from the table, he lifted the window to bring in some fresh air.

He went and opened the front door, staring out, hoping he'd see or hear Della coming. How long was the meeting with Burnett going to take?

He recalled her words and the pain in her voice. *He knows I'm a monster.*

Hell, he didn't have to wait for her. "Come on, guy. Let's go find her."

"Della," Steve said again, as if he weren't sure she'd heard him.

She pushed back the notion of just ignoring him, and turned to face him again. "Yeah?"

"You sure you're okay?" he asked.

This time she decided to go for the truth. "No. But 'okay' is overrated."

It was supposed to be funny, but he didn't smile. He just continued to study her with those dark, caring eyes. Eyes that seemed to see through her charade.

"It's just that you look . . ."

"Like shit? I know. Burnett just told me."

He smiled this time. "I wasn't going to say . . . that. You look beaten."

"Beaten? Me?" she asked, offended. "I prefer shit."

His smile widened. "Okay, not beaten, maybe just tired."

As good as it was to see him smile, she didn't have it in her to return the gesture. "Yeah, I need to hit the sheets for a while." Right then she recalled how many times she and Steve had hit the sheets together. They would hold on to each other, take things to a certain point—almost to the breaking point—but they'd never crossed the line.

She'd been scared. Scared it wouldn't last. She'd been right.

He claimed he couldn't handle her working with Chase, but the truth was he'd planned all along to go to Paris to a school for shape-shifters.

He glanced away for a second, and she could swear he'd read her thoughts. "Well, I gotta . . ." She waved. "Later."

He nodded, and his eyes met hers again. While she couldn't read his expression, something told her he wasn't any more comfortable with this conversation than she was. She turned and walked away. Walked. Not ran.

With every step, she felt him watch her go. It hit her that the last time he'd been at Shadow Falls, she'd watched him leave. She didn't know if it meant anything, but for some freaky reason it felt as if it did.

Instead of taking the path to cabin fourteen, Della cut through a patch of woods. The day was gloomy. And secluded in the alcove of the woods, it appeared almost dark. The damp earth scented the air. Some of the rain from earlier fell from the trees above and splattered on her forearms. A drop spattered onto her face and rolled down her cheek like a tear. She ignored it and kept walking.

Soon she realized something else she was trying to ignore. The feeling as if she weren't alone. Stopping, she turned a full circle, listening, looking, and inviting trouble to come on out if it lurked in the shadows.

Nothing.

Probably her lack of sleep.

Or the dead.

She evaluated the temperature. It was cold, but was that Mother Nature or a ghost?

"Mrs. Chi? Is that you?"

She got nothing again.

"Bao Yu?" she whispered her name.

Only a light breeze and a distant bird answered back. A few more drops of leftover rain hit her face.

Feeling silly, she took off again. The closer she got to cabin fourteen, the quieter she walked—watching her every step, being extra careful her black boots didn't snap a twig.

Oh, he would hear her and smell her before she arrived, but the thought of giving him less time to try to come up with a story seemed like a good idea.

She spotted his cabin, and took a deep breath to catch his scent. It lingered in the air, but weak. Stronger were spots where Baxter had lifted his leg and left the world a message that he was there.

She was glad she didn't have to squat and pee to be noticed.

She took a few more steps toward the wooden structure. Was Chase here? The closer she got, the more certain she was that he wasn't in. As she stepped up onto the porch, she inhaled again, checking to see if her canine friend Baxter waited inside.

When she'd been in the office, she'd heard Chase call the dog as if he'd wanted to see her. And the truth was, she'd like to see Baxter, too. She got a few feet closer.

No Baxter, either.

She almost left, then stopped.

It was wrong. But so was lying, and he'd done plenty of that.

She went to the door and turned the knob. He hadn't locked it. Practically an invitation.

Pushing the door open, she could swear she heard something. She stopped on the doorstep and listened. The only thing she could hear were nature noises: birds and critters scurrying around. Then she noted an opened window.

She looked around. The cabin's layout was the same as the one she shared with Miranda and Kylie. A joined living room and kitchen, two small baths, and three bedrooms. The furniture was different and newer. This must be one of the cabins built a few months back when the camp turned boarding school. Della inhaled, and the scent of paint hung heavy.

She continued to survey the home, and stopped when she saw the framed photograph of a family of four. A mom, dad, brother, and sister. Stepping closer, she recognized it as the one he'd kept at his other cabin, his much nicer cabin.

She picked up the picture. Chase had been young, fourteen or so. The photograph had probably been taken right before the plane accident that killed his family. As she brought the picture up, Chase's scent grew stronger. She let the scent fill her airway—even inhaled a little deeper.

On the glass, she saw a fingerprint smear as if someone had touched the image. She knew it had been him. Could see him doing it in her mind.

Did he still miss his family?

Of course he did.

Her heart ached for him, then she turned to her own family issues. Would the pictures of her family be all she had of them someday?

Putting the frame down, fighting the pain, she saw an opened laptop and some papers on the kitchen table.

Nudging the achiness away, she recalled the reason she was here. To see if Chase Tallman was hiding something about her uncle—to ultimately get her father off of a murder charge.

"What are you up to, Chase?"

She picked up the papers and read the name "Douglas Stone."

Immediately she remembered Burnett's words: *He's saying a man named Douglas Stone killed your aunt.*

She read on. Chase had several addresses and information on several different Douglas Stones in the Houston area. He also had the name "Don Williams." She didn't know who the Williams character was, but she'd bet a quart of O negative blood that he had something to do with her father's case.

And damned if she wouldn't find out.

She pulled her phone out and snapped close-up shots of the papers.

Della went back to the office to collect her things, then headed back to her cabin. She should try to rest, but the thought that Chase was somewhere hiding from her made napping impossible.

She'd drop her stuff off then find him. Then nap. She hadn't seen her cabin when her nose caught the scent of one particular dog's message. Then she was hit by the scent of his owner.

She took off, expecting to find him on the porch, but nope. Then she noted the door was ajar. The little twerp had just invited himself into her cabin. Who did he think—

Okay, maybe she couldn't bitch too much about that.

Not that she didn't have plenty of other things to bitch about. She flew up the steps, dropped her items on the porch with a loud thud, and went to confront the lying piece of poop.

Chapter Fourteen

When she flung open the door, he stood between the sofa and the coffee table. No doubt he'd heard her coming in time to make it to his feet. But the sofa hadn't had enough time to lose the six-foot imprint of his frame. His eyes, she noted, still carried the lazy look of sleep.

"Sleeping on my couch, huh?" she accused, and felt Baxter bumping her leg with his nose begging for a petting. Bending slightly, she petted the dog, hoping that bit of kindness didn't make her appear less than pissed.

Chase passed a hand over his face as if trying to wipe away the evidence. "I was waiting on you." He pulled his phone out of his pocket as if to see how long he'd slept. "What all did Burnett want?"

"Where's my uncle, Chase?"

He frowned. "I could swear we already covered that."

She opened her mouth to blast him with all the reasons she would never believe a word he said, when he spoke up.

"But I'll be happy to answer it again." He looked right in her eyes. "I don't know where he is. He didn't kill your aunt. And I'm here to help find the person who's guilty."

"By napping on my sofa? Uninvited," she blurted out, pushing aside her own guilt of snooping in his cabin. Baxter raised his paw and gently placed it on her knee. She offered him another soft scratch behind his ear.

"The door wasn't locked."

Yeah, she'd used that excuse, too. "It's still wrong." She lifted her hand from the dog and slipped it on her hip.

He stepped closer and smiled. "And it seems I'm not the only one . . . in the wrong. Did you go through my clothes? What? Were you curious if I was a boxers or briefs guy?"

How the hell did he know I was there? She tightened her eyes at him. "Your undies don't concern me."

"Not even a little bit?" His smiled widened. "Not that I blame you, I mean, I got to go through yours the first day we met."

"Still a Panty Perv, huh?" she asked through tight lips, remembering how he'd found her backpack and later commented about her underwear.

"Just a Della perv." He laughed.

When she shot him her best go-to-hell look, he stopped laughing. "Okay, so maybe you weren't going through my . . . undies, as you call them, but you were at my cabin. I smell the fresh paint." He reached for her.

"Stop!" She pointed a finger at him. "The only reason I'm tolerating your presence right now is that I need to get my dad off a murder charge. So either tell me something about that, or leave."

She stomped her foot and waited to see if he was going to tell her more about Douglas Stone and this Williams character. Not that any of it meant her uncle was innocent. But perhaps Chase thought he was. Perhaps her uncle had him fooled.

He held up his hands in surrender. "I'm here to help, Della." The tease in his eyes faded as he stared at her. "Did Burnett tell you that I resigned from the council and I'm working for the FRU?"

"Yeah, he gave me the bad news."

He cut his eyes up as if her answer annoyed him. "I thought that's what you wanted."

"Wanted. Past tense. You lied to me."

"I'm telling the truth now. I'm not hiding anything. Ask me anything, I'll tell you."

"Yeah, well, I don't belong to the truth-will-set-you-free liar's club." She growled. "Are you dense enough to think you can come back here now and things will be the same?"

He closed his eyes as if frustrated.

Good. He deserved to be frustrated.

He opened his green eyes and looked back at her. "Della, don't fight me. Work with me. We can do this. We'll make it right."

She shook her head. "There is no 'we,' Chase. There's you and there's me. I'll work with you on the case, not even because I believe you don't know where my uncle is. The only thing to make right is getting my father off. I don't trust you. But right now you are the only lead I've got."

He exhaled. "Then I guess I'll have to win back your trust."

"The likelihood of that happening is slim to none." She tilted up her chin. Never let him say she didn't give him fair warning.

He stood there, just staring. "Why are you still fighting what you feel?"

"Because I get to choose my destiny, not anyone else." The moment Della said it, she realized how true it was.

"Who else would be choosing your destiny?"

"You. This bond. You did it knowing what would happen."

"So you would have really preferred to die than to care about me?" He looked hurt, and while he deserved to feel that, too, she couldn't deny that hurting him . . . hurt her.

"I would have liked the choice!" she seethed.

"Life isn't always about choices, Della! Did you choose to be vampire?"

"No, and I hate that, too!" She swallowed the tears that threatened.

"So you hate caring about me?"

The question hung out there and she didn't know how to answer, so she simply didn't.

Eventually, he looked up. "It doesn't always happen like this."

"What?" she asked.

"The bond. Not everyone ends up together. You still have a choice." Honesty and hurt thickened his voice. "But I'm going to do everything in my power to prove to you that I'm the right choice."

"By lying to me?"

"I'm not—"

"You did."

"Look," he said, sounding frustrated. "The day Burnett gave you those photographs, I was going to tell you."

"Sure you were."

"I was. If you'll remember, I told you that we needed to talk. I called you early that morning and asked you to meet me earlier because . . . I wanted to come clean."

Feeling vulnerable, she tightened her fist. "Why don't you just leave?"

He shook his head. "Eddie had never told me about your aunt. I questioned him about it and that's when he told me. Then when I heard about your father being arrested, I was shocked. I went back to Eddie and that's when he told me what really happened. And all I've done since is look for that guy to get your dad off."

"There." She held up a finger. "You finally said something that I care to hear about. What does my uncle *say* happened? Not that I'm sure I'll believe him." She walked to the chair and dropped down.

"Why would he lie about that?" he asked.

"Because he's guilty of murder."

"He didn't do it."

"Yeah, well, I trust him about as much as I do you." She leaned back and her whole body melted into the chair cushion. Instantly, she felt the lack of sleep making her eyelids heavy.

He moved to the sofa and sat down. "He was at a party one night with his girlfriend. They were leaving and some guy was hitting on her."

"I want to know about the murder, not my uncle's love life."

"I'm getting to that," he said. "Eddie stood up to him and they fought. The guy was vampire. When he got sick later, his parents took him to the hospital. A young nurse there was fae. She told him what was happening and even gave him some blood."

Della sat there, fighting the compassion that stirred for her uncle. His story was so close to her own that her chest ached. She was so darn tired.

Then she felt Baxter's soft snout rest on her leg.

"The fae told him about a funeral home that would help him fake his death. They also offered him a few names of gangs he could join. He didn't want to go that way, so he went on his own, but he couldn't do it. He wound up joining a gang."

Chase folded his hands together. "It wasn't one of the good ones. The initiation demanded he kill someone for blood. He couldn't do it. They offered him one more chance. Told him if he didn't do it, they would kill someone he loved. He didn't think they knew anything about him."

Chase's voice deepened and Della could tell just by his tone how much he cared about Eddie, that it hurt him to recount the man's story.

Silence and emotion hung in the air, then Chase continued, "Eddie went to tell the gang leader he couldn't do it, and that he was leaving, but the guy laughed. Told him that the punishment was already set in motion. At first Eddie wasn't worried; he countered that there wasn't anyone he loved. But as he walked out, the guy called him by his real name."

"Realizing they knew, Eddie took off as fast as he could. When he got to the house, Bao Yu was already dead. One of the gang members, a Douglas Stone, was still in the house."

Della's heart gripped. "My dad? Did he see it?"

Chase shrugged. "Eddie said when he got there your father was unconscious. Eddie and Douglas went at it. But Douglas was a lot stronger. They were still fighting when the cops, sirens blaring, pulled up in front of the house. Eddie was in bad shape, but he managed to get out before they got upstairs. Unfortunately, so did Douglas Stone. He got away."

He paused. "As soon as Eddie was able, he went looking for Douglas Stone. But the gang had broken up. They'd all gone their own ways. A few months later, he found out about the Vampire Council. He went and appealed to them to help him catch the guy. They looked, but never found him. He's still on their most-wanted list."

Della just stared, trying to take it all in, her exhaustion level climbing. "Who called the police?"

Chase shrugged. "I don't know."

"It had to have been my dad."

"It's possible."

The images flashing in her head were almost too painful to stomach. She felt Baxter bathe her hand with his tongue. She stared at the dog, using his soulful, caring eyes as a touchstone as the story replayed in her head. Did she believe it? Maybe. Oh, hell, she didn't know what she believed.

She looked up at Chase. Did she believe in him? Hadn't he proved that she couldn't?

"Does my uncle work for the council?"

Chase nodded. "Sort of. But not as an agent."

"Then what?"

He smiled ever so slightly. "Eddie says he has more brains than brawn. The council put him through Baylor. Then he trained as a supernatural doctor around the world. He no longer works as just a doctor, but works trying to improve the health of vampires. He's the one who discovered the five different lineages who are carriers of the Reborn virus and discovered how to save Reborns. He's a good man, Della."

"If he's so good, why isn't he here? Why didn't he come looking for me instead of sending you? What's he hiding?"

She saw the way Chase looked away for a second. Then he turned back. "It's Burnett."

"He knows Burnett?"

"No, because he's FRU."

"But . . ." She paused as she tried to wrap her head around his answer. "You're here and you've even joined the agency."

"Some people are more political than others."

"That sounds like a pretty weak excuse." And damned if her eyelids didn't feel heavy as well. She really needed him to leave so she could rest. But she was finally getting answers that felt half true.

"Is he going to avoid you now?"

"He wouldn't do that."

Was that doubt in his eyes? "Then it doesn't make sense."

He ran a hand over his face. "I don't know why he hates the FRU." He exhaled. "But whatever that reason is, it's not . . . He's got a good heart."

"Who is Don Williams?"

"I think it's an alias that Douglas Stone uses. I've got addresses on some here in the Houston area. Tomorrow I'll go check them out. You obviously saw what I printed out."

She didn't deny it. They sat there for a silent few seconds, her body sinking deeper into the chair, her eyes growing harder to keep open.

"Any other questions, Della? I'll answer them. I'm not hiding anything."

Did she believe him? Oh, hell, she was too tired to believe or not believe.

Chase stood and walked past her. "I brought us something." He pulled out a bottle of blood from the fridge, unscrewed it, and took a sip. The tangy scent was O negative. He walked back and held out the container.

"Here."

The taste buds on her tongue tingled. She didn't take it.

"I don't need it." Her stomach grumbled in protest. "I had some last night." She looked back at Baxter.

"How long did you go without? Did you feed at all when you were at your parents'?"

"Of course I did," she said.

"You know if you don't feed regularly, you get worn down. Especially, when you're a Reborn."

She glared up at him.

"I should have brought you some blood while you were there. I didn't think. I apologize for that."

She rolled her eyes. "I'm not your concern."

"You will always be my concern," he said softly. Then he put the plastic container in her hand. The wild berry scent rose up and her mouth watered. Oh, hell. She lifted it and took a sip. The flavor sent her taste buds to heaven.

She looked up. The fact that he towered above her hit a nerve, but with zero energy, she didn't have what it took to stand.

"I don't need you to take care of me," she said.

"We all need someone, Della. That doesn't mean you aren't strong."

She started to stand up, but he knelt down. His green gaze locked on her face. "You're beautiful, smart, and funny. You care more about people than is required. You're the furthest thing from a monster that I know, Della Tsang."

An achiness swelled in her chest. "You were eavesdropping." If she weren't so tired, she'd give him a hard shove and knock him on his butt. Hell, if she weren't so tired, she'd come up with some rude remark about his compliments meaning nothing.

"Not really eavesdropping. Not intentionally."

Before she realized his intent, he brushed a strand of hair from her cheek and let his hand linger against her cheek. The touch was both painful and wonderful at the same time.

She cut her eyes to the side and glared at his hand. "That's a good way to lose a finger."

As if to prove he didn't believe her, he ran his index finger over her bottom lip. "Get some rest. I'll check on you later."

She watched him walk out. Why hadn't she bit him? Damn, she should have bit him!

It wasn't until she blinked that she realized she had tears in her eyes. Hell, she was so tired that she didn't even know why she was crying. Not that she was short on reasons.

Chapter Fifteen

Sleep had never felt so good. Della didn't want to wake up, but then she heard the voices. Miranda and Kylie?

She rolled over and forced her eyes open. Her gaze landed on a dresser. A big white dresser with matching vases of plastic yellow sunflowers decorating the top.

"Shit!" She jackknifed out of bed, her feet thudding down on light blue carpet. She stood there, arms out, mind racing, trying to come to terms with the fact that she didn't have a white dresser. That the walls in her room at Shadow Falls weren't a pale yellow.

Her gaze shifted around. She didn't have a white four-poster bed, either. She didn't have a pink quilt. Or . . .

A loud crashing sound echoed from somewhere inside the house. Then came voices. No, not voices: screams.

Real screams like someone was about to die.

Della's gaze shot to the mirror. Her heart stopped when the person staring back at her wasn't . . . her. It was Bao Yu, her aunt. Somewhere deep in her mind, behind the wall of panic clawing at her conscious, she realized this was a vision.

"You okay?" Another voice rang out from somewhere, somewhere that wasn't here. Somewhere that felt safe, but Della couldn't go there. She had to stay here.

"Della?" a voice said her name.

A hand came down on her shoulder. Della swung around, growled, and showed her canines.

Suddenly the pale yellow walls disappeared. Her vision swirled, blurred, and then transformed into tunnel vision. She blinked, felt as if she were moving. She closed her eyes, then opened them. For one second she thought she was back in her room, but then something changed, everything changed. She lay on the floor, a cold tile floor; above her a ceiling fan whirled around. And around.

She cut her eyes left and saw a basketball about a foot from her face, sitting in a puddle of something red. She glanced right and saw . . . she saw a red tabby. Della fought to make sense of this, and then she did. The cat . . . Chester.

The feline rested on his side, he shifted his paw at her, his breathing labored. Just past the cat lay her husband. No, Mrs. Chi's husband. But she was Mrs. Chi. She blinked, waiting to see his chest rise with breath. But no. He lay so still. Too still.

Someone's foot landed between her and the cat. The shoe was a bright red tennis shoe that appeared to be made out of snakeskin.

Am I going to have to cut you again? A voice asked. And then, *Shit, go get them before they go rattling their mouth. Take care of them.*

Get who? Della wondered. She tried to look up to see the face of the killer, but her vision went black. A light, a soft light, called for Mrs. Chi. The woman's fury at the killers swelled in her chest and she turned away from the light. She clung to what she knew. To the here and now.

A rushing sound filled her ears, the taste of blood filled her mouth. She felt it then, a kind of nothingness. Not fear. Not pain.

She was dying.

"No," she yelled. But nothing came out of her mouth. Everything went dark, and all she could see was that beautiful light leaving her, floating away. Her husband of over fifty years was in the midst of that light, motioning for her to come. To hurry. But it wasn't right. None of this should have happened. She needed to tell someone before these bad people hurt others.

"Della?" her name came again, but it was still far away. Her visions started to clear. She sensed she wasn't alone. She saw his shape floating toward her in another light. A different light. Not Mr. Chi, but someone else. Someone . . . familiar. Chase?

Then he was gone. So was the light. A knife, blood dripping from its tip was held right over her face. Fear caught her by the neck and pulled her under. She felt a drop of blood from the weapon fall against her cheek. She tried to bolt up, but there was numbness in her limbs. Another spatter of blood dripped from the knife's edge.

An odd déjà vu feeling pulled at her mind. She looked up from the blade, to the person straddling her. Feng.

Not Feng! See the freckle. There, beside his right brow. That's not Feng.

Suddenly fighting mad, Della lifted her head up and let go of another growl. "No! No! No!"

The blackness returned and she welcomed it. Let it swallow her.
One.
Two.
Three.

She wanted to stay there. In the nothingness, but something, someone, brought her back again.

"I've got you. It's over," a male voice said.

What's over?

Della sensed herself being lifted off the floor, cradled in someone's arms. Her cheek came against a solid male chest. A solid bare chest.

She heard a steady heartbeat. And no sooner than she heard it than her own heart changed its rhythm to follow.

She opened her eyes and saw Chase's green gaze on her. Worry etched his expression. She felt his arms around her. Felt the coolness of his skin against the back of her legs, her bare back. Felt the muscle in his chest, where her cheek rested. Another fraction of a second ticked by before she became aware of him lowering himself. He sat on her bed.

Just like that she recalled talking to him, remembered him leaving. She had a slight recollection of stripping down to her bra and panties before crawling under the covers. But other than that, everything else in her mind felt blank. How did he . . . Why was he . . . Surely they weren't . . .

"You okay?" he asked.

She blinked. Okay? She was practically naked and in his arms and didn't have a clue how she got there. How could that be okay?

Slowly the confusion started to fade, a memory lurked close. A memory of something bad. Something . . . Her heart started to race.

"No! Not okay." Her mind pushed at the cobwebs giving her only a glimpse of something terrifying.

Bolting out of Chase's arms, and not very gracefully, she landed with a hard thump on her ass on the floor.

Chase stood up. Her gaze shifted up. Shirtless. He wore jeans, but they were unzipped and hung open. A dark trail of hair traveled down from his belly, disappearing under the elastic-band waist of what appeared to be a pair of dusty blue, Calvin Klein, tight-fitting boxers.

She heard his words from earlier. *What? Were you curious if I was a boxers or briefs guy?*

She shook her head, thinking this might be a crazy dream. She looked at the clock: It was almost four in the afternoon. If this wasn't a dream, she'd slept for a good two hours. She closed her eyes and willed herself to wake up.

When she opened her eyes, he stood there watching her, a tight frown on his lips. Then, remembering her lack of clothes, she shot up and snagged the pillow and held it over herself.

Only then did she remember the vision. Or visions? The ugliness of it rained down on her like pitchforks. The air in her throat hung. She'd seen Chester, Mrs. Chi's cat, Mr. Chi, and she'd seen . . . her aunt.

Her knees gave and she dropped back down on the bed.

Chase sat down beside her. "It's okay. Breathe."

She looked up and recalled the shadowy figure she'd seen in the light. Recalled someone calling her name. Had he been here while she'd had the vision? Or . . . had he been . . . there? There in the vision?

"Were you . . . ? Did you see . . . ?"

He nodded. "It was different than what happened in the vision of Liam and Natasha. It was like a movie going in my head. But it wasn't your aunt, or the older lady, it was you. When I woke, I got here as fast as I could."

Tears filled her eyes, recalling bits and parts of the vision. Her heart ached for Mrs. Chi, and then she remembered . . . *Not Feng! See the freckle. There, beside his right brow. That's not Feng.*

She glanced up at Chase. Had he heard that too? Just like that, she knew he had. "My dad didn't do it. She's just confused. Holiday says it happens all the time."

She glanced up at Chase's green eyes. Was that doubt in his gaze? "He's not a bad man, Chase. He was the dad all my friends wished their dads were more like. Any kind of late-night event, my dad would be our driver. He'd pick up all my friends and drive us to and from wherever we wanted to go. Some nights, after a football game, he would take me and my friends out and buy everyone dinner and desserts."

She wiped the tears from her cheeks. "He never missed a father-daughter dance or one of my events. He was my champion. I've always known my mom loved me, but my dad . . . he adored me. If I had a problem, he was my go-to person. And there wasn't anything he wouldn't do for me. Once, when I was barely a teen, my mom was out of town, I ran out of tampons. I was too embarrassed to go to the store and buy them. He did it for me. And when I had my tonsils out, he wouldn't leave the hospital. He's not a killer, Chase. He's my daddy. And I'm his little girl."

Chase wrapped his arms around her. Pulled her against him. She was just too damn weak to fight him. "Douglas Stone did it." He pressed his face into her hair and kissed the top of her head. The gentleness of that kiss had her breath catching.

She looked up, swiping away at her tears. "Do you believe that or are you just saying it to make me feel better?"

"I believe it." He passed his thumb under her eye as if to catch a get-away tear. "It's going to be okay," he said.

Not everyone ends up together. You still have a choice. His words from earlier vibrated in her head and heart.

Then he leaned in—or did she?—either way, their lips touched. Somehow her pillow slipped to the floor.

The kiss was soft and slow, as if he were afraid she'd regret it. She probably would, but considering what she'd just been through she needed a distraction. That was what this was, she decided, nothing more than a distraction. A kiss didn't mean a lifetime. It was just . . . a kiss.

He slipped his tongue into her mouth. In the background, she heard footsteps in her cabin. But before she could wrap her head around anything other than Chase's lips, the door to her bedroom swung open.

Miranda stormed in. "Did you hear that Perry is—" The witch came to a screeching halt. Seriously, her tennis shoes probably left skid marks. Her hazel eyes grew wide; her mouth dropped open. "Oh, I'm sorry, I . . . you two just . . . uh, continue on."

Chase shot up off the bed, probably trying to help, but something about the way he quickly zipped his pants just made the whole situation appear worse.

Miranda took several steps back and slammed the door.

Chase glanced down at her. "I'm sorry," he said sounding genuine.

Della fell back onto the mattress, closing her eyes, and wondered how one's emotions could move from horrified to wanting to be kissed to being humiliated in seconds.

"Just leave," she pleaded and listened to see if he granted her request.

No footsteps sounded in the room. Instead, the mattress gave as he sat down beside her. "You sure you're okay? That was pretty damn scary. I just . . . I . . . you . . . the thing . . ."

When he stopped making sense, she opened her eyes and caught him noticing what she was wearing—or what she wasn't wearing—seemingly for the first time. "Please just go."

His eyes swept up to her face. Slowly. All that tender concern in his eyes had turned into something different. His pupils were large and the green in his eyes seemed to glitter with a different kind of emotion. "But . . . uh . . . Don't you think we should . . . talk about what all we saw?"

"Not now," she said through tight lips and covered herself with the pillow again. Her bikini would reveal more than her bra and panties, but because it wasn't a bathing suit, she felt more vulnerable.

"Okay." He turned toward the door.

"Not that way," she snapped. "The window."

He looked back, just a hint of a smile in his eyes. "If I sneak out, she'll really believe we were . . . you know."

Della sat up, and hugged the pillow. "You aren't wearing a shirt, your pants were undone, and I'm in my underwear. And for some unknown reason we were kissing. There is nothing in this world you could say to her that will convince her that we weren't doing . . . 'you know'! So just use the window."

He opened it and had one leg out when he glanced back, that teasing look now brighter in his eyes. "One thing."

"What?" She scowled.

He countered her expression with a smile. "Make that two."

"What?" she snapped again.

"One," he paused. "This . . . the kiss that just happened. It was your choice. You kissed me."

She frowned, because damn it, she didn't want to be reminded.

"Second. You got your days wrong."

"Huh?"

"You're wearing your Friday panties, and it's Sunday."

She tossed the pillow at him then glanced down to confirm it. Yup, she was wearing her day-of-the-week panties.

She threw her arm over her eyes and moaned.

Chapter Sixteen

Minutes later, dressed, but still not ready to face her friend's accusations, or the deadly cold that had returned, Della heard another set of footsteps move up on her front porch. She inhaled the frigid air, and recognized Kylie's scent, along with Socks, her cat.

She heard Kylie speaking with Miranda. Della purposely didn't listen, only imagining what the witch was telling her. Then a loud feline howl filled the cabin. Was the cat protesting Baxter's earlier visit?

Right then the chameleon knocked on Della's bedroom door.

"Come in," Della said, as if she really had a choice.

Kylie moved in first, her expression serious. She dropped on the edge of the bed beside Della. "Are you okay?"

"We were not doing the mattress mambo. I had a vision, he saw it too, and when he woke up he came here." Della looked at Miranda standing in the doorway.

Kylie sighed. "I don't mean—"

"I know it looked like it." She frowned at Miranda. "And if I'd seen what you saw, I wouldn't believe me either, but—"

"I'm not asking about you and Chase, I'm asking about the five spirits."

"Yeah, I had . . ." Five? *Five? Freaking five?*

Della caught her breath. "No!"

Kylie nodded.

Della shook her head. "Two yes, but not five. You must have brought three with you, because I only had two."

"There were definitely five. And they weren't here for me. I couldn't see them, only felt them."

"Well, I didn't see them either," Della said, not wanting to claim them.

"Did they say anything?"

"No." She popped up off her bed. "No. And no!" Della looked up at the ceiling. Not really sure who she was addressing, but looking up seemed appropriate. "Two is two too many. No way, no how, no hell, can I deal with five!" Then she glanced back at Kylie. "Are they still here?"

"No." Kylie stood up. "They left."

Miranda spoke up. "But they were here. The three Diet Cokes that I set out on the kitchen table for our talk—as soon as you finished what you were doing—burst. I swear I got frostbite!" She rubbed the tip of her nose.

Right then a loud thump landed on their porch, followed by a knock. Burnett.

All three of them walked into the living room. Miranda ran to the door. "Good thing you're here. We had an invasion of ghosts."

Burnett frowned, stepped into the cabin, and looked at Della. "Did you rest?"

"Yes." Why did she get the strange sensation that he wasn't just here to monitor her sleep? "Did Lucas's trip to the basketball court turn up anything?"

"No." From Burnett's expression, she knew he had more to say.

"Then what?"

"I just got called to a murder scene. Three young weres. I think they might be the three you saw and may be connected to the Chi case."

"At least we know who the three extra spirits were," Kylie said.

"Did they say anything?" he asked.

"I didn't even feel them," Della said, hoping to put distance between her and them.

"You're still not working the case," Burnett said, "but it'd help if you could confirm they were the same ones. You up to it?"

Della inhaled. "Yes. Of course." But everything inside of her screamed no.

No to not working the case. She wanted to catch the Chis' killers.

No to ghosts. They still freaked her out.

No to seeing more dead bodies. That was just wrong.

No to kissing Chase. She wasn't ready for that.

Now all she had to do was figure out why in the hell she kept saying yes.

"You sure you're okay to do this?" Burnett asked, right before they were about to cross the yellow tape.

"Would you stop worrying about me? I've slept. I've eaten."

His brow tightened. "I was referring to . . . Never mind."

She suddenly remembered the last body she'd identified. A young girl and her boyfriend had been murdered by a vampire. Della had puked her guts out.

She swallowed and vowed not to have a repeat performance.

"I can handle this." And to prove it to him, and maybe even to herself, she took the lead and stepped over the yellow tape, walking closer to the storage shed that was located on the far side of the park. The same park where she'd met Lucas and had saved the girl from the weres. The park close to her house.

As she took her final steps up to the building, surrounded by an array of other FRU agents, she recalled how many times she'd played right here as a child. Had there been werewolves hanging out here then? Did her sister ever come out here at night now? The thought sent a whisper of fear running through her. And she made a mental note to warn her.

Della spotted three sheet-covered bodies lined up. Blood, the victims' blood, filled her nose. With that smell came the horrid scent that Della recognized as death.

Burnett said something to one of the other agents. She should have been listening, but she was too worried about controlling her gag reflex.

One of the younger agents, Shawn, the warlock, who had a thing for Miranda, stepped closer and nodded at Della. Della returned the courtesy.

"You okay?" he asked.

Frowning, she nodded. She'd be a lot better if people quit asking her.

Another agent, a black-suited, older were, walked over to the three bodies and one by one pulled the sheets from their faces for Della to see.

Her stomach roiled, but she willed herself not to throw up. She looked from one tainted blue face to the other. As she worked at controlling her stomach, she lost control of her heart. She recalled seeing the three teens out for a fun Saturday night. They'd had their whole lives in front of them. More than ever, she wanted to catch the creeps who did this.

"It's them," Della said and heard footsteps behind her.

She glanced back at Chase and realized she should have known he would be here. He was working with Burnett now. Chase's gaze, filled with concern, met hers and she saw the "you okay?" question in his eyes. Seeing it fueled her vulnerable side, and the emotion in her chest doubled. She recalled how good it had felt to lean against him earlier.

Her sinuses stung. Mentally giving herself a big swift kick in the ass, she glanced away and stiffened her shoulders. The last thing she wanted was Chase coddling her in front of a bunch of agents.

On second thought, the last thing she wanted was to need anyone to coddle her. What the hell was happening to her? Realizing she didn't need to look at the bodies anymore, she walked a few feet away.

Burnett followed, and behind him, Della heard Chase's steps. "We can't prove it, but we're pretty sure this is connected to the Chis' murders."

"It is," Della said, remembering some of the vision. "I'm pretty sure these three walked past the Chis' shop, probably smelled the blood, and they saw the murder scene."

Burnett's eyes widened. "How do you know?"

"A vision," Della said.

"So you saw the killers?"

"Not their faces." Bits and pieces of the vision filled her head. "But I heard—"

"I saw one of their faces," Chase said.

Burnett's brow creased. "You told me you didn't see them."

"Not earlier, but . . . in her vision."

Burnett scratched his head. "You were in her vision?"

Chase nodded.

"It's true," she affirmed, even knowing it sounded bat-shit crazy.

It was dark when Della and Burnett got back to Shadow Falls. Burnett had sent Chase to the FRU headquarters to work with their sketch artist.

The camp seemed extra quiet as she walked to her cabin. Della could smell the bonfire, which meant everyone was in the woods cooking hot dogs and marshmallows. She debated going. Having something else on her mind besides her own problems might be nice, but the thought of trying to be friendly to everyone seemed too much.

The quietness of her cabin appealed more. She continued walking.

In the back of her mind, bits and pieces of the vision kept flashing in her head. Some little detail about the visions kept teasing her, as if it were important, but for the life of her she couldn't put her finger on what it was. She was almost to her cabin when a bird swooped down. It didn't hit her, but it came close.

Recalling the bird on the office porch earlier, she growled. "Is that you, Perry? This isn't funny! I'm in no mood for silly jokes!"

She stood in the middle of the darkness and waited for the shape-shifter to answer her. No answer came. Tilting her head to the side, she could still hear the birds, or maybe a bird—she couldn't tell if it was the same one—rustling in the trees.

She waited, impatiently, for another couple of seconds. Then she started off, swearing to give Perry some lip when she saw him. Her phone dinged with an incoming text.

She pulled it out and read Kylie's request that she come join them. Trying to think of a good reason not to go without sounding pathetic, she stood in the dark. Finally, just giving up, she tucked it back into her jeans.

She was just in front of the cabin when she spotted a figure on her front porch. She breathed in and immediately frowned. What was he doing here? Then a second scent came to her. What were they doing together?

Chapter Seventeen

He hadn't seen her. Hadn't heard her. She could turn around and head to the campfire. Pretend she never knew he'd been here. She remembered his words: *We'll talk later.*

She'd agreed. But she still didn't have a clue what to say. Did he want some kind of an answer? With so much going on, she was answerless.

But then Baxter barked, in her direction, and curiosity struck again. What was Baxter doing with Steve?

Steve turned and glanced her way. "Hey." His Alabama accent making the word sound longer than three letters.

"Hi," she said.

Steve stayed on the porch, but Baxter bounded over to her. For an old dog, he had a lot of bounce.

"You had company." Steve motioned to the canine who was leaning against her leg. "He was waiting on your steps."

"Really?" Della knelt down and looked the dog in the eyes, confirming he was okay. Had Chase not put the dog inside?

She felt Steve studying her. "He belongs to Chase."

Steve leaned back against the porch rail. "Yeah, I know."

"You do?"

"Remember, I knew where his cabin was? He had the dog then."

Yeah, she did remember now and could kick herself for asking. Steve had spotted her there with Chase. They hadn't been doing anything, but Steve had been hurt.

And she'd felt like shit because of it.

"I heard you went to a murder scene," Steve said.

"Yeah." Della looked up to the moon hanging low in the sky. Silence filled the night and the distant campfire smoke flavored the cool air.

"Do you want to talk?" he asked.

She looked back at him, and her panic must have shown.

"Not about us," he continued. "I mean, I know we need to talk about that sooner or later, but right now, I meant about the scene." He shuffled his feet. "We used to talk about things like that."

She looked at him and her heart skipped a beat with her next thought. *We used to talk about a lot of things.* And right then another painful truth hit. Steve was just another thing in her life that had changed. Yet here he was, not trying to pressure her, just offering to talk, to listen. To help.

Chase's words echoed in her head. *Not everyone ends up together. You still have a choice.*

"It had to have been hard," Steve said.

She dropped on her backside and leaned against the front of the cabin. Baxter dropped down beside her. "It was," Della said.

"But this is still what you want to do as a career." He stepped closer. "Why would you want to see stuff like that?"

She looked at him. "I don't want to see it, I want to stop it."

He sat beside her, but not so close they touched. She recalled sitting out here on the porch with him so many times. Feeling so . . . scared of what she was feeling.

"I don't get it." He picked up a piece of pine straw off the porch and started twisting it. "It hurts you, but you still want to do it."

"But it feels right when I find the person responsible. Doesn't it hurt you to see someone sick?"

He almost smiled. "Touché," he said. "I guess I hadn't looked at it like that, but you're right." There was silence. The night noises echoed around them. "I saved my first life while I was in Paris."

No, I was your first. He'd given her a transfusion that had saved her life, but bringing it up felt too personal somehow, so she let it pass.

"How did you do it? Save the life?" she asked.

"A were came into the clinic I was assisting at. The doctor was out on a call. He had internal injuries, was bleeding out. I had to operate to stop it. I was scared he was going to die on me. But when he didn't, it was . . . I don't know how to explain it, but it was a powerful feeling. I've never been surer about wanting to be a doctor. It was like being validated."

"You're going to make a great one." Della recalled what Chase had told her about her uncle.

"Now I just have to convince my mom that going the supernatural route to medicine is what's right for me."

"I'm sure she'll be proud of you either way," Della said.

"Oh, hell, no. She's doing everything she can to try to get me to enroll in regular medical school. I know she means well, but I just don't understand why she can't let me follow my own dreams."

"Most parents don't understand." She thought about her parents, her father, and wondered what he thought he understood . . . what he believed. In her mind, she saw the way he looked at her these last few months. Was he really afraid of her?

"How are things at your home?" Steve asked, as if reading her mind.

"Crazy," she said. "I'm guessing you heard about my dad."

"Yeah. I'm sorry. I know that has to be hard."

She nodded.

After a moment, he asked, "What changed?"

"What do you mean? I thought we weren't going to talk about us."

"No, I didn't . . . I mean you coming back to Shadow Falls. I heard you went back to try to help out."

She gave Baxter a slow pass of her hand across his back. "My being there wasn't helping. It made things worse."

"Not intentionally, I'm sure," he said.

She stared at the dog. "No." A bird called out in the night. "I think my dad knows."

"Knows what?"

"That I'm vampire." She glanced up, unsure why she'd told Steve this. She hadn't even told Kylie or Miranda yet. Chase knew, but only because he'd eavesdropped. But the second she looked into the shape-shifter's eyes, she understood her reasons. This was Steve. He'd always been so easy to talk to. He was safe. Even safer than before, she realized.

Perhaps he'd always been safe, but it hadn't always felt that way. Now it did.

She didn't have that need to run away, or to keep him at a distance. She wasn't the least bit afraid. That, she realized, was what had changed.

And just exactly what did that mean?

Chase finished up with the sketch. Once outside the headquarters, he pulled out his phone and checked the time. Looking around, he spotted a bird in a tree. Was it just any bird, or was Burnett still having him followed?

Was he taking a chance?

He remembered the kiss he'd shared with Della. The one that she'd initiated, not him. And damned if that hadn't felt good. Sooner or later, she'd understand that they were perfect for each other. She had to, didn't she?

Maybe after she got her dad off, then they could start all over. A fresh start—one where she knew he was her choice, one where kisses and having a half-naked Della in his arms weren't so uncommon.

And tonight's little excursion might bring that about sooner. It might lead him to Douglas Stone. Burnett would get pissed, but, in a way, it had been his suggestion.

He dialed Leo. "We still on for later tonight?" he asked as soon as the guy answered the phone.

"Yeah, but Chase, are you really sure you want to do this? I'm sneaking you in, so I can't send the guards in with you. I'll be the only one covering the back entrance, which means I can't go in."

"I know," he said. "I'll be fine."

"We've lost three people this year. They thought they would be fine, too. And they weren't in there alone."

"Let me worry about that."

"Okay, be here at eleven and don't be late."

"Got it." He hung up and looked at his cell again for the time. He had just enough time to go back to the cabin, feed Baxter and let him out, and then go off to the jail.

As he flew over Shadow Falls, he saw the campfire's glow. Was Della there? He envisioned her with Miranda and Kylie. But a less desirable image hit. One of her cozying up to the fire with Steve's arms around her. Jealousy filled his chest.

As tempting as it was to fly low enough to see, he knew he'd set off the alarm. So he flew past the orange glow and scent of roasted marshmallows and headed for the entrance.

Walking through the gate, knowing the camera had taken his picture and let him pass, he looked back over his shoulder to see if he had a tail. He didn't spot one, but that didn't mean shit. He hadn't spotted one last night, either.

He came to the trail and debated making a quick visit to the bonfire. Taking off in a quick run, he got there in less than three minutes. The fire was huge, flames reaching up to the sky, and the popping sounds of burning wood filled the night air. Laughter rang out from a group of girls roasting hot dogs on sticks. A few couples, arm in arm, enjoyed each other's company.

Lucas, hanging out by some trees, spotted him and waved. Standing close by the blue-eyed were was Kylie. But no Della. Chase walked over.

Kylie smiled. "Hey, I heard you're back."

"Yeah." He noted that the girl's smile seemed genuine. Did that mean Della hadn't badmouthed him too much to her? Chase glanced back at Lucas and remembered that Burnett had sent him to follow the lead on the basketball.

"Your trip back to the park lead anywhere?"

"No, I stayed there several hours. I think Burnett sent another were agent to keep an eye out."

Chase nodded and focused back on Kylie. "Is Della around?"

"I don't think she's back yet." She pulled her phone out.

"She should be," he said.

"I texted her a while back and told her to come here." The blonde looked up. "She hasn't texted me back. But she might have called it an early night. I think she had a rough day."

Her light blue eyes hinted that she worried he was part of Della's rough day.

"Thanks, I'll run by her cabin."

"Or just let her sleep," she said.

"I just want to check on her."

"Is something wrong?" she asked.

You mean other than me being worried about her cozying up with Steve? "No."

Walking away, he did one loop around the fire, moving in and out of the groups of people, hoping to spot Steve alone, or better yet with another girl hanging on him.

But the shape-shifter wasn't around. Were he and Della together?

Chase took off for Della's cabin. He landed on the porch. He tilted his head to see if he could hear anyone inside. Just a cat meowing. Then a scent hit. His nostrils flared. Blood.

And not just any blood.

Della's.

He grabbed the doorknob and shot inside. The door hit the wall with a thud. His eyes burned and his canines extended when the scent of blood grew stronger. A quick glance around and he noted the lamps on the end tables were turned over, a couple of the kitchen chairs were downed. There had been a fight here. And considering it was Della's blood, his heart jolted in his chest.

He shot into Della's bedroom. Nothing looked out of place. Whatever had happened must've been contained to the living room.

He went back there. A growl left his lips when he spotted drops of blood on the floor by the door. He moved outside, where he spotted more blood splatter by the steps.

Fueled by fury, and fear, he took off to follow the trail of Della's blood.

Chapter Eighteen

The blood led Chase through the woods. The thought that he should call Burnett and get help was countered by the thought of not wasting a second before finding her.

He ran through the brush, not caring when he got caught by a thorny bush. After about a minute he realized that unless the trail changed, he'd come out at cabin fourteen. His cabin.

Had Della been hurt and gone looking for him? The thought of her needing him and not being able to find him sent another jolt of pain through his chest.

He suddenly cleared the woods and could see the light on in his cabin. He hadn't turned a light on. Someone had been there. Or was there.

Shooting forward, he caught her scent, still mixed with her blood. Then he heard her say, "I'm gonna kill you. I am."

Who was she going to kill? Not that she had to; he'd do it for her. Too panicked to check for another scent, he bolted up the stairs and swung open his door, ready to defend her.

She swung around. She had on a bloody white tank top and a pair of pajama bottoms. Baxter sat in front of her.

"What happened?" he asked, his heart thumping against his rib cage.

"You happened," she seethed.

He stood there, the roaring panic that had tightened his muscles slowly fading. "Me?"

"Yes, you let Buster loose. And he ends up at my cabin."

Chase hadn't let the dog out, but . . . He blinked and again noted the blood on her white tank top. Then he glanced at Baxter sitting at Della's feet, his tail slowly swishing back and forth, his head hanging a little low. Definitely his guilty pose.

Was she saying . . . ? "Baxter would never hurt you."

"He wouldn't hurt me, but a cat is another question."

Chase shook his head. "No, he wouldn't hurt a cat. He loves cats. Eddie had one and they were best buddies. He used to pick it up and carry it around in his mouth."

"Well, I guess Socks isn't fond of a canine set of chops coming at her, even if it is for a joy ride."

"Shit. What happened?"

"Baxter showed up at my cabin. I forgot about Socks and I let him in. I went to get my pajamas on and hell broke loose. Baxter had Socks cornered. Socks ran. Baxter chased. They ransacked the cabin. And before I caught the cat, the cat caught me. She clawed her way up me to get away from your dog."

Chase frowned. "Are you okay?"

"Okay?" She pointed to her shirt. "I was used as a climbing post."

"Bad Baxter," Chase said.

"No!" Della seethed.

"You're right," Chase said. "It was the cat who did it."

"No! You're the one who didn't put your dog up."

"I did put him up." Chase inhaled and realized the stench of paint was stronger. "I bet the painters came and let him out."

"Oh, yeah, blame it on the painters!" she snarled.

"I'm not." He bit back his laughter. Even covered in blood, she looked adorable in her pajamas. The white tank, with the word "princess" written across it in pink, hugged her chest and showcased her breasts perfectly. It also fit against her waist. And her white bottoms had little pink crowns printed on them. They were a little big, and hung just low enough to expose a little flat belly. She looked sexy as hell.

He walked closer, pushing back the sexy thoughts, because now wasn't the time, and concentrated on the blood. "Have you cleaned the wounds?"

"No, I had to get him out of the cabin. And because I care more about him than his owner does, I wasn't going to just let him run loose. There are wolves out there."

"I'm sorry. Let me help you clean the wounds."

"No. I'm going home. I'll do it there."

"Wait," he said. "Let me at least give you some ointment."

"I've got some." She walked past him.

"This is better. It's especially for vampires." He darted over to his backpack and pulled a tube out. He walked over to hand it to her. She smelled so damn good, as if she'd just showered. Shampoo and feminine soap. When his fingers brushed her hand, his heart hiccupped and he could swear he saw her pupils grow bigger.

"Your uncle came up with it." He had to force his eyes away from her breasts, where he could almost make out her nipples.

She frowned, but took it. "Were you able to describe the face from my vision?"

"Yeah, the artist did a good job. They ran it through their database, but didn't get anything."

He ached to run his hand across her cheek. She looked so . . . touchable.

"So we still have nothing."

"We'll get them," he said. "We still need to go over the vision. See if we can remember anything different that could help us."

"Then let's do it." The fact that she agreed so quickly sent a tiny wiggle of pleasure to his chest. He'd love to stay here and enjoy . . . what he could almost make out under her shirt.

"I can't. I have to be somewhere, but I could come by your cabin when I get back. It might be late. Or we could do it tomorrow evening. I'm pretty sure Burnett has me working tomorrow morning."

She stood there staring at him as if trying to read him. "You're going somewhere?"

He nodded.

"Is it about the case?"

He nodded again.

"My dad's case?"

"Yeah."

"Then let me change my clothes and I'll come with you."

He shook his head. "No."

She frowned. "Why?"

"Because you can't."

Doubt filled her dark eyes. "Is Burnett going?"

"No. I have to do this one on my own."

"Do what on your own?" she asked, tilting her head to the left. Her right hand came to rest on her hip. Chase wondered if she knew how cute she looked doing that. Like a kitten trying to act tough. Someday when he knew her claws had been clipped, and he wasn't quite so afraid of her, he'd tell her that.

"Where are you going?" she snapped.

"Burnett mentioned something earlier. He said the best place to get information about lowlifes like Douglas Stone would be from other lowlifes. I called in a favor from a friend. A guard at one of the council's prisons. He's letting me in to ask questions. I was going last night but didn't make it. And I didn't mention it to Burnett because . . . there's no way they'd let him in."

"So you're hiding something."

Chase frowned. "From Burnett, not you. And if I get anything I'll tell him. I just . . . I'm afraid he wouldn't allow me to go. I'd rather ask for forgiveness than permission."

"Why wouldn't he let you go?"

Chase pulled his phone out and checked the time. He had three minutes before he had to leave or he'd be late. "The inmates aren't the best hostesses. Normally when someone goes in, they go with several guards. Because I'm not really working for the council anymore, he's going to let me sneak in, so it will just be me."

"Then take me," she said.

He shook his head. "He wouldn't let you in either." Not to mention Chase wouldn't let her near that place. These were the worst of the worst lowlifes.

"Then don't go."

Her stubborn expression made him smile. "Careful, Miss Sass, you almost sound like you care."

She scowled. "Don't make more out of it than it is."

He walked over to the kitchen and filled a bowl of dry dog food for Baxter. He felt her eyes on him and loved knowing he had her attention. She always had his whenever he was within a hundred feet of her.

She took a step closer. "Do you even know if someone there has information about this Stone guy?"

"No. That's why I'm going."

She stepped closer. Was that really worry in her eyes? Yup, it was. He'd kiss her if he thought he could get away with it. Problem was, he wanted to do so much more than kiss. He wanted to run his hand over that little splash of sweet skin low on her abdomen. He wanted to take that top off of her and . . .

"Why would they tell you anything?" She tugged down her shirt as if she sensed it distracted him.

But it was such a sweet distraction. "Because they don't have anything to lose. Because they might think it'll offer them some salvation. It's a long shot, but I have to do it. We want to catch this guy, remember?"

"Yes, but . . ."

Baxter brushed against his leg. Chase knelt down. As he gave the dog a good rub behind the ears, he pressed his forehead against the dog's snout. And damned if he didn't catch a different scent.

Disappointment tightened his gut. He stood up. All he could think about was where on Della's sweet body the shape-shifter had touched. His head said to ignore what he knew and leave. His heart didn't listen. "Can you do something for me?"

"Go with you? Yes." She tilted her chin up.

"No. It's a lot easier than that," he said between tight lips. "While I'm off risking my life to try to get your dad off of a murder charge, don't hang around Steve."

She opened her mouth to say something, but he didn't stay around to hear it.

Della stormed back to her cabin, wearing her bloody pajamas, and madder than a trapped raccoon. She'd already texted Chase and asked him to change his mind.

When she swung open and slammed the door, Miranda let out a loud yelp that could've woken the dead. And considering the dead seemed to hang out around here, that wasn't an exaggeration.

"She's here!" the witch screamed into her phone. "But—oh, God! She has blood all over her. And I still feel it."

Feel what? "I'm fine," Della snapped.

But too late. The door behind her swung open and Kylie ran inside. Whenever the chameleon was in protective mode, she lit up like one of those glow sticks that was losing its power.

"What happened?" She still held her phone to her ear.

"Nothing."

Kylie dropped her phone from her ear, pointed to Della's bloody tank top, and waved her finger around the disaster of their cabin. "Try again."

"Okay. Nothing much."

Both girls came closer and were looking at Della's bloody shirt. "See?" she flashed them. Boobs and all. Not that there was a lot to flash.

"It was just a few scratches and they're all healed now." She started to go to her bedroom, but both Kylie and Miranda barricaded her door.

Miranda held up a bag of something that looked like weed, did some kind of dance move, and sprinkled some of the green crap on Della's head.

"What is that?" Della asked.

"Herbs to chase away the unwanted. We got company." Miranda tossed another handful of the dried plant life into the air.

"Who?" Della snapped the one word question.

"You first, Della. What happened?" Kylie countered, no longer glowing, but still with that pissed-off-chameleon look about her.

Problem was, Della was still so pissed off at Chase she didn't have the patience to deal with anyone else's pissy mood. And she sure as hell didn't appreciate having green shit tossed on her by a witch who wasn't making a lick of sense.

She took a step closer to her bedroom, and her two roommates didn't budge. "Okay, here's the short version. Chase's dog came over and your cat wasn't in the mood for company."

"Is Socks okay?" Kylie's eyes widened and she swung around calling out, "Here, kitty, kitty."

"She's fine. See." The cat came strutting its stuff out from behind the sofa. With all eyes on the prancing cat, Della tried to make it to her room.

"Not so fast, vamp!" Kylie caught Della by the arm and looked at Miranda. "Get the Diet Cokes out. It's time we had a talk."

Chapter Nineteen

Kylie led Della to the table, then pointed to the chair. Della dropped down and set her phone in clear view.

Normally, Della didn't mind the Diet Coke round-table discussions. She'd learned that sharing helped a little. And commiserating over her two best friends' problems reminded her that everyone's life sucked too. Fate wasn't just picking on her. It was an equal-opportunity abuser.

But right now on top of feeling as if she were drowning in her problems, she was pissed. And . . . worried sick over the pisser. She should have followed him, but no, his little don't-hang-out-with-Steve bit had left her shocked. Who did he think he was, telling her who she could hang out with?

Still, she worried. Not by choice. Damn bond! She cut her phone a quick glance.

The temptation struck to call Burnett and tell him what Chase was doing. The only thing that stopped her was knowing that if he did that to her, she'd raise holy hell. But if Chase lived through this, she might just have to kill him. That'd teach him to take stupid risks, wouldn't it?

"Who's going first?" Kylie pulled the tab of her soda, sending a fizzy noise into the room.

"Let the witch," Della said. "I'm curious to why she's tossing dried herbs and doing the hokey pokey."

Miranda rolled her eyes. "You should be thanking me, not poking fun at me."

"I wasn't poking, just calling it like I saw it."

"No arguing at the round-table talks," Kylie insisted.

Miranda opened her drink.

The fizzy sound actually brought a sense of calm to Della's nerves.

But obviously not for Miranda, who glared at Della. "You scared the pee out of me," the witch bellowed out. "Since I got back this afternoon, I've been feeling an invader. And then I find—"

"Find what?" Della asked.

"An invader."

"Like a spirit?" Della asked. "Because, you know, between Miss Ghost Whisperer here," she nodded at Kylie, "and now me," she frowned, "there might be a few hanging around." She looked up at the ceiling. "Just not five."

"Not ghosts," Miranda said. "Just a strong intuition that something—or someone—is spying on us. Like when I felt that Mario creep here trying to kill Kylie."

"Have you told Burnett?" Della gave her phone another quick check.

"No, I . . . want to make sure I'm right before I get him all worked up. You know what he's like when he gets . . . worked up." Miranda frowned. "Plus, I could be wrong."

Della popped open her own soda. The sound tickled her ears and created a bit more calm. "Have you had these feelings before and were wrong?"

"Of course." Miranda pulled the soda up for a sip.

"How many times?" Della asked, wanting to calculate the odds that something really existed, or if Miranda was just a paranoid twit.

"I don't know exactly."

"Estimate," Della snapped.

"Ten maybe."

"Two out of twelve." *Paranoid twit.* "Good to know. Let's move on." Della glanced back at Miranda. "So what other issues do you have?"

"It feels real," Miranda insisted.

"We'll all stay on guard." Kylie looked at Miranda, and then added, "So how was your weekend?"

"I hate going first," the witch whined.

"Fine, I'll go." Kylie leaned in a bit. "My mom is dating a new guy. He's five years younger than her. Which means he's only fifteen years older than me. It feels weird. And get this, she met him at the grocery store. What kind of guys really go to the grocery store to pick up chicks?"

"A lot of them, from what I hear," Miranda said.

Kylie shook her head. "What kind of pickup lines do they use? Hey look at the size of those melons?"

Della glanced at her phone again. "As long as it's not the cucumbers he's interested in, she's safe."

"Ugh," Kylie said. "Then my dad comes over, and I swear he's flirting with my mom. When is he going to move on? It hurts to see him all gooey-eyed for my mom when I know all she's got eyes for is Mr. Meet-Me-in-the-Produce-Aisle."

"Do you think he still loves her?" Miranda asked.

"Yeah, I do. And I know he deserves to be a little miserable because he's the one who got caught playing pin the assistant to the elevator wall."

"Ew, they did it in an elevator?" Della asked.

"I don't know. I'm just saying that because he works in a high-rise. But I wouldn't doubt it. My point is that it's his fault, but he needs to let go.

"Oh, and Lucas came over and we went out on Saturday. Which brings me to my big complaint about you two."

"Us two?" Miranda asked.

Della pulled her phone a little closer. "What did we do?"

"You didn't notice something."

"You got another hickey?" Miranda turned her head to the side to check out Kylie's neck.

"No." Kylie reached up to swipe her hair from her eyes.

Which Della noticed was the third time. That's when she spotted it. And it only meant more change.

"Are you talking about the fact that you're wearing an engagement ring?"

Kylie's face lit up and she wiggled her fingers. "It's just a promise ring."

Miranda snagged Kylie's hand. "It's a pretty big promise."

"I know, isn't it beautiful?" Her smile widened.

"Yeah. It's great." Della did another check on her phone.

"What's that mean?" Kylie asked.

"What does what mean?" Della looked up.

"The tone. And don't deny it. I heard it."

Nothing," Della said, not liking that she was wearing her emotions on her sleeve. "I'm happy for you." And deep down it was true. It was just . . . change.

"But?" Kylie asked.

Oh, hell, why not be honest. "But it worries me that you and Lucas are going to end up getting married before we three get to go off to college. The three musketeers is gonna become two. And then one, because one of us," she pointed to Miranda, "will end up killing the other."

"I just said it wasn't an engagement ring. And just because I'm wearing a promise ring doesn't mean it's going to happen any faster."

"I'll bet Lucas has other thoughts."

"No, he doesn't. He knows we're planning on going to college together."

"And what's Lucas doing?" Della asked.

"He's going to go wherever we go. Like you, he plans to work for the FRU, and he's pretty much a shoo-in, so where he gets his education isn't all that important."

"I just think—"

"Then quit thinking," Kylie said. "Or I should say, overthinking. Just because we have boyfriends doesn't mean we aren't going to always be together."

"Yeah." Even as confident as Kylie sounded, Della didn't completely buy it. Everything in life changed. Most of the time, a person just had to accept it. And she was friggin' tired of accepting shit.

Kylie looked at Miranda. "How was your weekend?"

"Terrible," Miranda said. "Dad invited Tabitha over to the house and her mom came to drop her off. My mom had a conniption and wouldn't open the door. The way my mom acts, you would think Tabitha's mom was the other woman and not her."

And from the way Miranda said it, it was clear the witch was having a hard time coming to turns with her home issues. Della supposed learning you had a half sister and that your dad was still secretly married to your sister's mom would take some getting used to.

Miranda took a big sip of soda. "Then Mom and Dad argued. Dad spent the night as a donkey. Oh, but it gets worse. I had to explain to Shawn why I had a donkey in my living room."

"Shawn?" Della and Kylie said at the same time. Shawn was a warlock, Miranda's childhood crush, and now the new cute FRU agent who had a thing for the witch.

"You're seeing Shawn?" Kylie asked. "I thought you were going to see how things went with Perry first."

"I . . . well, I . . ."

While Miranda spit out random words that didn't make sense, Della took another sip of soda and then checked her phone to see if she had a text from Chase. She didn't. Damn him.

"He came over," Miranda said. "He even said he knew I was

trying to make a decision and he wanted to give me space. But not so much space that I'd forget about him."

"He's too cute to forget about," Kylie said.

"But so is Perry," Miranda said. "I saw him tonight and he was . . . sweet and said he'd be patient. But . . . if he'd known I was out with Shawn last night, he'd have a cow."

"Well, let him have a cow and a couple of bulls while's he's at it," Della said. "No one should tell you who you can spend some time with. I mean, who the hell does he think he is? You didn't ask to be bonded to him! And if he goes off and gets himself killed, that's his fault!"

Confusion appeared on her friends' faces and she realized what she'd said. She dropped her forehead down on the table.

"I think the vamp has some explaining to do," Miranda said.

"Yup," Kylie chimed in. "Start talking."

Chase landed in the back of the abandoned building on the out-skirts of Houston, where the Hell's Pit was hidden in some under-ground tunnels. Pulling his phone out to see who'd texted him, he saw Della's number and almost didn't read it.

Then, refusing to be childish, he read the message. "Text me that you're okay."

He gritted his teeth, fighting back the sense of betrayal. He felt like an idiot for being jealous. He'd always thought jealousy was a fool's emotion. If people wanted to be with someone else, it simply meant they didn't want to be with you and they weren't worth hurt-ing over.

Yet, here he was . . . hurting. Feeling insecure. Another emotion he wasn't accustomed to feeling. The last time he remembered feeling like this was with Tami, when he'd been fourteen.

Was this what it was like when you really cared about some-one? Damn, he cared about Della. And the thought of Steve put-ting his hands on her did a number to his gut.

Realistically, he knew the guy probably hadn't had his hands on her. Chase hadn't smelled Steve on Della. The shape-shifter's scent had just been on Baxter. But from the look in Della's eyes when he mentioned Steve, he knew the two had been together.

He had started to text her back when he heard someone in the distance. Putting his phone away, he listened. Was Burnett still having him tailed?

When the noise came from the shed, he relaxed and pulled his backpack off.

He moved toward the small building that he knew was the back entrance of the prison. Then Leo stepped out of the small door.

"Hey?" Chase walked up. The African American man, ten years older than Chase, stood about four inches taller than him and had the body of a football player.

Leo shook his head. "I don't know if I think you're stupid or if I'm impressed." He opened the shed's door, where a staircase led down.

"Let's go with the first one." Chase followed the guy down. The smell of unwashed bodies permeated the air. Leo got half-way down and turned, his eyes a brighter blue. "Is that O blood I smell?"

Chase nodded. "One for you and a couple for bribes."

Leo smiled and continued down. Their footsteps echoed through the concrete halls as they made their way to the small office. There stood a huge metal door with some serious locks on it.

"You been here before, right?" Leo asked.

"Yeah." Once. At the time, they'd only had two prisoners locked up.

"We supply soap and water, but they don't bathe. They know the smell gets to us."

"I'll deal with it."

"We lock 'em in their cells, but those bars are cheap metal and don't hold up to some of those prisoners. We're supposed to get up-graded bars next month." He looked at a small screen. "From what

I can see, no one has gotten loose. But every time I go down, I go with the notion that someone is loose. It's saved my life."

Leo reached over to the desk. "This here's a Taser. You ever work one?"

"No," Chase said, tempted to tell him he wouldn't need it. His hands, with his Reborn strength, could cause plenty of damage. But he decided to take it. He wasn't afraid, but he wasn't stupid, either.

Leo pulled off the tip of the gun to show him how to load it. "Just pull the trigger." He grabbed a few extra cartridges. "Put these in your pocket. Whatever you do, don't let them get their hands on it. It hurts like a mother. I learned the hard way."

"Got it." Chase tucked the extra cartridges in his pocket.

"Be extra careful of the weres. Tomorrow's their night and they're at their strongest. If one gets out, don't hold back. They are planning on killing you and you best be planning to do the same. They're all on death row anyway." Leo shook his head. "Seriously, kid, we've lost two guards and a visitor this year. You sure—"

"They have visiting privileges?" Chase asked.

"Yeah. The visitors sign waivers and pay for their burial before they go down. And it's nonrefundable. I always take my wife something nice when we get anyone stupid enough to visit."

Chase smiled. "Then I'm sure she wishes there were a lot more stupid people in the world."

Leo nodded. "Didn't you say it was Douglas Stone you were looking for? The same one the council is looking for, right?"

"Yeah," Chase said.

"Then you are wasting your time, they already checked out that lead."

"What lead?" Chase asked, unaware there'd been a lead.

"One of the guys had a cousin come see him. He put his last name down as Jones, but I heard the prisoner call him Stone. After he left, I recalled a Stone on the wanted list. I called it in, and was told they would look into it. Later, when the same dude came back,

I called again and they said this guy had checked out and wasn't our guy."

"Really?" Chase asked. "Who did you talk to on the council?"

"I don't know for sure, but maybe the blond guy?"

"Kirk Curtis?" Chase asked.

"Yeah, maybe. It's been a while."

Chase tried to wrap his head around that information. If Kirk had a lead, he would have told Eddie. Or maybe he didn't because it didn't check out. Still, something about this didn't feel right.

"How often does this guy come to visit?"

"Not that often. He came a couple weeks ago, though."

"What's the inmate's name?"

"Edward Pope," Leo said. "He's in cell number eleven. Ugly bastard. He likes to bite."

"Thanks for the warning."

"There's one main corridor. Cells on both sides. Stay in the middle, some of those guys are like octopuses and have tentacles with a long reach. They get you, they choke you to death if they don't have a makeshift knife to do the job."

"In the middle," Chase repeated.

Leo exhaled. "Don't get me wrong. I've heard you're badass, kid, but there's nothing but mean sons of bitches down there."

"I'm told I've got a mean streak in me too," Chase said.

Leo put his hand on a lever. "You step in; as soon as I lock this door, I'll unlock the second gate. To get out, you have to lock the second gate. I have a peephole here." He waved to the metal flap. "When I confirm it's just you behind the gate, I'll open this exit."

"Got it," Chase said.

Leo frowned. "I've got cameras, but I'll have to cut them off or I'll get my ass in a jam for letting you in. So I won't know if you're in trouble. You're on your own."

"Don't worry."

The door groaned as if it weren't accustomed to opening. Chase moved in and a wave of cold washed over him. A chill ran up his spine. Was this just the normal cold, or the deadly kind of cold?

The iron door closed with a loud, bone-chilling clank. He supposed this place had seen its share of deaths. But even the dead weren't going to stop him.

The noise rang louder. The second set of bars creaked as the last gate slowly opened. The smell of filth filled Chase's nose and he had to concentrate on not gagging.

Leo's voice echoed from the peephole. "Welcome to Hell's Pit."

Chapter Twenty

"Is she gonna talk or take a nap?" Miranda asked.

Della raised her head. She didn't know where to start, but then the words just fell out. "My dad knows I'm vampire."

"Damn," Miranda said.

"Crappers," said Kylie.

"I'm going to lose them." Emotion tightened her throat. "He's going to tell my mom and sister and then they'll never want to see me again."

"I don't think that would happen," Miranda said. "You just prove to them that being vampire doesn't make you a bad person. Everyone's scared at first. I'm a witch and I was frightened, and look at Kylie. You used to make her cry whenever you were in the same room."

"I didn't cry," Kylie said.

"They'll never understand," Della said.

"You don't know that for sure," Kylie said. "What did he say to you?"

"He didn't say anything." Della told them about the Chis' murder and how her father looked at her as if she'd done it. Then she told them what her mom had said about him being hospitalized after his sister's murder. "Why would he need to be hospitalized if he hadn't seen anything?"

Miranda made a face. "Because his sister was killed. I mean, that could be upsetting by itself."

"Maybe," Della admitted. "But if you could have seen how he looked at me. He's afraid I'm going to kill him or my mother and sister." Tears stung her sinuses and a lump formed in the back of her throat.

"So are you going to confront him?" Miranda asked.

"And say what?" Della snapped. "Hey, so you know I'm a monster?"

"You're not a monster," Kylie said.

"Right." Della swallowed down a lump of pain. "But I am the one who brought this whole court case down on him. What if they convict him? He could get the death penalty."

"Don't think the worst," Kylie said. After a second she asked, "Did Chase turn your uncle in?"

"No, he says he doesn't know where he is. But he also says my uncle didn't kill my aunt. That it was another vampire."

"Do you believe it?" Miranda asked.

"I don't know what I believe anymore," Della sighed. "Tomorrow we're getting my dad's case file from the DA."

Kylie turned the soda can in her hand. "Maybe you'll find out what he told the police and then you'll know for sure if he saw the murder."

"Yeah." Della looked again at her phone, and when she glanced up both Miranda and Kylie were studying her.

"Who are you dying to hear from?" the witch asked.

"I'm not. I . . . Oh, hell!" She pulled in a pound of oxygen. "Chase is doing something stupid." She told them about Chase's visit to the prison.

"And you're not going to call Burnett?" Kylie asked.

"No, because if the situation were reversed and he told Burnett on me, I'd never tell him anything again. He's working my father's case. I need him to trust me."

"But if something happens to him, you'll never forgive yourself," Kylie said.

"Do you see what a position he's put me in?" Della snapped.

"Well, maybe you told me and then I told Burnett. It wouldn't be your fault."

"He'd still be pissed."

"But at me more than you," Kylie said.

Della looked at her phone for the hundredth time. "Give him thirty more minutes. If he doesn't contact me, then you can call Burnett."

Miranda turned her Coke in her hands. "Have you seen Steve?"

Della frowned. "Yeah. He heard about me going to identify some bodies and he came to see if I needed to talk about it."

"That's sweet," Miranda said.

"Yeah," Della said. "Steve's sweet."

"But?" Kylie asked.

"But she cares more about Chase," Miranda said, putting words in Della's mouth.

"No." Della felt her heart thump to the tune of a lie. "I would be just as worried about Steve if he was in danger."

"Would you?" Kylie asked.

"Yeah," she said, but that came with a tremble of her heart as well. "And if I wasn't, it would be because of the bond. So that wouldn't count.

"Because . . . because . . . It wasn't my choice to care." But she heard Chase's words: *You still have a choice.*

Did she?

"Everything in my life feels like I don't have a choice. Everything is changing and I don't get a say in it. It's my friggin' life, and all I am is a spectator."

"I'd have to disagree with that," Kylie said. "I've never met anyone who fights as much as you do against anything."

"Yeah, but just because I fight doesn't change anything. I was turned into a vampire and no amount of fighting changed that."

"It didn't change it, but you're here at Shadow Falls because you had the nerve to call Holiday," Kylie said. "We can't always change what happens, but we always have control over how we deal with those things."

"You're channeling Holiday again and spouting all that psycho-analytical crap," Della accused.

"Sorry," Kylie said, smiling. "Sometimes her wisdom just takes me over."

"Nobody likes a wiseass," Della smarted back, only half serious.

"Did you kiss him?" Miranda asked.

"Duh, you saw it," Della said.

"Not Chase, Steve. Did you kiss Steve?"

"No," Della said. "We just talked."

"Did you want to kiss him?" Miranda asked.

Della squeezed the can. "I . . . I don't know. I didn't think about it."

"But you thought about it with Chase, right?"

"No," Della snapped. "I didn't think about it. It just happened."

"Hmm," said Miranda.

"Don't 'hmm' me," Della said. "Things between Steve and me are different now."

"Different how?" Miranda asked.

Della tried to define it and finally said, "He's . . . He feels safer."

"Safe is good," Kylie said.

"Is it?" Della wasn't sure. She hadn't had a lot of time to think about it since she'd been dealing with the cat/dog disaster right after he'd left.

Speaking of "safe" had her checking the time. Was it time to let Kylie call Burnett?

. . .

Chase stepped into the long corridor, where only two low-voltage lights lit up the space. The sound of feet shuffling echoed as the prisoners came to gape from behind the bars. The cold in the room held on, but Chase decided to worry about remaining with the living instead of looking for the dead.

"I smell fresh meat," a were said, his eyes already gold. With the full moon tomorrow, he would be at his strongest. He reached his arm out, and came within a few inches of touching Chase. He sensed another prisoner's arms reach out behind him. Leo wasn't joking about staying in the middle. One step to one side or the other and Chase would be within a prisoner's reach.

Still, Chase didn't react. He knew they could smell fear.

"Young meat," another prisoner said.

"I smell blood," said the occupant of cell six, his face pressed against the bars. Chase studied his forehead to see his pattern. Vampire.

He kept moving until he got halfway down the long hall, where he spotted cell eleven. The room was in shadows. Chase thought he could make out a man on the cot, but he wasn't sure.

"Yes, I've got blood." Chase pulled his backpack off his shoulder. That brought a few more of the prisoners shuffling to the bars. "And I'm sharing with anyone who can tell me what I want to know."

"For some of that there blood, I'd give you my mama," said a man in cell eight.

"I'm looking for a man named Douglas Stone. Vampire, probably in his mid- to late forties." Chase kept watching cell eleven, hoping Mr. Pope would show his ugly face and some interest. Chase unscrewed the top of the bottle.

The scent filled his nose, almost hiding the stench of this place, and he knew the others could smell it as well.

"I know him," said the guy in cell eight. "I'll tell you exactly where to find him as soon as you pass me that there bottle."

"Where do you know him from?" Chase listened to the man's heartbeat. And had to concentrate over the sound of one of the weres bending one of the bars. Chase just prayed the bars held up long enough for him to get the information.

Chase took a long sip of the blood. "Anyone else want to try?"

"Why are you looking for him?" The voice came from cell eleven.

"Got a few questions for him." Chase looked into the cell.

The man stepped out of the shadows. Jet black hair and dark blue eyes. His nose looked like it had been broken more times than it could be fixed. A scar ran from his eye down to his lip.

It must have been a dirty fight. Literally dirty, because vampires healed quickly and didn't normally get scars. They were sort of like cats, and if the wound was dirty it would get infected and abscess, requiring the wound to be reopened. From the looks of things, Pope's face had to be reopened several times.

The vamp inhaled as if just breathing in the scent of blood fed his soul. Leaning forward, he wrapped his fists around the bars, giving Chase an even better view of his scarred face.

"You know where I might find Mr. Stone?" Chase took another sip of blood, hoping Pope would be compelled to answer before Chase downed the entire eight ounces.

"I might be inclined." The prisoner licked his lips and his eyes turned light green from the smell.

"Do you know where he lives?" Chase listened to the man's heart.

"I know where he hangs out. He never lives in one place." He put his hand through the bars. "Hand me that blood and I'll tell you what I know."

"I told you, I know," yelled the guy in cell eight. His arm came through the bars. "Give it to me."

Chase ignored the older vampire. He drank all but the last few precious drops and only then did he hand it to Pope. "Here's a taste. If your info sounds legit, I got another one in my bag."

The man snatched the bottle.

Chase could hear him swallow, trying to suck down every last drop.

He heard the grunting and growling sound of the were in cell one as he attempted to bend the bars. Chase's time was limited.

"He buys and sells houses all over Houston," Poke said. "Now hand me the damn blood."

"I need more than that." Chase looked back at the were's cell and saw that he had his arm and part of his shoulder through the widened bars. Thankfully, his chest didn't quite make it.

Growling, he looked at Chase. His eyes glowed an evil orange color and he latched on to the bars and went back to working on the metal.

"There's a Douglas Stone somewhere in the old part of the Heights," said Pope. "Now give me more."

"Where in the Heights?" Chase pulled the Taser out from the waist of his jeans, just in case the were freed himself before Chase had the info he needed. Then with his other hand he pulled out the other bottle of blood.

"Last bottle," he said, unscrewing the top. "And I'm thirsty."

"He's got some whore he hangs with that lives in a house off Main and Chestnut in downtown Jamesville."

"Address?" Chase started to drink.

"I don't know the friggin' address!" he growled. "But wait. It's beside a cheap Mexican food joint. Right beside it." He stuck his hand out for the blood.

Chase heard the truth in his words and considered whether to hand it over. Then deciding he believed the man and figured the rogue had enough hell in life, he passed him the bottle. He looked over his shoulder at the were still pressing on the bars.

Pope gulped the blood down. Chase started backing out.

"You ain't got a chance, kid," Pope said, pulling the bottle from his lips long enough to speak. "You think I don't know who you are?" The scarred vamp laughed.

Chase stopped, almost certain the man was lying, but . . . "Who do you think I am?"

"He told me about you. You're that doctor's boy. Not really his, 'cause he's Asian. He knows you've been looking for him. He knows the doc's been after his ass forever. But he's not gonna find him, 'cause the council ain't gonna let him find him."

Shocked that he did know, Chase paused. "Why would they protect him?" Chase asked, sensing the temperature in the room drop.

Get out. Get out now.

Chase heard the female voice, knew it didn't belong to this world, but he couldn't listen, not now. "Why would they protect a murderer?"

"Don't matter," Pope said. "Ahh, but you shouldn't've poked around in the wrong places. He's gonna find your ass."

Right then came a metal screech, followed by the clank of a bar hitting the concrete. Chase swung around, or tried to. He must have forgotten to stay in the middle and moved a little too far to one side. An arm came around, locked around his throat and something sharp jabbed into his back, slicing through skin.

The pain in his back hadn't completely registered when he saw the were step free of the metal bars and charge.

"I got his liver," said the were with his arm around Chase's neck.

Damn it, Chase thought. No one was getting his liver.

Chapter Twenty-one

"That's it, I'm calling Burnett," Della snapped and threw the empty soda can that she'd been using as a stress ball across the room. Socks, still a kitten in spirit, charged after it. She reached for her phone.

"I thought you were going to let me do it." Kylie put her hand over Della's.

"No, Chase will know I forced you. I might as well own it." She grabbed her phone and was about to dial when a text dinged.

"It's from Chase." She smiled as the tightness in her chest lightened. But then she read the text.

In front of school. Need help.

"Shit!" Della bolted up.

"What is it?" Miranda asked.

"He's at the front gate. I'm gonna go meet him. I'll see you guys later." She shot out the door.

A red Corvette was parked in front. She walked through the gate, knowing the alarm would record her exit, but not caring.

A man got out of the driver's side. She recognized him as one of the men on the Vampire Council. Where was Chase?

She approached with caution. But the look of concern on his face, and the smell of blood—Chase's blood—had her stomach knotting.

"Hello, again," the blond vampire said. "I'm Kirk. I met you when—"

"I know who you are." Della recalled how small the council had made her feel. Her gaze cut to the car; no one else was in it. "Where's Chase?" She felt her eyes brighten.

"Relax. I'm not here for trouble. Chase is reclined in the backseat."

Della started to the car as her questions started forming. How had Chase ended up with this man? Had Chase been lying about going to a prison? Had he even quit the council?

"I wanted to take him to a doctor but he refused. Said you would take care of him."

Her questions stopped with his words. Take care of him? She was so not a nurse.

"He needs blood quick. He said he had plenty at his cabin."

"How bad is he?" she asked, but didn't wait for his answer. Instead she opened the car door and lifted back the seat to see for herself. The smell of blood hit and hit hard. Her gut tightened.

"It looks serious," Kirk said.

The words sent sharp pain to her heart. Chase lay there, dead still, his shirt covered in deep red stains. His eyes were closed. Was he even conscious? Could he be . . . ?

She didn't breathe until she saw his chest move to take in air.

"What happened?" She looked back over her shoulder at Kirk.

"Just a little trouble," Chase said before Kirk answered.

Della swung her head back around and saw his lids flutter open.

"And it's not that serious." He shifted.

"Do you need a doctor?" she asked.

"I would feel better if he allowed me to take him to one," Kirk spoke up. "I can get him there in less than five minutes."

"No." Chase's tone was so adamant that it seemed to mean something.

Della looked at the blood on his shirt and worried how bad the

injury was. Sure, vampires healed, but if something was really dam-
aged, they could still die. "But if you need—"

"No." Chase's eyes met hers as if trying to tell her something,
but damn it, mind-reading wasn't her specialty.

Chase pushed against the seat to sit up. "All I need is some blood
and the ointment." He slumped back down in the seat. "And maybe
a little help getting out of the car."

She moved the front seat up so she could reach Chase.

"Do you need me to help?" Kirk asked.

Chase looked up at her, and ever so slightly shook his head.

"No," Della said. "I can do it."

She got Chase out of the car. His arm came around her shoulders, and she had to latch her hand around his hip to keep him from
falling over. When she did, he flinched. That's when Della realized
his shirt was even bloodier in the back than in the front.

"Go home," Chase said to the older vampire. "I'll be fine."

As she walked Chase to the gate, she heard Kirk pull away.
When she knew they were far enough away that he couldn't hear,
she said, "You've got some explaining to do."

"Can I just concentrate on not passing out right now and explain later?" His pain sounded in his voice, and her chest swelled
with sympathy.

"You need a doctor," Della said, the smell of his blood overpowering.

"Give me fifteen minutes after I drink the blood and use the
ointment, and if I'm still bad, call your good friend Steve."

Della frowned at his tone and the idea of calling Steve. Not that
she doubted that he would help. He would.

Two steps after they got through the gate, her phone dinged
with a text.

"Probably Burnett," she said.

"Don't . . ." Chase didn't finish.

They continued walking, and when they got to the entrance of
the trail, Chase said, "Della?"

"Yes."

"She saved me."

"Who saved you?" She felt his weight fall on her a little heavier.

"Your aunt. She . . . she appeared and everyone could see her. I could see her. They all freaked out."

"Who all freaked out?" she asked, but she was more concerned about getting him to his cabin than hearing his story.

"They were attacking me. The prisoners. I think they thought she was a death angel. It gave me enough time to get to the Taser. I think the were shit his pants he was so scared." Chase chuckled, but it sounded weak.

"You should have taken me with you," she snapped. And then she was angry with herself for not following him.

"Della?" he muttered as if he hadn't heard her admonishment.

"Yes?"

"I love you."

"You are not dying!" she seethed.

He chuckled. "I didn't say I was . . . But just in case." His knees gave. She caught him, and realized he'd passed out.

She held his dead weight in her arms and ran as fast as she could to cabin fourteen.

She spoke to him the whole way, but he never once answered. Bolting inside his cabin, she nearly tripped over Baxter. She tried again to wake Chase. "Rise and shine, buddy. You hear me? You have to wake up!" Della headed straight to the biggest bedroom and put Chase on the bed. He didn't moan or even stir.

Baxter jumped up on the bed, came to rest beside him, and whined. The dog's dark eyes met hers, as if asking her to do something.

"I'm trying," she spit out.

Sitting on the edge of the mattress, panic building in her gut, she took his face in her hands. "Chase, open your eyes, damn it!"

Knowing he needed blood, she ran to the fridge and found four bottles. Not knowing what else to do, she sat down and filled his mouth with the blood. It ran out of his lips, and he never swallowed. Then, afraid he would choke, she turned his head. Blood dripped out of his mouth, turning the white sheet red. She noted another growing stain around his torso, darkening the light tan bedspread. He was losing way too much blood.

"Shit!"

Standing up, barely able to breathe, she remembered Kylie's ability to heal. She grabbed her phone and dialed Kylie. The phone rang once.

Twice.

Three times.

It went to voice mail. Damn it, the girl had just been in their cabin. "Where are you? Come to cabin fourteen. I need you!"

She paced the room, her gaze on Chase, watching to make sure he was breathing. Baxter had inched closer and now rested his snout on Chase's arm. But his big black eyes kept shifting to her as if telling her to do something fast.

Should she go find Kylie? Leave him?

Then she recalled Chase's words: *Give me fifteen minutes after I drink blood and use the ointment, and if I'm still bad you can call your good friend Steve.*

For one second, she worried how awkward that would be, but before that second ended, she had dialed and was waiting for Steve to answer.

He picked up on the first ring.

"Hey." In that one word, she heard how happy he was to hear from her.

"I need you to come to cabin fourteen. Chase's hurt . . . It's bad."

She pulled in a deep breath. "I'm sorry." She realized he'd hung up. Was he coming? Was he angry that—? Chase moaned. Della ran to the bed and caught his hand.

"Chase? Can you hear me?" She lifted his head and held the

bottle of blood to his lips. "Drink some blood. You need blood." He didn't drink and his head fell to the side.

She heard someone running up the steps. Inhaling, she got Steve's scent. He didn't knock, just ran in.

"In here."

"What happened?" Steve set a bag down and went to stand by the bed.

Baxter growled.

"No, Baxter," Della said, and then, "I . . . don't really know. He was going to a prison to see if someone there had information about my aunt's killer."

"I thought your uncle—"

"My uncle said it was another vampire."

"How long has he been unconscious?" Steve asked.

"Just a few minutes."

Steve spotted the bottle on the bedside table. "Did you get him to drink any blood?"

"No. He passed out."

Steve pulled out an IV line, needle, and bag. "Take his clothes off and see how bad his injuries are while I set this up. And . . . get the dog out of the bed."

Della motioned for Baxter to get down. He didn't like it, but he did it. Dropping down on the other side of the bed, he looked up at Steve as if to say he wasn't going any farther.

Della started undressing Chase, and the sight of the wound in his abdomen made her breath catch. "It's bad." Her voice shook.

"He's vampire." Steve grabbed the blood and poured it into a bag. "If it's just blood loss he'll be okay. Take his jeans off, too," Steve said. "To make sure he doesn't have more wounds."

The fact that she was undressing Chase only seemed awkward when she started unzipping his jeans. She saw his green fitted boxers, and recalled him joking about her being interested in his underwear. Now her only interest was making sure he lived to tease her about this. Her chest hurt again from the fear that he wouldn't ever know, that she'd never hear him tease her again, or see his eyes brighten with a smile.

"He doesn't have any wounds on his legs," she said, tugging his jeans off and tossing them on the dresser.

When she looked back, she recalled touching Chase's back and thinking he'd had wounds there as well. She turned him over. With her hands on his bare torso, she noted how shallow his breaths were. "He has another one in the back. Oh, God. It's bad, too." She clenched her fist. "Please don't let him die, Steve."

Steve's eyes met hers for one second. "I'll do everything I can." He looked away and hooked the blood bag on the back of the bed. He shifted Della out of the way. "Let me get the IV in and then I'll check his wounds."

Della called Kylie again. No one answered. "Where are you? Please come to cabin fourteen." If Steve's magic didn't work, maybe Kylie's would. But even Kylie couldn't heal Della during her rebirth, and Kylie hadn't been able to save Ellie the vampire, either.

Della felt a few tears roll down her cheek and she swiped them away. "Tell me he's going to be okay," Della said to Steve.

"Get me some hot water to clean the wounds," he spouted out.

"Oh, and I'll get the ointment. I think it's in the kitchen."

"What ointment?"

"It's especially for vampires." She took off out of the room.

Grabbing the ointment, she was almost back to the bedroom when Chase's growl echoed through the cabin.

She flew into the room. Steve was cleaning the wound on his abdomen. Or had been. Now he held the bloody cloth up above Chase, while Baxter had his front paws on the bed, his lips curled back in a growl of his own.

"Down, Baxter," Della said. "We're trying to protect him too."

Steve looked back at her. "You might have to hold Chase down." He frowned. "But then again, he might hurt—"

"Is he conscious?" She dropped the ointment in Steve's hand.

"Not fully. But he's reacting to the pain. It could be dangerous."

"He won't hurt me," she said, believing it with all her heart.

"He might not know it's you."

"He'll know." Della sat on the tiny space beside Chase and the edge of the mattress. When she first touched him, he growled again.

Steve caught her as if ready to pull her back if Chase attacked. "We might need to tie him down."

Tears came to her eyes, realizing how much pain Chase must be in. "He's too strong. He'll just break loose."

"Then let's call Burnett," Steve said.

She shook her head. "Chase won't hurt me. I know that."

Steve frowned. "But you're not the only one in the room," Steve said. "And considering the exchange we had earlier, killing me might not be too far off his bucket list."

"He came to and spoke with you?" Della asked.

"Not now. Earlier today."

Steve and Chase had talked? Della put that little piece of information in the back of her mind to ponder later. "He wouldn't hurt you, either." And damned if she didn't believe it. "He even suggested I call you if he didn't start feeling better."

Steve seemed to give in.

She leaned down. "Chase, it's me, Della, okay? Steve's here. He's trying to clean your wounds. I know it hurts. But it has to be done. So I'm gonna hold you down, so Steve can do this. Please, don't fight us."

"He might not be able to hear you." Doubt sounded in Steve's voice.

"He hears me," she said.

Slowly, she rested her hands back on his chest.

Chapter Twenty-two

"We have to do this," Della repeated to Chase in what she hoped was a calm voice, even though calm wasn't even close to what she was feeling. Guilt, she felt. Shit-loads of it. She looked at his face. His eyes were closed, his skin was so pale, and his expression was empty. Chase was never without expression. Why hadn't she stopped him? Or at least insisted on going with him? Why, damn it?

Then she tightened her hold. He didn't growl. She looked at Steve. "Try again."

Steve frowned as if he disagreed, but restarted cleaning the wound.

Chase moaned and arched his neck back, pushed his head into the pillow. Baxter jumped up on the other side of the bed. He didn't growl or bare his teeth. He seemed to understand that they were trying to help now.

"Does he need surgery?" Della asked, so afraid Steve would say yes.

"I don't think so."

"Stitches?"

"Normally, we don't do stitches on vampires. You guys heal quickly as long as . . ."

His pause gave Della concern. "As long as what?"

"As long as you haven't been deprived of blood for too long. And an infection doesn't set in."

"Does it look infected?" she asked.

"Not yet. But it wouldn't show up for a few hours. It's when it's healing that the signs of infection will show up."

"And if it does?"

"We'll have to open the wounds back up, clean them again.

"Turn him over," Steve said when he finished cleaning the gaping hole in Chase's abdomen.

"Put the ointment on him first."

Steve picked up the tube he'd dropped on the bedside table. "I don't know what this is."

"Chase says it works."

"But it could be—"

"It's okay. My uncle invented it."

"Your uncle?"

"He's a doctor, or medical research scientist."

"And possibly a murderer," Steve pointed out. "You trust him?"

Did she trust her uncle? She didn't know, but it hit her then that she trusted Chase—on this at least—and he believed in her uncle. "I trust Chase's opinion. Use it."

Steve opened the unmarked tube and swabbed the wound.

Chase let out another low growl. Baxter lifted his head and whined.

"Now turn him over. And I wish the dog would get off the bed."

Della turned Chase, and got Baxter down again. Chase moaned. Della's gut knotted, feeling his muscles tighten and knowing she'd caused him pain.

Steve cleaned the wound and covered it in the ointment. After she rolled Chase back over, Steve started to walk away. But then his brows creased and he leaned down to study the wound.

"What is it? What's wrong? Is it getting infected?" Della asked, not liking Steve's sudden interest.

He glanced up, puzzled. "No, but the wound is already closing."

"Is that good?"

"It's . . . odd." He looked at the bag of blood. "He's barely gotten any blood. Usually . . . it takes longer." He looked back at the wound. "But yes, I guess it's good. He won't be losing more blood. Let's just hope he doesn't get an infection." Steve picked up the tube. "What's in this stuff?"

"I don't know," Della said. "If it's already healing and doesn't look infected, does that mean he's in the clear?" She wanted to hear Steve tell her Chase was going to be okay.

"Not necessarily," he said. "But it's a good sign."

She tried to find peace in that, but it wasn't helping very much. "So how long before he's conscious?"

"That depends on how much blood he lost. He looked as if he'd lost a lot. I can stay with him if you want to go."

"No, you can go. I'm gonna stay. Please, I have this now. If I need you, I'll call."

He nodded, and from his expression she saw that he was reading a lot into her request. All of the awkwardness she'd feared from the situation bubbled to the surface.

Glancing back at the bed, she went over and lifted the cover over Chase's mostly naked body. Not because she thought he was cold, but for modesty's sake. She wouldn't want to think someone would let her lay there half naked and out of it.

She motioned for Steve to follow her out of the room. "I . . . Chase was hurt trying to help clear my father's name. I owe it to him to make sure he's okay." But that wasn't the only reason, and she knew it. The truth was there, deep in the pit of her gut, where she didn't have time to dig for it.

When Steve didn't answer, she added, "Chase and I aren't . . . together." It wasn't a lie, so why did that make her heart do a couple of cartwheels?

Steve smiled. Not a real smile, but something close. "It's okay, you don't have to justify it, Della."

Didn't she? She watched him go back into the bedroom and collect his bag, and another question hit. Wouldn't the old Steve need a justification?

When he came out, he hugged her. She closed her eyes and tried to find comfort in that embrace, but all she felt was the awkwardness. And then that same sensation from earlier hit, the one that said things had changed.

"Thank you." She pulled back.

"I think Chase is the one who needs to thank me." Steve ran his hand down her forearm. "We still need to have that talk."

"I know."

He grinned, and this time it was real. But his eyes still looked sad.

"Don't let him move around for several hours. As soon as he comes to, make him drink blood. If he hasn't come to by the time his IV is finished, call me and I'll come and set up another one. Check the wound at least every hour. If the wounds start looking red or inflamed, call me immediately."

She nodded, then stood there and watched him leave. For some crazy reason, while she hadn't actually decided how she felt about Steve, or what would or wouldn't happen between them now, she felt he had decided. Had he closed the door to the possibility of them being a "them"?

She still hadn't decided how she felt about that when she heard Chase moan. All thoughts about Steve shot out the window and she ran to check on Chase.

When she got to the bedroom door, she saw him trying to get up. "No." She ran to his side. "Don't get up." She eased him back down.

He looked up at her. Then he caught her hand. "Stay here," he said.

"I will." She squeezed his hand.

"Right here," he said.

"I'm not going anywhere," she assured him.

He took a deep breath. "You were right."

"About what?"

"The council. They . . . they aren't . . ." He slumped down on the pillow.

"Aren't what?" she asked. He fell unconscious again. "No! Chase, wake up." She touched his chest. "You need to drink blood. Please."

He didn't move. Baxter whined.

Frustrated, she lowered the sheet to check his wound. It didn't look inflamed, but damn it, now she wondered if she shouldn't have asked Steve to stay.

What if she missed something? What if he got worse?

A sound—a light thump outside the bedroom window brought her head up. She saw the bird, a black grackle, perched on the outside of the windowsill.

She recalled the bird from earlier. Also a grackle. And black. She took one step. The bird bounced back into the air and, after fluttering its wings and suspending itself in midair, it flew away. Same bird? Or just a coincidence?

Hell, no, Della didn't believe in coincidences. Who was watching her? And Chase? It had to be one of the shape-shifters here, didn't it?

She had no time to ponder. Something—or someone—heavy dropped on the cabin porch and the door to the cabin swung open with a whack. Della ran into the living room, her canines already lowering.

Kylie, obviously in vampire mode, stormed in. "What's wrong?"

Della breathed in and willed her fight mode to calm.

"It's Chase," she said, glad to have Kylie here. "He was hurt."

She turned and ran into the bedroom. Kylie followed. Della stopped at Chase's side and pulled the sheet down to show Kylie his wound. Amazingly, it looked even better than it had a few minutes ago.

Baxter still rested on the other side of the bed, wagging his tail at Kylie's presence.

"It was bad, but he's healing fast," Della said. "Steve said there's still a chance of him getting an infection. We don't know how much blood he lost, which is probably why he's still unconscious. Do you think you could help?"

Kylie looked at Chase's wound. "I don't know if my healing abilities work on blood loss. I'm willing to try."

Della watched Kylie sit on the edge of the mattress and gently rest her hand on Chase's shoulder.

Just then Della's phone dinged with a text. With it came another chirp from Chase's jeans. She pulled her cell from her pocket. "It's Burnett," she told Kylie as she read the message.

Have problems. Meet me at the office.

"What did he say?" Kylie asked.

"Not much, but it's after eleven and he's calling a meeting, so it can't be good."

"Crappers." Kylie stared at the jeans on the dresser that kept dinging. "It might be about Miranda's feeling as if someone were spying. That's why I didn't come earlier: I went with her and forgot my phone."

"Oh, great!" Della said.

Kylie sighed. "I think you're going to have to tell him about Chase."

"Yeah," Della snapped. "Isn't that just peachy?" She looked back at the half-naked unconscious vampire then back to Kylie. "Can you stay here while I go get my ass chewed out by Burnett? It shouldn't take long. He excels at it."

Kylie half grinned. "Sure, but you may want to change out of your bloody clothes."

Della looked down at the stains on her jeans and shirt. She

hadn't even noticed them. She gave Kylie instructions on how to care for Chase's wounds.

"I'll take good care of him. I promise. Now go, before Burnett loses it."

Della flew out of the bedroom, heading to her cabin for a wardrobe change, and then off to face the music.

Chapter Twenty-three

The small group of Shadow Falls students Burnett relied on to help keep the school safe were all crowded in the front waiting room of the main office as Della entered.

Burnett's voice rang out, then paused as he waited for her to join them.

Della walked through the door, nodding at Lucas, Chris, Fredericka, and Derek as she moved the rest of the way into the room. Miranda, with a big smile on her face, stood beside the camp leader. Pride glowed in her eyes, no doubt from giving Burnett the info about an intruder.

Burnett's gaze met hers with tons of questions flickering in his dark eyes. Her tardiness probably concerned him, because she always arrived first at meetings like these. The wardrobe change had taken longer than it should have. It took some time to dig out the cleanest dirty jeans and shirt she had. And with a vampire's sense of smell, her idea of dirty and someone else's didn't always match.

"Where's Chase?" Burnett asked.

Della's shoulders tightened. Why did he assume she was with Chase? The fact that she had been with him didn't mean shit. He still shouldn't assume.

She bit back her desire to toss him a condescending remark. "I'll explain in a minute." And hopefully only a minute. She didn't want to be here too long.

He hesitated as if he were considering pulling her into his private office, but then refocused on the group. "Like I was saying. We think it's probably a shape-shifter. The electricity flickered off yesterday. I'm thinking that must have been when he snuck in."

"How do you know it's a shape-shifter?" another were, a friend to Lucas, spouted out the question.

"We don't know for certain," Burnett said. "But our system measures a heat index put out by the number of individuals here and taking into account the different body temperatures. The system can be thrown off slightly by any shape-shifter shifting on the grounds. I checked yesterday and it was slightly off and didn't worry about it, thinking it was due to a shift. After Miranda came to me with her premonition, I checked it. It's over again, which is a cause for concern."

Della frowned. "It's a black grackle."

All eyes turned to her. Burnett looked half puzzled, half pissed. "You know about this?"

"I saw the bird. At first I thought it was one of our shape-shifters, but then it showed up a couple more times."

Right then two sets of footsteps sounded outside. All the vampires turned toward the door. A familiar voice rose in the night. One she hadn't heard in a while. Perry?

"Did you think I wouldn't recognize you?"

Della titled her head to see if she could hear who he was talking to. Their footsteps drew closer. All the way up the porch steps.

"Found the intruder," Perry said, pushing into the room with another golden-haired bright-eyed shape-shifter—except that when Della checked his pattern she realized he was half shape-shifter, half human.

Della could almost hear the thoughts of everyone in the room, and they matched her own. The guy standing in front of Perry could have easily been his twin.

"His name is Sam." Perry held the boy's arm, and eyed him with contempt. "He's one of my long-lost cousins."

"And you think he was here to see you?" Della asked, thinking that was what Perry was going to say, but her mind was already refusing that explanation. Why would he have been following her around, or have been at Chase's cabin? This guy was up to no good, and she had a feeling it somehow involved her or Chase.

"No," Perry said. "He didn't know I was here. He's already confessed that he was sent by some lowlife to spy on someone here. But he doesn't want to tell me anything else."

Just like that, Della knew. "Douglas Stone." She shot through the crowd to stand right in front of the twerp. "That's who sent you, isn't it?"

The way the Perry look-a-like cut his eyes away from her, she knew she'd hit the nail on the head. What she didn't know was if this meant that Chase was right. Her uncle hadn't killed his sister.

"Good job." Burnett focused on Perry. "Everyone leave except Perry and his cousin." Burnett motioned to the door leading into Holiday's office.

Della counted her lucky stars, wanting to get back to Chase, and zipped out the door.

She had one foot on the first porch step when she heard Burnett's growl. "And Della!"

She stopped, let out a puff of air, and did a U-turn, all the while wondering how two words could evoke so much frustration. She stepped inside. "You said—"

"I can stay, right?" Miranda interrupted. "I'm the reason we found him." The witch stood by Holiday's office door and watched Perry usher his very unhappy cousin into the office.

Burnett faced Miranda. Della could almost see him rein in his temper. His shoulders dropped and his jaw unclenched. Why didn't he ever rein it in for her?

"Yes, you did," he said. "And I appreciate that, but we'll take it from here."

Miranda made her frustrated face and started out, but stopped next to Della. "Everything okay?" she whispered, the question telling Della the witch had heard her phone message to Kylie.

"I'll explain later." Della cut her eyes up at Burnett, standing a few feet away and scowling down at her.

At least the big, bad vampire waited until Miranda had stepped out before speaking. "Actually, I think you're going to start explaining right now. And start by telling me why Chase isn't here. I texted both of you."

But damn, all this happened so fast, Della didn't know how to start to explain. "Yeah, but . . . uh, Chase kind of . . . He—"

"Spit it out," Burnett ordered.

Della would have commenced spitting, but a loud crash came from Holiday's office. Out of the corner of her eye, she saw a jet black grackle come flying out of the office.

Standing closest to the door, Della slammed it shut to prevent the bird's escape. Turned out, however, it wasn't necessary. Burnett, almost as if he expected it, or if he caught and ate birds for dinner most of his life, reached up and snatched the bird from the air.

"Go check on Perry," Burnett snapped, while he stared daggers at the feathered captive.

She found Perry a little woozy from taking a whack with a lamp across the head. But he was fine. After a few minutes, Burnett asked again about Chase. She spilled her guts. If his red face and four-letter muttering were any indication, Burnett didn't take the news well. Della, however, was too concerned about Chase to be traumatized.

The first thing Burnett did was call Holiday and ask her to go check on Chase. Then he called Steve to meet Holiday there, where she was to assess if another doctor needed to be called in.

"Can I go now?" She wanted to be there to hear Steve's assessment.

Burnett looked puzzled. "Don't you want to hear what Perry's cousin has to say?"

"You can just tell me, right?"

He studied her. "Just like you told me about Chase being hurt?" Frowning, he waved his hand. "Go. I'll fill you in. But we will talk about this."

Nothing like postponing an ass chewing. She flew off and arrived just in time to hear Holiday calling Dr. Whitman. Chase's wounds now looked infected.

Chase woke to an empty stomach, his need for blood almost painful.

He lifted his eyelids and stared at the ceiling, feeling disoriented. A vague memory of going to the prison, of . . . pain. Lots of pain. Bits and pieces of memory fell into place. The were had escaped, another had cut him with a knife. Then the ghost had appeared.

Leo, the guard, had called the council.

He tightened his muscles, preparing to shoot out of bed to find answers, when he caught two scents. Baxter. And then one a hell of a lot sweeter than his dog.

Della.

Careful not to move, he glanced to the side through his lashes. The need for answers faded against his growing need to just . . . linger here. In this moment, with her, beside him. Asleep. In bed.

A smile, the one that just naturally appeared when she was close, widened his mouth. He worked to keep his breathing low, so as not to wake her.

She lay on her side, both her hands tucked under her cheek. Her dark lashes so long that they rested against the tender skin under her eyes.

Skin with a little dark tint, a sign she hadn't gotten enough rest. How long had she been . . . here? How long had she been a hand's reach from him, sharing his bed and even his pillow? He resented sleeping, feeling the time wasted, when he could have been watching her.

She lay so close he could feel her breath, a light tickle, on his neck. A strand of dark hair rested against her cheek. He longed to reach out and brush it away. Touching her hair was one of the things she didn't balk about. Or at least not too much.

Little did she know how much he loved touching it. Not that there weren't other parts he longed to touch. Still, the dark strands were soft, a lot softer than his hair, and always smelled like . . . like a girl's hair should smell. A cross between a fruit and a flower.

He fought the need to run his fingers through the long dark strands, knowing that when she woke up this closeness would end. She'd pull back.

Della always pulled back. He just kept telling himself that the day would come when she wouldn't. When touching her wouldn't be risky. When she would touch him back.

He studied her lips—so pink, with the perfect shape. He wanted to press his mouth against hers. To taste her. He wanted . . . His gaze lowered to the scoop of her tank top, where the soft swells of flesh pressed against the cotton fabric. He recalled how she'd looked in just her panties and bra when he'd gone to her cabin the other night.

For that matter, he'd seen her naked when she'd been sick, in the beginning of her second turn. Mentally, he'd tattooed that vision to his mind, where he visited it often.

What he wouldn't give to take her clothes off—every stitch of material—then to remove his own and feel her against him, skin to skin.

The feeling of rightness shot to his chest and then whispered lower, where his body hardened from all his wanting. Closing his eyes, staring at the blackness in his mind, he willed the primal urges to lessen. The last thing he wanted to do was to come off like a pervert. She didn't deserve that.

He felt her stir, heard her breathing increase. Was she . . . He opened his eyes.

She stared at him, her lids still heavy, sleepy and sexy. He expected her to jackknife up, to put more space between them.

She didn't.

"You're awake." She smiled. Damn, but she was beautiful when she smiled.

"You slept with me." He reached to touch her.

That's when she did it. She pulled back. But at least she didn't leave his bed. She pushed up on her elbow.

A slight frown pulled at her forehead. "You begged me not to go."

He grinned. "So that's all it takes to get you in my bed? Begging? I would have done that months ago."

She shot up, but he noted her expression didn't get as distant as it usually did when she pulled away. "You need to drink blood."

As she walked out, he watched her. "A morning kiss would be nice," he called out and petted Baxter, who shifted closer.

She turned around and frowned. "I don't want to shit in your Cheerios, bucko. But you almost died last night."

He chuckled, then searched his mind for what else he could remember. He recalled insisting that Kirk bring him here . . . to her. And like he knew she would, she'd taken care of him. More proof that she cared. That the wall she'd built up between them was slowly crumbling.

"You saved me," he said.

"No, I don't like you that much," she said. "Steve and Dr. Whitman did that." She walked out.

He tossed the sheet off to get up. He saw that he was wearing only his underwear. Had she . . . ? A smile pulled at his lips thinking about Della undressing him and their earlier conversation about underwear.

He stood up. His knees gave, but he caught himself.

She walked back in, ignoring his lack of clothes, and handed him a bottle of blood. When her fingers brushed against his, a sweet bolt of attraction hit, tingled down his arm, and went straight to his heart.

Something about her being here, waking up with him, and even him being just in his underwear made the moment feel right. It would have felt righter if she were partially unclothed—or completely naked—but he'd take what he could get.

He reached for her. She stepped back.

"Get back in bed and drink your blood." She took the bottle, unscrewed it, and then put it back in his hands. "The doctor said he would be here this morning to check on you."

"I'm fine." He turned to the dresser to grab his jeans.

She shot between him and the piece of furniture. "Bed!"

The move had her so close again, he could smell her hair, or her shampoo, he didn't care which it was. All he knew was that he really liked it.

"If you come with me." He wiggled his brows at her.

She growled. Her eyes brightened, her mouth pursed into a beautiful bow, and her shoulder arched back, emphasizing her small breasts. They may be small, but they were beautiful. The image of her naked flashed in his mind again.

He grinned. "You would never get angry around me if you knew how sexy you look when you're mad."

Her frown tightened. "Would you quit making light of this? You almost died, Chase. First from blood loss and then an infection. And for the record, if I never have to see the insides of your gut again, I'll be okay with it."

"I'm not trying . . ." Chase paused and looked at her. "Does Burnett know?"

"I had to tell him," Della said. "Douglas Stone sent someone to spy on you. And he snuck through the alarm."

"What? Wait. Did they catch him?"

"Yes."

"And?" Chase asked.

"And he's Perry's long-lost cousin, and the last news I got, he still wasn't talking. Burnett's taken him to the FRU headquarters."

Chase reached around her and snagged his jeans. "Then let's go make him talk." He sighed. "Before I got ripped to shreds at the prison last night, I found out that Stone knows we're on to him, and it sounds like he's being protected. I need to find out what the Vampire Council knows."

Chapter Twenty-four

"Is that why you didn't trust the guy who dropped you off last night?" Della asked.

Chase frowned. "That was Kirk."

"But you didn't trust him. I saw it in how you treated him."

Pain flashed in Chase's eyes. The emotional kind of pain that she knew so much about lately. "He's been like an uncle to me. He practically helped Eddie finish raising me."

"He could still be hiding something," she insisted.

"Like I said, I need to find out what they know about Stone."

"You aren't going anywhere now." Della pulled his jeans out of his hands and paused when she heard footsteps on the front porch. One deep breath and she knew who it was. Holiday walked into the cabin.

"Look at me," Chase snapped. "Do I not look fine?"

The fact that he didn't know Holiday was there told her he wasn't fine. "Get back in bed."

Holiday walked into the bedroom. Something about her expression gave Della a feeling of alarm.

"I don't care how fine you look . . ." Holiday paused. Her gaze widened, no doubt taking in his lack of clothes. "Do as Della says. Get in bed."

Shorter than Della, and probably weighing less than a hundred pounds soaking wet, Holiday didn't have an iron fist, but she should have. When the red-headed fae spoke, people listened.

Chase started backing up and dropped onto the bed. Then, as if realizing what Holiday said, he snatched up the sheet and threw it over him. His face brightened.

The fact that he hadn't been self-conscious about being in his underwear with Della meant something. But it was just another thing she didn't have time to contemplate right now.

"This is ridiculous," he muttered.

"Ridiculous is you almost getting yourself killed. But I'll let my husband take that up with you. I'm here to check on you and give Della this."

She held up a large manila envelope.

"The DA's file on my dad," Della said, guessing, and hoping.

Holiday nodded. "It was dropped off thirty minutes ago. I made Burnett a copy. He'll look at it when he gets back. I would have waited to give it to you, but she seemed pretty adamant you get it now."

"She?" Della asked.

"Your aunt," Holiday frowned. "Obviously, there's something in here she wants you to see. And she's not patient. She knocked over my bookcase when I didn't immediately do as she said."

Della took the envelope.

Holiday continued, "Normally, a spirit attaches themselves to only one person because of limited energy. Your aunt is probably the strongest ghost I've seen. Plus she's angry and confused, which concerns me."

Della inhaled. "She's never hurt me."

"Yet," Holiday said. "I'm not saying she'd do it on purpose, but when a spirit gets that much power, they don't know how to use it, or when they're crossing the line." She sighed. "It's extreme, but there is an exorcism that we could try."

"An exorcism?" Della remembered the visions she'd had these

last few months. The things she learned about her aunt—how Bao Yu had been forced to give up her illegitimate child, how she'd lost her boyfriend because of it, and how at only nineteen she'd been brutally murdered.

Della had no idea what would happen to Bao Yu if she was exorcised, but hadn't she had enough done to her? Her aunt might be confused about who'd killed her, but the reason she'd hung on to this life was to deal with all those things that had been forced on her. To find the answers she needed. Who was Della to take that away?

"No." Della clung to the envelope.

"Wait," Chase spoke up. "If she's dangerous, maybe—"

"No. You even told me that she was responsible for saving you last night."

"Yeah, but like Holiday said, she might not mean to do something wrong. She might—"

"No." Della looked at Holiday. "It's not happening!"

Holiday left, but Chase wasn't going to drop the issue with her aunt. "I'm worried something could happen to you," he insisted.

"Then stop. I'm not yours to worry about," she insisted right back.

"Like I'm not yours? Right?" He let out a low growl. "Then what are you doing here, Della? Why did you stay the night?"

"Don't make more out of it than it is," she told him, then told herself the same thing.

Frowning, he slumped back on his pillows and closed his eyes. She didn't know if he was drowsy from the healing process, or if he was thinking.

She hugged the file to her stomach and considered leaving. She needed to read the file. Her gaze shifted to the door.

Chase's voice stopped her from leaving. "This guy, Perry's cousin, who showed up. He didn't hurt anyone, did he?"

"No. And I don't think he could. He's only half shape-shifter."

Chase nodded. His eyes met hers. "Are we going to read the file?"

We? The word caught in her head. She tightened her hold on the envelope.

She almost left then, but realized that they both had a reason to want to solve Bao Yu's murder. Chase to get Eddie off, and her to get her father off. It was the first time she realized she truly believed it. Believed her uncle hadn't killed her aunt. Had it been Perry's cousin showing up and his connection to Stone that convinced her, or was it that she just wanted to believe Chase now?

Oh, hell, it didn't matter why. And just because she believed it didn't mean she had forgiven her father's brother. If he was any kind of man at all, he would have come forward to help.

"Sit down and let's read it." Chase motioned to the chair. Della sat and started reading. She heard him stand up.

He didn't say anything, but she could feel his eyes on her. His words replayed in her head. *I'm worried something could happen to you.*

She could feel his concern for her. She wasn't ready to accept that he had the right to be concerned. And yet she understood how he felt, since she'd been worried sick about him for the last twelve hours.

She'd even climbed in the damn bed with him, so she could hear him breathe, afraid he would stop.

But now that she knew he wasn't dying, she wanted to deny those feelings.

Hadn't her plan been to push him away?

Not everyone ends up together. You still have a choice. His words echoed in her head, and they felt less true than when he had said them.

"Stop," she finally muttered, and looked up.

"What?" he asked.

"Staring at me. I can't read."

His green eyes tightened into a frown. "Then can I see what you've read so far?" He held out his hand.

She started back reading. The first few pages didn't offer anything new. Times, dates, what officer arrived at the scene. She passed Chase the page as soon as she finished. Then she came to the script of the 911 call.

Her heart stopped. She looked up. "My dad is the one who called 911," she said. "He wasn't unconscious the whole time."

Chase stared at her, his eyes round with concern and maybe even fear. Only then did she feel the room's temperature.

Only then did she realize he wasn't looking at her.

She looked over her shoulder, and there behind her, a knife jutting out of her chest, was Bao Yu.

"Do you see," the ghost said, tears running from her eyes. Reaching up, she pulled the knife out. Blood gushed from the wound.

She used the knife to point to the papers in Della's hand.

Do you see? He wasn't unconscious. He did this! He killed me!

"No," Chase said. "Douglas Stone did it."

Her aunt looked up at Chase. Fury rose in her eyes. She slung the knife. It sank into the mattress, right between Chase's legs.

Della was pretty certain that the knife, a part of the vision, wasn't real. It hadn't been a real threat to Chase or his boys.

But judging by his pale expression, Chase didn't see it that way.

Chapter Twenty-five

Where the hell was Burnett? Chase had even tried calling him, but he didn't answer.

Della had left after they'd argued about letting Holiday attempt to get rid of the ghost.

An hour later, dressed, bored, and furious that he'd been put in timeout, he dropped back on the bed and tried to lower his blood pressure by petting Baxter. The dog rested at his side on the bed reveling in the attention.

When Baxter fell asleep, Chase got up. Still sitting on the sofa were the papers Burnett had brought about the FRU. Needing something to bide his time, he opened and read the contract and list of FRU rules. Rule number twenty-six, the one about every agent being self-motivated and responsible for deciding which risks to take was especially interesting, and one Chase stored away for his defense when Burnett decided to come and chew his ass out.

Looking at his cell for the hundredth time, he growled. Someone needed to go find Douglas Stone. Someone needed to find out what the council knew.

The fact that Douglas Stone had found him first pissed Chase off—for several reasons.

Was being here putting Della and the others at the camp in danger? He wanted to be close to her, but not at the expense of putting her in danger.

His thoughts were interrupted by footsteps moving toward the cabin. Heavy steps. Too heavy to be Della.

Thinking it was the person he dreaded seeing the most— Burnett—and not wanting to appear weak, he jackknifed out of bed and started to the door.

By the time the footsteps arrived at the porch, Chase caught the scent. Not Burnett, but another person he didn't care to see.

Being beholden to someone never sat well with Chase.

He ran a hand through his hair and waited for Steve's knock.

Steve stood on the porch, looking about as happy to be here as Chase was to have him here.

"I came to check your wounds."

"It's not necessary. I'm fine."

"Humor me," Steve said. "I promise it won't hurt."

Chase clenched his jaw.

"Please," Steve said. "Dr. Whitman asked me to do it."

Chase pulled up his shirt. The shape-shifter leaned down to check the small pink mark on his skin that the wound had left.

"It looks good." Steve rose up.

Chase met his eyes. "Why did you do it?"

"Do what?" Steve asked.

"Save my life." Suddenly, Chase remembered something. "Or did you purposely not clean the wound well enough, hoping the infection would take me out?"

Steve frowned. "For your information, I cleaned that wound several times. And if I hadn't, the infection would've killed you before Dr. Whitman got here." He paused. "Now, turn around and let me check the wound on your back and I'll go."

Chase turned. Steve lifted his shirt. "Did you do it because Della asked you to?" he asked, hoping to point out to the shape-shifter that Della cared about him.

Chase felt his shirt fall back against his skin. Steve exhaled.

"I did it because I'm a doctor, because if I let you die just because I don't like you, I wouldn't have been able to live with myself."

Realizing he was acting like a jealous boyfriend, Chase pushed back the unwanted feelings and faced the guy.

"Sorry. Thank you." Chase held out his hand.

Steve didn't take it. "You don't owe me thanks."

Okay, so maybe after accusing the guy of trying to kill him, he didn't blame the shape-shifter for not taking his hand.

"Can I pay you?" Chase asked, still trying to make amends. "Name your price."

"Keep your money." Steve turned to leave, but before he reached the doorknob, he turned around. "Actually, there is a way you could repay me. Seeing that I saved your life."

Chase tensed. Now he was sorry he'd played nice. "If that payment in any way involves my relationship with Della, you can go to hell. And I'll be happy to help you get there if you—"

"Please," Steve spit out. "I'm not ignorant enough to believe any deal I make with you could influence Della. And I respect her enough to not even try. She'll make up her own mind who she wants to be with. You have no control over her decisions. And if you think you do, that just goes to show you don't even know her."

The words and the insinuation hit hard. "And you'll respect her decision when she chooses me?" Chase asked.

"I'll accept it. Just as I'm sure you will when she chooses me."

"Nope." Chase shook his head. "That's where I differ from you. I'll never stop fighting for her. You can believe it's because I don't respect her, but I think it's because I love her more. Because I know with every cell of my being that she belongs with me."

They stared at each other for several long, tense seconds, then Steve turned for the door. That's when Chase realized Steve had never told him what he wanted. And damn it, he really didn't like being beholden.

"If how I can repay you isn't about Della, then what is it? Owing people's not my thing."

Steve took another step toward the door, then turned around. The remnants of anger still tightening his eyes told Chase that whatever the shape-shifter wanted, he wanted it badly—if not, he would have left.

"The ointment," Steve said. "The one Della said her uncle invented. Would he be so inclined to share what's in it?"

Chase felt his shoulders relax. "I'll ask, but knowing Eddie, if he thinks it will save lives, he'll say yes. It might be a while. At least until this mess is over."

Steve looked ready to leave, but then spoke again, "You know, your opinion of Della's uncle is higher than hers."

"She doesn't know him," Chase said. "When she does, she'll see."

Steve shrugged. "For Della's sake, I hope you're right."

As the guy walked out, Chase said, "Thank you."

Steve kept walking but Chase heard his words. "You're welcome. But I still don't like your ass."

"Perry feels terrible," Miranda told Della as she dropped down on Della's bed. Della had come back from Chase's to read the DA's file over and over. Hoping to find something that would help get her father off. Miranda's footsteps on the porch had woken her from a dead sleep—only to face the dead.

Della could feel the fingers of cold getting closer.

"Did his cousin tell Burnett anything?" Della asked, looking around and hoping she was wrong.

"Perry said that Burnett hadn't finished talking to him. He was called away on another case."

Della tried to pay attention to the witch, but it was hard. She could hear Mrs. Chi in the living room. *Here, kitty, kitty.*

Socks came hauling butt into the room and jumped onto the bed.

"What's wrong?" Miranda asked the cat and picked her up.

"Be careful," Della warned. "She has sharp claws."

"Don't make her feel bad," Miranda said. "She only scratched you because the dog was here."

"Yeah," Della said. "But she obviously doesn't like ghosts either."

Miranda's hazel eyes widened. "Is there a ghost . . . here? Now?"

Della wanted to lie, for Miranda's sake, but she saw the girl shiver. From the cold as well as fear, so she nodded.

"Oh, crap." Miranda put the cat down.

Kitty. Kitty. Mrs. Chi's voice echoed again. The eeriness of it caused fear to tiptoe down Della's spine.

"Is it your aunt?" Miranda asked, and the witch's breath sent a wisp of fog.

A thud sounded from the living room.

Socks flew off the mattress, hit the wall with a thump, twisted midair, then scrambled under Della's bed.

If Della hadn't been embarrassed, she'd have followed the cat.

Another thud sounded and Della turned her gaze to the door just as a bloody basketball rolled into the room.

Then Mrs. Chi appeared, looking lost and pathetic. Guilt chased away Della's sense of fear. She'd been so worried about Chase and the DA's file, she'd put her elderly neighbor out of her mind.

Mrs. Chi's sad gaze met Della's. *Where's Chester?*

"That's not Chester."

"Who's Chester," Miranda asked.

"A cat," Della answered, but didn't take her eyes or heart away from Mrs. Chi.

"Your ghost is a cat?" Miranda hugged herself from the cold. "This is getting freakier and freakier."

They did it again, Mrs. Chi said.

"Who did what again?" Della asked.

"Are you talking to a dead cat?" Miranda asked.

They hurt someone.

"Who did they hurt?" When the spirit didn't answer, Della threw out another question. "Do you know the names of the guys who are doing this?" Della motioned for Miranda to be quiet.

No. The old woman looked down at the basketball. *But I showed you.*

"What did you show me?" Della asked.

You saw.

"What did I see?" Della stood up. "I didn't see enough to help me stop these creeps."

You saw, Mrs. Chi repeated and then she and the basketball vanished.

Della snagged her phone, and called Burnett. It went to voice mail. "Call me," Della said and started toward the door.

"Where are you going?" A scared Miranda popped out of the bed.

"To see Chase," Della said, realizing they'd never gone over the vision. Maybe Chase would have an idea what Mrs. Chi's words had meant.

"Can I come?" Miranda asked. "I don't want to stay here with a dead cat." Then the girl paused. "Or are you and Chase going to get naked again?"

"We weren't naked," Della snapped.

"If I'd been a few minutes later, you would have been."

Della growled and wanted to deny it, but wasn't sure it was altogether untrue. "There wasn't a dead cat. Just a . . . dead . . . person." Then, flinching at how that sounded, and hoping Mrs. Chi wasn't in earshot, she added, "A sweet ol' lady." She flinched again. "Not that old."

"I'm still coming." Miranda stood up, looking around the room as if afraid something might jump out at her. "Why did I have to get stuck with two ghost-magnet roommates?"

"You're just lucky like that," Della said.

And so it seemed Della was lucky too, because Kylie stepped up on the porch and the witch decided not to come.

Chapter Twenty-six

The heavy-footed steps moving to his door told Chase the identity of his visitor before he got Burnett's scent.

"Come in," Chase said, though he doubted Burnett considered an invitation necessary.

The man stormed in. Chase didn't waste a second. "Did you get anything from the guy Stone sent?"

"What the hell were you thinking?" Burnett thundered.

"I didn't know Stone knew where I was!"

"I'm not talking about that! I'm talking about you going to that damn prison!"

"I was acting on some advice I got from another agent."

Burnett stepped closer, his eyes bright with anger. "What idiot of an agent would have advised—"

"You," Chase said, proud of himself. "You told me that to find the scum, I needed to ask other scums. The prisoners at—"

"I would have never allowed you to go alone!"

"Alone was the only way I could get in." Chase held his shoulders tight and recalled his ammunition. "According to rule twenty-six, an agent is expected—"

"You are expected to have enough sense in your brain to know the risks."

"I was aware of the risks," Chase said.

"No, you weren't. You think you're invincible. You are young and dumb."

"It would only be dumb if I didn't get anything."

Burnett scowled. "And who would have given us this lead if you hadn't made it out?"

"I did make it out."

"You think I haven't seen this before? The first agent I was asked to train was nineteen. She thought nothing could touch her. She took a stupid risk and went after a killer by herself. By the time I got there, the only thing I could do was hold her hand while she died. They gave me the job of telling her mother that her daughter was dead. I refuse to have to tell another parent their kid is dead."

I don't have parents, Chase almost said, but caught himself. "I probably should have spoken with you. You win. I was wrong. But can we start working on my lead, now?"

"Probably?" Burnett groaned, then looked at Chase. "We're talking about Hell's Pit, aren't we?"

Chase nodded, a little surprised Burnett was aware of it.

"I weighed the risk and made the decision to go," Chase said.

Burnett exhaled. "You know what? I'm wrong. I apologize. I mean, weighing the risk is an important ability, isn't it?"

"Yes." Chase felt validated.

Burnett nodded. "How about we send Della in to confirm whatever lead you got? I'll call her right now." He pulled out his cell and started punching in a number.

Chase's breath hitched in his chest. Burnett hadn't dialed Della's number, he told himself. This was a ploy.

"Della," Burnett said. "I'm at Chase's cabin. Can you meet me here in five minutes? We need to discuss something."

"I'm on my way now." Della's voice rang out from the phone. Chase's blood fizzed with frustration.

Burnett put the phone back in his pocket. "I want her to know the risk before she decides to do it."

Now it was Chase's time to grit his teeth. In his heart, he knew this was just Burnett's way of bringing home his point. The man would never let Della go. Chase just wished the point wasn't so damn sharp.

Burnett lifted one brow. "What's wrong?"

Chase swallowed. "Okay. It was too risky. You win."

Burnett ran a hand over his face then met Chase's eyes again. "I don't want to win! This isn't some friggin' game. It's life and death. If right now I thought I could go to the FRU and get your ass tossed out, I'd do it. But no, it's too soon, and they'd just give you to someone else. Then when you ended up dead, I'd be stuck thinking I could have saved your sorry ass if I hadn't passed you on."

Burnett moved in, so close Chase could count the man's lashes. "But I swear to God, kid. If you do something else this stupid, I'll find a way to get your ass tossed out of the FRU. And don't for one minute think I don't mean it. I'll make some shit up about you and the council. I'll plant evidence."

He put one finger on Chase's chest. It didn't feel like a threat so much as a man bringing home his point again. "Because I can live with killing your career a lot easier than I can live with watching you get yourself killed. Do you understand what I'm saying?"

Chase nodded. "I understand." And as scary as it was, Chase believed Burnett meant it.

"Good." Burnett dropped onto the sofa. "Now, sit your ass down and tell me what you got out of your stupid mistake."

Chase told Burnett everything. Even what he didn't want to about his suspicions that someone at the council knew more about Stone than they were saying.

"I never considered that Stone would be looking for me. The last thing I wanted was to bring trouble here. If you think it would be best, I'll find some other place to stay."

Burnett seemed to consider it. "I don't think that's necessary right now."

"The last thing I want to do is endanger—"

"If this kid, Sam, is all Stone has up his sleeve, I'm not worried." Burnett leaned forward.

Chase hated to disagree with Burnett, but . . . "You may not be worried, but the kid managed to get in. And as nonthreatening as Sam might have been, the next guy—"

"His getting in was my own mistake," Burnett said. "I should have run a check as soon as the power flickered. I won't make that mistake again." The man leaned forward. "If I feel your being here becomes a threat, we'll revisit this discussion. Until then, you stay."

Burnett's tone made it sound like an order. One that Chase didn't think he had the right to give.

Della landed in front of Chase's cabin. She tuned her hearing to listen to the conversation and walked in. They both looked at her and Burnett motioned for her to sit down.

"Who on the council do you suspect of being dirty?" Burnett asked Chase.

"I'm not sure, but maybe I can investigate further by speaking to the prison guard. Maybe he knows more than he thinks."

Della didn't miss the fact that Chase wasn't willing to admit it might be Kirk who was dirty.

Burnett frowned. "You do not go back into that prison. Not even near the prison," his tone deepened.

"I understand," Chase said.

Della wasn't sure what had conspired between these two, but Chase seemed to be playing nice.

In the beat of silence, her patience snapped. "What did you need to see me about?"

"Let's start with good news," Burnett said. "I just heard back from the agent trying to fix things so Natasha can return to the human world. We tied up a few loose ends and now have her disappearance tied to Liam's."

"So she gets to go back home?" Della asked.

"We still have a few things to work out, but yes." He paused. "Now for the bad news. There's been another murder. We're thinking it's the same killers as the Chis and the young weres cases. A couple, early twenties, only a mile away from the other crimes, was found in another park."

Della nodded. "Mrs. Chi appeared to me about fifteen minutes ago and told me they had hurt others. I called you."

"I was on my way here." He hesitated. "Did she give you anything that might help us catch them?"

"No. But she still had the basketball. Did you keep the agent at the park at the basketball court?"

"I did. No one has shown up."

"Was there a basketball court at the other park?"

"I think so," Burnett said. "I'll put someone on it. And I'll see about putting other agents at any nearby park with courts."

"I'd be happy to do that," Chase said.

Burnett shook his head. "They might recognize you from when you rescued Della. Plus the doctor said you need to take it slow for today."

Della remembered the reason she'd come here to start with. "Mrs. Chi said something . . . something that led me to believe she thinks I didn't pick up on something in the vision. Because Chase was in the vision too, I thought if we compared notes we might stumble across something."

"You should have done it right afterward," Burnett said.

"Things came up," Chase said.

Changing the subject, Della asked, "Have the autopsies been done?"

"Of Mr. and Mrs. Chi, yes, but not the young weres." Burnett hesitated. "Definitely a were crime, a few bite marks but nothing distinguishable. So no evidence to help catch the killers. They are testing for DNA, but unless the killers were arrested by the FRU, that won't help us."

"So they just get away with murder?" Della snapped, and her frustration intensified not just from knowing the Chis, but from the fact that these killers were close to her parents' home—close to her sister, who probably visited both the parks where the murders happened.

"Not if I can help it," Burnett said. "The same examiner who did the Chis' autopsy is doing the young weres'. She's supposed to call when she's finished."

Leaning forward, Burnett cupped his knees in his palms. "Holiday told me she brought you the DA's file. I still haven't had the opportunity to read it. Did you find anything that might help us?"

Della's heart raced at his question. She hated saying it aloud. "Help us, no. Hurt him, yes." She took a deep breath. "My dad's the one who called 911. The DA had made notes that his story changed, because now he claims he was unconscious the whole time."

Burnett frowned. "At least his lawyer knows now."

Chase leaned in. "It was a very traumatic experience. People block things out. I think it will be understandable to any judge that the situation could have affected his memory."

Della's emotions pushed back her ability to hear the positive. "But that's not the picture they are going to paint. They're going to say he killed his sister and then lost his mind." Making it harder was that his own sister believed it.

Burnett seemed to read her mind, or at least the direction of her thoughts. "Holiday's worried the ghost is—"

"No," Della said. "I'm not letting Holiday send her away or chase her off." She stared at Chase, praying he wouldn't jump in and add fuel to the fire. He didn't, but his gaze said he wanted to.

She swallowed the need to give in to tears and faced Burnett. "Have you gotten a judge on board yet?"

"Not yet," Burnett said. "We're still working on it. But giving up hope isn't going to help."

"I'm not giving up; I'm worried."

"We've got the Douglas Stone lead. And now we have this cousin of Perry's," Chase said, as if to comfort her.

Della glanced at Burnett. "Has Sam given us anything?"

"I was pulled away to go to the murder scene. I'm letting him stew for a while." Burnett cupped his hands and glanced down. She knew that look. He had something else to tell her and it probably wasn't good.

"What else?" Her stomach muscles hardened to the point it hurt.

Chapter Twenty-seven

"I got a call from our guy in the DA's office," Burnett said. "They got the trial date. Two weeks."

"We've got two weeks to prove him innocent?" Della's voice shook. "We'll never do that."

"Yes, we will," Chase said.

"Listen to him," Burnett said. "All it takes is one lead."

Burnett took out his phone to check the time. "Why don't you two go over the vision? In about an hour . . ."—he glanced at Chase—"if you feel up to it, you two can come down and help me interrogate Sam."

"I'm up to it," Chase said. "Tomorrow, in addition to looking for Stone's girlfriend, I'd also like to start revisiting the Douglas Stone suspects, concentrating on the ones I've already visited."

"But I thought you didn't get anything from them," Burnett said.

"I didn't, but as Pope pointed out, Stone said I was poking around in the wrong places."

"Were any of these people you spoke to vampires or supernaturals?" Burnett asked.

"No."

"Then how would Stone have known it was you asking questions?"

"I don't know, but my guts say he did."

Burnett sighed. "Then I guess follow your gut."

Della sat up a little straighter. "I'd like to go with him."

"You have school," Burnett said.

"I could miss a day or two. Hell, I could miss two weeks."

Burnett frowned. "You can't—"

"What am I gonna miss? Lessons about Russian politics, finding what friggin' *x* is to *y*, and trying to decipher the theme of *Pride and Prejudice*? We're running out of time. This could mean my dad's life!" This time tears filled her eyes.

Burnett glanced at Chase, almost as if seeking his okay. What the hell? She sure as heck didn't need his permission.

"I've got her back," Chase said.

"Oh, please," Della said. "Excuse me while I go and grow a penis so the sausage-and-meatball-toting gender will stop thinking I need a man to protect me."

Both Chase and Burnett looked taken aback by her rebuttal, or perhaps it was her description of their genitals, but what the heck did they expect?

Burnett cleared his throat. "What matters is that both of you are safe. If either of you sense danger, I want you to pull back and call me."

Chase nodded.

Burnett stood up. "You two go over the vision and meet me at the office in an hour." Burnett left, and after about a minute, Chase started laughing. "Sausage and meatballs?"

They spent thirty minutes recounting the vision. It led nowhere. Chase offered nothing that Della didn't recall. Frustrated, and feeling as if time were running out, she got up and started for the door.

"Della?" Chase said, trying to stop her.

"I'll meet you at the office."

"Where are you going?" he asked and came to stand beside her.

"I need to think," she spouted out.

He put his arms around her. And she let him. But when she felt herself about to cry, she pulled away and shot out.

She ran. Once. Twice. All the way around the Shadow Falls property, hoping to work off some of her emotions. It didn't help, but at least she wasn't in danger of crying anymore.

She arrived at the cabin a few minutes early. Perry stood on the office porch.

Having not really spoken to him since he'd returned, she offered a quick "Welcome back."

He shrugged. "What a welcome." He frowned. She got the feeling he was talking about his cousin.

"Are you coming with us to talk to him?" Della asked.

He nodded. "Maybe I can talk some sense into him this time," the shape-shifter said. Pausing, he glanced down, and then added, "I'm sorry. You know I haven't seen him in over twelve years. I wasn't aware of any of this."

Della recognized the guilt in Perry's eyes. "I know. Nobody blames you."

He dropped his hands into this jean pockets. "I still feel bad. But . . ." he paused. "I don't think Sam's all bad. I think he's afraid, and not just of Burnett, but of that Stone character."

"Maybe he should have thought about that before he went to work for him." She instantly regretted her gruffness and recalled how she'd felt about Chan, her cousin. He'd tiptoed close to the line of going rogue, but she'd still loved him. His death continued to haunt her.

"True," Perry said, and got quiet.

"He's still your cousin. This doesn't change that."

Perry exhaled. "I know. And it feels . . . weird. Seeing him.

Crazy, how I recognized him right away. I never thought I'd see any of my family."

Miranda had confided in Della about how Perry had been abandoned when he was young. No doubt that had to sting. The only thing worse was being abandoned by your family when you were seventeen. But this wasn't about her.

"That has to suck," Della said.

"Yeah." Perry stared into the woods. "He knows where my mother and dad are."

Della heard his emotions, but was unsure what to say. "Are you going to go see them?"

He shrugged again. "I don't know. They sure as hell didn't want me then. Why would they want me now?"

She sensed the emotion stirring inside him. She couldn't say he had tears in his eyes, but his eyes looked brighter.

"Better yet," he said, sounding angry, "why would I want to see them? I don't care about them!"

She heard his heart jump the tune of his lie. She knew all about caring when it felt wrong. She gave him a nudge with her elbow. "You might want to see them because you're curious. Or maybe because you want them to know they were wrong about you. That you grew up to be someone they would have been proud of." She inhaled. "Or maybe you just want to call them mo fos, shoot them the finger, and then moon their asses as you walk out. Not that you'd have to do that. But you could."

He grinned, but when his gaze met hers again she saw a sheen of tears in his eyes. "Thanks," he said.

"For what?" Della asked.

"I don't know. Listening, maybe. Saying the right thing."

She frowned. "I pretty much suck at that."

"Nah," he said. "Actually, you're not that bad at it."

"You know who's better at it?" she said.

"Who? Miranda?" he asked.

"Uh, well, I was gonna say Kylie. She's like a little Holiday. She says all the crap you don't want to hear, but she's right, and while you don't like it, you need to hear it. But I'll bet Miranda is good too."

He shook his head. "I wish I could talk to Miranda. She's still playing hard to get." Shuffling his feet, he looked out at the sky. At almost five, the sun was a big ball of yellow.

"Do you know if Miranda's seeing that FRU agent?"

What could she say? *Yeah, she saw him last weekend and wanted to kiss him.*

Shit. Shit. Shit. Della so didn't want to get in the middle of this. But in a way she was. Smack dab in the middle, too. Worse than being in the middle, she's been the cause of it.

For the first time she felt guilty for encouraging the witch to give the warlock a chance. Perry would totally hate her if he knew that.

But at the time, the shape-shifter had practically dumped Miranda. And as good a friend as Perry was, Miranda trumped him.

"Is she?" Perry asked again.

"I . . ." As a shape-shifter, Perry couldn't sense if she lied, but lying to someone she liked gave her stomach cramps. But damn, this was why she didn't like listening and being someone's commiserating buddy.

Right then, Burnett landed on the porch. Saved by the vampire. Relief spiraled through her. Temporary relief, but at this point she'd take it.

"Where's Chase?" Burnett asked.

"Here," Chase said, walking up.

"Then let's go get some answers."

They had all walked into the observation room with a two-way mirror. Through the mirror Della saw Sam sitting at the table, looking lost and scared. Before anyone spoke to Sam, they were waiting on another agent, who'd briefly interrogated Sam. She hadn't arrived yet.

Another agent stuck his head into the room.

"If he"—the man pointed to Chase—"is working this case, you need to get him to sign a contract now."

"Let's get this over with." Burnett led Chase out, leaving Della with Perry. Before the door closed, Shawn—Miranda's Shawn—walked past.

After staring at his cousin for a few seconds, Perry started toward the door. "I'll be right back," he offered. He was almost out the door when Della realized what he might be doing.

"Hey," she said.

He looked back. "What?"

"Don't go looking for trouble."

"I'm not," Perry said. "I just want some air."

"There's plenty of air in here."

"I'll be back." He walked out.

Della stood alone in the room, then looked back at Perry's cousin.

The door opened, making Della realize the room was sound-proof. She hadn't been able to hear anything outside the walls. She looked back, expecting Chase or Burnett, but in walked a woman, a young woman, only a few years older than Della. Her fitted black suit identified her as an agent. Della automatically checked her forehead and noted she was half vampire and half fae.

"Oh, hey, I thought Burnett was in here," she said.

"He went to sign some of Chase Tallman's paperwork," Della answered.

"I'm Trisha."

"I'm Della—"

"I know who you are," the woman said.

Della studied her. "Have we met?"

"No. I've just heard about you. That you're planning on signing on with us."

"From Burnett?" Della felt a touch of pride.

Trisha nodded.

"Don't believe half of what he says," Della said.

"Oh, he had nothing but good things to say. He told me just enough to make me feel sorry for you."

"Sorry for me?" Della emotionally flinched. What the hell had Burnett told them? About her parents?

"Okay, that was a bad way of putting it. I meant I heard enough to know what you're up against."

Della still didn't understand, and her expression must have shown it, because Trisha continued, "When I first came to work here, I was assigned under Burnett." She smiled. "I requested a transfer."

"Oh, you mean about him being a male chauvinist pig?"

The woman grinned. "That might be a little strong."

"No, it's not," Della said. "I tell him that all the time."

She laughed. "Sounds like he met his match with you. But when you get here, if you'd like to train under me, I'd be honored."

"Thanks," Della said. She hadn't really considered the training period of becoming an agent, and for some reason it sent a thrill through her. As if that part of life was closer than she expected. With all her problems of late, she'd kind of lost the excitement of where life could lead.

She glanced back up at Trisha, who appeared to be waiting for Della to say something else. "But I'll probably just stick with Burnett. He's a pain in the ass, but I'm told I can be the same. So we're a pretty good pair."

She laughed. "Well, it sounds like you two belong together. To be honest, I've regretted my decision as well. He's a good agent."

"So the other agents here aren't as overprotective as Burnett?"

"Well, they all have a little bit too much testosterone—just not as much as Mr. James. But after meeting you, I think you have enough estrogen to put them in their places."

All of a sudden, in the other room, Sam stood and banged on the door. "Are you gonna keep me in here all day?"

Della and Trisha both glanced at the boy through the two-way mirror. "Looks as if he might be frustrated enough to talk now. Burnett asked me to soften him up earlier, but he wasn't responding."

"He has to talk," Della said, thinking of her father, and the ticking clock. In two weeks he could be sent to prison.

"I read him when I was in there," the agent said, and Della assumed she was referring to her fae ability to read emotion. "He's not a bad kid, mostly scared. But we're all scared, aren't we?"

"Yeah." The woman had probably read Della's emotions. But could she read her enough to know Della wasn't afraid for herself—only for her father?

Two weeks.

Chapter Twenty-eight

"Just go in and be honest," Burnett told Perry.

Chase stood by Burnett as he spoke to the shape-shifter.

"What are we doing? Good cop, bad cops? I'm nice to him, and then you two beat him up?" Perry asked.

Chase heard concern in Perry's voice, and obviously so did Burnett.

"We're not treating him as a hostile . . . *yet,*" Burnett said. "If he talks, we'll go extra easy on him."

Chase wasn't sure he agreed with that, but he didn't think he had the right to argue.

"Okay," Perry nodded at Chase. The quick duck of the head didn't come with any friendly pretense. The way Chase saw it, Perry was probably friends with Steve.

"Go with Trisha." Burnett motioned to the agent who walked up. "She'll show you the way."

"Congratulations," Trisha said, meeting Chase's gaze.

"Thank you." Chase shook the agent's hand, a real sense of pride filling his chest. He'd signed the papers. It was official. Chase Tallman was an FRU agent. He'd even be given a badge and a couple of black suits. Not that Chase wanted to wear them. But the badge, yeah, he kind of liked having it. It felt nice to . . . belong to something.

Sure, he'd belonged to the council, but it hadn't been so much his decision as it had been Eddie's. This was his own doing. This was, Chase realized, his first real job.

Not that he needed money. His parents had left him with more money than he knew what to do with. But then again, this wasn't just a job. It was a career. It was something that would probably define his life from now until he was ready to retire.

It hadn't been anything like a ceremony, but in a small way it had felt like it to him. Part of him wished Della had been there. Because she should have been. Their lives were connected.

He recalled the conversation with Steve, and the one with Della earlier. *You still have a choice.* He hadn't lied to her, she did, but damn it, it was his mission in life to make sure she chose him.

"Welcome to the team," another agent called out.

Chase nodded, but realized the one person who hadn't congratulated him was the one walking at his side right now: Burnett.

Was he still thinking about their earlier conversation about Chase's trip to Hell's Pit? The conversation had stuck with Chase, too. As much as he hated admitting it, Burnett had been right. Chase did feel invincible. No one had been more shocked than him when he'd felt that makeshift knife slice into his back. If it hadn't been for the ghost, Chase wasn't sure he'd have gotten out alive.

"I plan on making you proud," Chase said to Burnett.

"Do that by staying alive," Burnett said, confirming that Chase had been right about the man's thoughts.

"I will," Chase said as they walked back into the room where they'd left Della.

Della, phone to her ear, looked back at them and then down, as she held up one finger. "Yes. I shouldn't be too late. I'll stop by."

Chase tuned his ear to listen, hoping to hear who Della had made plans with and fearing it would be the good doctor, Steve.

"Great," a feminine voice answered. "Bring Chase with you."

He recognized Della's cousin's voice. Chase really liked Natasha and her boyfriend Liam. And remembering Perry's cold shoulder, he was glad to know he had friends.

Della looked up at him. He nodded at her to let her know it was a go for him, but she still said, "We'll see."

What the hell?

"Look, I'd better go now," Della continued. "I'll see you in bit. Oh, and again, I'm thrilled things worked out."

"Me too," Natasha said. "Don't forget to come by; I can't wait to see you."

"I'll be there." Della hung up.

"You ready to do this?" Della motioned to Sam behind the window.

"Perry's going in first," Burnett said. "Then Chase and I."

"Not me?"

"I think we have this," Burnett said.

Chase saw Della flinch, but she tried to rein her frustrations in. She was constantly doing that. Except with him. She didn't hold back with him. At least not with anger.

"Perry stepped out for air," Della said.

"Just met him in the hall." Burnett paused and glanced back at Chase. "Meanwhile, Mr. Tallman has just made it official. He's an agent. Got his badge, suits, and everything."

Della smiled at Chase, and it looked genuine—the kind of smile that reached her eyes, and made them twinkle a little brighter. He wanted to see that a hell of a lot more. See her happy, worry-free.

And he would, his gut told him. Just as soon as the problems with her father were resolved.

"Congratulations, Mr. Tallman," Della said, her voice sounding sincere.

"Thank you." If Burnett weren't in the room, Chase would have moved in for a kiss, because he'd learned that whenever she allowed herself to smile, it meant her guard was down. And only then did she let him close.

What he wouldn't give to knock that guard down for good. While he knew he needed to be patient, he couldn't deny growing frustrated.

"It feels nice," he said, and held out his hand, hoping a hand-shake would curb his desire for a kiss.

It looked as if she wasn't going to accept it when he literally saw her guard go back up. But she slipped her hand into his. He took advantage of the moment and gently ran his thumb over her knuckles, hoping she felt that same spark of something wonderful that he did. Touching her was like sticking his finger into a happy socket. Nothing made him feel more alive.

From the quick way she retrieved her hand and the way her eyes widened, he knew she felt the electricity too. So why the hell was she fighting it?

Then through the two-way mirror, Chase saw Perry walk in and sit down across from his cousin, Sam. The two of them looked enough alike to be brothers.

"They send you in here to soften me up?" Sam asked.

"Maybe," Perry said. "Look, you gotta tell them what you know, or you're going to go down for a lot of shit."

"I didn't do anything but break into that school. What? Is that gonna get me sentenced to life?" Sarcasm rang from the guy's voice.

"Don't you get it?" Perry asked, his eyes turning gold. "You were helping that Stone guy, and that means you'll be responsible for everything he did too. And from what I hear he's a murderer."

"Whoa. I didn't hurt anyone. And hell, yeah, he's a badass. And if I talk, he'll come after me."

"Then tell them what they want to know and let them catch him. If you go to jail, you know this guy is gonna think you'll cra-ter and talk. If he's half as bad as you think he is, he has friends in low places. He'll have you killed. Do you want to die?"

· · ·

Thanks to Perry, it only took Chase and Burnett a few minutes to get the shape-shifter to spill his guts.

"I met the guy at the Get-Along Bar. It's known to be friendly to half-breeds such as myself. He was vampire, but had a slightly weird pattern like . . . he had a bit of something else in him. He said his name was Michael Higby, but someone else told me he also went by Stone. I heard he hired a lot of down-on-their-luck bar patrons to do grunt work for him. That's how I got here. But rumor had it he has a gang called the Bastards."

"What kind of gang is it?" Burnett asked.

"I don't know. Like I said, he was . . . vampire . . . Mostly, anyway. He approached me and said he needed a shape-shifter to break into a school. I was to spy on a—" He looked at Chase. "You. He wanted to know what you were doing at that school. It didn't sound illegal. I thought you were like his long-lost kid or something. I was just trying to reunite a family, you know?"

"Just warms my heart," Chase said, not so warmly.

"What does this guy look like?"

"He's forty-something. Over six feet. Hasn't let himself go to pot. Has brown hair and, like I said, has that pattern that's just a little different." He exhaled. "That's all I know, so can I go now?"

"Uh, no," Chase said.

Sam frowned. "But I didn't do anything. I mean, yeah, I snuck into the school, but Higby or Stone or whatever you want to call him set it up. All I had to do was fly over the fence when he told me to."

"And how did you mess with our electricity?" Burnett asked.

"He had one of his other grunt workers do something with the power lines outside your school. I . . . didn't hurt anyone."

"What info did you report back to him?" Chase asked.

"None," the kid said.

Chase and Burnett looked at him in disbelief.

"I didn't. I swear. You can check my phone. I was going to, but I got sidetracked by that chick. Then I saw my long-lost cousin."

"What chick?" Burnett asked. "Did someone else come in with you?"

"No, the one that was there. Dark hair, vampire. Nice ass."

Chase let out a growl.

The kid gave them a telephone number and the address of the bar.

"So what now?" Sam asked. "Can I leave?"

"Not yet," Burnett said. "I'm sending in a sketch artist. Then I think we'll keep you here for a few days."

"But I told you all I know," Sam said.

"Yes," Burnett said, "but we may need you to help us snag him."

"I didn't agree to that."

"You didn't seem to like the idea of prison, either," Burnett said.

Sam frowned. "I might as well be in prison. Why don't you let me go back to that school? Has nicer scenery." He smiled. "Especially that girl with the hot ass. Was her name Delia, or something like that?"

"You're staying here," Chase ordered.

Burnett walked up to Sam and held out his hand.

"What?" the kid said.

"Your phone," Burnett said.

"Will I get it back?" Sam asked.

Burnett didn't answer, and he and Chase walked out. The older vamp stopped and typed on his phone as if sending a text.

He looked at Chase. "You ever heard of that gang, the Bastards?"

"Never," Chase said. "You?"

"No, which is strange, because we know the ones out there. But I'll put out some feelers and see if we've got a new one in town."

Another agent met them in the hall. Burnett handed him the phone. "Text me as soon as you have something."

"Maybe it was just Stone's way of impressing the kid," Chase said, seeing the agent with the phone hurry away.

"I hope so."

"Like I said before, I could leave the school and lessen the chance of—"

"Not yet." Burnett's cell phone dinged with a text. After checking it, he looked up at Chase. "You ready?"

"Yeah." Chase followed Burnett down the hall. "You want me to go check out that bar?"

"No," Burnett said. "He knows what you look like. I've already got two agents on the way there. We're going to the morgue."

Chase's steps faltered and just like that a fine sheen of sweat popped out around his neck. Well, shit! Not fifteen minutes after signing his contract, he wondered if it was too soon to resign.

"Are we going to the bar?" Della asked when Burnett walked back into the room. As far as Della was concerned, it was the best lead they had on Stone.

"No, I've got Trish and Shawn going there," Burnett said.

"But—"

"No," Burnett said. "And before you ask, I've got two agents checking out the telephone number. Meanwhile, they've finished the autopsy of the three weres. Perry's staying here; I thought we could all head over there."

"Why don't I go see if I can find any info on the Bastards gang?" Chase offered.

"I've got that covered too," Burnett said. "And you're on light duty. When we're done at the morgue, you can go with Della to see Natasha."

Della noted Chase's frown. "He doesn't have to come with me," Della said.

"It's a full moon," Burnett said. "No one goes out alone."

A short ride later, Della walked into the morgue with Chase and Burnett. They walked past the front desk and down a white hall that looked and smelled almost too sterile. He pushed open a heavy door and entered another room. A colder room.

A woman in a white coat stood in the room tapping on a computer. She looked back, and Della saw her witch pattern. Burnett did quick introductions that brought nods.

"Tell me you've got something for me," Burnett said.

"I've got something." She smiled. "A few hairs. I've already sent them off. Definitely were-related, and I got a few bite marks that we might be able to use. I just uploaded them." She motioned Burnett closer.

Della didn't follow. Instead, she stayed where she was and visually took in the room. Behind the woman were three tables, presumably holding the three young weres. The bodies were draped and covered with white sheets.

The shapes of the bodies reminded her of seeing her cousin's body in that tarp before they lowered it into the grave. Or was it the smell, she wondered, that took her back? Had Chan's body and tarp still carried this astringent smell of the morgue?

She inhaled, trying to push the cold, the smell, and the pain away. Then as always, her chest stirred with guilt for moving past the biggest portion of the grief.

She heard Chase shift, standing to her right. When she took in his face, she almost gasped. His complexion matched the sheets.

While it felt good knowing she wasn't the only one feeling vulnerable, she was surprised. Chase had worked with the council for almost two years; surely he'd seen death before.

"Chase and I are going to wait outside," Della spoke up and caught Chase's arm before she gave Burnett a chance to answer. Chase resisted only for a second, then walked out with her.

"New on the job, huh?" she heard the woman say before the door swished closed.

Della stopped in the hall. Chase pulled away and didn't even look at her. He leaned against the white wall and closed his eyes.

"You okay?" she asked.

"Fine," he said, his tone as cold as the air that had been in the room.

"You sure?" she asked when he didn't open his eyes.

"I said I was fine," he snapped.

"But you look—"

"Friggin' hell, would you drop it!" He pushed off the wall and started out.

She stood there for a few seconds, trying to decide if she was more angry at his reaction or more worried. Worry won and she took off after him.

She found him leaning against Burnett's car.

The night had chased away every sliver of color from the sky, but the full moon shone down brightly, giving the parking lot an almost silver glow.

He saw her, and his mutterings of some four-letter words reached her ears, making it clear she wasn't welcome. She didn't give a rat's ass, and she kept on walking toward him.

Chapter Twenty-nine

She was ready to give him some shit, until she got close enough and saw his expression. Pain, grief, guilt. Emotions she'd just pushed away herself.

So she resisted making her snide remarks. Her footsteps sounded too loud. She leaned against the car beside him. Her arm almost touched his. The dark cold surrounded them, and the lukewarm temperature of his body reached her.

For several seconds neither of them spoke. But oddly enough, she could feel his pain.

"It reminded me of Chan," she said, thinking that if she reached out, he might reach back.

He nodded, and she felt him shift his weight. "I was an ass," he said, his voice still holding the remnants of anger.

"Yup." She waited for him to explain.

He didn't. He didn't have to, she told herself. She wasn't a big fan of spilling her guts either.

But she wanted him to. And just how much she wanted him to, scared her. Scared her because it reminded her of how imbalanced, how undefined this thing between them was. She cared, but didn't want to. She trusted, but not completely.

He shifted again and she glanced at him, only to find him looking at her. But damn, it hurt to see it, the pain lingering in his eyes.

What was hurting him?

"I'm sorry," he said.

"Yeah, but you know when you're an ass to someone, it helps if you explain it."

Inhaling, he looked ready to spill when the sound of a door swishing open echoed into the night. Footsteps rang out.

"You two ready?" Burnett asked.

"Yeah," Della answered.

She got in the front and let Chase take the backseat.

"What all did you get?" Della asked, hoping to hide the awkward silence.

"Bite marks, a few hairs, and a confirmation that it was weres. Nothing that will hand the killers over on a silver platter, but it's a start. I forgot to ask, did you two discover anything when you compared notes on the vision?"

She saw Burnett glance up at the rearview mirror, as if checking on Chase. Did Burnett understand this more than her?

"Nothing new," Della said and resisted turning to check on Chase herself.

Burnett drove back to the FRU office. As they got out, Burnett said, "Be safe and don't stay out late," looking at Chase. "You are still recovering."

Chase nodded. As they moved around back before going into flight, she thought he might explain what had gone down at the morgue. He didn't.

She didn't say anything, but his silence hurt.

Five minutes later, Chase dropped down about a block short of his cabin, in a thick patch of trees. She landed with him, unsure why he'd chosen to walk the rest of the way.

The moment he landed, he started moving.

She set her pace even with his.

Their footsteps filtered through the night, accompanied by the scratchy sound of an occasional critter scurrying away. The cold air surrounded them, and the moon spilled down from dark sky, whispering through the trees like liquid lace.

Chase stopped walking. He took in a deep breath.

She stopped beside him, silently waiting.

"I don't like morgues," he said.

She looked up at him. She could see his eyes, and the pain still lingered in his pools of green. "I don't think anyone does."

He exhaled again. "I couldn't go to their funeral. I was supposed to have been dead too." He started walking.

And that's all it took for Della to understand. Hurt filled her chest. The image of young Chase saying goodbye to his family in a cold white room that smelled of astringent filled her mind and she had to swallow to keep the hurt from filling her eyes with tears.

"Eddie asked me if I wanted to see them for the last time. I said yes. The thought of never, ever seeing them again was . . . too much."

Della didn't even realize she was doing it, but she reached for his hand and took it in hers.

"Seeing their bodies was . . ." He inhaled again. "Mom was . . . missing an arm. Dad's body wasn't even all there. I couldn't even look at my sister. I remember wishing that Eddie hadn't saved me. That the fourth body that carried my name on his toe tag had really been me. I didn't want to live without them."

Della tightened her hold on his hand. "He should never have let you see that." Fury at her uncle filled her heart. Just what she needed, another reason to dislike him.

"No, I had to. I had to say goodbye. It wasn't Eddie's fault. He tried to prepare me."

"You can't prepare for that," Della said.

"I just . . . I haven't been to another morgue since then."

"I'm sorry," she said, and after several silent seconds passed she sensed he wasn't going to say anything else. But she didn't let go of his hand until they got to the cabin, and even then she hadn't stopped hurting for him.

Natasha met them outside on the porch. The porch light cast a halo around her. Dressed in a sleeveless yellow sundress, she looked clothed for the wrong season. She wore a smile, and her eyes, portraying her Chinese heritage much more than Della's, sparkled with happiness. No doubt the thought of going back home filled her cousin with joy.

Della hoped her cousin's adoptive mom would welcome her daughter home with open arms and not notice the changes that came with being a vampire. Had her cousin really given this thought?

"I'm so glad you came," Natasha said. "Liam and I decided to do some taste tests. And you two are going to be part of the experiment."

"Experiment?" Della asked.

"Yeah," her cousin said. "Since we've been turned, we haven't eaten real food. And for the next few weeks we're going to be living with our parents, so we decided to see which foods are still palatable. We've been cooking all day."

Della made a face. "I don't know . . ."

"She'll do it." Chase gave her a nudge up the steps.

"It'll be fun," Natasha said. "And you don't have to eat, just taste." She led the way inside.

The cabin smelled like a hodgepodge of different foods. Liam, dressed in jeans and a polo shirt, stood in the kitchen stirring something on the stove.

"Hey," Liam smiled. "My woman has me slaving away in the kitchen."

"Not true." Natasha moved in to kiss Liam. "I just took the first shift of cooking."

Her cousin appeared to be running on happy batteries. "We even have some adult beverages." She glanced at Chase. "I noticed that you had some beer in his fridge. So that tells me you still drink it, right?"

"Yeah," he said. "But it has to be really cold."

"Okay, beer's going in the freezer." She stuck some bottles in the freezer. "And Liam brought a bottle of wine from his mom's house."

Della made a face. "I didn't like the stuff before I was turned."

"Well, maybe it's changed." Natasha darted to the cabinet and pulled down four glasses.

Liam laughed. "I swear, she's been like this all day." His gaze turned to Della. "Especially since she heard you were coming. Someone's filled her tank up with happy juice."

"Well, yeah," Natasha said. "In a few days I'll have my life back, and then . . ."—she ran over and kissed Liam again—"you and I can start our own lives." She glanced back at Della. "Nothing's wrong with happy."

No, Della thought, except it made her realize she must have a hole in her own happy tank. Or maybe knowing she was responsible for having her dad arrested for murder just sucked the happy out of her.

Chase moved into the kitchen. "I don't think this cabin has smelled this good in a while."

"Yeah, but I'm told certain foods might smell good, but taste like shit," Liam said.

"True," Chase said.

Della watched Chase. This was his house, but he didn't seem to feel awkward at all as Liam and Natasha played hosts.

Chase's gaze met Della's and he smiled. The pain in his eyes had gone. Obviously, he didn't have a leak in his happy tank.

She glanced away.

Natasha looked at the food Liam placed on the table. "I'm curious if we will all like and hate the same things. Or if our tastes will vary."

Della moved in. "I think they vary. Some vampires at the camp love pizza. Me, not so much." She spotted a chocolate cake on a glass platter. "Once, Kylie was having a meltdown, she was eating the chocolate syrup with a spoon. I poured some into my blood and it went down smooth."

Natasha pulled out the wine cork, then filled four wineglasses.

"I like French onion soup," Della said. "It's one of the few foods I still enjoy."

Natasha handed Chase a glass of wine. "You first."

Chase raised it to look at it as if he were a wine connoisseur. His mind seemed to wander, and she could swear she spotted a flash of the earlier pain in his eyes.

"Snickerdoodle cookies," he said.

"What?" Della asked.

"My mom used to make them. She said they tasted like love. About six months ago, I saw them in a bakery. I ordered one. I thought it would taste bad. It didn't. Maybe it was nostalgia. I bought a dozen."

He sipped the wine.

"And? How is it?" Natasha asked Chase, and passed Della a glass.

"Well . . ." Chase smacked his lips. "It tastes like . . . sour crap." He turned to the sink and spit.

They all laughed and all agreed. Wine was a no-go.

The conversation went to Natasha going home. "As soon as Mom's over the shock, I'll bring Liam over to meet her."

"Yeah." Liam frowned.

Natasha rolled her eyes. "He's worried my family and friends won't like him because he's part African American. Duh, I'm half Chinese."

"It's not the same," Liam said, but he curled his arms around her.

"Not everyone is racist," Della said.

"But quite a few are," Liam said. "Still, I'm not going anywhere."

Liam brushed Natasha's hair to the side and kissed her neck. It was . . . somehow almost erotic. Just watching it sent tingles running down her spine.

"They are going to love you. Just like I do." Natasha arched her neck back and they kissed. One of those soft kisses that lasted a little too long to be in public.

Della cut her eyes away, and accidentally met Chase's gaze. The look he sent her was almost as disturbing at watching Natasha and Liam.

For the next few hours, they sat at Chase's large French farm table, sampled food, and laughed. At one point, Della realized that while they were four vampires sitting at this table, this was the most normal—human-normal—evening she'd had in a long time. There seemed to be something comforting about sitting around a dinner table with food.

The thought hit her that she probably hadn't tried hard enough to fit in with her parents. Instead of dreading dinners she should have found food she could stomach and cooked them for her family. She should have passed dinnertime encouraging conversation instead of feeling like a monster and hence coming off as one.

If only . . .

Her chest felt heavy when she wondered if she would get a second chance to make things smoother?

Della finally looked at her watch. It was after eight. "I'd better get back, or Burnett is gonna have a shit fit."

"Yeah," Chase said. "We'd better go. It's been fun. Thanks."

"No, thank you," Natasha said. "For everything—saving our lives, letting us stay here. It's been just what we needed."

"Well, you're welcome to come back anytime. Take the key with you," he said to Natasha, but he reached over and held a chicken finger to Della's lips.

Della was so surprised, she ate it. And it wasn't half bad. Then Chase ran his finger over her lip.

Della felt the blush hit her cheeks, and she realized Liam and

Natasha were watching and smiling. Didn't Chase know she could feed herself?

"Aren't you going to move back in?" Natasha asked.

"Not for a while. I think I'll hang out at Shadow Falls."

"What?" Della shook her head. She'd thought he'd been staying at the school because Liam and Natasha were here. "This place is ten times better."

"Yeah, but Shadow Falls has something this place doesn't." Natasha grinned.

"No," Della said. "You've seen the cabins there."

"It has you," Natasha answered.

Della glanced at Chase. He didn't deny it. And he winked at her. Winked?

First he feeds her and then he winks at her?

"You're crazy," she said.

"Here's to being crazy," Liam said and picked up a glass of blood for a toast.

They walked out on the porch. Natasha pulled Della to the side. "Is my mom . . . ? Do you still see my mom?"

Della nodded, and decided not to mention that Holiday wanted to perform an exorcism to send her packing. "Yeah."

"Can you tell her that I'm happy? Really happy."

"I'll tell her."

Her cousin hugged her. "Chase is a good guy," she whispered in her ear. "Stop fighting it."

Della didn't answer that, but the thought hit her that if she *was* fighting it, she was doing a piss-poor job of it. Every damn day he got closer . . . not even just physically, but emotionally. And what was this feeding-her crap?

She glanced over at the guys.

Chase shook Liam's hand. "Hey," Chase said. "I just noticed your shoes. Are those the Nike foamposite shoes?"

"A knockoff, I'm sure," Liam said. "My mom got them. She couldn't afford the real thing."

Della looked down at his bright blue shoes with weird soles and . . . bam. Just like that her world flipped. She wasn't even standing. But lying flat on her back on a . . . cold, bloody, concrete floor.

"Della?" she heard Chase say her name. "You okay?"

"Yeah." She blinked and things slowly came into focus. His face, and then the missing piece of puzzle just slipped into place. "We gotta go."

She waved, jumped off the porch, and started jogging.

Chase kept up with her. "What is it?"

"I know what I forgot about the vision."

"What?"

"Shoes." Della continued to run.

"Shoes?" His footfalls fell even with hers in the darkness.

"One of the killers had on a pair of very strange shoes. Red, and they looked like snakeskin. I could be wrong, but for some reason I don't think a badass were would wear a pair of knockoffs. He probably bought them. And if I'm right and they are as expensive as I think they are, then there may be only a few places that sell them. If we can find out who sells them, we might be able to find out who bought them. And we'll have at least one of the killer's names."

She took off in flight, dodging the tree limbs and trying to hurry to get back to do her Internet search. While it wasn't about her father's case, it still felt good to think she was closer to catching Mr. and Mrs. Chi's killers.

Chapter Thirty

Della and Chase landed in the parking lot of the school and walked through the gate. Voices, laughter, and music came from the dining hall. It smelled like a pizza party. Having stomached more food than she'd eaten in weeks, she headed straight to the trail. Chase moved right beside her. Occasionally, his forearm brushed against her shoulder.

Was he purposely doing that?

While her mind worked on the thought of identifying that mystery shoe, her heart seemed stuck on the things she'd learned about Chase tonight. He'd seen his parents' bodies in a morgue and it still hurt him. He occasionally drank cold beer. He associated snickerdoodles with love, and was staying at Shadow Falls just to be close to her.

She recalled holding his hand, offering him emotional support after he'd told her why he'd wigged out at the morgue. She remembered waking up in his bed next to him, being overjoyed that he was alive. She even recalled how it felt that brief second when he'd fed her that damn chicken finger.

Then came the reminder of how she'd sort of been happy when he'd been embarrassed being in his underwear around Holiday, but not around her.

And that last thought led to her remembering how good he had looked in his underwear. All that skin showing. The muscles rippling down his torso.

Oh, hell!

Remembering all that stirred up things she didn't want stirred.

She thought of Natasha and Liam. She'd bet those two were already in their underwear, or perhaps naked and in each other's arms.

Could she ever find that . . . again?

She took in a deep breath and repeated two words in her head. *Not now.*

Maybe.

Perhaps.

She might at least entertain the idea after she got her dad out of trouble.

And found Mr. and Mrs. Chi's killers.

When she trusted that what she felt was . . . real, and not just because of shared blood.

She glanced at Chase. He glanced at her. He smiled.

Her heart dipped.

It hit then. She'd felt this before, before she'd known he was still lying. She'd put on black underwear thinking . . .

Would she . . . could she trust this . . . trust him again?

Then she pushed all that aside. Why in Hades was she thinking about this?

Two weeks.

"Have you come up with a plan for tomorrow?" Della asked.

"A plan?" He sounded as if he'd been lost in his own thoughts.

"Where are we going first? Should we see if we can find this so-called girlfriend or should we go check out the addresses of the Douglas Stones?"

"I haven't thought about it yet."

She got a feeling the reason was because, like her, he'd been thinking of other things.

They arrived at the path that led to her cabin, and she started down it. Chase spoke up, "Do you want to come to my place and do this? My computer is ten times faster than the one at your cabin."

The thought of being alone with him—alone with no worries of Miranda or Kylie appearing—sounded dangerous.

"I like my computer."

"You like it?" He looked confused.

"Yeah," she snapped. "And if you ever try to feed me again, you'll be sorry." She took off.

Three minutes later, Della was on the computer at the small desk in her kitchen. She did a search on expensive snakeskin tennis shoes.

"Bingo!" She glanced at Chase standing behind her. "That's them."

"Okay." He looked impressed. "Now run a search to find out where they are sold in Houston."

As she typed in the question, she felt him lean in to see the computer. His hand came down on the back of her chair and his knuckles touched her shoulder. Tingles slow-danced down her spine and she misspelled "Houston" three times.

She would have snapped at him to move his hand, but then he'd know. Know that his touch did crazy—and wonderful—things to her skin.

Finally, she typed it in right. She waited for the computer to search.

"See, your computer is slow." His words stirred in her hair.

"What's a few more seconds?" Right then her computer dinged with a new email.

She ignored it and waited for the computer to finish its search.

It finally spit out the information. Della pushed the thoughts of Chase's touch away.

"Four places." She glanced back with a smile. "And look!" She pointed to the screen. "This one is about a mile from the park where the murders happened."

"Do you want to call Burnett?" Chase asked.

"You do it," Della said. "I'm going to make a list of these addresses, so we'll have them for tomorrow."

While she collected data on her slow computer, she listened to Chase give Burnett the lowdown. More than once, Chase gave her credit for finding the lead. Once or twice, she felt him staring at her. She looked back and found she was right. He leaned against the fridge, looking so at home there, his phone to his ear, but his eyes on her.

"You got anything on the gang or the number Sam gave you?" Chase asked.

Della heard Burnett's answer. "Not yet."

Turning back, she got the rest of the addresses copied to a Word document and then hit print. While she waited for the computer to wake up her printer, she jumped over to her email to see if she had anything from her sister.

Chase hung up and she heard his steps moving to her. He leaned over her shoulder. "Burnett said to email him a list of the stores."

As she opened her new email tab, and copied and pasted the info into the document to send, she felt Chase breathing down her neck again. That soft whisper of his breath made her mind go to mush.

She hit send. Or tried to. The computer had to think about that as well. Trying not to react to Chase's nearness, she stared at the screen without seeing anything. Then she felt Chase edge closer and heard him inhale.

"Are you smelling my hair?" she asked, hoping her tone came off as irritated, even though right now, the thing that irritated her was her lack of irritation.

In her mind's eye, she saw Liam brush back Natasha's hair and kiss her neck.

"Yeah," he said, and his smile came across in that one word.

"Then stop," she said.

"But it smells so good."

She felt him sweep her hair to one side, just like Liam had done to Natasha. The brush of his fingers felt like feathers.

"And your hair is so soft."

He pressed his lips against the back of her neck. "Your skin tastes . . . sweet."

She closed her eyes. "You should . . . probably stop."

"Probably?" he asked and then said, "How about if I do this instead?" His lips shifted to kiss the side of her neck, sending all kinds of wonderful tingles down her back, her arms, to her breasts, and even lower.

"Stop," she said, a little firmer.

He stopped, but he didn't move away. "Why, Della?"

"I'm not ready for this. I'm still . . ." *I put on my black underwear for you last time and look what happened.*

He shot up. Something about how quick he pulled away, felt . . . wrong. She looked back over her shoulder.

"Not ready? Because of him?"

She just stared. "What?"

"He wants to talk to you," he said.

"What are you talking about?"

"The email. Your damn email! Look at your screen," he snapped. "You've got three emails from Steve. All with the same subject line. "'We need to talk.' What the hell does he need to talk to you about?"

She frowned, faced the computer, and clicked off the screen.

"Oh, hell," he said. "I'll see you in the morning." He started for the door.

She let him get halfway out the door before she spoke. "Don't," she snapped.

He swung around.

His bright green eyes expressed his anger. "Don't what, Della?"

"Don't be like that," she said.

"Like what?" he asked.

"Like . . . like I'm doing something wrong. Like . . . you're jealous." *Like you have a right to be jealous.*

"I'm not jealous," he said and lifted his arms behind his head, and the muscles in his arms bulged.

She was so caught up in his muscles that she almost missed that little hiccup of his heart. And she wouldn't have wanted to do that. Because this was the first time she heard his heart jump to a lie.

So the amazing Chase occasionally couldn't hide the truth. She liked knowing that.

He must have felt or heard his heart skip, because his expression tightened. "Okay, I'm jealous. But how would you feel if we turned this upside down?"

"Upside down?" she asked.

"How would you feel if I told you Cindy was calling me and asking me to meet up with her?"

She stood up and before she could decide what to say, she'd said it. "That depends. Who's Cindy?"

"She's nobody. Just a name, just a name of a girl. A girl who wants me for my body."

For some reason that struck her as funny. She felt her lips twitch. "You've got girls wanting you for your body?" *Not that I blame them.*

He stared at her for several seconds and she saw the anger fade from his eyes. "Of course I do. Look at me."

A laugh slipped from her lips. "You don't have an ego problem, do you?"

"No," he said, smiling, but then sighed. "Just a Della problem."

He walked closer and stood right in front of her. He stared right into her eyes. "I want to touch you. I want . . . what Natasha and Liam have. I want to kiss you when I want to kiss you, I want to check and make sure you've got on the panties with the right day of the week, I want to make love to you, I want to wake up with you in bed like I did this morning. Do you have any idea how good that felt?"

She looked away and in her heart she heard those two words from earlier. *Not now.*

She faced him. "Not now."

"Why? Why not now? If it's not Steve, then what?"

"Because I don't trust—"

"Damn it!" He held up his hands in frustration. "I've done everything I could to show you that . . . that you can trust me. I've quit the council, I've answered all your questions. I haven't lied. Not once, Della."

"It's not you I don't trust." The moment she said it, she knew it wasn't completely true and her heart noted it. "Maybe it is you a little, but it's mostly this I don't trust." Her heart didn't disagree with that statement.

He shook his head as if puzzled.

"This." She waved a hand between them.

"What's this?"

"This . . . the feeling. The chills. The thrills. And the fear. All of it, Chase. You give me your blood and suddenly I'm obsessed with you. How do you know any of this is real? And what if you wake up one day and it's not there anymore?"

"You don't trust love?"

Della shook her head. "Hell, no, I don't trust love. Love's kicked my ass too many times to trust it."

"You can't—"

"Yes, I can," she snapped. "I can do anything I want." Her chest felt heavy, achy. "But we aren't talking about love, Chase. Why are you even throwing that demon into the mix? We're talking about a bond. A chemical reaction. Something that nobody can even define, that happens when one Reborn gives another Reborn blood. It hasn't been going on long enough for anyone to know if it really lasts."

"Della, I know—" He stopped talking and waved to the door.

"No, you don't."

He put his hand to his lips.

Della heard the thump on the porch.

Burnett walked in. "I said send me the names—"

His gaze flipped from Chase to Della. "What's wrong?"

"Nothing," they both said in unison and then the sound of two hearts skipping beats sounded.

Burnett just raised a brow. "Okay. But can you please give me the names of the stores that sell this high-priced tennis shoe?"

"I sent it." Della walked to her computer. Where she saw it hadn't gone out. "I'm sending it, now."

Della heard some more footsteps moving down the path outside. Then Miranda's voice echoed.

Burnett turned and walked out.

Kylie and Miranda walked in.

Everyone just looked at everyone and it just got more awkward.

Then Kylie and Miranda shrugged at each other as if agreeing something wasn't right.

Hell, no, it wasn't right.

"Uh, well, I guess I'll see you in the morning," Chase said to Della. "At seven?"

"Goodbye," she snapped, her chest so tight it felt like her heart might crack.

She waited until he was out of earshot and then she turned to her two best friends, who stood there waiting patiently for an explanation.

An explanation that they were not going to get.

"I'm going to bed. I don't want to commiserate. I don't want a diet soda. I don't want to explain what just happened, or why it feels like the awkward fairy just came down here and pissed all over the room."

She'd almost reached her door when Miranda spoke up.

"But I wanted to ask you about Perry. Did you talk to him tonight? Do you still think I should go out with Shawn? Can't we just talk about it?"

Her voice was just pathetic enough to send Della over the emotional edge. She swung around. All the guilt she'd felt when she'd spoken to Perry earlier came bubbling back up inside her.

"Yes, I talked to him, and no!"

"No what?" Miranda asked.

"No, I'm not gonna talk about it. As a matter of fact, I'm sorry I ever gave you any advice about Perry or Shawn. Don't listen to me. Never listen to me! Never! Never! Never!" She moved her arms up and down, feeling as if she looked like a bird trying to fly, but she couldn't stop herself.

"Why?" Miranda asked, staring at Della as if she'd lost her mind. And maybe she had.

"Because," Della snapped.

"That's not a reason. You are one of my best friends. Why shouldn't I listen to you?"

"Because I'm an idiot," Della spouted out. "If advice comes out of this mouth"—she pointed to her lips—"don't listen. Don't just walk away. Run. Fast. Because I don't know shit about love, or about romance, or about the difference between a bond and love. I'm eff-ing clueless! Clueless!" she repeated.

She took two steps and then swung back around. "And . . . I'm changing shampoo, so my hair doesn't smell like this . . . and . . . and if Cindy wants his body, she can have it!"

She stormed to her room and slammed her door.

Unfortunately, she slammed it too hard and it fell off its hinges and crashed on the wooden floor.

Growling, she turned around, propped it up against the door-way, then dropped face first onto the bed.

"Who's Cindy?" she heard Miranda ask.

Della moaned and pulled a pillow over her head.

"Wouldn't have a clue." Kylie's voice still got through the pil-low foam.

"Should we try to talk to her?" Miranda asked.

"Nope," Kylie said. "I think she just needs to stew."

And as Della lay in bed, that's exactly what she did for the next few hours.

Stew.

Chapter Thirty-one

She still didn't trust him. Chase rolled over for about the fifth time and tried to mold the pillow to fit his head. He couldn't sleep. His pillow smelled like Della and he recalled waking up and seeing her so close. He tossed his pillow to the other side of the room. He rolled over, only to realize the damn mattress smelled like her too. He ran a hand over it, where she'd slept beside him while he'd been unconscious.

Exhaling, he ran a palm over his face, only to realize that even his hand smelled like her.

With clarity he recalled that she'd held it on the walk to his cabin. While her support had felt awesome, the fact that he'd let his emotions get the better of him at the morgue left him feeling weak. And that was the last way he wanted her to see him.

It might be wrong, but he wanted to be strong for her, wanted to be there for her to lean on. Not that Della Tsang did a lot of leaning. But when she did, he wanted it to be on him.

It had been four years since the . . . morgue. One would think he'd have moved past it.

He closed his eyes and pushed away the images of his family in the cold white room and pulled up the images of them skiing in

Colorado. His dad kissing his mother. His mom serving them snickerdoodle cookies. His sister laughing.

Happy times.

Trying to hold on to the good thoughts to chase away the bad, he recalled how it had felt to sign the FRU contract today. A step toward his future. Sitting up, he turned on the light and grabbed the FRU badge Burnett had given him. He needed to get his mind back on the investigation.

Chase snatched his phone. It was midnight. A perfect time to call Leo. He found the guard's phone number.

"I thought you'd have had enough of Hell's Pit," Leo answered.

"But it's such a charming place," Chase said with sarcasm.

"Kid, I thought you were a goner. I seriously don't know how you came out of that room with any of your limbs still attached."

"I'm fond of my limbs," Chase said.

"Apparently," Leo said. "If you're calling for another shot at Pope, you're going to be disappointed."

"I'm not," Chase said. "But why would I be disappointed?"

"The ugly son of a bitch met his maker. Another were broke free last night."

"Did he take out several other prisoners, as well?" Chase asked.

"Nope. For some reason that were had it out for Pope."

Chase stored that info away. "Look, I was sort of out of it when I left your place the other night. Are you sure it was Kirk you spoke with about Stone?"

"That was Kirk who came out to get you, right?" Leo asked.

"Yes."

"Well, now that I think about it, I don't think it was him, but the old fart."

"Powell?" Chase asked.

"Yeah. The elderly dude."

Chase found a little relief that it hadn't been Kirk, Eddie's good friend.

. . .

The first thing Della did that next morning was go to her computer, pull up her email, and send Steve a message.

It was simple. Short. Two words.

Not now!

While Della was trying to put her bedroom door back on its hinges, Kylie walked in looking sleepy and wearing light pink PJs.

"Want some help?" the chameleon asked.

"If you don't mind," Della said, and instantly felt bad for going bat-shit crazy on her friends.

"Here," Kylie said and caught the door. "I'll hold it up and you put the bolt in."

In only seconds, they had the door up; only one of the hinges had actually broken, so while it wouldn't close, at least it didn't look broken.

"You okay?" Kylie asked, just like Della knew she would.

"No, but I'm getting used to faking it," she answered. "And I hear Chase walking this way, so I don't have time to elaborate on just how screwed up I am."

"He's walking you to breakfast?" Kylie asked. "You're gonna be early."

"No, I'm skipping school to help with my dad's case." She inhaled. "They set the trial for two weeks. Less than two weeks now." Saying it made the air in her lungs hitch. What if they didn't get anything? What if he actually got convicted?

"Sorry," Kylie said. "Maybe tonight we can grab some Diet Cokes and have a talk?"

"Maybe," Della answered in a low voice, hearing Chase get closer. "I'm still trying to figure out how I feel, and I don't know if I can explain it without having another hissy fit like I did last night."

Kylie bit back a smile. "Well, it was entertaining to watch."

"Don't remind me." Della started out the door.

The knob still in her hand, she saw Chase, standing at the bottom of the steps, his wide-shoulder frame backlit with the early-morning sun.

Instead of the jeans and T-shirt she was accustomed to seeing him in, he had on a black suit and a light blue chambray button-down shirt underneath—all of which fit him really well and had her recalling some of the hot models on a commercial for men's clothing.

Then for some crazy reason his pristine attire reminded her of things she would probably miss in this life. Things she'd lost forever when she left the human world behind. Things like going to the prom or those silly Valentine's dances. Getting a corsage and posing for those stupid pictures in front of some wall of flowers.

She hadn't thought she'd wanted those things, but seeing Chase looking so sophisticated in his suit, she wished she'd been given the choice. Wished it wasn't wrong for her to want to run her fingers under that suit coat and feel the six-pack and ripples of muscles. She wished her father's trial wasn't preventing her from finding something close to happiness.

After another head-to-toe glance of the man in black, she felt underdressed in her jeans and powder blue scoop-neck blouse. Still standing with the door open, she considered dashing in and changing into her black pants.

"Don't you leave without telling me who Cindy is!" Miranda called out from her bedroom.

Okay, nothing wrong with jeans.

Della shut the door with a little more force than needed. If Chase's half-assed smile and arched brow were any indication, he'd heard the witch.

It was a friggin' great start to her day.

Cindy? So Della had mentioned their conversation to her friend, huh? From what little bit he knew about girls with their friends, having her mention him was much more desirable than not mentioning him.

Which was the reason I was upset that she'd mentioned Steve to her human friend.

He pushed that thought aside and decided to focus on the positive and not his idiotic jealousy. He was spending the entire day with Della.

The positive also being his final conclusion about what she'd said last night. He heard her voice in his head: *We aren't talking about love, Chase.* He planned to talk to her about that, too.

He watched her stand at the door in a bit of a stupor and noted the way she eyed him. He'd felt kind of ridiculous dressed in the suit, but Della's appreciative gaze changed that.

"Good morning," he said, standing a little taller.

"Morning," she said, no doubt purposely leaving off the good.

"You're not going to say anything?" he asked.

"About?"

"My suit?"

"It fits you," she said.

He almost laughed. "Burnett wants to see us in his office before we take off." He waited for her to move down the steps.

"Does he have news?"

"He said it wasn't earth-shattering."

Frowning, she shut the door and moved down the steps, all the while working hard to ignore him—and, yeah, he could tell she was doing that. And while she did that, he worked hard to study her, without it being obvious.

Right away he noted the dark lines circling her eyes. Those light half-moons were almost hidden by her long bottom lashes, but he noticed. And he'd known her long enough to know it was a sure sign of a sleepless night.

He probably hadn't slept much better, but he didn't wear the evidence like she did.

Had she been thinking about him?

"I brought the addresses to the stores," Della said.

"I think that's part of what Burnett wants to talk about," Chase said, in a small way dreading telling him about Pope and what he'd learned.

When they got to the office, Chase bolted up the steps and opened the door for Della.

She rolled her eyes at his act of chivalry.

"Please, don't start pretending to be a gentleman just because you're wearing a suit."

"When have I not been a gentleman?"

"The first time that comes to mind is when you climbed up the stall in the girl's bathroom when I was trying to pee. But just give me a few minutes, and I'm sure I could come up with a top-ten list."

He laughed. "You've got the memory of an elephant." He walked in.

"And you have the manners of a baboon," she countered.

"The zoo's this way," Burnett's voice spoke from Holiday's office.

Della frowned. Biting back a smile, Chase followed her into the office. Holiday, positioned behind her desk, nodded and Chase felt his muscles tighten. Ever since she'd threatened him, or rather his male parts, he'd avoided her. Burnett sat on the edge of the desk with his daughter in his arms.

The baby squealed when they walked in and held out her arms. "I think someone wants you." Burnett held out the child toward Della.

Della took the baby from Burnett. "She has good taste."

Right then the child squealed again and stretched out her arms toward Chase.

"Yup," Chase said and laughed.

"I take that back," Della muttered.

Holiday chuckled. "You look . . . hot, Chase."

"Excuse me?" Burnett said, in humor.

"Thank you," Chase said, his uneasiness lessening. "And it fits, too." He shot Della a quick glance.

"Here." Della held out the baby. Chase took a step back. "I don't know how to hold it."

"It?" Della and Holiday said at the same time.

"I mean her."

Della made a face at him and then turned toward Burnett. The child looked at her father and started flapping her arms up and down. "Dada dada."

"Did you hear that?" Burnett smiled bigger than Chase ever remembered. "She's saying daddy."

"She's just making sounds," Holiday said.

"You're just jealous she said daddy before mama."

"I am not," Holiday said, but she looked it. "That didn't sound like daddy, did it?" She looked at Chase.

"No . . . I didn't . . . I don't think so."

"See?" Holiday laughed.

"Not to take the spotlight off our little princess here, but . . ." Della focused on Burnett and set the child on her hip. Despite seeming unsure of herself, the ease with which she handled the baby surprised Chase. She continued, "Did you get anything from the bar?"

Chase noted the smile in Burnett's eyes fade. "The number Sam gave is a throwaway phone. No one ever answered."

"Could he know Sam was caught?" Della asked.

"We don't know that, but it's a possibility."

"And I suppose he didn't show up at the bar, either?" Della asked, her tone mirroring Chase's frustrations.

"He didn't, but we did ask around and confirmed Sam's story."

"The gang?" Chase asked. "You got something?"

"We're still confirming some things," Burnett said. "Word on the street is the gang is new here. But it has roots in France. Most of the members are mixed species—meaning their powers are limited, so we're not considering it a huge threat at this time."

Burnett's direct eye contact with him seemed to mean he didn't think Chase should be concerned about staying here. Chase wasn't so sure he agreed.

"So Sam was a member?" Della asked.

"No, but Stone might have been trying to recruit him." Burnett's phone dinged; he checked it and then looked up. "I have something this morning to cover, but I wanted to go with you to the shoe stores. So check out a few of those addresses, and see if you can run down Stone's girlfriend. We'll meet up somewhere to hit the shoe stores together later."

"Got it," Chase said.

Della handed Burnett the baby.

Burnett took the child and made holding something so small and fragile look easy. "And remember, one hint of danger and you walk away and call me."

"We know," Della said.

Burnett frowned. "And don't cause a mess for me to clean up."

"Don't worry," Chase said.

"Right," Burnett said. "And in case you don't know, by 'clean up' I mean: no breaking and entering, no trespassing, no using excess force. You have your badge?" He looked at Chase.

Chase nodded.

"Everything you do reflects back on us. For all intents and purposes, you are to appear like humans. No jumping off tall buildings or bench-pressing cars. Keep your fangs in. You understand?"

"Yes." Chase resented the insinuation that he would screw up—but he knew better than to argue. Then he remembered: "I spoke with Leo last night. The guard at the prison."

"And?" Burnett asked, and his eyes widened with interest.

"He said that after seeing Kirk when he came to get me, he realized he had gotten him mixed up with one of the other councilmen. Councilman Powell."

"So someone's hiding something?"

Chase nodded, trying not to feel as if he were betraying the council. And he shouldn't, because if any of them knew about Stone, they had betrayed Eddie.

"Let me ask you something," Burnett said. "Since you still have connections with the prison and some of the council, what are the chances of getting them to transfer Pope into one of our facilities so we might question him?"

"Impossible," Chase said. "Leo told me last night that Pope was killed."

"Convenient," Burnett said.

"I wish I could disagree," Chase said.

Burnett nodded. "Well, you two get going, but I mean it: don't create any shit."

Hannah bounced up and down. "Chit. Chit. Chit!" she squealed.

Holiday glared at her husband. "I'm gonna wash your mouth out with soap for a month of Sundays!"

"Bye," Della said, shooting Burnett a parting smile, and walked out. Chase was right behind her. They laughed.

As soon as they were out of earshot, Della asked, "Do you think they killed Pope because he talked to you?"

"I . . . I'm suspicious," Chase said.

"So what are you going to do?"

"I'm trying to figure that out," he said.

Chapter Thirty-two

When they got to Chase's Camaro, he pulled his keys out. "You want to drive?"

He remembered her driving his car and getting caught speeding by the cops. The memory almost brought a smile to his lips.

"That's okay," she said and jumped into the car without opening the door.

And she landed on a bag in the front seat.

She pulled it out from under her and when she did a twelve-pack of hot dogs fell out.

"What's this?" she asked as he got behind the wheel.

"Oh, in case we meet up with trouble," he said.

"What?"

He ignored her question. "Do you mind the top down or are you worried about your hair?" When she didn't answer he added, "I still have some hair things in my glove compartment."

She made a face and dropped the hot dogs on the floorboard. "I don't care."

He slid the keys in the ignition, sat back in the seat a bit, then looked at her. "Yes, you do."

"Do what?" she asked.

"You care. And I don't mean about your hair." He held up his hand, and before she could argue, he continued, "I know, I heard everything you said last night. About you not thinking this is real, or that it's not love. But after I left, I realized what else you said."

Her brows pulled together. "What else did I say?"

He reached between the seats and got his sunglasses. Slipping them on, he glanced at her. "How did you put it? Oh, yeah: the chills, the thrills. Then there was something about you being obsessed with me."

He slid the glasses down his nose, and looked at her over the rims.

Her wide eyes and slacked mouth told him she was searching for a comeback but couldn't find one. Shocking—Della always had a wisecrack. He loved that about her.

He continued, "I just want you to know, I'm okay with that. It's a damn good start. And I know this because I feel the same way. The difference between you and me is that I know it's the real thing."

She still didn't say anything, so he went on, "Probably because I wasn't completely honest with you in the beginning. You need time to trust this, to trust love and to trust me, and I get that. And I'll be here when you finally do." He pushed the glasses up and started the car.

Forty-five minutes later they parked in front of the first house on the list of Stone residences. Della look around. This was a not-so-nice house in a not-so-nice neighborhood. A dog, which looked to be a cross between a pit bull and a Tasmanian devil, was chained to a metal pipe stuck in the ground.

Chase glanced at her. "Meet Trouble."

Della recalled the hot dogs and couldn't help but grin.

Then she looked around. The house next to it had a CONDEMNED sign in the yard. she glanced up and down the street. The place looked like a great location for a meth lab. But was it a great place for a vampire on the run? Perhaps. She sure as hell hoped so.

Two weeks.

When Chase cut off the engine, the dog rose up and let out a low, serious growl.

"Friendly sort," Della said and realized Chase could probably say the same thing about her. She hadn't spoken since they'd pulled out of the parking lot. What could she say? Oh, she wanted to tell him he was so slick that his own bullshit just slid right off of him. She wanted to accuse him of thinking he looked like hot stuff in that black suit and dark sunglasses. But he did look hot, and she knew him well enough to know he was being sincere. Her only answer was . . . *Not now.* And she kept that one to herself.

"Get the hot dogs," he said.

"You're gonna get past him by feeding him hot dogs?" Della asked.

"It's better than what I fed him three weeks ago."

"What did you feed him?" she asked.

"A bite of my ass." He chuckled. "I thought I could rub his belly and make a friend."

"He bit you?" Della couldn't help but laugh.

"He didn't get much," Chase said and reached behind to touch his butt.

They got out of the car.

"So this house belongs to one of the Stones you've already investigated?" she asked, catching the scent of garbage and seeing the two overflowing metal cans on the front porch.

"Yeah."

"Remember, Burnett has ruled them out and thinks we should move to the new list of Stones."

"He also said for me to follow my gut. I feel as if I might have missed something. I want to circle back around, just to be certain."

The dog barked, calling their attention again. He scratched at the ground like a bull ready to charge. Then he bolted toward them. The canine's lip curled and exposed teeth, the hair on the back of its neck stood straight up, and drool oozed from its jowls. He got closer. Then closer.

Shit! How long was that chain?

Della was about to do a quick step back when Chase said, "It's okay."

Then, unfortunately, or fortunately depending whose side you were on, about a foot from where they stood, the dog ran out of chain. When he hit his limit, he was yanked up in the air and landed with a thud on ground. He didn't stay down long.

"I think he was inbred a few too many times," Chase said.

"Poor thing," she said and meant it. Most animals were stupid or aggressive due to how their owners treated them.

"Open the hot dogs."

"Why don't we just fly over him to the porch? No one is out here." She waved around.

"Two reasons," he said. "One, we're supposed to appear like humans, remember?"

"I don't think Burnett meant—"

"Two," he interrupted, "that chain reaches the door. How do you think I got my ass bit?" He rubbed his backside. "Here's what we're going to do. You're gonna throw the Oscar Mayers, and while he's munching on them I'm going to pull out that pole and reposition it so his chain can't reach the porch."

"And if he's not interested in the hot dogs?"

"Then I'll try rubbing his belly again." He smiled. "I rub a mean belly. Just ask Baxter. Anytime you need—"

"My belly is fine." She tossed a half of a hot dog and then looked at Chase. "Don't let him bite you."

"Good plan." Chase took off. In record speed, he pulled the metal pipe from the ground and moved it closer to the dog to reposition it.

The dog, obviously feeling the chain's movement, turned toward Chase and growled. Della threw another wiener.

The animal was so hungry, he forgot Chase and went hot dog hunting.

Chase pushed the metal pipe in the ground. "Done." He bolted back.

Della tossed the rest of the wieners to the hungry animal and then walked across the yard to the porch. On the front door, hung crooked, was a sign: IF TROUBLE, MY DOG, DOESN'T SCARE YOU, MY SHOTGUN MIGHT.

She looked at Chase. "You think you could offer to rub the shotgun's belly? I fed all the hot dogs to Trouble," she said in almost a whisper.

He grinned.

"Did you actually talk to someone here last time you came?"

"Yeah, human, in his late fifties, about as friendly as the dog. When I asked if he was Douglas Stone he said no and that he was just staying here with a friend. He was lying. Thing is I don't know if the lie was about his name or staying here with a friend. Or both."

Della took a deep breath to see if she got a trace of a vampire scent. She didn't, but with the thick stench of garbage, it could be hidden.

Chase tilted his head to the side, listening to see if anyone was inside. Della did the same.

"TV's on in a back room," Chase said.

Della felt a thrill shoot through her. If this was Douglas Stone, her dad's ordeal could be over.

"You wanna knock and I'll go around back in case he tries to run?" she asked.

"Nah, if we hear him leave out the back, you go left and I'll go right."

She looked at the peephole in the middle of the door. "If it's the same guy, he might not answer to you. Why don't you stand over there and let me do the talking. If I get him to admit his name is Douglas Stone, then we know it's not our guy, right?"

"Yeah." Chase moved to a window a few feet from the door and peered in. Then he glanced back at her. "I can see the entryway from here. If he really has a shotgun, I'll say move. You do it."

"You think I should?" she asked with sarcasm and then motioned for him to move back a little. "Don't let him see you."

Della banged on the door. And listened.

When no one answered, she banged again.

"What the hell do you want?" someone yelled from inside.

Chapter Thirty-three

Chase stood at the very edge of the window, hoping he could see the homeowner, but the homeowner couldn't see him.

"He's coming," Chase said in barely a whisper. "Not armed." Chase tightened his eyes to catch the guy's pattern on his forehead. "Human." Chase was pretty sure it was the same guy he'd spoken with before.

"Go the hell away," the man yelled out, but he kept coming.

"I just need a few minutes of your time," Della said, and Chase noted she'd put a slightly flirty tone to her voice.

"Who are you?" The man put his eye to the peephole in the door.

"I'm a house flipper and wanted to ask you about a few of the empty houses on the street." Damn, Della could come up with a story quickly.

"You can flip me anytime," Chase heard the lowlife mutter and saw him run a hand through his hair and suck in a beer belly that appeared to have taken years to grow.

He opened the door. Chase eased closer, in case the lowlife put a finger on Della, but he kept against the wall where the guy couldn't see him.

"Hi," Della said as soon as the door creaked open. "My name's

Charlotte Nance." She smiled and tilted her head to the side like a cute puppy. "I'm interested in some of the properties on the street and wondered if you could tell me who owns them."

"You look kinda young to be in real estate," he said.

"My curse. My mama says I'll be happy about it in a few years."

"Your mama is right, honey. Besides, I like 'em young."

Chase saw a muscle in Della's cheek start to twitch. Something told him that could mean trouble.

"Are any of these houses for sale?" she asked, still managing to keep her voice flirty.

"Well, uh, there were a couple of druggies living in that one, but I think they were renting it. Seemed to take off about two months ago. No one has even been around to mow the yard. The one next door has been condemned. It caught fire last year and no one's even touched it."

The dog barked, and Chase saw the man stick his head out, probably wondering why the animal wasn't doing his job. "You might want to come inside. My dog eats pretty young things like you for lunch. I, on the other hand, don't bite. Not too hard, anyway."

Chase bit back the desire to show the guy how hard he could bite. Della hesitated for a second. The muscle in her cheek continued to twitch.

She put a smile on her face, but not a real one. "Are you the owner of this property? Mr. uh . . . I'm sorry, I didn't catch your name."

"Stone," he said. "But call me Doug. All my lady friends do."

Yeah, Chase bet the guy had a lot of those.

"Oh, well, that's okay. If you don't have the names . . ."

"I bet I have 'em in my address book." He poked his head out again, but thankfully didn't look Chase's way. "You here all by your lonesome, sweetheart?"

Something about that question put Chase on instant alert. He almost stepped out, but Della cut him a glance and shook her head.

The man's hand reached out, but Della moved faster. She bolted back and his grubby little hand missed her by an inch.

"Don't play hard to get," the man said. "I got a few beers and I could use some company."

"Sorry. Gotta find a house to flip." She started to walk off—none too quickly—and she sent Chase a look that said she had this.

The idiot reached for her. Della swung around and with one quick lift of her knee, brought the guy down on all fours.

No excess force had been Burnett's rule. And it hadn't been excess, just a direct hit. The guy rose up, but with his hands cupping his privates, his mouth wide open, he had yet to make a sound. No doubt, however, he was gonna be singing soprano when he found his voice.

"Sorry," Della said, sneering down at the man. "I think I'm allergic to perverts. I get involuntary knee jerks whenever one is around."

They walked back to the car, keeping to the far left, out of the dog's reach. "Remind me," Chase said smiling, "to never upset your allergies."

"We got lucky," Chase said twenty minutes later and followed behind a car into a gated apartment building complex. Della looked around. It wasn't high rent, but it looked decent. He parked right against the building and hit a button that brought the top up and over.

"I didn't realize something until now," Chase said.

"What?" Della asked, still scanning the area.

"This apartment is only a couple of miles from where Pope told me Stone's girlfriend lived."

"So this is another one that you already visited, right?"

"Yeah. Hand me those files under your seat. I can't remember why I dismissed him as a suspect." Leaning forward, he looked around. "If I remember correctly, a woman answered the door."

"And she was human?" Della asked as she pulled a folder from under the seat.

"Yeah." He took the file and opened it, scanning his old notes. "Okay, I remember now. The girlfriend claimed her boyfriend had run to the store for some parts to fix one of the other apartments. She said he was the handyman of the place. I didn't come back because I didn't think someone like Stone would actually work for a living or date a human."

"So let's not waste our time," she said.

He looked around again. "Maybe I'm wrong. But my gut says . . ."

"What does your gut say?"

"See that?" He pointed to the building.

"What?" Della asked.

"This place has cameras." He looked back at Della. "Do you remember what Burnett said? That it seemed like a long shot because if I didn't get any trace of Stone, how would he have known I was here?"

"And it's true?" she said, not following.

"Well, if Stone has access to the cameras, his girlfriend wouldn't have had to recognize me. He could have just looked at the film."

"Okay," Della said. "But what about him not being of moral character to actually work? That sounded logical. And the human girlfriend?"

He looked at Della, and his eyes widened as if he figured out something. "Remember the interview with Sam? He said he heard that Stone hired patrons to do his grunt work for him."

She nodded.

"Well, maybe keeping up the apartment is their grunt work. Look at the advantages. Stone gets to live here for free, has a camera to watch who comes and goes, and gets some of his not-so-smart friends to work for him for nothing. Or maybe he lets them live here for free."

"It's possible," she said, and right then a cool breeze brought with it the scent of a were.

"You smell that?" she asked and looked around, but didn't see anyone.

"Yeah. Were, but not strong," he said. "Maybe a half breed. And maybe a member of the Bastards."

"What apartment is it?" Della reached for the door handle, eager to catch this guy.

"Not so fast," Chase said.

"Why?" Della asked.

"I think we need to get Burnett."

"Why?" she repeated.

"If he's here, it could be dangerous."

"For him, not us," Della said.

"We don't know how many of his friends live here."

"All we're getting is one weak scent."

"Others could be behind doors. Especially if they are half breeds. Their scents can be undistinguishable."

She frowned. "Burnett might be halfway across town. I'm not going to just sit here and let this guy get away."

"He's not getting away. We'll wait here." Chase pulled his phone out.

Della listened as Chase informed Burnett and named off the address, a little pissed that Chase didn't think they could handle it themselves.

"Okay," Burnett said. "I'm ten minutes away if there's no traffic. I'm calling a few more agents to meet us there. Do not get out of the car. And keep Della on a leash. I know she's chomping at the bit to go in."

Chase's gaze shifted to her. "I will." He hung up.

Della glared at him. "Oh, you're gonna keep me on a leash, huh?"

"What was I supposed to say?" He shrugged.

"Maybe that you don't think I need a leash."

"He just wants to make sure you're safe."

"Since when did you start taking his side? I thought you didn't even like him."

Chase exhaled. "He kind of grows on you."

Della nodded. "True, but he acts like I can't take care of myself."

"If he really thought that, he wouldn't even entertain the idea of you becoming an agent."

"If he had his way, I wouldn't."

Chase cut his gaze back to the apartments for a second. "He lost a female agent he was training. Sounds like it was hard for him. I think you remind him of her."

Della sat there staring. "How . . . He told you this?" she asked.

"Not that you reminded him of her, but he told me about her. And I kind of figured it out."

"He just confided this to you?"

Chase looked at her as if she were jealous. And, yeah, maybe she was a little.

"It's not like he was sharing something with me. Except his temper. He was reading me the riot act about going to the prison and told me he'd lost one agent he was training and didn't plan on losing another."

They sat there in the silent car a few minutes. Della used her phone, checking emails to keep from letting the quietness chip away at her sanity.

But when she found an email from her sister, it no longer felt like a stress relief. She decided not to read it. Her new, two-worded litany worked well in this instance as well. *Not now.*

Della put her phone away. She felt Chase studying her. "Don't," she said.

"Don't what?"

"Stare."

"Sorry, I just wanted to say . . . thanks."

"For what?"

"Last night. The morgue thing."

Her heart got tripped on the memory.

"I still think Eddie should be shot for taking you there."

Silence filled the car. "He's not a bad person, Della."

"What did his wife say? A woman would know that it wasn't right."

"There was no wife."

"Ever?" she asked. "What? Is he gay?"

Chase's mouth dropped open. "No. He saw some girls, sometimes."

"So he's a womanizer."

"No. He used to be married. He said his heart belonged to one woman. He never got serious with any of the others."

"What happened to his wife?" Della asked. "Did she leave him?"

He shook his head. "She was a medical researcher like him. There was an explosion." Della saw Chase's expression get serious.

"Sorry," she said.

"Eddie had just walked out of the building. I think he felt as if he should have died with her."

"That's sad," Della said.

"Yeah," he said. "She was his bondmate."

Della looked away, not wanting to think about that. "He still shouldn't have let you go to the morgue."

"It's the same thing as going to a funeral," he said. "But I sort of understand. I don't like your father, either."

She looked at Chase. "I told you he wasn't always like this. He was patient, kind, and he thought I held up the moon."

"I'm sorry," he said. "It's just the way . . ." He let out a deep breath. "I'm just saying I feel protective of you, too. Like you do with Eddie."

She wanted to deny it, but couldn't. She recalled how she'd heard Chase's heart skip to a lie last night about being jealous. "You really don't know where Eddie is?"

"No." Chase looked at her and he didn't blink, as if letting her look him right in the eye meant he thought she'd see the truth there.

"You know, it hurts that you still don't believe me."

"I don't know what I believe." She paused a few minutes. "How are you going to find out if anyone on the council knows anything about Stone?

"I guess I'm going to see someone," he said and still sounded angry.

She hesitated. "You don't think . . . that they would hurt you, do you?"

"I don't think so," he said. But he didn't sound that sure to Della.

Another silence fell like soft rain in the car.

"Hey," Chase finally said. "Don't make it obvious, but look at the guy walking out of apartment ten . . . to your right. Can you read his pattern?" Chase lifted his nose and inhaled.

Della turned her head slowly. "You think it's Stone?"

Chapter Thirty-four

Let it be Stone. Let it be Stone. Della pushed her hair back, trying to appear normal.

"No, he's too young, but he might be one of his grunt workers," Chase said.

Della spotted him. The brown-haired guy, around twenty, wearing jeans and a dark black T-shirt, but he was too far away for her to make out his pattern. "He has a tool box in his hands."

"I know," Chase said.

Not wanting to get caught staring, she looked around for a few seconds, but when his footsteps brought him closer to their car, she glanced back again. "Half were," she whispered and looked away, because if she could read his pattern, he could read hers.

"Do you think he can smell us?" she asked.

"Not all half weres have the ability to trace," he said, but then muttered, "Shit. He's coming this way."

The next thing Della knew, Chase pulled her closer and had her in a lip lock.

"What are you doing?" Della asked when Chase's mouth melted against hers.

"He can't read our patterns this way." His lips continued to brush against hers. "Besides, you're the one who taught me this trick. At the bar, remember?"

She wished she couldn't remember. Footsteps outside the car grew closer. So did Chase's lips.

"Kiss me, Della." He ran his tongue over her bottom lip. "Don't make me do all the work."

She opened her mouth. His tongue slipped between her lips. He tasted a little like toothpaste, a little like . . . Chase. And a lot of something forbidden.

He ran his left hand through her hair and gently cradled her head. With a gentle pull, he brought her closer. She stopped fighting it, and let herself go there—go to a place where nothing but sweetness and possibilities existed.

Where those footsteps were hardly heard.

Where the line between faking a kiss and enjoying a kiss became blurred.

Chase pulled back. Della opened her eyes and looked at him. Her heart raced, and she felt lost in his taste, in the soft feel of his hand behind her neck. The smile in his eyes sobered her. She looked around.

"Where did he go?" she managed to ask.

"Apartment sixteen." He dipped back in for another kiss. And she let him. Then, realizing what she was doing, she put her hand on his chest and lifted her mouth from his. She didn't actually push him away, but she thought about it.

"You sure?" she asked.

"Yes." He brushed his lips against hers again.

"Then we should stop." She pulled back, just an inch. With his hand still curled around her neck, he moved in and reclaimed that tiny space.

"We don't have to." He smiled. His green eyes came so close, she could see his irises—still taste his tongue, still feel his breath on her chin.

"Yes, we do," she said, a lot more adamantly.

"Why?" He pressed his lips to the corner of her mouth.

"Because Burnett's standing at your window."

Chase, certain that being caught making out would bite harder than the damn dog that got him last week, stepped out of the car. He felt even worse when he saw it wasn't just Burnett, but the female agent, Trisha, he'd met yesterday and Shawn, the warlock agent, who had a thing for Miranda, Della's roommate.

"Have you seen Stone yet?" Burnett asked. "Or have you been occupied?"

"No Stone, but a half were, half human just walked into apartment sixteen. Which was why we were . . . hiding our patterns." And it sounded a lot more convincing when he'd suggested it to Della than it did now.

"Oh, that's what you were doing?" the female agent said and grinned.

Burnett frowned. "Did he get your trace?"

"He never appeared to," Chase answered.

"Which one is Stone's apartment?"

"Apartment two," Chase said. "Right beside the office."

"Okay," Burnett said. "You two—"

Burnett never finished. The door to the apartment swung open and four guys walked out.

Their gaze found them and all four shot in different directions.

"See if Stone is in his place or the office," Burnett ordered and took off.

"I got apartment two," Trisha said, running.

Chase took off after a different were, and saw Della and Shawn doing the same.

Moving fast, his feet pounding against the pavement, Chase felt his side pinch, reminding him he wasn't completely healed. He ignored it and kept going.

The guy was fast, but not fast enough. Chase got within a few feet of the guy, his dark hair flipping in the wind. The were's body odor and scent filled Chase's airspace. His nostrils flared, as the scent hit as familiar.

Right before he latched on to the guy's shoulder, he remembered exactly where he'd come across this were before.

This was one of the creeps he'd pulled off Della.

He brought the guy down. Chase landed on top of him. The half were tried to scramble away, but Chase put his hand on the back of his head and pushed his face down just hard enough for the guy to know his strength.

"Don't move," Chase seethed. "Or do, and it'll make my day." His fury rose now as he became even more certain this guy had been at the park. He recalled with clarity seeing one of the half were's fists swing at Della, and Chase had to work not to let his eyes grow bright.

Grabbing the guy by the arm, he dragged him across the parking lot to his car.

Burnett met him halfway, with one of the other runaways. Shawn was placing another one in the back of a black sedan. Trisha stood outside apartment two, shaking her head, as if to say Stone wasn't there.

Chase turned to look for Della. The parking lot was empty.

Where the hell was she?

Della moved fast, sniffing the air. The guy had disappeared between apartment buildings. She'd caught the were scent when she'd first leapt out of Chase's car, but she'd left that behind as she pursued the new scent. What she now tried to follow was vampire and maybe a trace of warlock. Definitely a mixed breed.

She moved around several cars, thinking the guy might be hiding. He wasn't there.

Then she heard a scream. A child's scream. Coming from one

building away. She took off, completely blowing Burnett's no-excess-force rule.

The scream stopped. Della kept moving. She saw an apartment door open. And she heard a muffled cry from inside.

She debated for one second to enter or not. The moan came again. Della shot forward.

She stopped as soon as she spotted him. The vampire had his arm around a child, his hand clasped over her mouth. He held a knife in his other hand. The girl, dark skinned, with yellow ribbons in her hair, had tears running down her face. She looked terrified. As she should be.

"Let the child go," Della said, and fought to keep her eyes from growing bright. Not because of Burnett's rule but for fear of scaring the girl.

"Get away from the door," he seethed, his eyes lime green and his fangs out. He moved his hand from the girl's mouth and pulled her closer. Then he put the knife to her throat.

The girl let out a light cry. Della checked his pattern as she shifted away from the door. She'd been right. Vampire. Dominant vampire with some warlock.

"I'm moving," Della said. "Just leave the kid and I'll let you go." Della's heart raced. If he tried to run with the girl, she'd have to stop him. There was no doubt he'd kill the girl if he got away.

Della didn't lack the strength to catch him, but did she have the courage to do it, knowing how fast that knife could slice the child's throat?

The little girl's gaze met hers. The rogue pressed the knife closer.

"Go," Della said. "I won't chase you. Just let her go. She's a kid. She didn't do anything."

The vamp picked up the child and slung her across the room.

Della jumped up in the air and caught the girl right before she hit the wall, landing in the middle of the living room.

She pulled the little girl against her. "It's okay," Della said, but she had to look away from the child's face because she felt her eyes grow hot with fury.

But it quickly didn't become an issue, because the girl buried her face in Della shoulder and started sobbing.

Seconds later, Chase rushed in. His eyes were bright, his fangs half out.

She shook her head. He nodded and darted off.

Seconds later, Shawn came in. He nodded at Della and she knew what he meant. She should turn the child over to him and get the hell out.

Before she did, she gave the girl one last pat on her back. "It's all over now."

"You did the right thing," Burnett told Della, thirty minutes later.

The van had shown up and taken the three half weres away. The little girl had been taken by ambulance just to make sure she was okay. Stone wasn't there. The apartment manager, a human older woman who kept an unlit cigarette dangling from her lips, gave them the bad news. Douglas Stone had packed his shit and left a couple of weeks ago. And all but these four of his "friends" who had helped him out around the apartment had left with him.

Burnett had Chase take Della across the street, where they parked beside a fast food restaurant and watched Burnett, Trisha, and Shawn handle the police.

With Della being a minor, he didn't want her involved. They had changed the story; now Trisha had been the officer who saved the girl. Not that Della cared. The kid was safe, that was what mattered. But it wasn't all that mattered.

"He got away," Della said. Amazingly, her voice sounded calm, but her insides hadn't stopped shaking. She kept seeing that little girl and the knife to her throat.

Chase stood at her side. Too close. She felt his shoulder against hers. But she didn't have the strength to push him away.

"But it could have ended so much worse," Chase said.

"He's right," Burnett said. And then asked, "Are you okay?"

"I'll be okay," she assured him, and her heart didn't race to the lie. She would be okay: she just wasn't right at this moment.

"Did you get anything from the weres?"

"Not yet," Burnett said. "But we will." He walked over and put his hand on Della's shoulder. "You saved that girl, Della. You did the right thing."

I know," Della said. "But we still don't have Stone. And in just days my dad is going to go to trial for murder."

"And none of us are giving up." Burnett looked at Chase. "Why don't you take her back to Shadow Falls?"

"No," Della said. "Didn't you hear me? Time's running out."

"But—"

"No," she said. "We still haven't gone to Stone's girlfriend's place."

For a second, Burnett looked like he was going to argue with her, then he let go of a deep gulp of air. "Fine, let's go," Burnett said. "I'll meet you there."

"We could handle it if you wanted to go get the interviews done," Chase said.

"No," Burnett said. "I'm going. It shouldn't take long."

"Wait." Chase touched his forehead. "I just remembered."

Della looked at Chase. "The guy I grabbed. I knew him from somewhere else."

"What?" Burnett asked.

"The half were I snagged. I recognized his scent. I was going to tell you, but then all this happened. He's one of the guys I pulled off Della that night and the one I smelled with the animal blood on him earlier that same night. He's part of the group that killed the Chis and those other weres."

"Are you sure?" Burnett asked.

"Positive he killed the Chis? No. But I'm positive he's the same one with blood on him and the same one who jumped Della in the park."

Della heard him, but had to work to get it. "Wait. Are you saying Stone, or at least his gang, is mixed up in the Chis' murder, too?"

"Top up or down?" Chase asked Della a few minutes later as they got into the car to go see if they could find Stone's girlfriend. He wished Burnett had insisted he take Della back to Shadow Falls. He could tell she was still shaken. And rightfully so.

He'd have been shaken too. He'd rescued a woman from a rogue before, but something about a child made it more intense.

"Don't care," Della said.

Chase reached over and caught her hand. "It's going to be okay."

She shook her head. "Not if we don't find Stone it won't be."

"We'll get him." Chase's gut knotted when he saw the sheen of tears in her eyes.

She wiped a few tears from her face. "The new manager said Stone took off, and most of his workers did too. What's the chance these guys know where he is? They obviously don't know since they weren't important enough to go with him."

"I'd say it's pretty good," Chase said. "They were obviously in the gang."

"I wish I believed that," Della said. A few more tears slipped from her lashes. And for one second he wanted to tell her that Eddie wasn't going to let her father go down for this murder—that he would sacrifice himself, but Chase had vowed not to let that happen. And still planned to stop it.

"It's not over." Chase started his car. And he was determined to find Stone and make sure that neither Eddie nor Della's dad paid for his crime.

. . .

Della tried to push the feeling of doom and gloom away as Chase drove. But all she could feel was a ticking clock. Thanks to her, her dad could be convicted of murder. Thanks to her, he might get the death penalty. There was no pushing that gloom away.

Chase parked on the side of the street.

"Which house is it?" she asked, looking out.

"Pope said her house backed up to a cheap Mexican restaurant. All three of these houses are adjacent to this strip center."

Della climbed out of the car; the Mexican food scents flavored the air. Onion, grilled meat. Even though she might like the taste of onions, the smell was almost overpowering. Then again, it might be because of the scent of garlic mixed in.

Or was it?

She got a light scent of something really terrible. She saw Chase lift his head as if trying to decipher the smell as well.

Burnett parked beside them.

The three of them walked around the corner. No one said anything; as crazy as it seemed, it was almost as if they all sensed something bad was about to happen.

The three houses lining the street were each painted a different shade of blue.

Two kids played outside of the first one. Della's mind went back to the little girl with the knife at her throat. She blinked, pushed the thought away, and fought the desire to tell the kids to get inside.

The second house had a FOR RENT sign nailed to the front door. Burnett headed for the porch. Della saw him tilting his head to the side, listening if anyone was there. Then he lifted his face again as if trying to catch a scent.

Della and Chase continued on and moved up the porch steps of house number three. Della hadn't gotten both feet up the last step when the smell grew tenfold. A really, really bad smell. She took another step to the door.

"Wait." Chase caught Della's arm and stopped her from getting closer.

"Why?" Della asked and put her hand over her nose. She'd barely got her nose covered when the noise hit. The buzzing noise. She looked at the window on the porch and her first impression was that the glass had turned liquid and moved. But no, it was not moving glass, just flies. Thousands of insects, buzzing around and covering the inside of the window.

The stench found its way behind her palm. And Della instinctively knew that Stone's girlfriend was going to be another dead end.

"Dead" being the key word.

Chapter Thirty-five

Following Burnett's orders, Chase dropped Della off and then came right back to the murder scene. He got there just in time to see people in hazmat suits take out a body, piece by piece.

Chase had seen a lot of ugly crimes, but this one took the cake.

He stood by Burnett. "I'm not staying at the school any longer," Chase said. All he could think about was Della or someone else there meeting up with the lowlife monster who did this.

For once, Burnett didn't argue. "At the office we have a couple of rooms in the back."

"No, Natasha is leaving today, right?"

"Yeah," Burnett said.

"Then I'll stay at my cabin."

Burnett frowned. "I would prefer that—"

"I know you would prefer it, but I prefer to stay there. And I'm an agent, not a Shadow Falls student."

Burnett nodded. "Fine." The man ran a hand through his hair. "Don't mention this to Della. She's got enough on her mind right now, but I just put two agents on her parents' house."

"Why?" Chase asked.

"Because I don't believe in coincidences," Burnett said. "If you're right about the half were being a part of the group that murdered

Mr. and Mrs. Chi, then it's probably the Bastard gang doing it. All three of the murders that we're looking at them for were less than three miles from Della's home. It got me thinking, why there? Maybe Stone wasn't so much looking for you, but for Della's uncle. He might be watching Della's house, thinking one of you would show up there. If we suspect that Della's father saw the murder, then Stone might think Della's father knows about his brother and has contact with him."

"The examiner listed the girlfriend's cause of death as homicide," Burnett told Della the next day when she walked into the office.

Yesterday, Burnett had made Chase bring her back to Shadow Falls, before he'd called the regular police and other agents to come help out with the murder investigation of Jamie Brown, Stone's girlfriend. Della spent the afternoon and last night mulling over everything and worrying. Kylie and Miranda had tried to get her to talk, and Della had pretty much lost it. Again.

Knowing Miranda, she was probably pissed, but Kylie . . . Kylie was always more forgiving, and she probably told the witch to just give her some space. But it wouldn't last for long.

With no other leads to hunt down on her father's case, Della had been expected to go to school today. Fifteen minutes into English, she'd gotten up and walked out.

"Did either of the half weres give us anything? Have you proven that the two cases are connected?" she asked, and bam, just like that, the smell of death found its way back into her sensory memory. She'd actually thrown up twice today.

The look in Burnett's eyes told her the answer before he did. "No, but I'm going back in a while and taking another go at it."

"I heard you chose not to go to school," Burnett said.

"Couldn't do it," she answered.

After she'd left English she'd gone back to her cabin and written her sister another email, asking if things were okay. The email she'd gotten yesterday and hadn't read until the middle of the night when she'd given up trying to sleep was just another angry message about how she wouldn't forgive Della for abandoning her.

Della had written her back and tried to explain that it hadn't been her choice, but of course her sister wouldn't believe it.

This morning Della had also called her mom to see how things were. Nobody answered.

Was it already happening? Had her father forbidden either of them to communicate with her? The possibility that he knew she was vampire seemed more and more likely.

Della dropped into the chair across from his desk. "We already knew the girlfriend was murdered. How does that help?"

"We can have the FRU investigate it."

Tears filled her eyes. "We're not getting anywhere. We don't have anything to prove my dad innocent."

"We have Mr. Timmons—he's a damn good lawyer—and we have a DA assistant working with us."

"The judge? Any news on that yet?" Della asked.

Something in Burnett's eyes told her he had news about that, but bad news. "They've assigned a judge to the case."

"And he's not one of us?" she asked and felt a tear slip from her lashes.

"No, but the FRU is still trying to get that changed."

She shook her head. "If he's convicted, Burnett, I'm not going to be able to live with this. I swear, I'm not."

Burnett frowned. "Della, I know this is hard, but you're looking at this all wrong. Even if we went to court right now, Mr. Timmons says he feels certain that we have a good case."

The knot of pain rose higher in her chest. "They have what they think is his blood on the murder weapon."

"I know, but he was there during the attack. I spoke with Mr. Timmons this morning. He said the police forgot to take pictures of your dad, or they got lost. He's going to argue that your father tried to defend his sister and received a small cut that went unnoticed."

Della stopped to consider it. "The police file didn't say if he went to the hospital," Della said, remembering.

"I know. The lawyer has asked your father; at first he claimed he didn't remember, then said everyone was just so upset about his sister."

"Mom said he went in later, like to a mental hospital." She considered that. "What if he remembered something then and told them about it? That would look bad. Does the doctor-patient privilege law prevent them from getting those?"

Burnett's brow tightened. "You dad didn't mention that hospital stay. So far the DA hasn't brought it up. We don't know if they are just being sloppy and haven't discovered he went in, or if the lead DA is afraid of opening up those records for fear it might persuade your father to change his plea to insanity."

Della concentrated on that for a second. "But Mr. Timmons could get them. Maybe there's something in there that could help my dad's case."

Burnett leaned back in his chair. "If he gets them he'll be required to share them with the DA."

Della swallowed. "He's not getting them because he's afraid there's something bad in there? So what you're saying is that the lawyer thinks my dad's lying. And if that's the case, then my dad saw his brother in vampire mode and he knows what I am. I was right: He's scared of me."

Burnett frowned. "Mr. Timmons is just being cautious. I know this is hard, but don't look at the negative. How about I give you some good news?"

"About my father's case?" Della asked.

Burnett sighed. "Your lead about the shoes gave us the name of a were. And he has a record. There's an APB out on him and I have several agents looking for him now."

Della had forgotten all about that. "So the one Chase caught and recognized wasn't one of them?"

"We don't know for sure. They aren't talking yet. But what we believe is that the guy with the shoes and the one Chase took down were both in on it."

"Is that what Chase is working on?" Della asked. He'd dropped by her cabin last night, and she'd refused to see him. After their little make-out session in the front of his car, and after everything that happened after that, she didn't know what to say to him.

He hadn't tried to come see her this morning, and part of her had been disappointed.

Burnett hesitated. "No, he has something else he's looking into."

"About my father's case?"

Burnett nodded.

"Then why am I not with him?" She sat up. "You said I could work this case."

Burnett held up his hands. "He had to do this alone. He went to try to find out what the Vampire Council knows."

"Alone?" Della asked.

"Chase trusts one of the councilmen, a Kirk Curtis. He's hoping Curtis will shed some light on why Mr. Powell would have tried to protect Stone."

Della inhaled. "But what if this Kirk guy is in on it too? It could backfire and even put Chase in danger. You shouldn't have let him go alone."

Burnett frowned. "Chase was adamant that Mr. Curtis isn't behind it."

"And what if he's wrong?" Della asked.

On the way back to her cabin, Della texted Chase. *Call me!*

She held her phone in her hand waiting to see if he would text or call her back. He didn't. Just what she needed. Another thing to worry about.

She got all the way to her cabin and the phone didn't ding. She walked in, stood in the middle of her living room, and instantly felt as if the walls would close in on her. The thought of going for a run to expend her energy tempted her, but then why spend her energy on exercise when she could spend it on something more useful?

She went to her room, snatched up her father's case file, and went back outside to read it.

She read a few lines, then looked at her phone. "Please let me hear from you," she muttered.

She picked the phone up and was in mid-text, insisting Chase be careful, when it rang. She hit receive call and put it to her ear. "Chase?"

"Della?"

"Mom." Della closed her eyes.

"Who's Chase?"

"A friend," Della said. "Is everything okay?"

"Yeah, I'm returning your call from this morning," her mom said.

"I know, I just . . . I wanted to see how you're doing."

The silence on the line had Della's eyes stinging again. Knowing her mom, she was either trying to figure out a way to sugarcoat things or trying to come up with an out-and-out lie.

"The truth, Mom."

"We're dealing with things. You shouldn't worry."

Della heard the lie in her mom's tone. Just as she heard the pain in her voice. Her mom was about to break, and Della wasn't there to catch her. Nobody was. Her sister was wrapped up in her own concerns. Her dad was drowning in emotional crap due to the murder case. And it was Della's fault. All of it. She'd done this to them.

"How can I not worry? Is Dad okay?"

Her mom's breath shook, a telltale sign she'd succumbed to tears. "Uh, I'm getting another call, I need to go."

There was no other call. Della would have heard the click. "Please, Mom," Della said, but it was too late. Her mom had hung up.

Della called back, but it went to voice mail. She pulled her knees up and let herself cry right along with her mom.

Kirk wasn't at the council's office. No one was. And when Chase looked in the window, the furnishings were gone.

They'd moved. They did so regularly, fearing the FRU might catch up with them. And no doubt, with Chase working for the enemy, they were probably worried about him turning them in. While he wasn't second-guessing his decision, and he understood their reasoning, it still hurt knowing they'd consider him their enemy.

He'd been relieved that the FRU hadn't asked him to hand over info about the council. But surprisingly, Burnett, meaning the FRU, had more information on the council than he would have guessed. He'd known the location of Hell's Pit.

I trust Kirk, Chase had told Burnett. And he did. Kirk, a friend of Eddie's, had always been around when Chase was growing up. But did Kirk know Powell was protecting Douglas Stone?

Chase got back in his car and drove toward Brown Lake, Kirk's home for the last ten years. The place Chase had spent many of his summer vacations since he'd been turned.

Chase's only worry was that the lake house might be where Eddie had gone. He hoped not. He didn't want to have to lie to Della or Burnett about knowing Eddie's location. Nor did he want to hear Eddie say he was turning himself in.

Chase knew Eddie had his finger on the pulse of his brother's case. But it wasn't over yet. Chase still had a little over a week to track down Stone. And Chase wasn't going to slow down.

While his tires ate up the pavement, his phone in his black suit coat pocket beeped. He pulled it out and read Della's two-word text.

If he called her she'd ask him where he was going. He wouldn't lie. But he didn't want to talk about this now.

He'd call her later, when he was sure Eddie wasn't there. When he knew he didn't have anything to lie about.

Sitting on the porch, Della had read over the file so many times she practically had it memorized. But she reread it again. And she finally found something that she hadn't noticed before. In the transcript of the 911 call, her father had said *he* had broken into the house, but that *they* had hurt his sister. They being more than one.

What had her father really seen? She tried to imagine what her father must have thought seeing his twin brother, who he thought was dead.

She tried to envision what Bao Yu must have thought, facing a vampire. Had Bao Yu seen Feng at all? Was it the shock that made her want to blame Della's father?

A piece of the puzzle was missing. A cold breeze brushed past. "Is that you, Bao Yu?"

Della recalled Holiday's concerns that the ghost could somehow hurt her. She didn't believe it, but neither could she deny the prickle of fear that tiptoed down her spine.

Della was so caught up in thinking about her aunt that she didn't hear the person approaching until a shadow fell on the porch.

Chapter Thirty-six

Chase parked his car in front of Kirk's two-story cabin that was built on stilts. Its balcony actually hung over the water. The noon sun was centered in the sky and water reflected it in diamond sparkles. No cars were parked in the driveway.

But Kirk and Kirk's friends didn't always travel by car.

He cut the engine off and got out. He lifted his face in the breeze and caught the lake's scent as well as a fleeting trace of vampires. More than one.

He relaxed when he didn't detect Eddie. Another intake of air and he recognized the scents of the council members. Others were strangers.

Chase debated leaving. He really wanted to chat with Kirk, alone.

Of course, since he'd gotten their scents, one of them had surely gotten his.

Leaving wasn't an option now.

"Hey," Della said and looked up at Steve, trying to suppress a frown at seeing him. If he'd come to "talk," well, he'd come at the wrong time. Because damn it, she just had too much on her plate to deal with this right now.

"Can I join you?" he asked.

"I'm not in any mood to—"

He dropped down anyway. She stopped trying not to frown and let it happen.

"How are you?" he asked and he looked at her like Steve always looked at her, with concern and patience.

"Terrible," she said. "And I'm not very good company. So why don't—"

"I heard some of what happened. That had to be hard."

"I know, but—"

"Della, you're avoiding me. Sooner or later we need to talk."

"Then later it is." She shot up to her feet.

He caught her. "Don't do this."

"Don't what?" She jerked free and then felt like a bitch again, but she wouldn't have to be a bitch if people would just leave her the hell alone! "Look, I'm sorry, but I've got too much shit going on to pile more shit on top of my other shit."

"Fine!" he snapped. "But don't run off. Sit down. Please." His warm brown eyes looked up at her. "Talk to me."

"Are you deaf? Did you not just hear me? I don't—"

"Not talk about our shit, about the other shit. You don't have to go through this alone."

She wasn't, the thought hit. She had Chase, but she might not when he returned, because she was gonna kill him for not texting her back. And she had Kylie and Miranda—though, after being such a bitch yesterday, they might not be on her team anymore. But she didn't say any of that.

Looking at him, she blurted out, "I'm sorry."

She dropped down and hugged her jean-covered knees. "My dad's murder trial is days away. My sister hates me. My mom is dying inside. I know my dad's going crazy. I'm pretty sure he knows I'm vampire. And it's my fault. I've done this to them all."

She could have kept going and told him about almost seeing a little girl get her throat slit, about how the smell of death kept following her around, but she didn't. Even she couldn't handle that much pathetic.

She pressed her forehead to her knees and swallowed, trying to fight her need to cry.

"What is Burnett saying?" Steve asked.

"He just keeps telling me it's not as bad as it seems. But the police have a weapon with my dad's DNA on it. Or rather my uncle's DNA, but they don't know he's alive."

Steve frowned. "I can see how that's hard on you. What is this?" he asked, pointing to the papers.

"That's the DA's file on the case."

"Wow, you got it?"

"Burnett did. I've been trying to find something that might help."

Steve picked it up. "Do you mind? Maybe you need a fresh pair of eyes."

Chase clicked the button to put the top up on his car. He hit the locks, and then started walking toward the door. No doubt they were waiting for him by now.

He tilted his head to the side and listened to see if they were talking. He heard a duck call to a mate on the lake, a fish splash in the water, and a motor on someone's boat move down the lake.

But not a word came from the house.

He walked up the length of the driveway. The hair on the back of his neck stood up. Sensing that someone was watching him, he looked up, and just then the drapes in the front window fluttered back into place.

He ran a hand over the back of his neck, fighting the crazy sensation that trouble waited. But this was Kirk, he told himself. He trusted him.

Didn't he? Right then Chase saw two guards standing at the back of the property.

"Is this a bad time?" Chase asked, knowing the council inside were listening.

"Yeah, but you're already here," came Kirk's reply. "Come on in."

"They never arrested your dad back then, right?" Steve asked Della when he finished reading.

"No," Della said. "But according to Derek's detective buddy, who read the old case file, he was the only suspect. They just didn't have enough proof to take it to court."

Steve looked back at the file. "So we know he called 911, but then he says he couldn't remember anything. Was he checked for a concussion? "

"The file doesn't even say if he was taken to the hospital. My dad's not much help. He says he doesn't remember, and my uncle told Chase that when he got to the house my dad was unconscious."

"And you don't believe him? Or you do?" Steve asked.

"I don't know," Della said. "I mean, this Douglas Stone guy really exists. He's bad, and he was out to stop Chase from trying to prove this. So maybe I do believe my uncle didn't do it. Oh," she grabbed the file and flipped pages and pointed down, "and I just found in the transcripts of the 911 call that my dad told the operator 'he' broke in but that 'they' were hurting his sister. Doesn't that mean there were two people there that night? And that kind of supports my uncle's version, because he said Douglas Stone got there first and then he arrived."

Steve sat there thinking. "But why would he think your uncle was hurting his sister?"

"I don't know. Maybe he was unconscious when Feng got there and just heard them screaming or something. But the thing is that my mom said that shortly after all this happened they had to put my dad in St. Mary's hospital, that hospital for crazy people. Which is more proof that he saw something. But my dad's lawyer is afraid to request the files because he thinks something in there could hurt the case."

"Or it could prove that he got attacked and that's the reason his blood was on the knife. Those files might help his case."

Frustration welled up and started spilling out of her and she moaned. Really loud.

Realizing how crazy she looked, she said, "I'm sorry."

"For what?" Steve asked.

"For bitching. I told you I wasn't good company."

Steve hesitated. "Are you sure it was St. Mary's Psychiatric Institution?"

"That's what my mom said, why?"

"Well, what if you could get your hands on those files and find out if they would help or hurt your father's case? And if they help, you can tell the lawyer to get them opened and used for evidence."

"How?" Della asked.

Steve shrugged and looked hesitant to say it. "My mom works there one day a week. Well, she volunteers and visits some of the people who don't have insurance. I don't know if they have the old files there, but they might."

"Your mom would actually give them to me?" Della asked, not believing it.

"Oh, hell, no," Steve said. "I'm thinking if I found out where they keep the files, I could go, then leave a window open and you could take a peek at them."

"God, I love you," Della said and hugged him.

It only took a second for Della to realize what she'd said and to realize how awkward it felt. Her arms around Steve. Steve's arms around her.

Surely Steve didn't think she meant that she loved him like . . . "love" love.

Or did he?

Oh, hell!

. . .

Chase moved faster up the steps. He saw the two guards start toward him as he entered the door.

Kirk, along with the other councilmen, waited in the entryway.

Chase stared at Kirk's face, trying to read him. "What's going on?"

Chase heard the guard's footsteps move up the porch.

"Stop," Kirk growled. "There will be no bloodshed!"

The two sets of footsteps halted.

Chase looked at the man whom he'd grown to love and trust, and just like that he knew he'd been wrong. Kirk knew about Stone. The whole council was in on this. "Why are you protecting Douglas Stone?"

Councilman Powell's shoulders gave, as if in defeat. "The guy you call Douglas Stone is my son."

Chase looked from Powell to Kirk. "And you knew who killed Eddie's sister and you lied to him all these years?"

"I didn't know at first," Kirk said.

"None of us did," Powell snapped.

Chase felt his eyes grow hot and stared at Powell. "Your son is a monster. He not only killed Eddie's sister, but he recently killed another woman. I watched them take her body, piece by piece, out of a house just yesterday. And someone in the gang he runs nearly killed a child."

"I'm not surprised," Powell said. "I stopped trying to excuse his behavior years ago. I know what he is. I know he has to be stopped."

Chase looked back at Kirk. "Then what's the problem? Tell me where he is and I'll bring him in."

"That's the problem," Kirk said.

Chase's fury rose higher. "You're protecting him, even knowing what he is?"

"We're not protecting him," Kirk said. "Stopping him. Killing him isn't a problem. But you can't take him in to the FRU."

"Why not?" Chase asked.

As soon as Steve left, Della went inside. When Miranda and Kylie walked in from their last class three minutes later, Della sat at the kitchen table. She had three Diet Cokes waiting in the fridge and an apology resting on the tip of her tongue.

"Looks like the vamp has finally decided to talk," Miranda said.

Kylie elbowed her. "Yes, and being her friends, we're here to listen."

"I'm sorry." Della stood up and got the three Diet Cokes out. "I was a real shit, wasn't I?"

"Yup." Then Miranda ran over, throwing her arms around Della in one of those bear hugs that just about hurt. "But like Kylie said, we forgive you. We will always forgive you. But I hate it when I see you're hurting and you won't talk to us!" Her hug actually got tighter. "So can you please not do that anymore?"

"I'll try really hard," Della managed to say. "But, speaking of hurting, can you stop hugging me now?"

Miranda released her.

They all sat down in their designated places.

"Who's going first?" Kylie asked.

"I think Della should," Miranda announced. "She's the one who is worse off."

Della didn't like to go first, but she put that aside. "My life is effed up."

"We're gonna need more than that," Miranda said.

"Every time we think we have a lead on Douglas Stone, the guy who probably killed my aunt, it goes away. Now, not only is he responsible for killing my aunt but his gang is the one who killed Mr. and Mrs. Chi. My mom is losing it. My sister hates me. I'm pretty sure my dad thinks I'm a monster—of course I told you that, right?"

Kylie nodded.

Della inhaled and continued, "Chase thinks the Vampire Council knows something about Stone and he left to go there this morning and we haven't heard a peep from him. I'm worried sick something has happened. And you might think things couldn't get worse, but they do! I told Steve I love him."

Chapter Thirty-seven

"Why can't Stone be handed over to the FRU?" Chase asked, his patience waning, and waning fast. "Someone better start explaining."

"Eddie had been with us for almost a month," Powell started talking. "We were helping him look for a man named Douglas Stone. It wasn't until I saw the sketch that I became worried, but it wasn't a perfect match for my son's likeness. I confronted him. He swore it wasn't him. I believed him. His mother lives in France. He went to live with her. But four years later, he came back to the States. Some old friends of his showed up. One of them mentioned a gang that they had belonged to. It was the gang Eddie had joined. That's when I knew for sure."

The old man had to stop to catch his breath. If Chase hadn't personally seen what a monster his son was, he might have felt sorry for him.

"I told him that he needed to turn himself in. That I would go to Eddie and maybe he would find it in his heart to ask the rest of the council to go easy on him."

The old man closed his eyes. "He called me a fool. Told me that I would never turn him in. He said to go check the files and see what had been taken."

"What files?" Chase asked.

Kirk stepped forward. "All of them, Chase. Every job the council had done for over fifty years had been cataloged in those files. Powell's son swore that if anything ever happened to him he would leak the information to the FRU."

"But you never told Eddie?" Chase asked.

"No. Stone left the country. We actually thought he'd been killed. But a few months ago, he came back. We got the files, but Powell's son got away."

"But he knows things, Chase," Powell said. "If the FRU got him, he could bring us all down."

"If you're guilty of things like he did, then maybe you need to go down," Chase snapped.

Kirk shook his head. "It's not like that, Chase. The things we did wrong were justified. It was war. We were protecting what we believed in."

"Then why are you so worried?" he asked.

"Because it wouldn't look like that to the FRU or the government," Kirk insisted.

"Tell him everything," the elderly Powell said.

"What?" Chase insisted, staring at the oldest of the councilmen.

Powell looked at Kirk, who nodded, then the old man started talking. "It wasn't just us. It was Eddie, too."

Chase curled his hand into a fist. "He wasn't an agent, why would he be in there?"

"Kirsha," Kirk said. "Eddie's wife. She was killed by an FRU agent."

Chase recalled the stories Eddie had told him. "No, she died in an explosion at the medical lab. Eddie told me."

"Yes," Kirk said. "But it was intentionally set by the FRU. Eddie had just discovered the treatment for AIDS. He was about to release it. They didn't want the council getting credit, so they stole his work, and then, afraid we would claim rights to the work, they put the bomb in the lab."

"Eddie and Kirsha weren't supposed to be there, but Kirsha had left her purse. When they entered the building they heard someone run out. Eddie made Kirsha wait inside while he ran after the intruder. He had just caught the man when . . . the building exploded. Eddie lost it. He killed the FRU agent."

Chase could barely breathe. He didn't want to believe it, but with Eddie's dislike of the FRU it made sense.

Chase turned and stared out the window at the water, his heart on Eddie. On how crazy it was that he hated the FRU because they'd taken his bondmate from him, and Chase had joined them to win his bondmate?

Was there justice anywhere in this world?

"But you see," Kirk said, "all of this will go away if you can make sure Stone is dead before the FRU get him."

Chase turned and faced Kirk. "You're not asking me to get justice. You're asking me to kill."

"He deserves to die," Kirk said. "You'd just be saving the FRU the money it would cost them to incarcerate him and hold a trial."

"Wow," Miranda said. "You love Steve. I've been thinking it was going to be Chase. I'd practically written Steve off."

"I didn't mean it," Della said. "I mean, I love him, but I don't . . . love him? You understand?"

If the expressions of her two best friends were any indication, they didn't. And maybe she shouldn't be surprised. She sure as hell didn't have a friggin' clue what she meant.

Or did she? She heard Chase's words.

You need time to trust this, to trust love and to trust me, and I get that.

"Of course you don't understand." Della dropped her head on the table with a loud thump.

"Wait," Kylie said. "Don't panic, I'm trying to understand. You love Steve, but you don't love him, like . . . true love, right?"

Della raised her head. "Yeah, kind of."

Kylie spoke up again. "Earlier you said that Steve made you feel safe. Does he still make you feel safe?"

Della considered the question and remembered sitting with him on the porch. "Yeah, still safe." She recalled when she hugged him. It had been awkward, but not unsafe.

Miranda piped up. "And safe's good, right?"

"Yeah," Della said. "But love's not safe. Not for me. You get it?"

"No." Miranda looked at Kylie. "Do you understand any of this?"

Kylie looked back at Della and made her "sorry" kind of face. "Not a bit."

"Okay," Della said, trying to think of how to explain. "Steve used to be scary. I mean, I was always scared because I had feelings for him. It was like a shadow following me around and it made me want to run and keep running."

"And now Steve doesn't scare you," Kylie said, but still looked unsure.

"Right." Della inhaled.

"I'm still lost," Miranda said.

Kylie held a hand out to Miranda. "I think I'm figuring it out."

Chase walked out. He saw two vampire guards standing on the side of the porch, and he walked past them. Part of him wished they'd try something; a good fight would suit him right now.

A fight. But he wouldn't kill them. He wasn't a killer. He went down the stairs.

"Chase?" Kirk shot in front of him. "I know this is hard."

Chase stared at him. "Hard is knowing you've deceived Eddie all these years. Which means you deceived me."

"I was protecting Eddie, Chase," Kirk's eyes grew bright with anger at the accusation. "What do you think would happen to him if the FRU found out he killed one of their own? You've preached your justice talk for years, Chase. But where is the justice in Eddie being put to death? And that's what they will do. You know that." Kirk shook his head. "Eddie killed the man who murdered the woman he loved. Can you fault him for that?"

Chase stared out at the water. His chest hurt. "Maybe there is no justice in this world."

"Don't do it for the council. Do it for Eddie. Word is that the FRU are after Stone. We can't get any of our guys to go after him for fear they'll get tangled up in this. You could do it."

He handed Chase a piece of paper. "Here's all of Powell's son's hangouts. A list of all his friends. Take care of this."

Chase curled his fist around the paper and stared at the man he no longer respected. "If I kill Stone without handing him over to the FRU Della's father will get tried for murder. And—"

"And you would choose him over Eddie?" Kirk spouted out.

The love and devotion Chase carried for Eddie rose in his chest until the point of pain.

Chase scowled at Kirk. "Don't you get it? Eddie told me his plans. If it appears his twin brother will go down for this murder, he's going to come forward and confess to a killing he didn't do. Either way, I lose Eddie!"

"No, you won't," Kirk said. "I'll talk to Eddie. I can talk him out of it. Besides, you don't even know they will convict her father. The lawyers can get him off. We know the FRU are on it. You take care of Stone. I'll take care of Eddie."

Chase stood there and wondered how the man he had once respected so much could ask him to do this.

"Promise me, Chase," Kirk said. "Promise you'll take care of this."

Without saying a word, Chase got in his car and drove off.

. . .

Why had Della tried to explain this? She couldn't.

"Yup, I think I got it," Kylie said and looked back at Della. "Steve doesn't scare you, but Chase does, right?"

Della took a deep breath. She didn't want to admit that, not because it wasn't true, but because admitting it seemed awful close to admitting something else. But she couldn't lie to her friends.

"Right." Della dropped her head back down.

"I thought so," Kylie said.

"Thought what?" Miranda asked.

"Della's afraid of falling in love. And Steve doesn't scare her because she's not falling. She's falling—or has fallen—for Chase. So she's in love with—"

"Don't say it," Della said. "Please. Just don't say it."

Right then Della's phone rang. She nearly jumped out of her skin. She snatched it up.

"Is it Chase?" Miranda asked. "Just tell him you love him."

Della looked at the number. "No." Della stood up. She wouldn't. Couldn't tell Chase she loved him. Because she still didn't trust love. "It's not Chase. It's Steve. I need to talk to him . . . in private." She started to her bedroom, but remembering her door wouldn't close all the way, she took off outside.

"I don't get it," Della heard Miranda say. "She thinks she's in love with Chase, but Steve calls, and she bolts out because she needs privacy. That girl is missing a few of her marbles, if you ask me."

Worried Miranda might eavesdrop, Della took off for a long stroll in the woods. She'd just hung up with Steve. He had spoken with his mom. She was going to be at the office in St. Mary's tomorrow. Steve was going to skip his morning class and was going to visit his mom. Before he left, he planned on transforming himself into something small so he could sneak around and find where the old files were kept. If he found them, he'd leave a window open so Della could get in and read the files for herself.

At first Della considered going to Burnett, but what if Burnett refused to let her do it? She couldn't let him stop her.

But she trusted Chase to understand. The realization hit, and hit hard. She trusted him. He would help her.

He would if he were still alive. Why the hell hadn't he texted her or called her?

She texted him again. *Where are you?*

Then she tucked her phone into her pocket and started walking back to her cabin. She cleared the woods, and had just gotten on the trail when she heard someone walking down the path. She turned. Listened to the footfalls. Raised her nose in the air. And then took off.

"Where have you been?" she asked him.

"I was just texting you," Chase said.

"But I texted you like five times."

"I'm sorry," he said, but he didn't sound all that apologetic. "Crazy day."

She looked at him, noting something different. "What happened?"

"What do you mean?" Chase asked.

"I mean what happened? Burnett said you were going to confront Kirk. Did you?"

"Yeah," he said.

"And?" she asked impatiently.

He ran a hand through his hair. "And Douglas Stone is Powell's son."

"Shit," Della said. "Did my uncle know this? Was he protecting—"

"No!" Chase snapped. "He doesn't know. The council deceived him."

"So they've been protecting Stone all these years?"

"He left the country. They couldn't find him."

"But he's here now. Are they're hiding him?"

"No. Even his father knows he's bad. He wants him stopped too."

Della tried to understand. "But then why did Powell not look into the lead about Stone at the prison? Are you sure his father doesn't know where he is?"

"I don't think he's lying," he said. "They've agreed to help us find him. They want him stopped too."

"Did you tell Burnett?"

"Yes. I just left his office and if you don't believe me you go ask him."

"I didn't mean . . ." Della kept looking at him. Something wasn't right. Then it hit her. He wasn't smiling. He almost always smiled.

"Did something else happen?" she asked.

"No," he said.

She moved in and got right in his face. "Don't lie to me."

He frowned. Then suddenly, he lifted his face and his eyes went from green to a bright neon green.

"How about you don't lie to me?" he growled.

"I haven't," she said, unsure what the hell was happening.

"Okay, tell me, Della. Why is it that I smell a certain shape-shifter all over you?" He leaned in. "Your hair." He leaned lower. "Your chest?" He turned around and ran his nose over her shoulders. "Your back. You were in his arms, weren't you?"

She swung around and stood there, not sure what she could or should tell him. But not appreciating him sniffing her like she was some dirty slut.

"You know what?" he seethed. "I've had a pretty miserable day and I'm done. Screw it." He took off.

Della started to fly after him, but then stopped. She hadn't done anything wrong. Yeah, she'd hugged Steve, but not like a hug-hug. Oh, and she'd told him she loved him, but as she'd finally admitted to Miranda and Kylie, she didn't really love Steve. She was . . . this close to admitting she loved Chase.

And if Chase had asked her in a reasonable way about Steve's scent, she would have told him. Hell, she'd been planning on telling Chase about Steve's plan, and getting him to go with her.

But if he was going get all pissy about Steve, he'd probably find a reason she shouldn't go get her father's files.

She turned and stormed back into her cabin.

Miranda and Della were still at the kitchen table. "Forget what I said," she snapped. "Chase doesn't scare me anymore. He just downright pisses me off!"

She took off for her bedroom and slammed the door, forgetting it didn't shut. The last sound she heard before she landed facefirst on the bed was the door falling and hitting the floor.

Chapter Thirty-eight

As angry as Della was, she left her phone on her bedside table so she would hear it when Chase texted or called with his apology.

It was almost three before she fell asleep. Not that it had been just him on her mind. He wasn't even in the top five. Or maybe he was.

Her phone never rang, never dinged with a text. But she still checked it first thing when she woke up.

Nothing.

That hurt, damn it. Where did he get off being such a jerk?

She got ready for school early, thinking he might come by before he went to work. Wrong again.

Jerk!

At lunch, Steve texted and said his plan had worked. He found a room on the tenth floor where all the old files were boxed up. He'd even left a window open for her.

She texted him back and asked if he would go with her tonight.

And just as she knew he would, he said yes.

When she got out of school, she walked by Chase's cabin, but he wasn't there. So she took off to the front of the school, to see if Chase's car was there. It wasn't. But Burnett's was.

"In here," Burnett said as she moved inside the office.

Della stepped into Holiday's office, not really sure what she planned on saying. Then she remembered she needed to let him know that she and Steve were going out.

"You back from work?" she asked, not wanting to blurt it out first thing.

"Yeah," he said, looking up from his laptop. "You okay?"

"Not really," she said. "Tell me we got a new judge on my dad's case and I'll be better."

He frowned. "I haven't heard anything yet."

"So no luck finding Stone?"

"No. Chase did get a few more addresses from someone on the council to check. But—"

"Is that where he is now?" she asked.

"No, he covered that this morning. He didn't find anything." Burnett looked back at his computer.

"So is he working the Chi case now?"

Burnett looked up as if almost confused. "No, we did that earlier too."

She didn't want to ask, but it just leaked out. "So where's Chase now?"

Burnett hesitated. "I'm assuming he's at his cabin."

"No, I went there, and his car's gone."

Burnett frowned. "I didn't mean here, I meant at his cabin." He sat up. "Did he not tell you he was moving back?"

She recalled Chase's words: *I'm out of here. Screw it.* "Yeah, he kind of did," she said, hurting.

"Is something up between you two?" Burnett asked.

"I wouldn't have a clue what's up with him," she said to keep from lying. And it was true. She didn't know what had gotten into Chase. Sure, he'd been jealous of Steve before, but never so . . . so crazy.

"He wasn't himself today," Burnett said.

Della almost tossed out that she and Steve were thinking of going out, but it just seemed too weird after talking about Chase. "Well, I've got homework."

Not that she planned on doing it.

She took off, and almost as if wanting—hoping—to prove Burnett wrong, she went to cabin fourteen.

She stepped in. Looked around. She went to his bedroom. It was empty.

She looked at the bed where she'd stayed with him when she didn't know if he was going to live or die. Her next intake of air brought on his scent. He wasn't here, but his scent lingered.

Her heart almost broke then.

He'd done it to her again. Stormed into her life, made her start believing his talk about loving her, and then disappeared.

Her chest filled with a deep kind of pain and it just curled up and joined all the other pains and regrets she had.

Would she ever learn to stop letting herself care about boys?

"Where are you going?" Miranda asked Della that evening when she walked out of the bathroom with her jeans and black button-down on.

"Out." She had her phone in her hands. She planned to text Holiday and tell her she was going out for coffee with Steve, right before she walked out of the gate. She'd rather ask for forgiveness than permission. And who'd said that to her? A certain vampire who'd skipped out on her!

"You seeing Chase?" Miranda asked and Kylie looked up from the computer.

"Did he apologize?" Kylie asked.

Della had confessed to them last night about Chase's little tantrum. But she hadn't mentioned his moving out. Who wanted to admit you were an idiot? And that's what she'd been. Believing in Chase. Believing he really loved her.

"No." He didn't apologize. Della felt bad, or at least a little bad, about hiding her excursion tonight, but she knew Kylie was

one of those non—rule breakers and she'd try to talk her out of going. Or at least try to convince her to tell Burnett.

Della didn't want to chance that he would have a problem with
it. Nope. She knew it wasn't exactly legal. But this was to help her
father.

"No, I'm going with Steve to grab some coffee." And it wasn't a
lie, because she'd told Steve they had to so that she wouldn't have
to lie.

Della heard both her friends' little gasps of surprise.

"With Steve?" Miranda asked.

"See ya." Della started out.

"Not so fast," Kylie said, after having shot across the room and
blocked the front door. "What's going on?"

"We're going for coffee, that's what's going on."

"Is she lying?" Miranda asked Kylie. "Get your vamp on and
find out."

Frowning at the witch, Della said, "Bye, guys. I won't be late."
She gently picked up Kylie by her shoulders and set her away from
the door.

Then suddenly sentimental, she was tempted to blurt out, *I love
you,* or *thank you for being here.* But she couldn't find the words. So
she just left.

Della followed Steve into the coffee shop, right around the corner
of St. Mary's hospital. She was instantly hit by the smell of freshly
ground coffee beans. How could something smell so good, but
taste so bad? She moved with Steve up to the empty counter and
tried to decide if she wanted to "fake drink" something, or if she
really had to with Steve. He knew she hated coffee.

Steve gave the girl his order.

"And you?" the girl asked.

"Nothing," Della answered, but then her eyes lowered to the

bakery stuff under the glass counter. Her heart dropped a few inches. *They tasted like love,* Chase had said.

"Wait," she said as the lady started to turn. "I'll take a snicker-doodle cookie."

"I've never seen you eat sweets," Steve said.

"Is it against the law for me to want one now?" she snapped and wanted to die for being such a bitch.

Ding. Ding. Ding. The awkward bells started ringing again. She was going to have to stop those damn bells. But the only way was to have that talk Steve had been pushing her to have.

Not now.

Really bad timing. How did you tell someone helping you, *Oh, by the way, you know how I said I love you? Well, I don't really love-love you.*

And yeah, that was what she needed to tell him. It didn't matter what was happening with Chase. The fact was, she didn't love-love Steve and he deserved someone who did. He was a great guy.

The woman put the cookie in a bag on the counter, and Della reached for some money.

"I got it," Steve said.

"No, uh, I'm buying it and I'm buying yours, too."

"No, I can . . ."

"You're helping me." Della threw a twenty-dollar bill on the counter. "Keep the change," she told the girl. Then she went and found a corner table.

Steve walked over a few minutes later with a steaming cup of good-smelling, bitter-tasting stuff and a slice of cake.

"Thanks," he said.

She nodded and reached for a napkin, suddenly wishing she had bought a coffee just to have something to keep her hands busy. But then again, she had the cookie. She glanced at it, still in the bag.

She looked up, and his soft brown eyes met hers. *Not now.* She glanced away.

Then Steve reached for her cookie. He had it halfway across the table when she put her hand on top of his and stopped him.

"What?" she asked.

"Nothing, I was going to try a bite."

"No."

He looked odd. "Okay."

Ding. Ding. Ding.

She pulled the cookie back to her side of the table.

She glanced up. "I don't love you," she blurted out. Oh, friggin' hell, why had she done that?

Steve had his cup to his lips. Her words must have shocked him because he apparently swallowed wrong. Coffee spewed out of his mouth, and . . . maybe even his nose. So not pretty.

Then he went from spewing to hacking.

"Shit," she muttered and handed him her napkin.

He took it and put it to his lips.

"Sorry," she said as he turned his face away and used the napkin to clean off his face.

When he turned back, he had tears in his eyes. Surely it was from the hacking and not . . . Let it be from the hacking. Please!

He met her gaze and then . . . then laughed. Real deep, belly-type of laughing.

She stared at him. "What's so funny?"

"You," he said. "Us."

"I guess I don't see the humor in it." She ran her finger over the edge of the table and looked down at the cookie again.

"Hey," he said, his voice pulling her eyes up.

"I knew what you meant last night. And I also knew you felt weird about saying it."

"You did?"

"Yeah, I did."

She nodded. And just like that she remembered some of the vibes she'd gotten from Steve since he'd come back. "You don't love me either, do you?"

That chased away the humor in his eyes.

"Well, I . . . care, but . . ." He turned his cup in his hands. "Are we finally having our talk?"

"As long as you aren't gonna be pissed at me and not help me tonight." No sooner had she said that, did she wish she could unsay it.

He frowned. "You know me better than that."

"Sorry. I do. I'm just . . ." dying inside. "I'm messed up right now."

"Do you want to go first?" he asked.

"I hate being first." She looked down at the bag with the cookie and reached in and broke a piece off. "I'm sorry. You can have a piece of you'd like."

"That's okay." He smiled.

She took a bite. The sugar and cinnamon had her taste buds dancing, but then the other stuff, the doughy middle, tasted like paste.

But she forced herself to swallow.

"Okay, I'll go first." He took a deep breath. "Here's the thing. I care about you. A lot. And if . . . some things didn't happen, things might be different now."

"Things?" she asked.

He let go of a deep breath. "Sorry, that's not what I want to say." He frowned and looked down at his cup. "I'm sort of messed up too. A little bit. Not so much that I wouldn't share my cookie with you." He grinned and she knew it was a joke.

She also knew that sometimes Steve joked when he was nervous.

They stared at each other for several minutes.

"Here's the truth," he said. "There's a part of me that is still pissed about Chase. But something you said to me before I left has stuck with me."

She bit down on her lip. "I said a lot of things." She wasn't even sure she remembered them. She'd been really pissed.

He smiled, his sad smile. "You asked me why I had made you care when I knew I was leaving."

She nodded and the hurt from before whispered over her heart.

"You were right. I was planning on leaving. I didn't know for sure if I would get the Paris gig, but I was hoping I would. And I think I just sort of thought you'd understand because it was about my career. I want to be a doctor. I want it more than anything."

"If you'd told me—"

He held up his hand. "Let me finish, please. I think I didn't tell you because that would have made me realize how my fantasy future—the one I dreamed I'd get—didn't really match my . . . Della future. The one I was kind of hoping I'd get too. I knew that if I got the Paris gig there was a slight chance that I might get chosen for the International Training Academy . . . and I was." His eyes sparkled with pride.

"Congratulations," Della said.

He nodded. "After I graduate from Shadow Falls, I'll be moving to France for a year to train under one doctor, then for the next four years I'll be moving to Germany, Japan, and then Switzerland."

He picked up his coffee. "So while it ticked me off that you sort of chose Chase over me, I—"

"But—"

He held up his hand and silenced her. "I finally realized that I sort of chose my career over you. Or I was going to if it happened."

Nodding, but still needing something to do with her hands, she pulled her phone out and ran her finger around the case.

"That doesn't mean I don't care about you," Steve continued. "As crazy as this sounds, I still kind of love you. And I'm still kind of pissed about Chase, but . . ."

"I understand." She looked up, trying to think of something to say that would make him feel better. "You just love your career more."

He frowned again and she realized that might not have been

the right thing to say. "And you love Chase more. And maybe even your career."

She looked down at the cookie. "I don't know . . . Chase and I . . . I don't know if it's love." *He's already left me.* "I mean, the bond just—"

"Stop," he said. "And look at me," he insisted.

When her gaze raised, he continued, "I don't know what or how the blood transfusion affected you two. But Della, you had eyes for him when he first showed up. You were halfway in love with him before you got his blood."

She didn't deny it. "It's still complicated. He deceived me and now . . ."

"And now he's working for the FRU, helping you get your father off, and . . . and he loves you. He told me, Della. And he's not going to give up on you."

He already did.

"But that doesn't mean you have to make it so hard on him. I know you. When someone gets a little too close, you start pushing them back. Stop it. I know you've been hurt, but other people, people who care about you, shouldn't have to pay for the mistakes some idiots made in the past."

Emotion tightened her throat. Had she run Chase off? She recalled telling him she didn't love him, but hadn't he told her he'd wait?

Maybe waiting didn't include thinking she was snuggling up with Steve. Maybe she should have tried to explain right away. But if Chase was able to just walk away after a little misunderstanding, was she that important to him?

"Thanks for the advice," she said, and for some crazy reason she reached over and took another bite of the cookie. Then another. It didn't taste any better, but it didn't stop her.

She wanted to like it.

She also wanted to know what love tasted like.

Chapter Thirty-nine

Chase parked in front of his cabin. He got out and stood by the open door waiting for Baxter to get out.

"Come on," Chase said when the dog just plopped back down in the seat as if to say he planned on sleeping in the car.

"We're gonna sleep inside tonight. I promise." Baxter hadn't found the porch all that comfortable. Neither had Chase, but what did that matter? He'd barely slept these last few nights. He'd spent his eight hours working with Burnett, then took off and worked another twelve combing Houston searching for Stone. He still didn't have a friggin' clue what he was going to do when he caught the bastard.

Kill the man before he took him in, knowing it might prevent Della's dad from getting off, or take him in, and let Stone take down the council and Eddie?

"Come on, get out," Chase told the dog. Baxter had been depressed since he'd brought him here. Probably pissed at Chase's long hours, or maybe the dog missed Della.

Chase did too.

He was friggin' miserable, too miserable to deal with a depressed dog.

Damn, Chase missed her. But he'd promised her he wouldn't

lie. And if she questioned him about what went down with Kirk, he'd have to lie.

"Come on, Baxter. Let's go."

The dog did as requested.

Chase walked around the back and got out his two purchases in separate bags.

He'd gone to a store to buy air spray—so he could sleep in the house. But when he passed the diner inside the grocery store he saw their sign announcing the sale of their French onion soup. So he picked that up too.

Della said she liked it. Maybe he would too.

He walked inside, Baxter at his heels. He pulled the Lysol out of the plastic bag. "You might want to go back outside," he told the dog. This stuff stinks, but he'd rather smell it than the alternative.

The dog dropped down, so Chase commenced with spraying. First one room and then the other. He practically emptied the can in the bedroom.

He just hoped the stuff got rid of the smell.

The place smelled like pheromones. Happy, happy phero-mones. Liam and Natasha must have done it like rabbits. Oh, they'd washed the sheets and even lit a candle. But he could still smell it.

Normally, the smell wouldn't have bothered him. Chase liked sex. Especially if he was having it. But all it did was make him miss Della even more. Want Della even more. Want to have sex with Della even more.

Not that he would pressure her. Never. He figured it would happen sooner or later. He'd been hoping for sooner, but hey, he always was an optimist.

He loved her. And he was keeping his damn promise, not lying to her even if it meant he couldn't see her until all this was over.

But then that smell would also take him back to finding Steve's scent all over Della. They hadn't had sex—he would have smelled that—but thinking about her in Steve's arms pissed him off.

The one thing Chase was really good at when he was pissed off was acting like an ass. And he had. He'd out-assed himself.

He should have given her a chance to explain. He should have apologized. But he hadn't, because walking away mad had been an easy out. From the moment she'd seen him, she'd started asking questions about his visit with Kirk. If he'd stayed there, even a few minutes longer, she'd hit a question he couldn't dance around and he'd have ended up lying to her. And nope. He wasn't doing that.

He'd promised her.

And Chase may occasionally be an ass, but he didn't break promises. Which was why he didn't make them very often. Why he'd refused to give Kirk his promise.

Walking into the kitchen, he dropped the can in the garbage. Then he grabbed a spoon and slid his bag with his soup over and dropped down in the chair. The chair Della had sat in the other night.

Kirk's words echoed in his head. *Besides, you don't even know they will convict her father. The lawyers can get him off. We know the FRU are on it.*

Could he take that risk? Was he planning on purposely killing the man? Could he commit murder? And yes, no matter how Chase looked at it, that was what it was.

Murder.

He dropped the spoon, then pulled out the piece of paper Kirk had given him from his black coat pocket. Six out of ten places were crossed off. After a couple of hours of sleep, he'd go back out.

He pulled the Styrofoam cup of soup out and opened the top. It was still hot, steam billowing out of the top. But the cheese he'd seen the woman put on top was stuck to the lid.

He tried scraping it off, but it wouldn't come. He gave up and grabbed the spoon.

Chase took his first bite. And looked at the lid. Maybe the cheese was what made it good, because without it, it tasted bad. Really, really bad.

He spooned himself another bite. Logically, he knew that just because he loved Della didn't mean he had to like everything she liked.

He still didn't stop eating. Because . . . because . . . Hell, he didn't know why. Other than that Della liked it.

Nope, he never stopped. He finished the whole damn thing. Every disgusting spoonful.

Steve and Della walked out of the coffee shop. The sky was dark. The moon still hung big in the sky, only a sliver of its fullness missing. But it was probably the safest night to be out, because the weres were all hung over from their monthly shift.

The wind was cold, but not deadly cold. It reminded her that she hadn't seen a ghost in a while.

When they cut around to the back of the hospital, the darkness became denser. Only their footsteps echoed in the night.

"Right there," Steve said and pointed up. "Tenth floor. Second window to the right." He looked around as if to make sure no one was watching. "I'll meet you up there?"

Della nodded and flew up.

There was a ledge, about a foot wide, but it gave her just enough space to park her butt. She had just perched herself when she realized just how much pigeon poop she'd just sat on.

Oh, and it smelled.

Nasty.

Just as Steve had said, the window was left partially opened.

Della raised it another ten inches. The smell of old paper, reminding her of how an old library smelled, filled her nose. She turned her legs around and slipped inside. Her feet had barely hit the floor when Steve landed on the windowsill, looking regal as a peregrine falcon. Her heart did a little tug. She did almost love him.

But it still wasn't love-love.

He swooped inside.

With his wings fluttering back and forth, the magic bubbles appeared around him as he transformed back into human form.

"I found a flashlight when I was here," he whispered and turned to look around. "I thought I left it right—"

"There," Della said, spotting in on the floor below the window.

He grabbed it and turned it on. He cupped his hand over it as if it were too bright. His nervousness made her antsy. She tilted her head to listen for anyone nearby. She didn't hear a sound.

"Is someone else supposed to be in here?" she asked.

"There's a laundry room next door. For all I know, people are there at all hours. And the place has like three security guards. So we need to be careful."

She tilted her head to the side. "But I don't hear anyone. So we can relax."

He frowned. "We're breaking and entering. We can't relax."

"Let's find the file." And when she turned around she realized just what a job that would be. Row upon row of metal racks filled the room. And each rack held boxes stacked on top of boxes, reaching almost to the ceiling, which was at least thirty feet high.

Her gaze shifted from one end of the room to the other.

"Are they marked?" Della asked.

"Some have dates on them," Steve whispered.

They walked into the front of the room, stopping when she got to first row. She took the light from Steve and shined it at the stacked boxes.

She could barely make out the writing. She had to get closer to the box to see the year, nineteen sixty, scribbled in pencil.

"What year are we looking for?" he asked.

"Nineteen ninety-five," Della said.

It took fifteen minutes to find the right year. Unfortunately, it appeared it had been a busy year, too. There were over forty boxes.

Talk about a needle in a haystack . . .

She climbed up the metal rack, and brought down a box. Steve took it from her. Frowning, she realized that if they didn't get lucky, it could take forever.

Making it worse was that whoever had packaged the files hadn't taken care to put them in any order. Some were alphabetized and others random.

They were on the last six when Della started to worry that it wouldn't be here. That she'd dragged Steve out and forced him to help her break the law for nothing.

But then when she picked up one of the remaining boxes to open, she felt it. A chill.

"I think it's in here," she said. She pulled off the top. One file was standing up higher than the others.

The name of the file tab read: CHAO TSANG.

Chase paced. He took Baxter for a walk. Then he went for a run.

He wanted to see her. Just tell her he was sorry for acting like an ass. If she started asking questions again, he'd leave.

Running inside, he filled Baxter's bowl. "I'll be right back," he told the dog.

A few minutes later, he walked through the Shadow Falls gate. Burnett looked at the window as he walked through. He just waved.

As he got closer to Della's cabin, he heard voices. Taking the steps, Chase had already knocked before he took in a breath and tasted the air. He got some odd scent—probably the chameleon chick—and a witch. Miranda.

What he didn't get was Della.

The door opened and Miranda stood there. She smiled. Then her smile faded. No, not faded; vanished. Like bam! There one second and gone the next.

"Chase?" she said. Panic filled her eyes. Then she looked back. "Kylie, look who's here. Chase. Come talk to Chase."

Kylie appeared at the witch's side. "Hi, Chase," she said, but like her friend she appeared . . . not herself.

"Do you know where Della is?"

"Nope. Don't have a clue," the witch blurted out. And her heart did a tumble.

His gaze shot to her wide hazel eyes.

Kylie cleared her throat, obviously trying to communicate to the witch not to lie. But it was too late.

"Is she okay?" he asked the witch.

She nodded.

"Is she here at the school, or did she go out?"

Her head didn't budge. But her eyes cut to the right to peer at Kylie. "It's your turn." Then the witch ran off. Disappearing into a bedroom.

Chase looked at Kylie.

"What's going on?" he asked.

"Oh, Miranda acts weird like that sometimes," she said.

He studied her. "Where's Della?"

"I'm not sure exactly where she is."

Her heart didn't skip.

"Is she with someone?" he asked.

She blinked. "She was alone when she left."

Clever girl, but he knew a cover-up when he heard one.

"Thanks." He walked off straight to cabin nine. To the cabin Perry, Steve, and a new were named Caleb were staying.

He knocked. Caleb opened the door.

"Is Steve here?"

"Nope," he said, completely honest, and unconcerned.

"Do you know where he is?"

"Went out on a date, I think."

Della stared at her father's name on the file. That whisper of cold became a bone-chilling cold.

She reached down and pulled it out, but it was empty. Completely empty.

You keep looking for proof. It doesn't exist. Why can't you believe me?

Della looked up, frosty air hitched in her lungs when she spotted her dead aunt stretched out on the floor, a knife in her chest. Blood was slowly leaking out and turning the white nightgown red.

He did it. I see him over and over again. I feel the pain, the betrayal, and I see him pulling the knife out of my chest. I see him standing there with blood dripping from the blade.

"He would not do that," Della snapped.

"What?" Steve asked.

Bao Yu jumped up. *Go ahead, look. Look in every box there is. You won't find it because the proof doesn't exist.*

Her aunt climbed up the metal rack and started throwing the boxes. The sound echoed in the big room.

"What . . . what's happening?" Steve asked.

"Shit," Della said, realizing that wasn't a vision, that the boxes really were moving. She climbed the rack. "Stop," she said to her aunt as she picked up and tossed another box. It landed with a loud thump.

Della moved in front of her and tried to catch the box, but she couldn't.

Steve yelled something from below, but Della was too busy trying to rein in an angry spirit to listen.

Then all of a sudden six or seven boxes floated up in the air. And they started flying across the room. They hit the walls with loud thumps and papers started raining down.

Steve yelled to her again. Della jumped down. Her heart raced as she watched her aunt send more boxes flying.

"We have to go," Steve snapped.

But it was too late. She'd been so involved trying to stop her aunt that she hadn't noticed they had company until now. She looked at the officer standing in the door, a gun and a flashlight pointing at her.

"Don't move," the guard said. "I swear to God I'll shoot."

Chapter Forty

Della's heart pounded against her breast bone. The guard was a good fifty feet from her. She debated making a dive for the window, but how would that be explained? And while she was fast, she didn't know if she could outrun a bullet.

She cut her eyes to the window where Steve stood, waving for her to come.

The tall shelves hid him from the officer's line of vision.

"Go," she whispered.

"What?" asked the guard.

"No," Steve whispered.

"Go. Get help," she said and watched as some more loose paper fell from the ceiling.

"Don't move. I'll shoot. I swear I will," the guard yelled.

"Burnett?" Steve asked.

"Chase," she said without thinking. And in the corner of her eyes, she watched Steve transform back into a bird and he took flight.

"Is someone else with you?" the guard asked.

"No one else," Della said to the guard and raised her hands. "Just me. Little old me." The ghost tossed another box from the top of the rack and it crashed at the guard's feet.

"Who else is here?" the guard asked, looking at the top of the rack.

"Just me," Della said again and glanced up at the ghost. *Please stop it. Please.*

The next box that came down hit the guard on the head. Della saw him lose his footing as if slipping on a banana peel. His feet came out, his arms extended.

And right then the gun exploded.

Chase had fallen into bed, not that he planned to sleep, but to wait out the need to puke. The three ice cold beers and nasty-tasting bottle of wine didn't sit well. Or maybe it was that damn soup.

He closed his eyes to stop the spinning, then heard a tap against his window. He shot up and saw the bird. Then he saw the bubbles popping against the window pane.

Two seconds later, he caught the shape-shifter's scent. What the hell did Steve want?

Wasn't it enough that he'd just taken Chase's bondmate on a date? Did the guy want to gloat about it? Was he an idiot?

He grabbed his jeans and shirt and went to the door.

Steve stood there. Breathing hard.

Chase stood there. Breathing hard too, and trying not to throw up.

"What?" Chase asked and right then he caught it. Della's scent. He tightened his fist and fought the urge to hit the guy.

"Della," Steve said, trying to catch his breath.

"Della what?" Chase asked, getting a bad feeling.

"She . . . she needs you."

Chase ran to the porch rail and threw up all of the alcohol he'd spent the night consuming.

Then he turned back, wiped his mouth off with the back of his wrist, and asked, "Where is she?"

. . .

Della sat in front of a desk, at the hospital's main office, trying as hard as she could to be supremely polite and perfectly poised. Not easy, because neither came naturally to her.

Especially when her little trip here had offered her nothing.

And now she couldn't help but wonder if someone hadn't already snagged her father's files.

Was it the DA? Did they now have evidence in their hands to make sure her father went down for murder?

Della had refused to give anyone her name—hoping that alone would hold them off from calling the police.

Not that she had remained silent the whole time. She'd apologized profusely and explained that she'd wandered in earlier that day before closing hours and somehow found herself locked in the room upstairs.

The woman in charge, Mrs. Applebee, if the name tag was correct, kept asking Della if she was a runaway. She told her no. The woman didn't actually believe her, but considering the guard's story, she didn't look all that bad.

"She can move things," the guard started up again. "I'm telling you, she was throwing boxes at me with her mind. She'd look up and down would come a box. And that's when my gun went off."

Della wasn't certain if that was actually what had happened, but she had seen the box hit. What she had been certain about was that the bullet had missed her by a few inches.

Right then she noticed that the guard had moved his chair another inch away from her. He'd probably pee himself if Della growled at him.

She might have felt sorry for him if she hadn't smelled the whiskey on his breath. And from Mrs. Applebee's expression, she'd gotten a whiff of the guy's breath as well. That might even be why she was hesitant to call the police. That and the fact that he'd used his gun while intoxicated and shot at an unarmed teen.

Hell, maybe she could use that in her favor.

So far Della hadn't tried to explain the mess of the upended boxes and files littering the floor. But if the guard kept talking crazy, maybe Della wouldn't have to.

She glanced at the clock on the wall. How long would it take for Chase to get here? Any minute now, the woman would be calling the police.

Della had hidden her driver's license, credit card, and phone in her bra, but if they searched her and found them . . . and, God forbid, attempted to call her mom . . . No way could Della let that happen. Her mom had enough problems to last a lifetime.

She looked at the door, wondering how much trouble she'd be in if she ran. And she could run: Mrs. Applebee had confiscated the guard's gun and put it in her desk.

Just when the idea of running seemed like a real option, she recalled the cameras on the outside of the office. They had her face.

Where was her rescue?

Right then her left breast started vibrating. Well, her phone started vibrating. Luckily, she'd silenced it before breaking and entering.

She glanced again at the door. What was taking them so long? Crap. She suddenly remembered that Steve probably thought Chase was still at the school. Which meant Steve would have sought help elsewhere. Her chest tightened and she expected to see a very pissed off Burnett walking through the door any second.

But right now, she'd even take him.

"I'm telling you, she was throwing boxes at me using her mind. She has powers. I've seen shows about people who can do that."

Mrs. Applebee frowned. "Mr. Kelley, just how much have you had to drink tonight?" Then the woman's gaze shifted to Della. "Tell me your name or I'm calling the police, young lady!"

. . .

After Steve had finally spit out the words, Chase went inside and in less than thirty seconds dressed in his official black suit. Tasting his breath, he reached into the garbage can, grabbed the Lysol spray, and gave it a shot. It was mostly air, not disinfectant.

Or maybe not. He fought the urge to puke again.

Handing Steve his car keys, Chase told the shape-shifter to meet him at St. Mary's. Face it, in the dark sky, there was no speed limit or rules about driving after one too many drinks.

In record time, he landed to the side of the hospital. He ran a hand through his hair and patted down his suit. Amazing how flying at a hundred and forty miles an hour could sober a person up.

Not that he knew a lot about sobering up or being drunk. Sure, he drank a glass of Eddie's Scotch when offered, but this had only been his second time to ever drink enough to cause a buzz. And, like the first time, he didn't like it.

He walked around to the front of the hospital, relieved there weren't any police cars. God, he prayed they hadn't already come and taken her away.

Della needs you. Steve's words echoed in his head. He'd never heard sweeter words. And hearing them from Steve made them all the sweeter.

He went to the glass doors, picked up the phone, and pushed a button.

"Can I help you?" a male voice asked.

"Yes, I'm here about the situation. The break-in. Here," he said, looking around for a camera. "I'm holding out my badge."

The bell dinged and Chase walked in.

He figured he had a snowball's chance in hell of actually pulling this off without someone calling the FRU office and eventually getting Burnett involved, but Steve had said she'd asked for him, not Burnett. Since her life wasn't in danger, and no risks were involved, there was no way he was going to disappoint her.

Never mind that she'd disappointed him by trusting Steve with this whole plan without even telling him about it. Chase just hoped the whole date thing had been part of their cover-up.

A knock came at the office door and Della held her breath with hopes that it was her savior. She wasn't even picky. She'd take anyone. Anyone over a real cop who would call her parents.

"Yes," Mrs. Applebee called out.

A nurse popped her head in the door. "Someone's here about the girl."

Della took in a deep breath. Relief went through her when she picked up Chase's scent—along with some disinfectant.

"Who called the police?" Mrs. Applebee asked and then glared at the guard.

"She probably did it with her mind," the guard said.

"I don't know," the nurse answered.

"Let them in," Mrs. Applebee said.

Chase walked in. Della's heart did a few somersaults. His gaze landed on Della for only a second, then focused on Mrs. Applebee. "Madam," he said and held out the badge.

The woman glanced at it and looked up as if content, or maybe not content. Nervous.

Chase wore his black suit—it looked a little wrinkled, but the disheveled look fit that of a tired officer. His hair was pushed back, a little mussed as if he were coming off a hard shift. He looked official. His height and shoulder width in the suit, accompanied by his five o'clock shadow, hid all signs of his true age. He looked . . . wonderful. Like her knight in shining armor.

It hit her then. Hard. She loved him. A knot appeared in her throat and she swallowed. *Not now! Not now!*

"I hear you have an intruder?" Chase said. Mrs. Applebee waved a hand toward Della.

"Yes, I wasn't aware that you were called."

Chase eyed her. "Looks like a runaway."

He must have overheard some of the dialogue before he came in.

"She swears she isn't, but . . . she's not talking."

"They never do," Chase said. "A night in a real cell usually loosens their tongues."

"What's your name?" Chase asked her.

"I'm not a runaway," Della said, repeating her concocted story of how she'd wandered in and gotten locked in the room. Then, feeling as if Chase might need the ammunition, she said, "He shot at me. With a real gun. Real bullets. And he's drunk."

Chase's eyes brightened. She saw his eyes shift down her body as if checking for blood. Then he turned to the guard. "You shot at her?"

"No! She threw a box at me and the gun went off."

"I never threw a box. They must have fallen off," Della said.

"I . . . I'm aware how this looks," Mrs. Applebee said. "I apologize."

Chase turned back to the woman and Della could see his mind ticking on how to play this. "Did she do any damage?" Chase asked.

"Made a mess of our old files," the woman said.

"She did it with her mind," the guard said.

Chase glared at the guard and then at Mrs. Applebee. "You realize you could both get in big trouble. This girl could have been killed."

Mrs. Applebee's face turned white while the guard's turned red, or redder. "Fine, I'm a little drunk, but I know what I saw. She was throwing boxes at me and she was on the floor and the boxes were coming from the top."

"I apologize for him," Mrs. Applebee said. "We have a service who hires out security. We weren't aware that—"

"She's telekinetic or she's a witch." The guard shot up and walked out.

Chase looked back at Mrs. Applebee. "Obviously, this could be trouble. For you and for our . . . runaway. Are you pressing charges?"

"Well, I . . ." Her gaze moved to Della. "I tried to solve this without getting the police involved. But she wouldn't give me any information."

"If I could get this young lady to give me her information and get her home, would you be willing to drop this?" Chase asked.

The woman looked shocked, but relieved. "Why . . . yes, I mean nothing bad has happened. Right?" She looked at Della and smiled.

"Will you do that?" Chase asked Della in an official tone.

"I just want to go home." Della tried to sound desperate. Then again, that wasn't too hard. She was desperate.

She'd broken into a hospital and didn't have anything to show for it.

Chapter Forty-one

They left the office. Della couldn't walk fast enough.

The moment they were alone, Chase asked, "Are you okay?"

"Yes." Her heart pounded and ached. As they made their way to the exit, his shoulder brushed against hers and the touch sent sharp jolts of pain right to her chest.

Chase waved at the guard and the doors opened.

They walked through. The cold air hit Della's face and it felt and tasted like freedom. Chase kept going until he reached the end of the sidewalk. He stopped and looked out into the parking lot across the street.

"The guard really shot at you?" He continued to look around.

"Yeah, but the box did hit him. It could have been an accident."

"You threw the box at him?" Chase glanced up and down the street as if looking for something, or someone.

"No," Della said. "The ghost did."

He looked about ready to say something, but itching to put miles from this place before Mrs. Applebee changed her mind, she asked, "What are you looking for? Can we leave and talk later?"

"Steve drove my car. He should . . ."

An engine sounded in the night, and Chase's car pulled into the parking lot across the street.

"Shit," both Della and Chase said at the same time. Because the scent that reached them at the same time wasn't Steve's.

"What in the hell were you thinking?" Burnett asked as he drove out of the parking lot. Chase had quickly explained that they'd let Della leave without involving the police. Then Burnett told Chase to get back on his own, but to meet him at the school.

The moment Della had crawled into the car, she'd started explaining that this was on her, not Chase, but then she realized that if Steve had been driving Chase's car Burnett probably knew what had happened.

"I was thinking my dad could get the death penalty." She looked away, afraid he'd see tears in her eyes. And not because she'd been caught. She'd didn't give a flying flip that she'd been caught. It was the fact that she still had nothing. Nothing that would help her dad.

After blinking, she looked back at Burnett.

"The files were gone. Someone took them. What if it's the DA? What if—"

"It's not," Burnett said.

"How do you know?" she asked.

His hands tightened around the steering wheel. "Because I've already got them."

Her heart dropped. "You got them?"

He nodded.

"When . . . But . . . why didn't you tell me? I wouldn't have done this if . . ." She saw his expression harden. His silence said so much.

"There's something bad in there, isn't there?"

Burnett let go of air. "What matters is if the DA does go to look for them, they won't find them. I destroyed them."

"What was in there? Did my dad see the murder? Does he know about . . . vampires?"

She saw Burnett's Adam's apple go up and down.

"Damn it! Tell me."

"He talked about being attacked by what he referred to as a monster, but then . . . he claimed he killed his sister."

"What?" she gasped. "He didn't do that." She curled her hands into fists and wanted to hit something. Yanking at the seat belt, she broke it.

"Della, I'm not saying he did it. I . . . I'm saying he told the doctor he did it. But that will never come out. I destroyed the file."

"You did?"

"Yes," he said.

"Did he say why he thought he did it?"

"No. He just said he did it. That's all he said."

She sat there, hurting. "He didn't do it. We know this other guy did it. Stone did it."

"I know. That's why I didn't tell you."

She inhaled a shaky breath and they drove in silence for the next fifteen minutes. Her mind continued to race. She tried to understand. She couldn't.

"Why would he say that?" she muttered.

"Because he was confused," Burnett said. "Maybe in his mind, not protecting her was the same as killing her."

It sounded as if Burnett had already tried to rationalize it. But did he believe it? Did he think her father had killed his sister? She remembered Bao Yu and the visions. The accusations.

None of it could make her believe that her father was a murderer.

A few minutes later, another concern hit. "What if his doctor testifies?"

"He passed away last year. Unless they can find a nurse—and that would be hard because I looked, and couldn't find one—this won't come out. Like I said, I destroyed the file. This will not come out."

Della pulled her knees up in the seat and hugged them. Right then, she knew that Burnett was doing this for her. And she'd bet he hadn't gone through the FRU, either.

"Thank you." She leaned her head against her legs and gave in to the tears. Silently.

"What happened in there?" Burnett asked. "Did they take your name? Did they call the FRU office?"

Della told him about the ghost, about the guard shooting at her, and how everything played out.

Burnett gritted his teeth. She could actually hear it. He couldn't jump on her about what she'd done. Because he'd done the same thing. Only he'd been successful.

"You're lucky that guard didn't hit you," he said through tight lips.

"I know." She looked out the window at the passing terrain and tried not to think.

"We're going to have to do something about the ghost."

"She didn't hurt anyone. She wasn't throwing the boxes at him, just tossing them out." *Go ahead, look. Look in every box there is. You won't find it because the proof doesn't exist.*

"But Della—"

"Give me this, Burnett. Please. She just wants answers." *We all do*, Della thought. Why would her father think he'd killed his sister? It didn't make sense. Because she knew, she knew with every ounce of her being, that her father wouldn't kill anyone. The man had even purchased live traps to catch a rat that had taken up residence in their attic. Then he took it off in the woods and let it free. Her mother had teased him about it, and he'd teased back that the rat had reminded him of her mother.

They drove the rest of the way in silence. When he parked the car, Della looked for Chase. She didn't see him. She inhaled. His scent lingered. Probably waiting in the office.

"Go get some rest." Burnett got out.

She started to walk off and then turned back. "Do you believe me now? My dad said he saw a monster. He saw Feng that night and you remember I told you he told my mom that his brother got cold like me. He knows that I'm vampire?"

Burnett exhaled. "We don't know that."

But Della did. She knew it just like she knew her own name. Her father thought she was a monster. And this, this was why he didn't love her anymore.

Della was almost to the cabin when Chase dropped down right in front of her.

She didn't have time to brush off her tears.

"I'm sorry," he said and pulled her against him.

She let him.

His scent filled her, and she gave in and cried some more.

She stayed there for several long seconds. His arms around her. Her head on his chest. Her heart breaking.

Her mind ran laps around what she wanted to say.

She loved him.

She hadn't done anything wrong with Steve.

Her father knew she was a monster.

"It's going to be okay," he whispered, close to her ear.

She pulled back. "No, it's not. He knows, Chase. My dad knows. And in the file, it states that my dad said he killed his sister. Why would he say that?"

"I don't know." He brushed tears from her cheeks. "Della, listen to me. I promise, I'll fix this. Okay?"

She looked up in his eyes. "How?"

"I just will," he said.

She blinked and there was something in his eyes, something in his tone.

"What are you going to do?"

"Just trust me. Can you do that?" he asked.

And of all the things he could have said this gave her more pause. "If you have a plan I need to know."

He stood there, his firm hands on her shoulders. "I haven't got it all figured out yet, but I'm working on it."

"Working on what?"

He dropped his hands from her. "I need to go see Burnett." He started to leave.

"No." She grabbed his arm. "You know something. What are you not telling me?" He looked away from her. "Don't lie to me, Chase. What's going on?"

"I have not lied. I promised you I wouldn't lie. And I haven't."

"But you're not telling me something."

"Della, I'm trying to work this out. Can you just give me some time? I'll do the right thing."

"What's the right thing?" she asked, now certain he was hiding something. "What are you planning?"

"I'm planning on doing everything earthly possible to get your dad off. I believe he's innocent."

"I know he's innocent," Della insisted. But there was still something Chase wasn't saying. Her mind raced. "Did Kirk give you something? Does he know where Stone is?"

When Chase didn't answer, she asked, "Have you talked to Burnett about it?"

"No." He sighed.

"You know where my uncle is now, don't you?"

"No. Della, please, just . . ."

"Just what? Trust you? You are asking me to trust the guy who's done nothing but lie to me? Who's walked out on me twice? No, let's make that three times, because you left me again."

"Burnett thought it was too dangerous for me to be here."

"Why didn't you tell me? Why haven't you called me, or texted me? Why didn't you text me the other day when you went to see Kirk?"

When he didn't say anything, she just stared at him.

"I have to go," he said. "Burnett's waiting,"

"What the hell are you not telling me, Chase?"

He leaned down and kissed her. "That I love you."

He flew away.

Della stood there in a world of hurt. Was it possible to love someone and not trust them?

Chase landed on the office porch. He heard Burnett stirring in Holiday's office. Chase raked a hand through his hair. Looking over his shoulder, he checked to make sure Della hadn't followed him.

Then he glanced back at the office door. Right or wrong, he had to do this.

He walked in and heard the chair in Holiday's office shift as if protesting the person's weight.

"In here," Burnett said, in his normal pissed-off tone.

Chase walked in. The man sat there, his shoulders straight, arms crossed, and looked up at Chase with the same expression his tone carried.

"You should have called me. This whole thing could have been bad."

"Yeah. I probably should have."

Chase sat down. The chair groaned in protest. And so did Chase's heart. Eddie had saved him. Taught him. Protected him.

He looked at Burnett.

"Something wrong?"

Chase felt a knot tighten in his throat.

"I need some help," Chase said.

"With?" Burnett unfolded his arms, and leaned forward, now more curious than angry.

"I've found myself in a very bad position." Chase ran a hand over his face.

"What position is that?"

Chase looked away, unsure how to start. His gaze landed on a picture of Holiday holding Hannah.

He sat up. "What . . . what would you do if someone killed Holiday?"

Chapter Forty-two

Della dreamed it. She was Bao Yu. So she woke up and refused to sleep. Then she saw it when she wasn't asleep.

She saw the knife being yanked from her chest. The blood dripping from the blade. Her father's face staring down at her. She struggled to take her very last breath of air.

Then she died. Or her aunt died. Over and over again.

And each time she went through it, right before she lost her life, Della felt her aunt mourn and grieve for something different.

People she would miss. Love she'd never be able to give. A child she had given up and would never be able to say "I love you" to. The chance to make all of the things she'd done wrong, right.

Della went to school, hoping it would stop. She walked out of science when it didn't.

Exhausted, mentally, physically, and emotionally, she headed to the office. On that walk, one footstep after another, all Della could hear were Burnett's words. *He said he'd been attacked by a monster.* Did her father really suspect she was vampire?

Holiday looked up when Della walked in, then gasped.

She must have felt what Della was feeling.

"I can't do it anymore. I just can't."

Holiday ran to her and wrapped her in her arms. "I got you. I got you."

Della leaned against her and sobbed. She didn't care if she looked weak. Didn't care if she was getting tears and whatever else on Holiday's pretty green sweater. She simply didn't care.

Or was it that she cared too much?

She cared about Bao Yu. She cared about her dad. She cared . . . that he considered her a monster. She needed to fix this. All of it. But how?

"It's okay." Holiday brushed her hand over Della's back.

Some of the pain left with the touch, but not nearly enough. Especially when she saw it again. The vision hit. She was her aunt, and the knife was being pulled out of her own chest.

Della pulled out of Holiday's arms and pushed her palms deep into her eye sockets, wishing it would go away. "I've seen it at least fifty times today. I'm seeing it now. What does she want from me? Does she want me to say he's guilty? I can't. He never even spanked us. He wouldn't do that. And it doesn't make sense. Why would he have killed her? When someone else had gone there to do it? What does she want?"

"I don't know." Holiday moved in and stroked Della's back.

Della opened her eyes. "Is she punishing me because I still love my dad?"

"No. She's not punishing you," Holiday said. "She wants to understand too, and she thinks you can help her."

"But how? What can I do?" And right then Della had her answer. It scared the crap out of her, but it was the right thing. It was going to happen sooner or later.

"I know what I can do," Della said. "Talk to my dad. He has to know he didn't do this. If she hears him say it, she'll believe it."

Holiday frowned. "Okay . . . I see why you think that would work, but . . ." She paused. "How are you going to explain any of this without telling him—"

"Telling him the truth?" Della finished for her. "Maybe it's time I tell him."

Holiday shook her head. "I'm not sure, with the trial and an angry ghost, that this is the time for that kind of talk."

"Will there ever be a right time for this kind of talk?"

"There might be a better time. I'll tell you what. Instead, why don't you let me try to make her go away? I've been reading up on it. It wouldn't be hurting her. Just blocking her."

"And you don't think that would hurt her?"

Holiday made a face, but couldn't deny it.

"No," Della said. Her idea was better.

Looking over her shoulder, she noted the sun streaming into Holiday's windows. The bright rays hit the crystals hanging around her office and sent spirals of color dancing on the walls.

Not the weather to attempt a daylight flight.

She could wait until tonight, but damn it, she might lose her nerve. Plus, she wanted to talk to him alone, not with her mom. He'd be at work. That was the perfect place. He wouldn't freak out too much. Not with his coworkers around.

"How about a cup of chamomile tea?" Holiday suggested.

She didn't want tea, but a glance at Holiday's desk and Della changed her answer. "Tea sounds good," she lied and felt guilty for it.

Of course, lying was a sin, and grand theft auto was a felony. But it didn't stop her from snagging the keys to the school's silver Corolla and getting the hell out of Dodge before Holiday called out asking if she wanted sugar with that tea.

Della's phone rang. Holiday's number flashed on the screen.

Della cut it off, with good reason. It was dangerous to talk and drive. Oh, yeah, she'd use that excuse.

Trying to fight the urgency flowing through her veins, she drove, never passing the speed limit. It was bad enough she was driving a stolen car. She didn't need a speeding ticket on top of it. Nope, Chase wasn't here to pick it up for her.

Not now. Not now! She didn't want to think about him. Her heart could only break so much. He was keeping something from her. And if he'd been thinking about her, couldn't he have sent her a text? Given her a call? Yeah, he could have. But he hadn't.

An hour later, Della parked her car at her dad's work.

She leaned forward and looked up at the high-rise in the northeast side of Houston. She felt a slight breeze of cold air. That's when she realized that since she'd come up with this plan, the flashes of death had stopped. It seemed her aunt was happy with her decision.

She got out of the car, walked in, and hit the elevator button for the ninth floor. Cool air brushed against her skin as the floor numbers flashed.

She recalled Holiday's warning about having an angry ghost and it not being the time to talk.

"No throwing boxes! No throwing anything!"

The elevator doors opened.

Della stepped out and into her father's workplace.

The receptionist, an older half-Chinese lady who went by the name Lucy looked up and greeted her with a fake smile. That smile changed into a real one when she recognized Della.

"Well, Miss Tsang. You're growing like a weed. Look at you. You're practically an adult now."

Yeah, there was something about stealing a car that probably was going to get her tried as an adult. Of course, the breaking and entering she'd done last night was an adult crime too. She was just a regularly criminal now.

"It happens." She forced a smile. "I was hoping to see my dad. Can I just walk on through?" She started for the door. It didn't make that clicking sound saying it was unlocked.

She took three steps back and looked at Lucy.

The woman shook her head and had a sad face. "Well, I . . . I . . ."

Had her dad told them not to let her back? Was he that afraid of her?

"Your dad isn't in."

"Late lunch?" Della asked.

"No. He . . . hasn't been in for two weeks. He said he needed to focus on the . . ."

"The trial," Della said. But there was a problem. And a big one. She'd been home last week, and he'd left for work every day. Had he just not told her mom? Embarrassed that he couldn't handle it?

Probably.

Della faked another smile and hurried back down and sat in her stolen car. Her chest ached for her dad. For her whole damn family.

She almost changed her mind. Confronting him about this would hurt him. But was it so wrong to need the truth?

And that's when it hit. Bao Yu needed the truth. Della didn't. She knew the truth. Her father hadn't killed his sister.

But she hadn't come here just about that. *He talked about being attacked by a monster.* It was about making him see her. Making him know she wasn't the monster he considered her to be.

Della inhaled. "Where are you, Dad? Where are you hiding out?"

Just to make sure her dad hadn't already come clean about his nonwork status, she dialed her mom.

She answered. "Why aren't you in school?"

"Taking a break." *A long one.* "Is Dad there?"

"No, he's at work. Is something wrong?"

Hell, yes. "No. I just missed him." Her heart dropped when she realized how true that was. She'd missed him for months. "Later."

She heard her mom say her name.

"Later," Della promised.

She rested her head on the steering wheel and tried to think. Where would her dad go to spend his days if he wasn't at work?

Chase and Burnett walked around the empty house with a foreclosure sign out front. They had taken Chase's car, but Burnett had insisted on driving. Chase didn't know if Burnett didn't trust Chase behind the wheel or if he just liked his car. He hoped the latter.

This was the third place they'd gone today from Kirk's list and it appeared to be another one to simply scratch off his list. He couldn't help but worry that this was a wild goose chase.

"You know, I don't get why he'd be at any of these places and live and work at the apartment."

"I checked, and all of the addresses you have were recently purchased, in different people's names—but one of them was Don Williams, the alias that he used in France. He was either putting up his gang, or making sure he had several hideouts."

Burnett hadn't promised to ignore any information about Eddie that Stone might give, but he had promised to personally do the interview with Stone, and not hand anything over until he'd looked into it himself.

And since Burnett had called Chase at five this morning and told him to meet him at the FRU office, Chase suspected Burnett had already investigated some things.

They walked up onto the porch, both of them raising their faces to catch any scents and listen for any signs of someone hidden inside.

Chase got nothing.

"Where to next?" Burnett asked, and they started back to Chase's car.

Before Chase could answer, Burnett's phone rang. "Hey, babe," the man answered.

Chase walked ahead to give Burnett privacy. But he stopped walking when he heard Burnett's signature word for trouble.

"Shit!"

. . .

Della parked in front of the restaurant. The smell of fried rice filled the air. It was the same restaurant her grandparents used to own. The top floor was now used for storage, but it was where her father had lived for the first seven years of his life.

The Chinese couple who'd bought the place from her grandparents still owned it. And her dad brought her here regularly. And while they ate hot and sour soup and fried rice, he'd always tell her about his mother and father and his sister. Little did she know that during all of those talks, he'd been deceiving her about his other two siblings.

Yeah, the fact that he'd had a twin and another sister never came up.

Pushing away anger, she leaned forward, trying to see through the glass window to check out the patrons sitting at the tables.

In the back table, sitting by himself, she saw him. He had a paper in his hands, but she could see the side of his face, and his posture. And the way his hair stuck up in the back gave him away.

Tears filled her eyes. He'd been hiding out every day so he wouldn't have to tell her mom he couldn't face the thought that his associates might think he was guilty. Squaring her shoulders, she pushed the pity away, because she was about to upset him a lot more.

But it was time.

For Bao Yu and for Della.

"What is it?" Chase asked when Burnett hung up and started for the car.

"Your girlfriend," Burnett said.

"My . . . Della?" No one had called her that, and Chase liked it.

"Yes. Or do you make out with any girl while you're on a case?"

"No." Chase smiled. "Just her." Then he noticed Burnett's expression. "Is something wrong?"

"Yes. She took the school's car and is going to confront her dad."

"About the murder?"

"Probably about everything."

"It was bound to happen sooner or later. She's pretty sure he knows she's vampire," Chase said.

Burnett shook his head. "Yeah, and her biggest fear is that he thinks she's a monster. She doesn't need to know how right she is."

Burnett dialed a number. "Della's on the loose, she's trying to go see her father. Do you have him in your sights?"

"Yes," Shawn said on the line.

"Della's in a 2013 silver Corolla. Don't let her talk to him. I'm heading that way just in case."

Burnett hung up. "Let's see if the little spitfire will answer me."

Spitfire, Chase thought. Yeah, that was Della.

Chase heard it go to voice mail. "Della, I need to talk to you. Now!" Burnett growled. He looked at Chase. "Do you think she'd take a call from you?"

Considering their last few conversations, Chase doubted it, but he pulled out his phone. He left almost the same message.

He met Burnett's gaze. "What do you know?"

Burnett started walking to Chase's car. "I know that Della's father is an idiot. And I know Della has a pissed-off ghost following her around."

"What else?" Chase asked, knowing there was more.

Burnett frowned. "When I called to tell her father that Della needed to come back to school, he informed me that he didn't want her coming back to his house again. Ever."

Burnett raked a palm over his face in frustration. "Then yesterday he sent an anonymous email to the police naming Della as a suspect in the Chis' murder. He gave the cops the name of the school."

"Goddamn him!" Chase seethed, his eyes growing hot.

"So far they haven't contacted us," Burnett said, "but if the Chis'
case doesn't get wrapped up quickly, they will."

"Someone needs to teach him a lesson!" Chase said. "And I volunteer! Let's go." Chase stopped at his car. "Maybe that bastard
did kill his sister!"

Burnett shook his head, and opened the locks but didn't get in.
"He didn't. Something happened that night, however, that makes
him think he did." He exhaled and blinked as if trying to control
his own anger.

"Believe me, I've looked under every rock, every leaf that man
ever walked past. I've searched everywhere, hoping to find the smallest reason to beat the holy shit out of him!"

"How he treats Della isn't enough reason?" Chase snapped.

"Yeah, but the kicker is that he's a decent man. He's a good husband, and until Della got turned, he was practically up for the
father of the year award. Why else do you think she loves him so
much?"

"But what about how he treats her now?"

"I know. I'd like to knock some sense into him too. But the only
thing that makes sense is that her being turned somehow brought
back all of these terrible memories. I think until then he either managed to forget or believe it was a dream. Now he's scared. And not
for himself, but for his family."

"Then let's not beat the crap out of him, let's just talk to him."

"Not now," Burnett said. "We need to get this trial over with.
If he loses it, he could hurt his case. And we both know if he gets
convicted Della wouldn't be able to handle it."

Della walked to the door. Put her hand on the handle. *I love you,
Daddy. I just need to understand and you need to understand.*

She'd practiced what she'd say on the ride over here. Now she
took a deep breath and, holding it, she walked inside. She walked
past the booth where her dad had told her he had done his

homework every evening. She walked past the huge lion that her dad claimed he used to climb on as child. She walked past the picture of her grandparents that still hung on the wall.

Finally, she plopped her butt across from her dad.

She saw his paper stiffen. And only then did she breathe.

Only then did she realize her mistake.

The scent of vampire filled her nose.

"Hello, Della," her uncle said.

Chapter Forty-three

Della sat frozen as her uncle lowered the paper. His eyes, his face, all his features were a dead ringer for her dad. Every reason she disliked this man ran through Della's mind, but her heart recalled how in the beginning she'd longed to know him. Longed to have a family member who would understand, who wouldn't look at her like a monster.

She couldn't speak.

He studied her. "You thought I was your father, didn't you?"

Unable to lie—literally unable—she simply nodded.

"Sorry to disappoint you." He smiled. "Would you like some tea?"

She shook her head, still trying to figure out what to say. Hell, what to feel.

"Does your father come here?" he asked.

She nodded.

"It brings back memories." He looked around. "It hasn't changed that much. That booth over there is where we did our homework. You father and I would climb on that lion. Mother used to scold us and say the lion would get one of us one day." His gaze landed on the photo. "You know that's your grandparents."

His voice even sounded like her dad's. Her chest tightened more.

"Why?" she forced that one word out. "Why didn't you come to me earlier? Why did you send Chase and not come yourself? Why didn't you save Chan?" Tears filled her eyes. "Why didn't you go to the FRU when my father got arrested for murder? And why . . . why did you let Chase go see his parents in the morgue?"

He stared at his cup. "That's a lot of questions."

She brushed away a tear. "I deserve answers."

He inhaled. "Where do I start?" He paused. "I did not come to you because you were connected to the FRU. I have reasons not to trust them." He looked down again. "I wanted to save Chan."

"Then why didn't you?" Della sensed a decrease in the room temperature. She ignored it to listen.

"The last time I attempted to bond with someone, they died. My blood is no longer useful. Understand, it would have been unfair of me to ask Chase to bond with either of you. And I didn't. One should only bond with someone you care about. You give up powers. You give up a part of your soul."

Della recalled Chase telling her about Eddie's wife, but she held back her words of sympathy and waited for him to continue.

He added a pack of sugar to his cup. Bits and pieces of tea leaves swirled on top. The spoon clinked against the cup. "I asked Chase to prepare you and Chan to face it on your own. Chase said Chan was too weak to survive even if someone bonded with him. It hurt Chase. He found you were strong. He felt you might survive it. But you intrigued that boy." Her uncle smiled. "He would tell me some of your antics. I heard it in his voice. I knew he would do it, even before he knew." He held up his cup. "He said going in that you were going to fight him. He had you pegged."

Her uncle paused again. "Let's see, what was your other question? Oh, yes. The morgue? Now there is a question I did not expect. But I like it, because it tells me you have stopped fighting the bond."

"That is yet to be seen," she said, remembering how Chase had pulled away again.

"Okay, how can I explain the morgue?" He looked up. "Not my brightest idea. But as someone who had to walk away from my family, I had no closure. So I offered him this choice."

Feng picked up his tea and took a sip. "There, are you happy? Now I'd like to hear about—"

"You forgot one."

He arched a brow.

In the corner of her eye, she saw Bao Yu sitting in the booth. The one they had done homework in, staring. Just staring. She was young, and had some books with her. Did she recognize Feng?

Pushing her aunt from her mind to focus on her uncle, she leaned forward. "Even if you don't like the FRU, when my father got arrested for murder, why didn't you step forward? All of this would have gone smoother. Instead of wasting our time looking for you, we could have been looking for Stone."

"I told Chase that if it appeared my brother would be convicted, I'd come forward and confess to the crime myself. To the police, not the FRU. I've already figured out how to make it believable."

Della sat there, her heart aching. "It would have been nice if Chase would have shared that with me."

"He probably didn't because he swore that wouldn't happen."

Della shook her head. It didn't matter why. It was just another secret he'd kept from her. Another lie.

She met her uncle's gaze. "What is Chase hiding from me now about his meeting with Kirk?"

Her uncle sat back. "What meeting with Kirk?"

Della looked at her uncle. "He really hasn't spoken with you? You don't know, do you?" *At least he hadn't lied about that.*

"Know what?"

"Douglas Stone is Councilman Powell's son. The whole council has known this for years."

"No," Feng said. "They wouldn't . . . Kirk wouldn't."

Della saw the sense of betrayal in his eyes. They grew brighter.

"Why would I lie about it? And it gets worse. I think Kirk is trying to get Chase to do something. And I don't like it."

Her uncle threw a five-dollar bill on the table and shot up. He took one step and looked back at her. "You coming?"

"Where?"

"You want answers or not?"

Almost an hour into the drive, Della broke the apparent code of silence and asked, "Where are we going?"

Her uncle drove a gold Malibu. Nothing flashy, but it still smelled new. He'd been quiet, and for some reason it disturbed her. As had Bao Yu in the backseat.

Della cut her eyes back to her aunt. Still a young girl, still silent.

The insides of Della's palms started to itch. Hadn't her mama always told her not to get into cars with strangers?

This man driving might be her uncle, but he was still a stranger. Considering Chase had told her that he'd lost most of his Reborn powers, she could probably take him.

But laying a hand on a man who looked so much like her dad wouldn't be easy. Not that it was really him she was afraid of. It was what he planned on doing that scared her.

"I told you. To get answers." He put both hands on the wheel and stared straight ahead.

Della noticed the window starting to fog up. "Can you elaborate?"

He finally glanced at her, and the hurt in his eyes told her that he was thinking of his friend's betrayal. "First we're going to go have a chat with Powell. Then I figured we'd go see my pal Kirk."

And that's what she was worried about—seeing Kirk. "Why don't you just call Chase? He'll tell you everything."

"He asked me not to call him, or contact him. He didn't want to have to lie to you."

And how did that make her feel? Chase had purposely cut off contact with someone who might have helped her father's case. She pushed that aside.

"How about if I give you permission to call him? You can tell him we're together, so he wouldn't have to lie."

"I'd rather get the whole story. I expect they'll tell me more than they told Chase." He leaned in and turned on the defroster.

"You think they'll just tell you?" She saw steam leave her lips and she tried not to visibly tremble.

"With some convincing," he said.

"Okay," Della said. "I'm just gonna be honest here." She stuck her hands between her legs to keep them warm. "I want to know the truth, but in the last twenty-four hours I've committed breaking and entering and grand theft auto. And assault and battery might be included, but that wasn't me. Not that anyone will believe it. Anyway, I'm at my limit for committing crimes. I mean, if I do any more, I'm gonna go down. It's a Murphy's Law kind of thing."

He looked at her. His eyes were bright and serious. Then he laughed.

And God help her, but it was the first time she'd heard her father's laugh in so long that she laughed with him.

"You really haven't done all that, right?" he asked when the humor faded.

"Yeah, I kind of have." She gave her aunt a quick glance and then looked back at Feng.

He frowned. "Okay, not to worry. I think I can get you through this without being arrested. And if I can't, I'll say I forced you."

She wasn't sure if he was joking, but she said, "Okay."

"Now, can I ask you a question?" He swiped his hand over the windshield. "Who the hell is in the backseat with us?"

"Come on, let's go finish what we started," Burnett said to Chase.

Chase looked away from the house and back at Burnett. It was after five. Della's father had returned to his house. Briefcase in hand, as if he'd been working all day and not hanging out at Starbucks.

"What if Della comes back?"

"My agent will stop her. And I've got someone combing the streets. Our time is better spent finding Stone. And we need to go by another address that we have on our expensive-tennis-shoe wearer. If we catch him, the police can't suspect Della for the murder."

"Since this guy was in the gang, he might be with Stone," Chase offered.

"The others who we are pretty damn sure participated in the murder got left behind. I'm following my gut that he got left behind too. I'm thinking Stone had people around Della's house, and a couple of his guys lost it and committed the murders. This might even be why they got left behind. Stone doesn't want to draw attention to himself right now."

"Okay," Chase said, seeing logic. "But why don't we separate? We'll get more done."

"Too dangerous." Burnett started walking back to Chase's car.

"I'm not one of your students anymore. I'm an agent." He pulled on the label of his jacket. "In case you haven't noticed the suit."

"You think I'd send a junior agent out alone on a case?"

"I'm not a junior. I worked two years for the council."

"Yeah, but oddly they have failed to send over your files." Burnett stopped by his car.

Chase frowned. "Can I at least drive my own car?"

"No," Burnett said. "You aren't thinking about selling this, are you?"

"No." Chase got in the passenger seat and called Della. It went to voice mail. Again. Where the hell was she?

Della felt her phone in her pocket vibrate again. Who was it this time? Not that she'd check. As long as she didn't know, she wouldn't feel guilty. Or too guilty.

Holiday was going to hate her. Burnett was going to whip her butt. Kylie and Miranda wouldn't speak to her. Chase was . . .

Not now.

Della's gaze shifted to the sky painted with reds, purples, and grays. Only a sliver of big orange sun hung over the western horizon. It reminded her of the few fishing trips she'd taken with her dad. She hated fishing, but being with him all day, just sitting by the water and discussing everything from fish to future boyfriends, had been some of her best childhood memories.

"You gonna tell me? Who's back there?" her uncle asked again.

Della inhaled. "Do you have a firm grip on the wheel?"

"Yeah. Why?" She saw his hands tighten.

"Because . . . I've seen her do crazy things to cars." Della swallowed and gave the girl in the backseat another quick glance. She looked so young and completely innocent, popping gum and enjoying the ride. This wasn't the same spirit who'd destroyed St. Mary's file room. Was it Feng, or was it seeing her childhood home that had changed her?

She glanced back at her uncle. "So you can feel ghosts too?"

"Feel them, not so much. But I can feel temperature, and it's colder than a witch's tit in here. Plus, you've been eyeing someone back there this whole time."

"It's Bao Yu," Della said.

Della saw her uncle's shoulders drop an inch as if the weight of the world had just sat on them. "I thought she would leave after you and Chase found her daughter."

"She needs answers too." Della suddenly realized that her uncle might be able to give them to her.

"Tell her I'm so sorry. I'm responsible. They did it because of me. I wouldn't do what they asked. I went to help, but I got there too late."

Della shot her aunt another glance. She was older now, but not wearing the white bloody gown. It seemed that when she had the gown on was when she got out of control.

He was dead. How can he be alive? Bao Yu asked.

"He wasn't dead. I told you. He's a vampire like me. Like Natasha."

Her uncle looked at Della, then glanced in the rearview mirror. "Do you see her?"

"Yeah." Della answered and hesitated to bring it up, but decided it had to be done. "She thinks my father killed her."

He did! He even admitted it! When I found him at the hospital. He told the doctor.

Della inhaled. "In the doctor's notes. When my father was hospitalized, he admitted it too."

Her uncle shook his head. "No. Douglas Stone did that."

"You saw it?" Della glanced over her shoulder and as expected, the bloody gown was back.

"No . . . not exactly. But when I got there Chao was unconscious, on the floor by the phone. I heard someone in my old room. I found . . . Stone was standing over her. She had the knife in her chest. It was my knife." The sound of grief echoed in his voice. "I chased him out of the room."

"Did my father see you?" Della asked.

Her uncle nodded. "We were fighting in the hall. I saw him run into the room where Bao Yu was."

He did it. I showed you!

Della saw it again in her head. Her aunt flat on the floor. A knife jutting out of her chest. When she reached up she found another hand on the knife. The knife pulled out. The pain hit. The numbness started. The last thing she saw was her brother, holding the knife. Blood dripping from the blade.

Just like that, Della realized something. In every vision she'd showed Della, her father had never . . . stabbed her.

"I know what happened." Tears filled Della's eyes and she looked first at her uncle and then back to her aunt. "You were trying to pull the knife out. He saw you and he thought he was helping. But you died then. You thought he killed you. He thought he killed you."

The car spun out of control—Della saw Feng fighting the wheel—then the last thing Della saw was the tree rushing toward them before everything went white. All white.

Chapter Forty-four

Chase watched Burnett cut the engine off. About a dozen mobile homes filled the small park. Gold light beamed out of the windows. Both he and Burnett pulled in air at the same time, testing it for any weres.

Burnett's gaze shot to Chase.

Chase nodded. "It's him."

"You get anything besides were?"

"Humans. And it might be more than one were." Chase looked down at the paper Burnett had handed him. "The address says number eight. It must be one in the back."

As Burnett reached for the door handle, his phone rang and he checked the number. "Make it fast," Burnett said into the phone and got out of the car.

"We found the Corolla, but not Della." Shawn's voice reached Chase's ears.

"Where did you find the car?"

"We looked at all the places her father hung out these last few days, thinking Della might have gone looking for him. The car is parked in front of an old Chinese restaurant in Chinatown."

"Have you checked the area?" Burnett frowned at Chase.

"Yes. She's not here. Do you want us to get the car?"

"No," Burnett said. "She'll come back for it. Leave someone there, and . . . keep looking. Find her." Burnett hung up.

Chase heard Burnett's concern and he felt it tenfold. He also knew what scared Burnett the most was that Stone had somehow gotten his hands on Della. And damned if it didn't terrify Chase. He'd seen what that man was capable of doing to his own girlfriend. He could only imagine what he'd do to a stranger.

They walked past the first five trailers. Chase heard people milling around inside.

"You go to the front door and knock," Burnett said. "I'll go to the back and stop their asses when they run."

"I could do the back," Chase offered.

Burnett frowned. "I got it." Then he glanced around. "We've got to do this with no show. Not too many witnesses. You understand?"

Chase nodded and started to the front porch of trailer number eight as Burnett went around the back.

He stepped on the porch and right before he knocked he heard the telltale sound of a shotgun being cocked.

Chase moved. Just not fast enough.

Della pushed the airbag out of her face and looked at her uncle. He was doing the same thing.

Della smelled blood before she saw it ooze from his brow. "You okay?"

"Yes. The wheel went crazy." He touched his brow. "Just a bump. You?"

"Fine." Only after declaring it did Della move all her arms and legs. Nothing hurt.

The car engine spewed and sizzled. She glanced to the backseat with concern—only to feel like an idiot because her aunt was already dead. But she wasn't even there.

Her uncle got out of the car. Della did the same. Or would

have if the car door would have opened. She gave it a shove and the sound of screeching metal filled the night. They stood outside the car.

Feng looked at the vehicle.

"I warned you," she said.

He nodded. "Never liked that car anyway." Then he looked up at the sky. "It's still quite a few miles from here." He looked her up and down. "Sure you're not hurt?"

"Sure," she said.

"Then you're okay to fly?"

She nodded.

Chase lurched back, landing on his feet.

Pain hit his shoulder as one tiny shot grazed him. But if he hadn't moved he'd have been a goner. He growled and caught the scent of his own blood.

Pissed off, he leapt back onto the porch. He pushed through what was left of the door, hoping the shotgun wasn't a double barrel, ready to give someone hell.

But hell had already been given. Burnett had the two guys down, FRU cuffs on their wrists. Chase saw the back door of the trailer on the floor.

Relief filled Burnett's eyes when Chase appeared. Then he scowled.

"You're hit!"

"Just grazed." He went over and picked up the shotgun. Adrenaline still fired through his body, his shoulder stung, and he fought the desire to kick the two half-weres now stretched out face down on the stained carpet.

Then he noticed what was on one of the guy's feet. "Nice shoes," Chase said.

"Real nice." Burnett stood and snatched his phone from his coat pocket and made a call. "We need a wagon to bring in two."

. . .

They landed in a wooded lot, close to a fence. Her uncle took one step, then stopped. Della wasn't quite sure where she was, but the neighborhood looked upscale. They'd passed over several nice estates. Houses as big as apartment buildings.

"You see that house?" her uncle asked.

Della looked between the metal slats of the fence. She could see it, but it was half a block away. "Yeah."

"How fast can you make it there and knock down that door?"

Della looked at him. "More breaking and entering?"

"I don't think he'll call the police."

She hesitated. "Why don't I just knock, ask if I can come in? I can be convincing."

He frowned. "Because the second one of us gets any closer to that house, it will set off a lockdown mode and a metal plate with electrical current will come down on all the windows and front door."

"Oh." She grimaced and looked back at the house.

Feng continued, "It will take thirty seconds for the metal to lower and get the power to it. Back in the day, I could get to that house in fifteen seconds. You that good?"

Della sighed. "Maybe. Whose house is this?" She inhaled, but wasn't close enough to get any scents.

"Powell's."

She bit down on her lip. "Do you think Stone's in there?"

"I don't know. But I'd bet my canines Powell knows where his son is."

The thought of snagging Stone and stopping the trial before it happened had Della pushing away the feeling that she was crossing over the line.

"He's the old guy, right?" Della asked.

"Yeah."

Della looked at Feng and tilted her head to hear his heart. "You're not going to kill him?"

"No. I promise."

Della nodded. "Then I'm ready."

"You might as well confess," Chase growled down at the barefooted rogue sitting in the interrogation room. "We got you. You're going down."

"You ain't got shit," the were said.

"Really?" Chase, feeling his canines lower, pulled the picture from the file he held. "Do you know what this is? It's a picture of a shoe print, idiot! And guess what? By tomorrow, our guys will have matched it to your shoe, and you're going down."

"I'm not the only one who wears those shoes!" the half were said.

The door to the room opened. Burnett waved Chase to come out.

Chase slammed the door on his exit.

"What?" Frustration and worry over Della had his whole body knotted. "You found her?"

"No, but you've been going at him for thirty minutes. He's not going to talk. And as you said, tomorrow they'll identify the shoe print and we'll have him. Don't waste any more energy on him."

Chase didn't hate it so much that Burnett was right, he just hated that he was wrong. "Okay, let's go back to our last two addresses to find Stone."

Burnett shook his head. "I haven't slept in thirty-eight hours and I'm betting you're going on forty-eight."

"And I'm not going to sleep until we know where Della is," Chase said.

"Neither am I," Burnett said. "But we both need to drink some blood and at least try to relax, or we're likely to mess this up. I've already sent some agents out to the other two places on the list. Right now, both residences are empty. I've got them on watch, and if anyone shows up, they'll call me first thing."

"But—"

"Don't argue," Burnett said. "We did good tonight. Tomorrow, when the evidence comes in, I'll mark the Chis' case solved. Della will never have to know that her father reported her to the police."

Della started to step back.

"Wait," her uncle said. "If that metal plate comes down, stop. You got that?"

Della nodded.

"It probably wouldn't kill you, but it would hurt like hell. And if I hand you back over to Chase with a scratch on you, he'll have my head."

"You won't hand me over to anyone," Della said.

"I didn't mean . . . Sorry," he said.

"Let's do this," she said.

She moved back several feet to get a running start. She heard the alarms as soon as she crossed the gate. The wind tossed her hair in her eyes. As she came closer to the porch she heard clicking sounds as if things were about to come down.

She sped up and hit the door with her shoulder full force.

It hurt like hell, but the door cracked. She landed on her side on the floor of the home.

The clicking noises stopped. She heard her uncle land on the porch and he rushed inside.

She bolted to her feet, and the smell hit.

It wasn't as bad as the smell at Stone's girlfriend's house, but close. She slammed her hand over her nose.

"Well, you don't have to worry about me killing him," her uncle said.

Della turned around, and there, on the hall floor, was the old man she remembered from her one and only council meeting. Considering his age, Della might have suspected he'd gone of natural causes. But there was nothing natural about the knife sticking out of his back.

"What's the address here?" Della asked, looking away.

"Why?" her uncle asked.

She reached for her phone. "Because I'm calling Burnett."

Chapter Forty-five

Begrudgingly, Chase stormed out of the office. He'd just dropped his ass on the seat behind the wheel. He hadn't even shut the door when Burnett shot beside his car.

"Let's go," he said.

"What?" Chase climbed out.

"Della," Burnett said. "She's at a murder scene."

"Stone?" Chase asked, slamming his car door and putting his keys away.

"No, Logan Powell." He pulled out his phone and spouted out an order to someone.

"What? How did Della meet up with Powell?" Chase asked.

"Don't know. She was short on details." Burnett took off.

Chase took off after him.

Ten minutes later, Chase and Burnett landed in front of a large two-story house.

"Does this belong to Powell?" Burnett asked.

"I don't know," Chase said. "I've never been here." And he sure as hell didn't understand how Della had gotten here.

As he got closer, he spotted Della sitting on the edge of the porch. The muscle in his chest—his heart—released for the first time since he'd known she was missing.

The smell of death hit. As he moved closer, Della's scent reached him. But then another scent hit, a weak vampire trace, meaning he was no longer on the premises, but it certainly answered the mystery of how Della had gotten here.

Eddie.

"What happened?" Burnett asked as they got closer.

Della stood up. "I don't know, I just found him."

Chase walked over, wanting to hold her, but her angry look stopped him. He waited for her to mention Eddie. She didn't.

"Who was with you?" Burnett lifted his face again to draw in air.

Della's gaze met Chase's. He nodded.

"My uncle."

Burnett shook his head and looked at Chase. "Did you know she was with him?"

"No," Chase said at the same time Della did.

"I found Feng when I went looking for my father."

"And why would he bring you here?" Burnett asked.

"I told him that Stone was Powell's son. He thought maybe Powell could tell us where Stone was."

Burnett looked at the door.

"Was the door broken in when you got here?"

"No, I did that."

Burnett shook his head and exhaled loudly. "Have you touched anything else?"

She shook her head.

"Okay. Go back to the school."

"But—"

"Don't you even think of arguing with me!" Burnett seethed. "Do you have any idea how worried we've been about you? Go back to the school. Straight back!"

"The car," she said.

"I said get to the school!"

"It's on Peach Street and—"

"I know where it is!" He raked a hand through his hair. "Some more agents will be showing up here any minute now. If you want a career with the FRU, you'd better get your ass out of here now."

Chase saw Della nod. He also saw the tears in her eyes. He took one step toward her. She took off.

"Did you have to be so hard on her?" Chase growled.

Burnett ignored him and stormed inside the house. Chase followed.

He stopped when he saw Councilman Powell's body in the hallway. Chase hadn't been close to the man, but seeing him dead pulled at his heartstrings.

Burnett looked up. "We need to mask Della's scent. Go to the kitchen, find some seasonings, anything with a strong odor, add water to it, and boil it. Then wipe your prints off and put it all way. Fast."

Forty minutes later, Della landed in the school's parking lot. As good as home felt, right then she'd rather be anywhere but here. She knew what, or rather who, waited for her.

Della had grown accustomed to butting heads with Burnett. Holiday was another story. Burnett got mad. The kind of mad Della could handle. Holiday mostly got disappointed. That was harder.

A night breeze brushed against Della's face and she hesitated, closing her eyes. Her heart ached, her mind raced. Then, knowing she couldn't postpone it, she walked through the gate. The slight click of the alarm announced her entrance.

She heard the creak of one of the white rockers on the front porch. Through the darkness she could see the shape of one small woman.

Della didn't know what to say. She wasn't sorry she'd done it. Even considering everything that had happened, meeting her uncle was . . . good.

Holiday stood up.

Della stepped up on the porch. The red-haired fae frowned. Holiday didn't frown a lot.

"I'm sorry I upset you," Della said. "I know you were worried. But I had to go. And . . . the car's fine."

"It's not the damn car I care about!" Holiday seethed, and she wrapped her arms around her. "You don't do this to people who love you!"

Della rested her head on her shoulder for a few seconds before pulling away.

"I know what happened now," Della said.

"Happened?"

Della nodded. "The night Bao Yu died. My dad didn't kill her. Well, not . . . really. He wanted to help her. He found her and she was trying to pull the knife out of her chest. He did it for her. And that's the last thing she remembered."

Holiday sighed. "Does she know?"

"I think so. I don't know if she believes it yet."

"If that's what really happened, she'll realize it now."

Holiday stepped back and looked at her. "You're exhausted. Have you fed at all today?"

Della shook her head.

"Do you have some blood in your cabin's fridge?"

Della nodded.

"Then go feed and get some sleep. Kylie and Miranda are worried sick about you, but don't let them keep you up too late. Burnett said he'd talk to you in the morning."

Della had barely stepped off the front porch when two cars pulled into the parking lot. One of them was a police car with its lights flashing.

At almost ten o'clock, at least six agents moved around the house. Chase kept his mouth shut and let Burnett do all the talking. When one agent asked how they'd found the crime scene, Burnett said he could read it in his report later. What they needed to do now was collect and find any evidence.

Thankfully Burnett's order wasn't questioned. Chase still didn't know how Burnett was going to explain it.

So far, nothing appeared in Powell's home to prove he was part of the council. But since Burnett had known Powell's full name, someone at the FRU would probably put it together.

Wearing gloves, Chase helped two agents go through a desk off the back of the kitchen. He found an address book. When he flipped through it, he found Eddie's old addresses. Not wanting them looking into him, he almost attempted to pull the page, then decided against it and bagged the whole thing for evidence. Even if they went there, they wouldn't find anything.

The agent in charge of removing the body estimated that the murder had happened about seventy-two hours ago. That meant Powell had probably died the same day Chase had seen him.

The fact that Powell was probably killed by his own son made Chase feel a little sorrier for the old guy. Did Stone know his old man had turned on him?

"Chase?" Burnett called to him from another room.

Chase walked out and when he saw the look on the man's face, he knew something else was wrong.

Burnett was ending a call on his phone. He turned to Trisha. "We've got something we need to handle elsewhere. Can you take over?"

"I got it."

As they left the house, Burnett muttered, "The cops are at the school questioning Della."

Chase's chest filled with hot anger. If she learned her father had turned her in it might just break her heart. And if that happened, Chase just might have to break something of her father's. Preferably his neck.

. . .

Holiday had sent Della to wait in one of the conference rooms housed in the main office cabin, with strict orders to stay put. Then she'd heard Holiday walk out to the parking lot to talk to the police.

It was just far enough away that Della couldn't hear what was being said. She almost went outside, but considering she'd already disobeyed the woman once today, she decided against it.

A short time later, footsteps moved inside. A crazy thought hit. Were they here about her?

Two cops walked in and sat across from her at the table. Holiday sat beside her. One of them must have been a detective, because he was wearing a suit; the other wore a uniform.

"Ms. Tsang." The detective introduced himself and the other officer.

"Yes," Della inhaled, her heart hammering in her chest. She wondered if this was about the hospital break-in. Then another thought hit. Had Holiday called them when she took her car? No, she wouldn't.

"We're here about Mr. and Mrs. Chi. Are you aware of what happened to them?" the guy in the suit asked.

Holiday's palm rested on Della's hand, offering her some calm.

Calm that Della didn't want. What she wanted was to understand. She pulled her hand down in her lap. "Yes, I'm aware." She looked at Holiday and then back at the cops.

"Why are you asking me about this?" Della leaned in.

The dark-haired heavy-set uniformed guy sneered at her. He didn't have a pretty face, and sneering just made it worse.

"I think you might be confused," he said. "We didn't come here for you to ask us questions. We came to ask you questions. And you can play nice and answer them or we can take you in. Ever been in jail, Miss Tsang? It's not a nice place."

Della's breath caught.

"Just answer them," Holiday said in a calm voice. But Della saw the fury glittering in the woman's eyes. This time, there was no concern or love mingled with it. Just plain ol' fury. And it wasn't targeting Della.

Della recalled hearing Holiday call Burnett before the policemen had left their cars. Their dialogue had been quick. "The police are here." It was almost as if she'd been expecting them.

"You knew Mr. and Mrs. Chi, right?" the other officer asked.

"Yes," Della said. "They were my neighbors and I pet sit for them."

"And where were you Friday night?"

All the air in Della's lungs came out. "You think . . . you think—?"

"Just answer our questions, Miss Tsang," the ugly officer snapped.

"I was out . . . with a friend. I saw Mrs. Chi at a restaurant."

"What restaurant?"

Della was about to answer when she heard a loud thump on the office porch. The door swung open, and she caught Burnett's scent.

He stormed into the room, holding his badge out.

"Hello. I'm Burnett James, part owner of Shadow Falls Academy, and I'm with the Federal Research Unit. I was recently assigned to the Chi case and just picked up the killers tonight."

The sneering uniformed cop stood up. "You're with who?"

"FRU," said the detective. "They're an offshoot of the FBI." He looked back at Burnett. "I didn't know the case had been reassigned."

"It wasn't." Burnett gazed at Della, almost as if he were checking on her. "We were asked to assist. One of my students"—he motioned to Della—"was friends with the victims."

"We haven't seen anything about the killer being caught," the uniformed cop said.

"We just brought them in tonight, haven't done the paperwork yet. If you'd like I'd be happy to see you out." From his tone it wasn't a suggestion. Burnett waved at the door.

"Wait!" Della said.

Everyone looked back her. "Why did you think that I . . . ?"

"We should just let them go." Holiday put another hand on Della's shoulder.

"No," Della said. "Who . . . who said I was involved?"

"Someone named you as a suspect," the detective said.

Things suddenly became clear. And damn, it hurt. "My dad?" she asked. "He said I did this, didn't he?"

Tears filled her eyes. The memory of how he'd looked at her before she left walked across her heart.

"Why would your dad say you did this?" the fat cop asked.

"Because he thinks I'm a monster." Della looked at Holiday and remembered the call she'd made to Burnett.

"You knew, didn't you? You knew he told the cops I did this!"

Della stormed out of the room before everyone got to see her cry. Before they got to witness her heart breaking.

As she ran, her feet pounding on the cold hard ground, the absurdity of it hit. She was trying to get her father off for murder while her father was trying to get her convicted. Maybe it was justice. It was her fault he'd been arrested.

She had to stop and catch her breath when she realized that her father actually thought she'd killed someone. Even with all of the evidence pointing to him, she'd never believed he could have done that. What had she done to make him hate her so much?

The answer came, with clarity. She was a monster.

She was almost to her porch when she saw Kylie standing at the window, phone to her ear. Holiday had probably called her.

Della didn't want anyone trying to make her feel better. They couldn't.

"Della," someone called her name.

Recognizing his voice, she swung around and faced Chase. "Go away. Go! I don't want to see you. I don't want to see anyone!"

"You're hurting," Chase said. "I know. I just want to sit with you. Hold you."

"I don't want you to sit with me. I don't want you to ever hold me again! My uncle told me, Chase. You knew he said he would come forward and wouldn't let my dad go to jail. Why didn't you tell me that?"

He ran a hand over the back of his head and guilt filled his eyes. "Because I wasn't going to let that happen. He didn't kill his sister."

"Neither did my father!" Admitting it aloud made all this hurt so much more.

She shook her head. "And you purposely forbade him from getting in touch with you. Because you knew if he did call, you would lie. Lie to me, just like you always lie! And whatever Kirk told you, you are keeping that from me too."

He shook his head. "Della?"

"No!" she screamed and lurched forward, knocking him on his ass. "Leave! You excel at doing it, so do it one more time. And this time, don't come back."

"You don't mean that," he said, but he didn't get up. "You're just upset."

She shook her head and went and stood over him. "Listen to my heart, Chase. Hear the truth." She wiped her tears away. "You said it was my choice if this bond lasted. I'm choosing, Chase. It's over. Leave me the hell alone!"

She shot up the stairs, past Kylie, who stood in the doorway, and went to her bedroom.

Chapter Forty-six

Chase stood up. Della's words sliced through him like a dull knife. But it was her pain that he felt the most.

He started up the porch, but Kylie stepped into the doorway.

"I think it might be best if you let her be alone for a while."

He raked a hand over his face.

"She's just upset," Kylie told him and touched his arm. She'd turned fae. He could feel her trying to soothe him.

He shook his head and had to swallow not to let his emotion turn to tears. "She wasn't lying when she said . . ." Damn, that hurt.

Kylie stepped closer. "Sometimes when the heart breaks, it doesn't know what it wants and it doesn't recognize the difference between the truth and a lie. Give her some time."

"Time." He turned and walked away.

Holiday came running up. "Is she okay?"

"No," Chase said. "She's not. Somebody needs to be with her, but she definitely doesn't want it to be me."

Chase stopped off at the office to see Burnett.

"Can I kill her father now?"

Burnett frowned. "Go home and sleep. I'll call you when and if anyone shows up at the two houses where you think Stone might be. If I don't call, I'll pick you up at six."

Chase hadn't even remembered he'd left his car somewhere. Hell, he didn't care. "I feel like I should be doing something."

"Go rest so you can do something later."

Chase started out, and Burnett said, "Wait."

He looked back. "Do you have a way of contacting Eddie?"

"I could call Kirk. Why? You want to arrest Eddie?" *Wouldn't that be the perfect ending to all of this?* Chase thought.

Burnett shook his head. "No. I won't let anything Stone says come back to him. But I would like to talk to him. I'm not going to ask you to give me his number, but could you ask him to call me?"

Chase ran a hand over his face. "I don't think he'll do it."

Burnett sighed. "Look, I can't blame Eddie for what he did. If it had been me, I would have killed him too. But I'd like to at least know that Eddie doesn't plan on trying to exact some revenge on the FRU later on."

"Don't you think he would've already done that if that was his plan?"

"I'd still like to talk to him."

Chase went to his cabin. He fed and walked Baxter. He drank a glass of blood. Then he went to bed and watched the ceiling fan spin.

You said it was my choice if this bond lasted. I'm choosing, Chase. It's over. Leave me the hell alone!

Baxter jumped up on the bed and rested his head on Chase's arm. It was as if the dog knew he was dying inside.

Picking up his phone, he considered calling her, but what for? She'd only tell him to go away.

Then, because he figured he couldn't hurt any more than he already did, he dialed Kirk's number and left a message that he needed to speak to Eddie. Hell, for all he knew, Eddie wouldn't talk to Kirk.

But ten minutes later, his phone rang.

"Hey," Chase said.

"Son?" the man answered. And it was the voice of the man who had been there for him since the plane crash. The man who had held him when he'd wept over losing his parents.

Chase started to say something, but his voice broke.

"What's wrong, Chase?" Eddie said.

"Everything," Chase said, not knowing how to explain any of this. Would Eddie think Chase had sacrificed him to save Della's father? The man didn't deserve to be saved.

How could Eddie not feel betrayed by Chase? Especially when he probably already felt betrayed by Kirk.

"What is it? Talk to me."

After a few minutes, Chase asked, "Did you talk to Kirk?"

"For the first time, right now. Just to tell me you called. He wouldn't answer my calls and he wasn't at his lake house. But he said I could call him after we talk. How could a friend do this?" Eddie asked.

Chase pushed his head into the pillow. "I don't know."

"What did Kirk ask you to do, Chase?"

"To kill Stone and not hand him over to the FRU. Kirk promised to talk you out of confessing to killing your sister."

"I don't understand," Eddie said.

"He took the files, Eddie. Stone was blackmailing the council not to turn him in."

"That's not an excuse. Kirk should have told me. I thought he was my friend."

Chase swallowed. "Kirk told me about Kirsha. About the agent who planted the bomb."

There was silence. "He shouldn't have told you."

"Look, I can understand why you did it. And I went to Burnett. He's going to try to fix it."

He heard the man who had been his father for the last four years let out a low growl. "I don't need an FRU agent to try to fix it, Chase," Eddie seethed. "I killed the guy who killed Kirsha and I'd do it again if he showed up today. And again tomorrow."

"I know. And I don't blame you. That's why I told Burnett. He doesn't hold you responsible either. If I catch Stone, I'm not going to kill him."

"Kirk should have never asked you to do that," Eddie said.

"I know." He inhaled. "Look, Burnett has agreed not to let anything Stone says about you to come forward, but . . ."

"What?" Eddie asked.

"He wants to talk to you. I'm going text you his number. You should call him."

"I can't promise that," Eddie said.

"Try."

Eddie hung up.

Chase texted Burnett's number, then went back to watching the ceiling fan.

Somewhere around three that morning Chase finally fell asleep. At five thirty his alarm rang. He sat up, hoping that big knot of pain in his chest had released.

It hadn't.

His phone dinged with a text. His heart leapt, thinking it would be Della.

It was Burnett. *Be there in thirty.*

Chase texted back one word. *Della?*

His cell dinged back with two. *Not talking.*

Tossing his phone down, feeling helpless, he went to shower.

By eight, the shoe imprint had come in that matched the half were's shoe. Chase got to give him the news. That felt good and he wished he could be there when Della's father got the news that they'd caught the murderers.

At nine Burnett had Chase doing some filing. *Filing?* When that was done, Burnett had him fetching breakfast for Sam, Perry's cousin, who was still being held in a temporary cell. Chase was beginning to feel like Burnett's secretary.

When Chase returned, Burnett met him at the entrance. He handed the bag of food off to the receptionist—delivering the orders—and motioned for Chase to follow.

"We got something?"

"A cleaning lady just entered the house on Vermont Street," Burnett said. "When she leaves we're going to snatch her up and see what she knows."

Burnett stopped at a white van parked out front. "Here." He handed Chase a cup he'd been holding. "It's for you. My personal breakfast blend. O negative with some B positive."

Chase got in. "I'm not really hungry."

"Drink." Burnett cut his eyes to Chase. "Eddie says you can be an ass if you don't feed a little in the morning."

Chase looked up. "He called?"

"Yeah."

"And?"

"I have a plan." He started the engine.

"And you aren't going to share it with me?" he countered.

"First we need to catch Stone."

Frustrated, Chase stared out the window. Then realized he was being an ass. Burnett was helping him. "Thank you."

"It's not a favor. It's what's right."

Silence filled the van, and then Burnett spoke up. "This agency does a lot of good, but I don't always agree with their policies."

It was the thing he respected about Burnett the most. The man valued rules but bent them when needed. "How do you know when to do it?" Chase asked

"Do what?"

"When to break policy? I mean, do you ask, 'What would Jesus do?' or what?"

"Everyone has a moral compass," Burnett said.

"But not everyone's is pointing in the same direction."

"You only worry about your own direction." He exhaled. "I ask myself, if my ass gets caught, will it be worth it. If the answer is yes, I do it." He glanced at Chase. "And don't for a minute think they won't fire you."

Chase stared out the window at the blurred landscape: trees, buildings, cars, people. The world hadn't stopped, so why did it feel as if his had? A vision of a dark-haired spitfire filled his mind.

He hated to ask, but his concern outweighed his pride.

"Any news on Della?"

Burnett didn't look at him, but his jaw tightened. "Holiday said she still hasn't come out of her room. Miranda and Kylie are planning an intervention if she doesn't surface soon. Is she not answering your calls or texts?"

Chase swallowed. "She . . . asked me to stay away."

"Sometimes women say shit they don't mean," Burnett said.

"Yeah," Chase said, but she'd sure as hell sounded like she meant it.

The sun poured through Della's window, proof that while she felt dead inside, life went on.

It was late. She'd actually slept. Well, some. At least visions of bloody knives hadn't kept her awake. Not that she hadn't thought about death. Just not about Bao Yu's.

Had her aunt accepted the truth that Della's father hadn't killed her? Della didn't know, but she had done her own accepting.

She knew what she had to do.

Getting out of bed, she tilted her head to make sure Kylie or Miranda wasn't out there waiting to pounce. As much as she loved them and knew they only wanted to help, she didn't need the hold-hands-and-sing-"Kumbaya" kind of help.

There was only one kind of help she needed.

No noises echoed from the cabin, so Della went to shower. She reached into a drawer and pulled out clean underwear. Written across the front of her high-top panties was the word: "Tuesday."

She recalled Chase seeing her in Monday panties and laughing that she'd had the days of the week wrong.

She remembered telling him it was over.

Not now. Not now.

She finished dressing, and headed to the office to start putting her decision in motion.

"I do nothing wrong. I clean houses," the young Hispanic woman said, looking at Chase and Burnett sitting across from them at the hamburger joint they'd followed her to.

Chase saw the fear widening her brown eyes. She kept one hand on the wiggling infant in the baby carrier.

"We aren't saying you have," Burnett said. "We just need to ask you a few questions."

"I file for citizenship. I wait for my papers. But I have to work now, my baby need diapers and to see doctor. Her daddy not help me."

"Ms. Galvez, we are not with Immigration," Chase said. "We do not care about your papers. We are investigating the man who owns the house you just cleaned. We need to know about him. Do you understand?"

She nodded. "I do not know him well. I work for him only two months. I get job because I cleaned the house for the señora who live there before. I go to clean the house the day she move out and he see me and ask me to continue to clean for him. He and his friends come and go."

"How many of his friends stay with him?" Burnett asked.

"Many friends."

"How many approximately?" Chase asked.

"Sometimes twelve, sometimes eight. House only have four beds. They sleep on sofas and on floor." She leaned in. "They make big mess. Not very clean people."

Burnett leaned forward. "How often do you clean the house?"

"Every two weeks."

"No one was home today, right?" Chase asked, just making sure.

"Right."

"Is that unusual?" Burnett asked. "Is he usually gone? How does he pay you?"

"He sometime there, sometime not. I like it better when he not home. He leave money on kitchen table."

"Was your money there today?"

She nodded. "I tell him, no money, no clean."

Chase looked at Burnett and knew the man was thinking the same thing. No way would Stone leave money for the maid if he'd skipped town.

Burnett looked back at the young mother. "Do you know where he works or where he might be when he's not there?"

She shook her head. "I not get too friendly with my men clients."

"But have you seen something in the house that could have told you anything?"

She shook her head. "I sorry, I do not know."

"Thank you," Burnett said.

"I go now?" she asked.

"Yes," Chase said. "And if I were you, I'd stop cleaning for him."

She stood. "Is he bad man?"

Burnett nodded.

She exhaled and Chase saw in her eyes that she needed the money from the job. She walked away with the baby carrier that almost looked too heavy for her. She didn't appear to be much older than him.

"Wait." Chase pulled out his wallet. "Thank you for speaking to us." He handed her all the money he had in his wallet. Probably only a couple of hundred, but it might hold her over until she found another cleaning gig.

She looked hesitant.

"Please take it. It's reward money for speaking to us."

"Thank you." Nodding, she took the bills from his hand and walked over to the counter to order her lunch.

"I'll pay you back," Burnett said.

"You don't have to," Chase said.

They started out.

"Sir, sir." Mrs. Galvez came hurrying over to them. "I just remember. Last month, I take my sister to help me clean. She see Señor Stone and some of his friends at his house. She tell me he has another house next door to one she clean. The next week I ask him if he want me to clean other house, too. He tell me he not own other house. I think my sister has good eyes. Maybe he has a friend who own house."

"What's the address?" Burnett asked.

Chapter Forty-seven

"I need your help." Della dropped down in the chair in front of Holiday's desk.

Pity, empathy, and a whole shit-load of emotions filled the camp leader's face. Della could tell the fae was aching to touch her to try to ease her pain. But sometimes pain was a good thing. It forced one to focus on the problem. Maybe even to find a solution.

"You got it," Holiday said. "Anything. What do you need?"

Della picked up a pen from Holiday's desk. The words sat on the tip of Della's tongue. All she had to do was spit them out. She clicked the pen. The tiny noise filled the small office. Click. Click. Click.

"I . . . I need you to help me plan my death."

Holiday's eyes widened. "Anything but that."

"That's not acceptable." Della frowned. Click. Click. Click.

"But Della—"

"You gave me your word that if I tried it your way—that if I attempted to stay connected with my family and it didn't work, you'd help me fake my own death." She put her finger back on the tip of the pen. "You even helped Jonathon."

Click!

"Jonathon's home life was dysfunctional."

"And mine's not? My father thinks I could slice and dice a sweet ol' neighbor and her husband." She gripped the pen so tight that she thought she heard the thin plastic crack.

"What about your mother, Della? And your sister. You love them."

Della felt a lump form in her throat. "Why the hell do you think I'm doing this?" Click. Click. Click. "They'll be better off without me. If I'd done this when I first came here, none of this would have happened. My dad wouldn't be on trial for murder."

"But, right now—"

"I don't mean right, right now. After the trial. But right after it." She tossed the pen back on Holiday's oak desk. It bounced once, rolled off the desk, and fell apart in about four different pieces.

Della got up and walked out.

Della went for a run and was almost back to her cabin when her phone rang. Her heart hurt, her head hurt. There wasn't anyone she wanted to talk to. They'd just try to talk her out of dying. And the truth was she felt like she was already dying inside.

She let it ring. It stopped. She waited to hear if they'd leave a message. It didn't ding.

For a reason she didn't even understand, she checked to see who she'd ignored. Her heart hoped it was Chase. Not Chase. Her breath caught.

What about your mother, Della? And your sister. You love them. Holiday's words echoed in her head.

She hadn't expected it to be her mom.

Was something wrong?

Oh, hell, she hit redial. Her mom answered.

"Della," her mom's voice shook, tears sounded in her voice.

"What's wrong?" Della's grip on the phone tightened right along with her heart.

"You need to come help me talk some sense into your dad."

Della talk sense into her father? He hadn't even spoken to her in months.

"What's wrong?"

"He just . . . he fired his lawyer, and said he's going to the police station to confess to the murder."

"What?" Della asked.

"You heard me."

"He didn't do it, Mom. He just pulled the knife out."

"What?" Her mom sounded confused. *Oh, hell!*

"I'm on my way. Do not let him go to the police station. I don't care if you have to hit him over the head and sit on him. Do not let him go!"

Della started to take flight, but the day was too bright. Shit! Shit! Shit! She flew back to the office and ran inside.

"Holiday, I need—"

She wasn't there. Della pulled her phone out and dialed Holiday's number. A phone rang on Holiday's desk. The camp leader must have forgotten it.

Della's gaze fell to the car keys in the wooden box on the desk.

Her hesitation lasted one second. She snagged them up, and wrote a quick note. *Trouble at home.* She left.

Adrenaline flowed through Chase's veins as Burnett slowly drove by the two-story house. The structure looked like a tired white elephant. The brick had been painted white and the roof on the garage sagged. The yard looked overgrown.

Three cars were parked in front of the house and some hard rock music pulsed through the air. In the distance, some thunder seemed to play the same tune.

"Someone's home," Chase said.

"Yeah." Burnett parked on the opposite side of the street.

"Front or back?" Chase asked.

"Not so fast." Burnett dipped his head down and eyed the house. "There could be a dozen of them in there."

"Let me take a stroll and I'll tell you what I hear and smell."

"You get closer and if Stone—or a full were—is in there, they'll catch your scent."

"Then let's just storm the place. I think we can handle them."

Burnett frowned. "I think you could have died last night if you hadn't heard the crack of the shotgun. If they had guns, these guys could be toting too."

"So, what? You calling for backup?" Chase asked.

Burnett's frown deepened and he stared again at the house, as if considering it. "If Stone's in there, it would be easier if we didn't have company."

He pointed to the back of the van. "There's a briefcase in the back. Pull it up here and grab those two vests in that seat."

Chase dropped the case and one of the vests beside Burnett.

"That thing weights a ton. It'll slow me down."

"It'll slow down a bullet, too."

Burnett slipped the vest on over his suit. Chase tried, but the dang thing was too tight.

"It's too small," Chase said.

"Take your coat and shirt off," Burnett said.

Frustrated, Chase did it. Then he slipped his black jacket back on.

Burnett looked around. "Lucky for us, it doesn't appear that any neighbors are home."

He opened the briefcase. In it were two strange-looking guns that looked like they'd come out of a sci-fi flick.

"Tranquilizers?" Chase asked.

Burnett nodded. "Six-shooters, too. All you have to do is aim and pull the trigger."

"Easy enough."

Burnett nodded. "Important to remember—"

"Shoot them before they shoot you," Chase said.

"I was going to say, hit upper torso so it will work faster, but your point's good too."

They got out and started across the street.

Burnett spoke again as they stepped onto the front lawn. A mist of rain fell. "The drug in our bullets takes about five seconds to take effect. It only takes one for them to pull a trigger. So it's not a fair fight if they have real guns."

Chase nodded.

"You take the back this time." Chase started to the back. "Careful," Burnett whispered.

"It's my middle name."

Della parked in the driveway. Had she gotten here in time? Jumping out of the car, she got a scent of blood. She looked over her shoulder, almost certain the smell came from across the street. But it scared her nevertheless.

She rushed inside. "Mom?" she screamed.

The sound of a door slamming filled the oddly disturbing silence. She moved toward the kitchen, thinking she might find her mom there. But she never got past the entryway.

"Oh, goodie," a male voice said, coming from the dining room.

Della took a noseful of air to see what she was up against. But her mom must have cooked spaghetti because all she smelled was the nauseating odor of garlic. She swung around. A quick check of the intruder's forehead showed he was half were.

She could take him.

Still, heart pounding, fear triggering her inner vamp to come out to serve and protect, she tilted her head to the right, hoping to decipher if anyone else was here.

The sound of heavy breathing came from the den toward the back of the house.

"We have the whole family here now," the were called out.

In one hand he held a baseball bat; in the other, he held a framed photo—a family portrait of them posing in the park taken right before Della had turned.

Fury rose in her chest. She loved that picture. "Put that down!"

"What? This?" He held up the frame. "Or this?" He held up the bat.

"Actually, both," she seethed.

He took a swing. Della caught the bat and spotted a touch of fear in his eyes. For good reason. But oddly, he didn't think to check her pattern. His mistake.

Hit again by the smell of blood, she instantly became aware of the thick slickness on the bat. Her heart gripped.

Who had the dirty rogue already hit?

Chapter Forty-eight

Chase moved along the side of the house, ducking down below windows, to get to the back. Misty rain thickened the air. The music played so loud, he could feel the ground below his feet vibrate. He hoped he could hear when Burnett pounded on the front door.

Inhaling, Chase caught were scents, weak ones, like half breeds—five, or maybe six. But no vampire trace reached his nose. He only hoped that Stone was somewhere upstairs and his scent simply didn't reach.

He heard voices behind the music. The loud bass prevented him from deciphering what they said, but he knew one of them was female. Was she part of the gang?

Chase emotionally flinched. He hated fighting girls.

He continued to the back and jumped over the gate to the yard, making his way to the back patio. In the distance, he heard more thunder. A storm brewed. He looked up and saw the dark clouds rolling in. The smell of real rain scented the air.

Right when he spotted the back door, he heard the hammering of Burnett's knock. He ducked behind a rosebush and held out his tranquilizer gun.

Footsteps came rushing toward him.

"That's right," he muttered quietly. "Come on out."

The door swung open. Three figures appeared. Two guys. One woman. One guy held a pistol. Chase hit him with a tranquilizer first.

The guy stopped, looked down as if he couldn't believe something had hit him.

The girl slowed down; the other guy booked it to the fence.

Chase booked it right behind him. He caught the guy by the feet and yanked him back. He hit the ground. Hard.

But obviously not hard enough.

The were bolted up and took a swing. Chase beat him to the punch . . . literally.

The guy dropped.

Hearing yells from inside the house, Chase swung back around to take care of the girl and check on Burnett.

The girl was hunched down beside the tranquilized were.

"Stop right there." Chase ran over. "I don't like hurting girls, but—"

"Please don't hurt me," she begged in a soft voice.

"I won't. Just don't move," he ordered.

She moved.

She shot up. Chase's reaction came a fraction of a second too late. He spotted the gun in her hand. Almost like slow motion, he saw her finger twitch, and saw the gun go off.

Della, poised to remove the bat from the were, stopped when she heard another stranger's voice from the den.

"Bring her in here."

Marla's squeal and her mom's and dad's gasps filled Della's ears and banged into her heart.

Swallowing, she dropped her hold on the bat, wiped the blood from it on her jeans, and turned around.

The were used the bat to push her forward.

Her mom and dad were on the sofa, and another half were stood beside them holding a gun pointing in their direction. Her mom's skin lacked color. Her blue eyes were wide, and Della saw the handprint on her face. Somebody had hit her. Her stomach knotted.

Her dad had blood oozing from his lip, and his eye was swollen, evidence he'd tried to fight. Was that his blood she'd wiped on her jeans?

The sandy-haired vamp, or at least mostly vamp, stood by the big bay window. Stone.

The murdering lowlife had Marla's arm. No doubt, his firm grip would leave bruises. Her sister had tears running down her face and kept her head turned away from Stone.

Only then did Della notice that the man's eyes glowed, and he'd let his canines come out to play. He obviously enjoyed scaring people. And he was succeeding.

"Let her go," Della told Stone.

Marla let out another cry.

"It's gonna be okay," she told her sister, but didn't take her eyes off Stone, all the while fighting to keep her canines in and her eyes from brightening.

"Of course it is. Big sister is gonna save the day." Stone laughed, the sound heavy. Evil. Della's heart thumped against her breast bone.

"I love spunk," Stone said.

"But you only get one of them. I get the other?" said the were holding the gun on her parents.

Her father shot up.

"Down!" The were put the gun to her mother's head. "Or I'll blow her head all over the house."

Her father dropped down and Della saw the raw torture in his eyes.

He'd seen what had happened to his sister. Now it was happening to his own family.

Her mind raced. Her gaze shot around quickly and she decided that getting the gun was the first order of business.

But then she saw the were's finger on the trigger. Was she fast enough to rip it out of his hands before . . .

The impact of the bullet knocked Chase flat on his back. And every bit of air in his lungs gushed out.

Had the vest stopped the bullet? Probably, but he still couldn't breathe.

"That's what you get for being a puss where girls are concerned." The girl darted for the fence, thinking he was dead, or close.

Now pissed, he felt more alive. He rolled over and aimed his gun. She'd just pulled up on the fence. The dart got her right in the ass.

She stopped, her legs dangled, then she slid back. She remained upright, leaning on her good butt cheek, swaying as if fighting the drug.

One hand on his chest, Chase jackknifed up, yanked the gun out of her hand. "I'm not a puss!"

She fell back, unconscious.

Bumps and clanks sounded from the house. Still fighting for air, he took off inside.

Burnett swung around; his eyes glowed and his fangs were all the way out. Blood dripped from his arm and Chase saw a bloody knife beside the unconscious guy with a tranquilizer dart in his throat.

Two other guys lay out cold on the wood floor.

"You okay?" Burnett asked, the brightness in his eyes fading.

"You're not?" Chase said.

"Just a cut."

"I'll check upstairs." Chase took the stairs three at a time. His nose told him no one was there. But damn, he wanted Stone.

He checked every room.

When he got back down the three guys inside were wearing FRU cuffs, and Burnett was outside restraining the other three.

"No Stone," Chase snapped when he walked out.

"Help me get these guys inside," Burnett ordered. "We've got another problem."

"What now?"

"Della left the school forty minutes ago. I called to warn Shawn that she might show up. He's not answering. I got agents coming to pick these guys up."

A cold fear ran through Chase's body. "That's where Stone's at."

Chase didn't wait to hear Burnett tell him he couldn't fly. Hopefully there were enough clouds to keep him out of view. Less than two minutes later, Burnett was flying right beside him.

Della breathed air through her teeth, focusing on not losing control and letting her vamp take over. Face it, her family was traumatized enough, they didn't need more.

Behind her, she heard Stone inhale, deeply, as if he were just now getting her scent. "Look at me!"

Della turned around. He squinted at Della's forehead, and his eyes widened. He might know she was vampire, Della thought, but he didn't have a clue she was Reborn. She planned on making sure he knew it the first chance she got.

"My, my," Stone said. "It runs in the family. Now, can you tell me where your uncle is? 'Cause if you can I might be so inclined to let one or two of you live."

Her mom let out a sob. "I told you his brother died years ago."

Della heard her father lose a little air from his lungs. He knew, Della thought. Or at least a part of him knew that Feng had never died.

Stone glanced at the two weres. "Why am I just now finding this out?" He motioned to Della, obviously meaning her being vampire. "Weren't you watching the house? I know you guys can't smell worth a shit, but can't you read a pattern?"

"Joey and the other guys were doing that," the were holding the gun said.

"No," Stone snapped. "What they were doing was causing trouble. And I told you to watch them."

Della considered now would be the time to pounce, grab the gun. But Stone moved his hand up to Marla's neck.

"I've got to get some new help," Stone said, looking at Della. Then he focused back on her parents. "Wait? Why aren't you showing your true colors?"

A grin spread his mouth. "They don't know, do they?"

Della glared. Fury filled her chest.

"Well, don't you think it's time they found out?" He shoved Marla into a chair and grabbed Della by her hair, turning her so her parents and Marla could see her.

"Make your eyes pretty for them!"

Chapter Forty-nine

Pain shot up the back of Della's neck. Stone pulled her hair harder. Della could feel her hair being ripped out of her scalp.

She studied the were with the gun; he still had it pointing at her mom.

Could she move fast enough?

"Come on, show 'em!" he yelled in her ear.

Tears filled her eyes. Fury filled her chest and she couldn't stop it. Her eyes grew hot. Her canines lowered and she heard her mom gasp.

Stone laughed.

"Stop hurting her," her father shot up.

Della saw the were start to pull the trigger. She reached back, grabbed Stone by the neck, and threw him at the guy with the weapon.

The gun exploded. The were fell, but popped back up, gun still in his hand. Della bolted over the sofa, over her parents, caught both Stone and the were by the necks, and flew them to the other side of the room, slamming their bodies against the brick wall.

Still hovering midair, she heard the front door bang open. Thinking she might have more rogues to fight, she looked over her shoulder. Chase stormed into the room. His gaze met hers. Relief filled her chest. She wasn't alone anymore.

Then she heard her mother scream. Della looked back, thinking her mom was frightened of Chase, but that's when she saw her sister slump forward in the chair. The smell of new blood filled Della's nose.

"No!" Della screamed and let go of the two scumbags, and flew down to her sister. Her parents stood over her. Della saw Marla breathe, but blood oozed from her shoulder. Lots of blood.

"Give her to me," Della said. "I can get her to a hospital fast."

Her parents hesitated.

"I'm not a monster! *They* are the monsters," Della screamed and for the first time, she believed it.

Her mom touched her father. "Let Della take her."

Chase stood over Stone and the others were as he looked out the window and saw Della carry her sister out the back door and fly off.

Della's mother and father stood up as if to go to the hospital. The front door swung open and two more agents walked in.

One was a female agent, a fae, and she went straight to Della's parents.

She put her hands on them. Both Mr. and Mrs. Tsang's postures changed immediately.

"Come," she said to them. "Let's talk." She ushered them into the kitchen.

Burnett shifted closer. His eyes were bright red. He crouched down and looked at the three rogues. "Which one of you is going to tell me where my agent is that was sitting in that car out front?

"I'm counting to three, then I start shooting." He pulled out his gun.

"One.

"Two."

He shot Stone. "Oops, I forgot to say three."

The two other weres gasped.

Stone tried to get up, but fell back down. The two weres looked terrified, not realizing it was only a tranquilizer gun.

"Should I start counting again?" He looked at the other two, and Chase guessed he was sizing them up for which one was more likely to talk.

"One." He shot one of the half weres.

"He's in the shed across the street," the other were blurted out.

Burnett looked over his shoulder. "You get that?" But the other agent was already heading out.

Then Burnett looked back and shot the second were. Then he leaned in. "How well do you know that guard at Hell's Pit?"

"Pretty well," Chase said.

"Think you can remember how to get there? Eddie said he and Kirk would meet you there. Give him a call."

Della paced the small room. A whole team of people was working on her sister. She'd stayed there with them until one of the doctors noticed her. "Get her out of here."

At first she'd fought them, but then one said, "Do you want the best care for your sister?"

Della nodded and two other nurses brought Della in here. Oh, they pretended to just be comforting her. They didn't know she'd heard the doctor tell them to detain her, and call the police.

"You want anything to drink?" the nurse asked.

"No." Della kept blinking, and staring at the ground hoping to hide her bright eyes. Blood—her sister's blood—soaked her blouse. Each time she walked back and forth, she repeated her prayer. *Don't let her die. Please, God, don't let her die.*

She heard voices on the other side of the door. Probably the police. Della didn't care. There would only be a problem if they tried to take her out of the hospital. She'd have to hurt someone then. She would.

All of a sudden the door in the tiny waiting room flew open and Burnett walked in. He flashed his badge to the two nurses.

Della burst out crying, and he pulled her against him. "They tell me she's about to go into surgery," he said. "Kylie is on her way too."

Della pulled back. The air she tried to pull into her lungs shook. "My parents?"

Burnett glanced at the two nurses. "Can we have a minute?"

They walked out.

"I have an agent with them. I'll bring them here as soon as . . . it's safe."

"Safe?" Della asked, and her first thought was something else had happened, but then realized what he meant. He wouldn't—couldn't—let them come here screaming about vampires.

"It's not their fault," Della said. "You can't keep them from here. I know they're worried sick. If Marla doesn't make it . . ." Della's throat knotted.

"I think they'll be here shortly. I'm just making sure."

Della noticed the blood on Burnett. "What happened?"

He frowned. "Shawn. An agent. He'd been watching your house. They got him. I just brought him in."

"Shawn, Miranda's Shawn?"

Burnett nodded.

"Is he . . ."

"No. They're taking him into surgery too."

Five minutes later, Kylie showed up.

No sooner had Kylie walked in than the doctor stuck his head in.

"We're prepping her for surgery. I'll have the nurse give you updates."

"Can we see her?" Della asked.

"I really don't think we can spare the time."

Burnett looked at Della and Kylie and glanced to the door that still stood open. "Doctor, can I please have a word with you?" he motioned the doctor over.

Della and Kylie ran out. Della led Kylie to the ER where they'd taken Marla earlier.

Two nurses were standing around her, monitoring her and wiping something around her chest.

"You can't be in here now," one of the nurses said.

"We just need to see her for a second. Please," Kylie said. "It's her sister."

When the nurse reached for a phone to call someone—probably to toss them out—Kylie moved in and put her hands on Marla's feet.

"We need someone in here, now," said the nurse on the phone.

Della got between the nurse and Kylie, prepared to fight if she had to.

After only a couple of seconds, Kylie said, "We can leave now."

Della looked back and Kylie was glowing.

The two nurses gasped.

"Did it work?" Della asked, chewing on her lip as they went out.

Kylie smiled. "I'm pretty sure. I think all they need to do is take the bullet out."

Della, realizing Kylie was still glowing, pulled off her hoodie and handed it to her.

Two hours later, Della sat at her sister's side in the recovery room. She hadn't woken up, but the surgeon—who'd been shocked at how little damage the bullet had done—had assured her that Marla would be fine.

Burnett had popped in and told her that Shawn was going to make it. "My parents?" Della asked.

"They should be here soon. It's going to be okay," he said. But Della was afraid to believe it. It didn't feel okay.

He left. Della looked back at her sister and worried about what she was going to say to her.

In just a few minutes the curtain shifted again. Della expected it to be a nurse, but her mom walked in.

She looked terrible. Her face was pale, her nose red, and her eyes wet.

Della waited to see the fear, the repulsion, appear in her mom's eyes, but it didn't. Or Della just couldn't see it. Her mom moved in, albeit a little slowly. She glanced at Marla, and didn't look away until her sister's chest shifted to take air into her lungs.

Her mom let go of a deep, sad breath.

"They say she's going to be fine," Della said.

Her mom met her gaze again.

"I'm so sorry," Della said.

Her mom pulled Della into her arms.

"For what? You didn't do anything wrong. If you hadn't come, we'd have died."

Della leaned in and for the first time since she'd been turned, she didn't worry about her mom touching her, or that she'd freak out at Della's lack of body temperature.

Her mom pulled back and she brushed Della's tears from her face. "I'm the one who needs to say I'm sorry. I . . . we . . . I wish you could have told us. These last nine months shouldn't have been like this."

"It's not an easy thing to tell," Della said.

Her mom nodded and said, "It wasn't an easy thing to hear, either. But things are going to be different now."

Were they? Della wondered. Her father wasn't here. And she was pretty sure she knew why.

Her mom inhaled. "Your father is in the chapel. He did something terrible, Della. I'm furious at him, but he wants to apologize."

Della figured it was about telling the police she might have killed the Chis.

"Why don't you go and I'll stay with Marla," her mom said.

Della nodded, but when she walked out, she stopped and just leaned against the hospital wall. More tears fell from her lashes. What in the world was she going to say to him? Would he ever look at her and not see a monster?

Miranda and Kylie walked up. Miranda hugged her. Della hugged her back and hung on.

"You okay?" Miranda said and was the one who ended the hug.

"My dad wants to talk to me," she said.

"Then go," Kylie said.

"If he says anything mean to you, I'll give him jock itch." Miranda twitched her pinky.

Della, with tears still running down her face, couldn't help but smile. Then she remembered. "How's Shawn?"

"He's out of surgery and doing well," Miranda said. "His parents said I could visit him in a bit."

"Good."

"Go see your dad," Kylie said.

Della nodded and took off, but when she came to the waiting room, she heard voices. She stopped and pushed the door open—just a few inches. Her gaze shifted around the room looking from one concerned person to the other.

It took her a second to realize who was she was looking for.

He wasn't here. Not a vampire in the room.

She recalled some of the things she'd told him. And she supposed she didn't deserve to have him here. But she remembered that second when she'd seen him walk into her parents' home. She'd felt . . . Well, she hadn't felt alone anymore.

Then she remembered the things she'd learned from Eddie. Chase had still been keeping things from her. Didn't she have a right to be upset?

Stiffening her backbone, pushing Chase problems aside to worry about Daddy problems, she followed the signs to the chapel.

Chapter Fifty

Kirk and Eddie had met Chase at Hell's Pit. He'd signed the papers for Douglas Stone, or Connor Powell, to become a regular resident.

Chase hadn't said anything to Eddie about him talking to Burnett with Kirk around. But with their brief conversation, Eddie didn't appear to hold any grudges against Chase.

However, Chase had sensed some tension between the two men. Eddie told Chase he'd meet him outside, and Kirk went with him through the prison's back door to sign Stone up for his new residence. The paperwork was done and the guard led Stone to his cell.

When Chase went to leave, Kirk called him back. "I was wrong to have asked you to take care of this the way I did."

"Yes, you were," Chase said.

Kirk looked toward the exit and frowned. "I never meant to deceive Eddie. It was always more about protecting him."

Chase sensed honesty in the man's tone, but that was for Eddie to decide.

"It's late," Chase said.

Kirk held out his hand. "Can I say that knowing you work with the FRU, I'm hopeful that there might be some changes for the good?"

Chase recalled the times Kirk had been there for him and Eddie, and he couldn't help but shake the man's hand.

"Thank you."

Once outside, Eddie met him. "You okay?" his surrogate father asked.

Chase nodded. "You?"

"Yeah." Eddie put his hand on Chase's shoulder. "I'm proud of you, son."

"Even if I work for the FRU?" Chase asked.

"Even if," he said. "How's Della's sister?"

"Burnett texted me that she's going to make it."

"Good."

"Thank you for calling Burnett," Chase said.

Eddie nodded. "If he wasn't an FRU agent, I might even like him."

"I told you. He's a good guy."

Eddie smiled. "He reminds me of your father."

"Which one?" Chase asked. "I have two." He met Eddie's eyes, letting him know what he meant.

"I love you, son!" Eddie said and the two of them embraced.

Della walked into the chapel. Her father sat in the first row. The lights were out, except for some flickering candles. She wiped the tears from her eyes.

She saw him look over his shoulder. Her chest swelled with emotion, but she forced herself to go and sit down beside him.

He had his head down, his hands folded. "I am a terrible person," he said.

More tears came. "No, you're not. You saw some terrible things a long time ago and I reminded you of it all over again."

He still didn't look at her. "I'm the one who told the police that you might have killed Mr. and Mrs. Chi."

"I know," she said.

He looked at her. "You knew?"

"Yeah," she said. "And it's because of me that you were arrested for murder. I'm the one who had the file pulled so I could find out . . . about Feng and Bao Yu."

"Yes, but Mr. James tells me you never thought I did it. Even when he got the file with my confession. You believed in me, and I turned you in."

She felt another wave of emotion fill her. "It's different," she said. "I didn't witness something terrible that gave me doubt."

"Yes, you did." Tears filled his eyes. "You witnessed me these last nine months. I treated you so badly. How can you forgive me?"

She reached over and took his hand in hers. "Because that was nine months, and you treated me so wonderfully for over seventeen years."

He wrapped his arms around her and there, in the small hospital chapel, she got her daddy back.

After a few minutes, Della felt the temperature go down in the dark room. She looked around, almost afraid of what her aunt might do if she still didn't believe.

"You didn't kill your sister," she told him and hoped Bao Yu would hear as well.

"I pulled the knife out," he said, and his voice shook a little. "I might have killed her. She was trying to do it and I just . . . It looked like it was hurting her." He cupped his hand over his eyes and the sad sound of her father's cries filled the small dark room.

I was already dying, Bao Yu said. *I'd seen the light already. He was trying to help me. I wanted it out. It's not his fault.* Her gaze met Della's. *I finally remembered. Thanks to you.*

Della stared at the altar and the cross and where her aunt stood. She smiled at Della. She had tears in her eyes and mouthed the words, *Thank you.*

"She was already dying," Della said. "I'm sure you did that because she . . . because you thought it would help." She squeezed his hand. "The man who came into your house, the really mean one, he was the one who killed her."

Her father shook his head. "Mr. James told me that too."

Della looked back at her aunt.

Bao Yu turned and looked over her shoulder, and Della almost gasped when the wall behind her aunt seemed to open up. Where the Sheetrock had been was now what looked like the most beautiful sunset she'd ever seen. Colors so brilliant, so . . . unlike any she'd ever seen. Bao Yu turned, and suddenly Mrs. Chi showed up. They both waved at Della, then walked away, and the colors slowly faded.

But the warm, soft feeling swelling in Della's chest didn't fade.

"Did you see that?" her father asked.

"See what?" Della asked, shocked.

"Those colors, like a rainbow flashed on the wall."

"Yeah," Della said. "I saw that."

"Maybe it is a sign that good things will happen from now on."

"Yeah," Della smiled. "I think it was a sign."

They sat in the peaceful silence. Both looking at the wall, as if waiting for more colors to appear.

Her father spoke again. "Mr. James also told me that you saw Feng."

"I did," she said. "He's a very nice man. A lot like someone else I know," she said and smiled.

"I would like to see him," he said.

"I'll bet he would like to see you, too."

Four days later, Chase poured Eddie a glass of blood and they sat down at his French farm table. Baxter rested at his guest's feet. The dog loved Eddie almost as much as he loved Chase.

"Della called me today," Eddie said.

Well, that hurt. She hadn't found the time to call him. Chase picked up his glass and took a slow sip to hide his emotions.

"The courts have dropped the case against Chao. His lawyer

requested a new DNA test to be done on Bao Yu's gown, and when they went to do it, it was missing. Fearing he would look bad, the DA decided to drop the case."

"Really," Chase said, and took another long sip. "Funny how things like that happen."

Eddie looked at him. "I see you used your fireplace recently."

"It got cold."

"Right," Eddie said. "You could have gotten your ass in a lot of trouble."

"Yeah," Chase said. "But I asked myself, if I got caught would it be worth it? It would have been. Besides, I didn't do it alone."

"Who?"

"Della has a lot of friends at Shadow Falls."

Eddie nodded. "Della says that my brother wants to meet with me."

"That's good," Chase said. He'd heard through the years how Eddie missed his twin.

He'd also heard from Burnett how Della's father had admitted he'd been a total ass and was seriously trying to make amends with his daughter. So maybe the man wasn't such an ass after all.

"Have you called or texted her?" Eddie asked.

Chase took another slow sip. "She told me not to."

"And since when do you do what people tell you? You sure as hell didn't listen to me."

"She knows where I am. I've told her how I feel many times." *And she never told me she felt the same. That hurt.*

Eddie leaned down to pet Baxter. When he sat back up, he dropped Baxter's dog collar on the table. "Never turn your back on a challenge," he said. "Isn't that what the collar says? There was a day when you said you lived by that. Don't stop doing that now, son."

"Checkmate," Della said, and smiled at her dad.

"Okay, I clearly need to brush up on the game," her father said.

Della just grinned. She knew he'd purposely let her win, and she loved him for it. God, she loved him. Loved her whole family.

"One more game?" he asked.

"I should go." Della frowned. "I promised Mom I would help her cook chicken fingers for dinner and I promised Marla I would watch the *Twilight* movie with her." Della made a face.

Marla had gotten to come home yesterday. The doctors were still stunned at her recovery.

Her father grinned. "Your sister is trying to show that she accepts you."

"Yeah, well, she could just say that. We watched those movies years ago. Whoever heard of a vampire sparkling?"

He leaned in. "Marla's like your mom. She has a hard time saying things sometimes. Not like you and me."

It was true, Della realized. She and her dad didn't sugarcoat things like her mom and sister did.

Her father leaned back in his chair. "Are you sure I can't talk you into staying home and finishing out the year at your old school?"

Della made a face. "I kind of like it at Shadow Falls. I have my best friends." *Chase lives close.* Though why that mattered she didn't know. At least a hundred times, she'd written him a text, only to delete it.

He'd kept stuff from her. Wasn't that the same as lying?

"Okay, I'm not going to try to talk you out of it. But I'd buy you a new car if you reconsidered."

"That's bribery," Della said. "And it's a low blow."

He sighed. "Okay, I just can't stand the thought of you leaving."

"I'm almost eighteen."

He sighed and held up his hands. "You know I'll still buy you a car. I was going to when you graduated high school."

She stood up and hugged him. "Can I have stick shift?"

"You don't drive a stick shift," he said.

"I learned." She remembered her driving lessons with Chase. Her heart did another tumble. Would she ever stop missing him?

"I'll let you help pick it out."

"Thank you." She hugged him again.

Funny how lately she'd become almost as much of a serial hugger as Miranda.

Sunday, at almost eight that night, her whole family drove to drop her off at Shadow Falls. They hugged, kissed, and Marla even cried.

"I'll be back in two weeks." Della stayed at the gate and watched them leave. Then she cried. For the first time, she actually knew they were going to miss her. She knew she still had a place at home. Would always have that place.

She turned around and stared at the Shadow Falls Academy sign. This was home too.

Oddly, she was surprised when Kylie and Miranda weren't at the gate waiting for her. They had called five times today, asking when she'd get there.

She walked through the gate.

"Hey," Miranda called from the dining hall. "I was just grabbing us some Cokes, can you help?"

"Sure." Before she walked through the door, their scents hit. Vampires, shape-shifters, faes, witches, werewolves, shape-shifters. The whole bunch of them. She was still surprised when they all yelled, "Welcome home!"

She almost got a little teary eyed. Everyone was so nice. Over the next hour she spent time laughing with all of her Shadow Falls family, Holiday and Burnett, and little Hannah, Jenny and Derek, Perry and Miranda. Lucas and Kylie. Jonathon and Helen. Even Fredericka and Chris came over and welcomed her back.

When Della was ready to head back to her cabin, Burnett asked if he could see her in the office.

"Is there a problem?" She walked into Holiday's office.

"No," Burnett said. "Well, a little one."

"What?" Right then something rubbed against her leg.

She looked down. "Chester? What?"

"Remember you asked me to find out what vet the Chis' cat was at?"

"Yes," Della said.

"Well, I don't know how I got to be the person responsible. But the Chis' daughter called the vet and said they couldn't have a cat at their apartment. So I got stuck with Chester. Holiday doesn't trust Hannah with a pet yet. Do you think Chester could hang out with you?"

"That's a great idea!" Della picked up the cat.

"There's a carrier."

She started out, cat in tow. "Della?" Burnett said.

"Yeah," she said.

"Have you spoken with Chase?"

A lump filled her chest. "No."

"Oh," he said.

She started out again and stopped when he spoke up.

"It just seems odd."

"Why?" she asked.

"He worked so hard on your dad's case."

"And he kept things from me. Eddie had told him that he was going to come forward and confess. He didn't tell me that."

"Yeah, but do you know something else that's odd?"

"What?"

"You both were doing the same thing. Trying to save your fathers. But only one of you seemed to support the other one."

She stood there, feeling her emotions well up. When it was put like that, she really came off as a bitch.

"Stone was blackmailing the council. He had files that put them all at risk, even your uncle. The council promised Chase that they'd protect Eddie if he'd kill Stone. He didn't do it, because he knew that if Stone died, your father might still get convicted. He risked Eddie going to jail to save your father from the same thing."

"He did?" she asked and realized she didn't just come off as a bitch, she was one. A full-fledged bitch.

"Yup."

She looked down at Holiday's desk. A plan started to form.

"Do you think I could borrow the car later? I might . . . run out and get some food and stuff for Chester."

He grinned. "You're going to ask? I thought you just took the keys and ran." He picked up the keys and tossed them to her.

Smiling, she started out, then turned. "Burnett?"

"Yeah."

She searched for the right words. "During some of this time, I felt like I lost my father. But you were sort of a backup. And still are. Thank you."

He smiled. "I feel the same way."

Chapter Fifty-one

Della went to her cabin and had a round-table Diet Coke session with Kylie and Miranda.

They laughed, listening to Miranda whine about her love life. She'd been spending time with Shawn since he'd been hurt. As friends. Just friends. But now Perry announced he was going to be gone for another month to try and find his parents.

"He said you're the one who told him he should do it." Miranda frowned at Della. "Not that I think it's wrong, I just . . . I'm confused."

They talked for a few more minutes. Della put her soda can down. "I'm confused too. I'm about to do something and it might be stupid."

"What?" Kylie asked.

"I'm going to go see Chase."

"That's not stupid," Kylie said.

"I don't think so," Miranda said.

They agreed to watch Chester, and Della went back to her room.

"I thought you were going to see Chase."

"I am, but I'm going to shower first."

Miranda's mouth fell open. "You aren't just going to talk, are you?"

"Shut up," Della said.

"What kind of underwear are you going to put on?" Miranda teased. "Just in case you don't know, it's Sunday."

"I should have never told you guys that," she said.

"You have to, it's in the rule book for best friends," Miranda said as Della walked out.

Della drove to the grocery store. Not the closest one, but the one thirty miles away. The other store would have what she needed. Items purchased, she got back in her car. Her phone dinged with a text.

She figured it was either Marla or Kylie and Miranda.

It wasn't.

Chase. It was short, sweet, and right to the point.

Still here.

Still miss you.

Still love you.

She started to text him back, then decided to just surprise him.

Twenty minutes later, she parked in front of his cabin.

He stepped out onto the porch. He wasn't wearing a shirt. Not that she minded. The guy carried off shirtless really well.

He stood there and stared as if he couldn't believe she was there. Then he and Baxter finally came hurrying down the stairs.

"You're here." He didn't try to kiss her. So she leaned up on her tiptoes and kissed him.

He pulled her against him. "God, I missed you."

"Me, too."

Once inside, he pulled her against him. She leaned her head on his chest. His bare skin felt so good.

"Oh, I forgot." She ran outside, snatched the bag, and hurried back in and handed it to him.

No sooner had the bag left her fingertips when she remembered what else she'd bought.

"Wait!" She snatched the bag back. Unfortunately he still held it and it ripped open. The twelve-pack of condoms and the bakery container fell to the wood floor.

Chase looked down. Della snatched the condoms. But not before he saw them.

"Don't you dare say a word, or I'll change my mind."

"Not a word," he said, but he had a silly grin on his face. "You know, I had some."

"Oh, you thought you'd need them, did you?"

"I hoped I'd need them. So why did you buy them? You collect them or something?"

"I . . . Forget it." She grinned.

He laughed, then picked up the bakery box that Baxter had started to sniff. When he opened the box, his smile vanished. He glanced up, and he looked . . . not sad, but serious. "Snickerdoodles?"

Holding the condoms behind her back, she nodded. "You . . . you said they tasted like love."

He put the cookies on the table and kissed her—a warm soft kiss. "They do." He reached for a cookie.

"Taste one," he said. He reached back and held on out.

She shook her head. "Sorry, I tried one last week and it tasted terrible."

He laughed. "Well, that's okay. I tried French onion soup and I puked. It could have been the wine, though."

She laughed and leaned in, setting her chin on his chest. "We don't have to love the same kinds of foods. Just each other."

"I do," he said. "Love you."

"I love you, too." She put one hand on his chest. The one not still hiding the condoms behind her back. "I'm sorry I was a bitch. I was scared, and confused."

"You're not a bitch," he said and put his hand on top of hers.

"No, let me finish. I need to say this." She swallowed. "All I could think about was that if my father got convicted, it would be my fault. And while I knew you considered Eddie like a father, I never really took into consideration that you were just as scared about him. I mean, I sort of knew it, but I was being selfish and—"

"Stop," he said and brought her hand to his lips. "You are the least selfish person I know."

"I pushed you away," she blurted out. "I didn't want to admit how much I cared. And it's not just the bond, Chase. Steve set me straight about this. He told me that I was crazy about you before you ever gave me your blood. And he's right. I was . . . crazy about you."

He smiled. "I'm crazy about you, too."

Leaning down, he pressed his lips to hers. The kiss was soft, sweet, but quickly moved into hot. And Della became more and more aware that she was holding a pack of condoms behind her back.

Somewhere in his cabin she heard a clock hand move, counting down seconds.

She pulled back. "What time is it?"

He looked over his shoulder.

"Eleven fifty-eight—why?"

"We need to get this show on the road, then."

"What?" he asked.

"Can I take my clothes off?" She tossed the condoms on the sofa.

His eyes widened. "Well, I . . . Sure."

She glanced at him and giggled. "I think you're blushing."

"I am not," he said.

Yes, he was. But she kind of liked knowing that. Knowing he was sort of new at all this too. At least a little new.

She pulled her T-shirt off, then wiggled out of her jeans. Then stood before him with only her underwear on.

His gaze shifted up and down, and she could tell he liked what he saw.

He inched closer. His hand moved gently around her waist.

His soft touch brought goose bumps to her skin and anticipation rippled through her, but she pushed his hand way. "Hey, Panty Perv, you're missing the point." She backed up and waved her hand up and down her partially naked body.

His brow pinched. "Missing what . . . point? Other than . . . you look amazing."

She shook her head. "I got the day right." She pointed to her panties.

He dropped his head back, and laughed. The sound rang like music to her ears. And being here with him felt like magic. Then he pulled her against him. They laughed and held on to each other all night long.

Della couldn't remember anything feeling this right. Being with him, beside him. Feeling his bare skin against hers. She loved him. Loved how he made her feel beautiful and sexy. Loved how he took his time and made touching her feel like an art.

Nine months ago, her world had turned upside down. She'd hated that everything had changed. Hated who she was. What she was. And yet now, she realized that those changes had led her here. Led her to Chase. Led her to the career she wanted. Led her to two best friends and everyone at Shadow Falls.

Sometimes, she supposed, change wasn't so bad.

Read the series that started it all

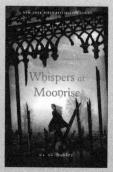

Available now.

Quiz#:181369
BL:4.0
16pts